PRINCES OF WAR

A NOVEL OF AMERICA IN IRAQ

Claude Schmid

WARRIORS PUBLISHING GROUP
NORTH HILLS, CALIFORNIA

PRINCES OF WAR

A Warriors Publishing Group book/published by arrangement with the author

This is a work of fiction. Names, characters, military units, places, events, and incidents are either the products of the author's imagination or used in a fictitious manner. Any resemblance to actual persons, living or dead, or actual events is purely coincidental.

PRINTING HISTORY
Warriors Publishing Group edition/June 2016

All rights reserved.
Copyright © 2016 by Claude Schmid
Cover art copyright © 2016 by Gerry Kissell (gerrykissell.com)

This book may not be reproduced in whole
or in part, by mimeograph or any other means,
without permission. For information address:

Warriors Publishing Group
16129 Tupper Street
North Hills, California 91343

ISBN 978-1-944353-10-0
Library of Congress Control Number: 2016939528

The name "Warriors Publishing Group" and the logo
are trademarks belonging to Warriors Publishing Group

PRINTED IN THE UNITED STATES OF AMERICA

10 9 8 7 6 5 4 3 2 1

To Kevin Walter Schmid, the greatest soldier who
never wore a uniform.

DAY ONE

1

I CAME HERE TO STICK a thermometer in you," said Brigadier General Vincent Craig, the 1st Infantry Division's Assistant Commander, in the laconic, no-bullshit style that was his calling card. "Up north here, your brigade sits atop one of Iraq's human volcanoes. Ethnic tensions, fanatic ideologies, regime holdouts, thugs, and criminals—you guys have it all. After six months of living that, you tell me how it feels."

BG Craig—all white-haired, six-foot-three, 225-plus pounds of him—sat in the front middle seat of an audience of 30 to 35 soldiers assembled in the brigade headquarters. The senior leadership and a few selected staff members of the three brigade battalions were in attendance. On the agenda today was a six month review; the brigade was due to give a mid-tour accounting of its performance, and the Assistant Division Commander was here to receive it.

He wanted the thermometer reading.

For the next 45 minutes, the parade of briefers presented systematically, each armed with a set of PowerPoint slides and a laser pointer. The briefers, mostly men and mostly officers, stood in what the brigade staffers affectionately called the "mosh-pit"—named after the aggressive, full-contact dancing craze popular in the late 1980s—and delivered their slice of information, trying to look and sound competent, while remaining agile enough to field questions.

First Lieutenant Nathan Petty, 2nd Battalion's Assistant Intelligence Officer, sat in the audience on the right flank. He listened to the briefings, periodically taking notes, and he studied the audience, especially the main attendee: BG Craig.

Petty noticed that every time Craig questioned a briefer, the general would, while listening to the answer, suck on the frames of his eye glasses, as if by doing so he could measure the man.

Three large computer screens hung on the wall behind the briefers. The middle screen displayed the PowerPoint slides and the outer screens showed maps. The map farthest away from Petty displayed all of Iraq, the country wedged into the center of the Middle East, surrounded by other mostly Arab countries—except Iran—with boundaries drawn by post-World War I colonial powers. Graphics on this map showed 1st Infantry Division's area boundaries and the other larger commands. Nearest to Petty was another map, much more magnified. This one showed the brigade's area on the northern edge of the division's operating area, and was further subdivided by the boundaries of the respective battalion task forces. Here he could locate Bajanas and other familiar towns and landmarks. When he peered and used a little imagination, he could see the ground his close friend, First Lieutenant Christian Wynn, patrolled—even at this moment—since Wynn had responsibility for all activity in that area.

It didn't take long before Petty was staggered by the magnitude of what the brigade had attempted, and what they had experienced.

Most comments, although delivered with relatively positive wrapping paper, revealed statistics of toil and blood.

Major Stewart, the Brigade Intelligence Officer, now had the mosh-pit. He spent several minutes summarizing the enemy activity. Then, with his eyes locked on BG Craig, he said, "Sir, in the last six months, reports have confirmed seven different insurgent groups operating in our battlespace. These range from groups claiming a handful of attacks to groups claiming dozens. All are Anti-Coalition. Most have Sunni origins. Reports suggest most receive outside help. Each—every damn one—has our blood on their hands. We're studying them all, but it's challenging to get inside the workings of these groups. Here, Sir, it's worth emphasizing that the war in our area is changing. It's a true counterinsurgency. Almost no sizable enemy concentrations. It's all small-group action, focused and deadly. Some days our guys think their uniforms should say U.S. Police instead of U.S. Army."

"Tough situation out there, no doubt about it," BG Craig began. "Your people, and American soldiers all across Iraq, have been bombed, rocketed, and shot at. You've lost friends. You've seen folks you love hurt and maimed. You, many of you, have ordered men into situations that ended with someone dying or getting seriously hurt. The call was yours, your responsibility, you think." Craig paused, and turned left and right to check his audience. When he continued, his voice was several decibels quieter, his tempo more restrained. "Any deaths—you tell yourself—are on you, too. But that would be an incomplete sentiment. The truth is this, and never forget it: the United States Government sent us here, sent us here on behalf of the American people. Just like it did with every previous war. And that core truth doesn't change, no matter what kind of war we're fighting."

As the briefing neared its end, Petty looked down at his notes.

"Brigade area now is 610 square miles…"

"Iraq population estimated at 1.5 million…"

"3,315 US Soldiers…"

"13,256 patrols completed…"

"1,420 engagements with tribal leaders…"

"1,115 civilian construction projects initiated, 318 completed, 402 underway, 395 waiting funding…"

"Population census underway in 30% of the urban area…"

"Five lines of brigade campaign plan: security, governance, population services, economic, communications…"

Then he looked at statements he'd underlined.

"In the last six months…IEDs detonations: 915, VBIED detonations: 34, direct-fire engagements: 538, sniper reports: 221, insurgents confirmed killed: 345, estimated Iraqi regional casualties from all violence: 1,000-1,500…"

Then Petty looked at a statement he'd underlined twice.

"U.S. dead: 28, U.S. wounded: 182..."

At the bottom of the page he wrote in capital letters: SEVEN INSURGENT GROUPS! He circled that and closed his notebook.

2

Cole "Moose" Murphy surveyed the view in front of him for maybe the hundredth time. Before him lay a dusty street lined with non-descript rectangular one- and two-level Iraqi houses. The morning sun colored the arid landscape cinnamon, scorching his kevlar helmet and every other exposed surface. He scanned the usual pedestrian traffic and occasional car, looking for anything that might be irregular, that might be a threat to the platoon's security. And threats there were. In the past week, within a 25 mile radius of where Moose now stood, 23 bombs had exploded, 11 more bombs had been discovered and disarmed, eight reports of rocket or mortar fire, 73 reports of gunfire, and 16 dead bodies found on the street. His platoon leader, 1LT Christian Wynn, went over those unsettling statistics that morning.

All four of the Humvees on this mission, D21 through D24, belonged to 2nd Platoon, Delta Company, which called itself the Dogs. Each platoon chose the name of a dog breed to further identify itself. 2nd platoon was the Wolfhounds.

Today the Wolfhounds worked a mixed neighborhood of Kurds and Arabs. The Kurdish areas were considered relatively safe; the Kurds resisted any Al Qaeda presence. In the predominately Arab areas of Iraq, however, a smorgasbord of insurgents and conspirators hid more easily and vast regions were poisonous cauldrons. Many Arabs in the area were better off than others in Iraq and so maintained a low profile. Some worked for the Iraqi Oil Company which explained the area's relative affluence. The fault lines imprecisely separating various religious groups and ethnicities were turbulent and dangerous, like fault lines everywhere.

Standing up in D24's turret, Moose looked down the long black steel barrel of the .50 caliber machinegun he manned, tracing the gun receiver to the end of the barrel and into the neighborhood of flat-roofed houses crammed together like sardines. He felt invincible. He looked to his right, then coolly walked his gaze from right to left. Nothing abnormal.

Moose was a big man, though not tall, with massive bulging shoulders like whole hams. He had a large blunt nose, large ears, flat green eyes, and chestnut-colored hair. Though he could run fast, he lumbered when he walked—a bit slower than normal—giving him the gait of a bull moose. Someone in the platoon started calling him "Moose." The name stuck. Back home they said he came from good stock. He'd been raised as a strict Southern Baptist, had gone to church most Sundays, and still got "Dear Son" letters twice weekly from his mother. But at 16 he rebelled, thinking he had all the answers. Now he took to church as a cat takes to showers.

A few weeks before joining the Army, he'd quit a dead-end job at Benson's body shop because the owner promised him a three-day weekend for the opening of hunting season, and then reneged. Then 9/11 happened. The following week he went to the nearest recruiting station. No terrorist was going to attack America and get away with it. Fourteen weeks later, he started basic training. Now, almost three years later, Moose was in Iraq.

He thought of the United States Army as an adventure club—the biggest and strongest club of all, with common ideas and principles and a shared purpose. He was young and unconquerable and wanted his war.

1LT Wynn was meeting with an Iraqi Sheikh inside one of the houses while the rest of the platoon provided security outside. Each of the Wolfhound trucks were manned by four or five soldiers. Their plan positioned one truck and crew at the far end of the street and a second truck at the other end, about 75 meters away from Moose. Two Humvees, including Moose's, parked adjacent to the meeting house. Two soldiers went inside with 1LT Wynn, providing close security.

Moose didn't understand why the lieutenant thought they needed to sit and talk to so many locals. They did this almost every day. Leadership called it engagement, designed to help community relationships. This policy sounded too much like politics. Moose wanted more fighting and less talking.

Glancing around at the other Humvees, he could see two of the other three turret gunners. Specialist Ulricht hunched low in D22, his gloved hands gripping the truck's .50 caliber. Ulricht had ears big enough to fly with, and he acted as if talking were a sin. He was the quietest man in the platoon. He scrutinized his zone, an I'll-kill-you-fucking-now look stamped on his face. D21's gunner, Sergeant Singleton, bulging with body armor, his chin firm with resolution, scanned a distant intersection like a hawk watching for ground varmints. Moose wondered whether Singleton was listening to music. He took it everywhere, even to the latrine. Every Wolfhound did his job; they'd be fearful of letting their buddies down if they didn't. They could be me, Moose thought, as if a mind-weld took place, an invisible solder joining each man to the other.

He and the others had left the civilian world far behind. The Army's world was different, both more constrained and wilder. Wartime service in Iraq magnified those differences. Here, you could get rimmed out one minute for not sweeping out your living trailer, but be expected to crush an insurgent's Adam's apple the next. Here the soldiers kept the beasts inside them close to the surface, but let the Army maintain the keys. Extra deprivation—no tenderness, no love, no freedom— shaped and toned the men, their combat experiences and isolation intensifying their connections. Some men felt closer to each other than to their own families.

Moose's eyes again swept the area before him, his mind continuously processing details of what he saw. An old pickup truck loaded with butchered lamb carcasses stood in an alley about 30 meters away, blood dripping through holes in the truck's rusty bed onto the street. An open sewer bisected the street. A dozen or so thin mattresses with colorful slipcovers were stacked on the curb beside the truck. Must be an Iraqi version of a mattress sale, he thought. Instead of a man in a funny costume swinging a sale sign, they just stacked the mattresses outside. Nearby, a boy swept the curb with a bundle of dried sticks.

A few Iraqis walked the street, some alone and silent, others in small groups, talking. Their clothing varied from western-like business suits to traditional Arab dishdashas, loose flowing garments which some of the soldiers called tents.

A big truck loaded full of decorative tile, with five laborers in the back, drove through the intersection in front of Murphy, shaking up another cloud of dust. A dog ran after the truck. One man threw something at the dog.

Moments later, a mosque began the call to prayer. The muezzin's high-pitched passionate voice carried into the neighborhood like a metaphysical mist. Moose didn't understand the prayer. Whatever was said stilled the anxieties of some, admonished others, and had little effect on many more. Moose accepted the barracks' view of Islam: the religion was a cover for politics and the purpose of politics was power. Religious leaders in Iraq were deep into the contest for power. Most folks just struggled to survive, to feed their families, to live in security, hoping to prosper.

The mosque—small, well-maintained, and crowned by a lean and elegant minaret—looked surreal, an architectural jewel suggesting improbable affluence, glorifying the skill of man as much as the purposefulness of Allah.

Across the street from the mosque was a large empty lot that had once been a block of homes. Saddam had razed the neighborhood because a family living there was implicated in a plot against his regime. Then he ordered the homeowners to haul the broken remnants away. Rebuilding had been forbidden. Yet signs of returning life could now be seen around its edges. It had taken nearly a year after Saddam's overthrow before Iraqis got up the courage. Poor Kurds were moving in and building modest homes—often shacks assembled of uncemented concrete blocks, cardboard, and scraps of plastic and sheet metal. Chunks of brick held down the tin roofs of several shacks. Others had tarps for roofs. Some sported a faded UN logo.

Moose looked again at the upscale house where Wynn was meeting. Moose's family's Kentucky home would have fit inside it. Four round columns held up a portico, and vertical strips of colorful tile highlighted the façade. Ornate molding trimmed the flat roof. Many houses along this street had small courtyards and gardens. The immediate area seemed miles away from the neighborhood Saddam had destroyed, but wasn't. In every country one finds sharp contrasts between the haves and the have-nots, he thought.

Wynn sat so close to Sheikh Amir that you couldn't run a pencil between their arms. He sat close by design, wanting Amir to know he wanted to be on good terms. Without a personal connection, cooperation from any Iraqi would be fragile or non-existent.

Amir had just returned from praying in another room while Wynn had waited. As a senior sheikh of the Joubari tribe, Amir was an influential local leader. Though Westerners often viewed tribes as relics of antediluvian social networks, Arabs considered tribes a kind of extended family.

As they talked, Amir periodically touched Wynn's hand. Physical contact between men was common in the Middle East, the act of touch enhancing human connections and facilitating trust, like two dogs sniffing.

The contrasts between the men were sharp: Wynn, at 25, stood nearly six feet tall, fit and wiry with a runner's build. Short curly blond hair and almond skin gave him a from-the-far-north appearance. He had thin lips, a strong high forehead, and an angular face. His eyes were most striking, set deep in his face like small turquoise stones.

Years of adversity and responsibility had stamped Amir's face with an abundance of terrain. Probably 60, he had old boot-leather skin, dark and tough and worn by heat, moisture, time, and more time. Coarse tangles of hair advanced aggressively from his ears and nostrils, like wild vegetation. He had wire-brush salt-and-pepper hair and a big mustache and a large plow-shaped nose. His eyes were coal black, as impenetrable as a collapsed tunnel.

Next to Sheikh Amir sat one of his key assistants, a man named Haider. Haider was tall and dour-faced, not a man you could see leading any revelries. His right hand had been mangled, reportedly in a childhood farming accident, leaving him with a stubby fingerless palm and a long thumb shaped like a chisel. The Americans nicknamed him, "Mr. Thumb." He rarely spoke.

Wynn had an interpreter—a terp—named Cengo with him, who sat to his right. Cengo, 20, looked older than his years, and permanently tired. Wynn constantly reminded himself not to look at Cengo during the dialog but to keep his focus on Amir, as he'd been taught by the Army.

Amir, animated and generous, appeared to relish the meeting. Wynn could tell the Iraqi felt possessive of Wynn's time and interpreted these meetings as giving each man part ownership in the other.

"America is strong country," Cengo said, translating Amir's latest statement. "America rich. This make America strong. This good, Amir say," Cengo said in a clipped voice, sounding like an airport announcer.

Amir again leaned closer, his face brightening as if he was about to share an exclusive insight, and spoke. Both men waited for Cengo to translate. Amir's eyebrows arched like stretching caterpillars.

"We Iraqis are old people. We have long history. Arab people have great education from this long history. It make us wise. We want help America by teaching her about our country. We good people. We want help you, Sheikh Amir say," Cengo translated.

"This is helpful," Wynn commented. "When we work together, we can accomplish a great deal. Americans are good people too. They want to help Iraq."

"It good that American people want help Iraqis, but how you think I can help you?" asked Amir, through Cengo. "I have nothing to hide. We good people. We want peace."

Wynn answered. "But Sadi," addressing Amir with the Arabic word for sir, "you know some Iraqis don't want peace. Some are committing acts of violence. They want to undermine the new Iraqi Government. They attack Americans. They attack Iraqis. If you can help us with any information on insurgent groups, we would greatly appreciate it."

Amir turned briefly and spoke firmly to Cengo.

"These people foreigners. Not Iraqi. No Iraqi people," Cengo translated.

"Yes and no," Wynn replied gently. This was one of the important questions, he realized. How much of the insurgency was homegrown, and how much was done by outsiders?

"Not Iraqis." Amir shook his head, as if reading Wynn's mind, struggling to answer in English.

Amir spoke in a voice heavy with caution and reputation, like a man never hurried, like a man always heard. As a sheikh, he had the luxury of talking only when he wanted to. He said a little or a lot, depending on how he assessed his position.

Wynn visited Amir because he wanted information and cooperation. After seven months of being in the country, and months of preparing, Wynn knew this war was more about accurate information than about firepower. Counterinsurgency theory required they act like doctors: treat carefully and do no harm. This sounded fine, but no one considered it easy.

Amir wanted security and money. Money meant power and influence, the ability to have his way, to sustain his authority.

The discussion continued. Amir said he took great risks by meeting with Americans. Wynn didn't doubt this. By now the whole neighborhood would know about this meeting. A neighboring tribal sheikh had recently been beheaded for reportedly cooperating with the Coalition, the title given to the allies fighting in Iraq. Before killing him, terrorists had visited the sheikh one night and warned him to stop talking to the

Americans. He said he would but didn't. Though dangerous, cooperation with the Americans tempted prominent Iraqis for financial reasons. Americans brought projects and money. The Takfiri—the name Iraqis used for terrorists—brought intimidation and death.

Double-dealing was as common in this part of the world as sand. Amir would be tempted to cooperate in as small a way as he could and still get what he wanted. Later that night, Amir might also be cooperating with Takfiri. The tactics would be similar. Give as little as possible to get more in return. These were rules of survival in a dangerous world.

So far they'd been sitting in a small room on western-style furniture. Now a young Iraqi boy, age maybe 14, came into the room and walked over to Amir and whispered something. Amir looked at Wynn and said, "We eat." He led the way to another room.

"Iraqi food good. Very good. You must eat," Amir said with pride, looking back over his shoulder at Wynn.

"I know, Sadi. I enjoy it."

The group of seven men—four Iraqis and three Americans—entered a long narrow room. A thin carpet bisected the room, and seating pillows lined the walls. Amir motioned to the party to assemble in two rows, separated by the carpet.

"Sit down, please."

Everyone sat, Amir directly across from Wynn, and Mr. Thumb to Amir's right.

Within minutes, several large metal pizza-like plates loaded with food were carried in and placed on the carpet. Custom called for the meal to be served family style. No one had individual plates. The largest plate, placed between Amir and Wynn, was piled high with a mixture of rice and raisins and pieces of roasted chicken and lamb. Smaller plates held cold vegetables and flat bread.

Amir, sensing Wynn's hesitation, picked up a piece of flat bread with his right hand and, using his hand like the mouth of a pole digger, plunged the bread into the huge mound of rice and meat. Rice and other pieces of food fell off indiscriminately as he scooped up a handful and ate.

The meal was a gesture of hospitality to the American guests. Amir orchestrated everything. The Americans drank cans of Turkish soda while the Iraqis drank bottled water—the Americans avoided most local bottled water because the bottles were often reused and refilled from questionable sources.

Wynn enjoyed the meal. The food was fresh and each man took what he wanted. Of the vegetables—probably washed in unsanitary water—he ate a few, not wanting to appear to his host as ridiculously careful.

Amir wiped his mouth with the back of his hand and picked up a particularly juicy piece of meat with his hands and put it on piece of flat bread before Wynn.

"Eat. Eat," he said. Wynn smiled.

As they ate, the conversation sparse, Wynn studied Amir, keenly aware of the differences separating them. Different worlds made them; that indisputable fact lay in the room like a carnivore. One man grew up in a life dominated by past glories and what it had once again released, looming dangerously over the present. The other came from a new glittering and diverse place, bred on confidence and exceptionalism, yet constantly bumping into hard realities. Although he wanted and accepted the hospitality of the older man, Wynn felt as if he was being feted by an anachronism. Part of Wynn hoped that one way or another the modernity and power of America would make everything about this old man irrelevant and absurd, that newness and youth should triumph. Another part of him knew better. Nevertheless, he hoped the pragmatic nature of Americans gave them a solid chance to succeed.

When the main party finished eating, servants carried the platters out. Nothing remaining was likely to be wasted. Tradition held that after the men ate, the women would eat. The animals got what was left.

Amir, noticing the Americans were increasingly uncomfortable sitting on the floor pillows, suggested they move back into the other room. Soon came hot tea, served in tiny glass cups and saucers resembling the accessories of a doll house. Small talk resumed.

A feeling started to grow in Wynn that, so far, little had been gained from the visit. Again he carefully contemplated Amir. Wynn had hoped his respect and concentration would draw out Amir's inner feelings and motivations. Amir appeared to detect Wynn's uncertainty and a careful smile creased his face. His eyes narrowed into little black slivers, as if refreshed by wet ink.

Wynn asked several more questions circumspectly. The back and forth of the terp and the complications of the language barrier forced an extended deliberateness and succinctness to the interrogation. But were they really communicating? Could Amir be playing him? Wynn was sure about nothing.

He asked about Amir's sons. Were they still in the area? He didn't ask about his daughters. Amir spoke for several minutes in response. All Arabs liked talking about their sons. He asked Wynn whether he had sons.

"No. I'm not married. I have no children."

For an instant, Wynn thought about Clare Baldwin, his old girlfriend back home, and about whether things could have been different. His mind retrieved her flashing smile, her soft skin, the way she stood up slowly, the way she walked so portentously. Maybe yes; maybe no. He couldn't let that distract him now.

"You are young, my friend. Still time," Amir said.

Amir reverted to Arabic again, speaking to Cengo. Suddenly Amir brought his hands together conclusively, as if he'd just closed a deal, and a smile of collusion crossed his face. Cengo translated.

"He say you must not wait long to marry. You wait too long, it sad. Our culture say marry young. Sheikh Amir say he can get for you special Iraqi wife, if you wish."

Wynn laughed.

"Tell him thanks but no thanks. Beautiful women live all over the world, but I don't have time for that right now."

Wynn changed the subject again and asked about the area's population. Had it changed? Had any foreigners moved into the area? Amir said no. Hardcore Al Qaeda members were generally not locals. Most were not even Iraqis.

Amir answered each question carefully, but he always seem to be leaving half the answer out. Then Amir asked a question.

"He say there no work for the men of his tribe. Can we find help getting jobs?" Cengo translated. Moments later Amir asked when the "friends" would fix the irrigation canals. Iraqis frequently used the word friends to refer to the Americans.

Wynn answered without commitment. "We should help each other, Sadi. Iraqis help Americans. We will help you." He wanted to convey the message that both sides should benefit. Easy generosity might undermine cooperation.

Wynn checked his watch. Time was wasting, and so far Amir had given him no important information. Wynn wasn't surprised. It was all process, and process eats time. They would meet again soon. He took modest satisfaction in feeling he had at least furthered the connection.

"This time is now," Amir said suddenly, with an air of finality. He struggled to speak in English. He spread his hands widely is if he was welcoming someone. "We go. We go."

Wynn didn't understand. Amir surely didn't mean that he wanted anyone to leave.

"In...future...we go. Back," Amir threw his hand over his right shoulder as if tossing trash.

"Back. No good. Back. Finished," Amir said sharply. Doubting he'd communicated clearly, he turned and spoke to Cengo in measured Arabic, gesticulating with his hands.

"Amir say that the past is finished. Whatever happened in past is finished forever. He say even we want change it, we cannot. Saddam gone."

Amir spoke again for nearly a full minute, before letting Cengo translate.

"Amir say that if we could go back in time, there many things we could do, do differently. He say that his oldest daughter marry weak man, and that if he knew that before, he would not take this man as his daughter's husband. He say that if he had the power he go back and heal the eyes of his father. He mean get operation for his father. His father go blind. Operation maybe fix. But he say this we cannot do. He say that if it possible to go back and change, to fix, our past mistakes we would not be in our world. That different world. Would be God's world. He mean only God can fix things. Not man. Only God."

Amir reached over to a side table and picked up a silver cigarette case and lighter. He would have offered Wynn one, but he knew Wynn didn't smoke. Amir selected a cigarette, lit it with unhurried precision, and took a deep draw, blowing the smoke overhead in wisps of satisfaction.

"My brother," he began again in English, more softly, as if he was taking Wynn into a special confidence. "Something else. America bring princes of war."

"Who is that?" Wynn asked, curious.

"Killers, bombers, kidnappers, thieves. All terrorists. And you. Princes of War."

Amir stopped talking. Condescension climbed out on his face. He smoked his cigarette contemplatively, studying Wynn like a man studying a zoo animal. He never looked at Cengo. Amir continued.

"These people live from war."

Outside, Moose and the rest of the platoon watched their assigned areas, looking for any suspicious activity. This was no easy task. Right and wrong was never entirely clear. And terrorists choose the time and place of attack.

He looked right. The street was mostly empty. A few cars were parked along the curb, near houses. He checked several roofs and saw nothing. About 100 meters up the street, an elderly man walked slowly down the north side. He looked steadily skyward, as if searching the heavens for something important.

Thinking about highbrow's theories about Iraq, Moose smirked.

Here he was: he and other American soldiers in this ass-backwards hellhole of a place, looking to kill bad guys while avoiding being killed. They were instruments of the counter-insurgency campaign. "Instruments?" No way. That was a different world. Didn't make sense here. Instruments were for cleanly dressed fresh-faced sensitive folks aspiring to be doctors or musicians or such, while sitting comfortably in nicely lined-up seats on manicured lawns or polished stages. They were for highly educated, clean-hand types working proficiently and delicately in temperature-controlled white rooms with lots of lights and tons of electronics. Not for him. Not for the Wolfhounds. Their world here was blunt, raw. A word like instrument carried too much precision. Here everything was rough and outlandish.

He looked left. At the far end of the street block, Humvee D22 waited. Its crew had the responsibility of watching two directions, northeast and southwest of the intersection. Three soldiers now manned the vehicle. Two men had dismounted and taken overwatch positions on a nearby house roof. Higher roofs provided superior observation positions.

The Americans called the crossing street Route Blueberry and had long since come up with their own road naming convention. A grid system, beginning with the letter W, numerically identified sectors in all the battlespaces. Unknown were the Arabic names, or if it even had a name. Americanization of area geography was necessary for basic communication and navigation.

Moose thought he made out Specialist Brett Kale's profile on top of a house. How was he holding up? Others had recently asked that same question. Ever since Ramirez, mental fractures of some sort were messing with Kale.

Kale watched the southeast. From his rooftop vantage point he could see if someone approached from an area not observable by the teams on the ground. He was of medium build, solid, lean, and fit, but had always wanted to be bigger.

Kale knelt on the rooftop. It was hot, so hot that he felt he was weeping sweat. A small boy dashed around the edge of a house. The boy, maybe five years old, rushed to the corner of the yard, lifted his little dishdasha, and relieved himself. From the boy's location he could see D22, but seemed not to notice it. He was dirty and shoeless and about the age of Kale's stepson, Wilson. Kale pondered the harsh distance between this child and Wilson, a distance measured in centuries of time and furthered by the science and technology extravaganza of the western world. Did fate put one boy in this world and one in the other? Kale had an urge to go down and talk with him. He might make the boy laugh, make him forget this harsh place. What was his name?

The radio squawked and Kale turned to his left, reacting to the noise. Haller, his partner on the roof, picked up the radio handset and listened. Haller, who invariably had a wad of paper in his mouth that he chewed like tobacco, was called "Halliburton" by the platoon—a nicknamed spun off the multinational corporation of the same name—after claiming once that if all were right in the world, he'd be the heir of a great fortune.

Kale wondered whether it was another report on IEDs—Improvised Explosive Devices. During the Wolfhounds' drive here, Charlie Company discovered an IED on Route Marlin, which ran several kilometers east of Route Blueberry. Their report included a request for an Explosive Ordinance Disposal or EOD team. The intersection of Routes Marlin and Blueberry was a frequent insurgent target. In the last 6 months, upwards of 20 IEDs had been hidden there. That statistic infuriated the soldiers; it meant insufficient surveillance. Yet Coalition convoys kept using those routes. Kale shook his head in disgust.

He looked again at the Iraqi boy, who had changed his focus. He now watched D22. What did he think? The child's concentration had shifted from the simplicity of his life to the alien Americans and the steel monster Humvees.

Inside, the meeting neared closure.

Wynn knew he shouldn't linger longer. His platoon had been providing security outside for almost an hour. Standard operating procedures required that they avoid remaining static in an area for too long, as this invited too much attention and could give the enemy time to react.

In order to wrap things up, Wynn returned to points the sheikh had raised earlier. He summarized Amir's requests. Regarding two civilians that had been arrested—unfairly arrested, in the sheikh's view—Wynn promised to look into their cases. Amir requested continuation of the trash removal program because it brought jobs and money to his tribesmen. Most importantly for the sheikh—or so its emphasis made it seem—Amir wanted the right contractors chosen for construction projects in the area. The right contractor meant someone Amir favored. To all these things, Wynn said he would do what he could.

"I enjoyed the meeting, Sadi."

"Welcome. Welcome."

"I hope you will call me when you can help. America wants to help make Iraq a great country."

"Thank you. Thank you." Amir took Wynn's hand in both his. Saggy bulges of yellowish flesh hung under both his eyes, as if egg yolk had been injected under the skin. Haider, watchful, stood close by.

Despite the inconclusive meeting, Wynn accepted why he was here. Iraq was where the war was, where the action was. Since childhood, he was imbued with a respect for martial combat, of strong men standing against bad. Now in Iraq, he was where he wanted to be: in the thick of the fight. He had the opportunity to test himself before the eyes of the world.

3

The Wolfhounds remounted their Humvees and drove west towards Route Blueberry, then Blackberry, heading back to FOB Apache, their base. Within minutes, local conditions worsened. Raw brick shacks, no exterior stucco, no decorative tile, no gardens—as if they had just left a gated community for the 'hood.

The convoy passed under an unfinished bridge where construction had stopped before the war. Naked rebar stuck out vertically from the unfinished girders like the legs of giant spiders.

Three hundred meters beyond the bridge, traffic slowed the platoon. Staff Sergeant Turnbeck, commanding the lead Humvee, D22, came up on the radio.

"Accident ahead. More than one car," he said.

Wynn, from the second Humvee, tried to see the scene. He hoped the convoy would not stop; vulnerability to IEDs or rockets was greatest at stops.

The convoy picked up speed again. "We clear?" Wynn asked D22.

"Yes."

Wynn saw a crowd ahead. Like back home, onlookers gathered at accident sites. As the Wolfhounds passed, a legless beggar zipped around the crowd in a wheelchair, looking for donations.

Sergeant Singleton, up in the gunner's turret of Wynn's truck, said, "That man got dealt a fucking bad hand."

Once on Route Blackberry, the Wolfhounds passed beyond the town into open country on a road the locals considered a highway. Wynn had heard it described as "a bad road cut over a dragon's back." Knots of defiant earth bulged up from underneath the barren land stretching for miles into the distance, scaring the dry landscape like old wounds.

The battalion's total area of responsibility included all of Bejanas—a city of about 275,000 people—and the ground west, halfway to the Tigris River. To the north, Route Cherry was the main east-west road.

Their convoy turned north on Route Grape. Sergeant First Class Cooke, Wynn's platoon sergeant, called Wynn on the radio to report that the last truck had made the turn. From here the drive back to FOB Apache would take about 20 minutes, when they were due to take over part of FOB security for 12 hours. A quarter of the Wolfhounds would rotate into the base security plan, assisting with perimeter guard duty. Men not on guard duty got time off.

Wynn adjusted his eyes to the road ahead. Soon they arrrived at an Iraqi checkpoint. The Iraqi soldiers waved through the lined-up civilian cars. The road narrowed at the checkpoint, not enough room for two cars to pass. Hundreds of cars passed this way daily, and the Iraqis checked few closely. A vigilant Iraqi soldier could notice a suspicious accent. Arabic, like most languages, had many dialects. Americans couldn't do this, Wynn knew. A capable Iraqi guard would also know whether the tribal part of a passerby's full name was common to the surrounding area. Americans didn't. But all these native advantages depended on the Iraqi soldier being serious about his work, trained, and loyal.

Kale, manning the turret gun in D23, remembered a recent nearby IED attack on a U.S. Army Hemmit Truck. A subsequent investigation determined that the IED had been buried in the road during a pothole repair, and covered by asphalt. The attackers had been patient, only detonating the bomb several weeks later, killing an American that had three kids.

Kale and the others were mistrustful of the road repair crew. Could terrorists have placed an IED in the hole without their knowledge? Were the repairers questioned? Surely yes?

Frustrated by all the things he didn't know, Kale traversed the gun turret to the right, orienting towards two o'clock instead of one o'clock, hoping to move his thoughts onward. He couldn't flounder on unanswerable questions; he must do his job right. He thought about what he and others were doing.

Eyes focusing between away and near, looking for things of interest, checking anything or anyone approaching, hunting danger. In the rear vehicle the gunner usually looks backwards, guarding the rear. Most men were alert, making a quick registry of what they see, then either discarding or selecting it for closer scrutiny. They studied each oncoming car. If the car had more than one person in it the odds of it being a threat diminished. Suicide drivers drove alone. If just one person was in a car, the men tried to ascertain the person's age. Young drivers were greater threats. Old people were less likely to blow themselves up. Stationary vehicles without an occupant were the most concerning. The eyes moved on. All the while the soldiers reported back and forth succinctly on the vehicle radios.

They looked for indicators of hidden bombs on both sides of the road, as the drivers tried to keep their vehicles in the center to reduce the strength of any blast coming from either roadside. Broken road surfaces were studied. Anything on the road surface was suspect. Cans, jugs, boxes, discarded tires, even animal carcasses had been used to hide bombs. The eyes moved on. When possible, the Wolfhounds drove fast.

Kale figured they'd driven past hidden bombs that didn't explode because the trigger man wasn't there or the device was defective. The two most common forms of IED attack were command detonation and remote detonation. Command meant the device was hardwired. Remote meant the device relied on a wireless signal, like a cell phone. One attacker initiated many IEDs. Others had timers or pressure plates. Eyes moved on. They drove on. Just too damn much to take in.

It felt like swimming with sharks. And recently, he felt more and more like his blood was in the water.

There was some positive news. The Task Force regularly rolled up IED manufacturing operations. Often informants revealed their whereabouts. A typical raid might uncover caches of old artillery rounds, batteries, cell phones, wire, various ancillary components to making the bombs. The bad news was that such raids confirmed that extensive amounts of artillery and mortar ammunition had been buried by Saddam's forces and were now available to the insurgents.

After passing through the Iraqi checkpoint, Wynn came up on the radio.

"Speedy and aggressive, that's how we're going to take it, man. Speedy and aggressive,"

"Uh huh," grunted Gung, Wynn's Chinese-American driver.

The traffic thinned and the platoon drove faster.

D22 still led. D21 followed, then 23 and 24.

"Love ya, baby," said Moose. His crew knew he was referring to the big machine gun.

Each man shifted in his seat, charged by the intensity and adrenalin this ride had unleashed.

Turnbeck restarted the reporting chatter. "Friendly convoy ahead. Coming this way."

The convoy drove 45 miles per hour, the four trucks spaced at 50-meter intervals.

"IA vehicle ahead."

An Iraqi Army truck was stopped on the roadside. The Wolfhounds slowed, curious. Two Iraqi soldiers were changing a tire.

"Go, go, go!" blurted Turnbeck, prodding his driver to the right side of the road, away from the down Iraqi truck, not wanting to slow down too much.

"Those guys actually look like they're working," commented Halliburton, Turnbeck's driver, as he blew paper spittle from his mouth into a soda can.

"Female ahead, two o'clock," Turnbeck reported. A lone female walked on the left shoulder of the road. "Not displaying anything in her hand."

"She's displaying something else," Halliburton said.

"Meaning?" asked Moog, a back-seater in D22.

"Dumb fuck! I mean she's got something I need."

"Keep your mind on the business, man."

"Thicker traffic ahead," reported Turnbeck.

"I got something thick for ya!" Halliburton said.

"Right." Moog scratched his crotch.

Traffic increased. The convoy slowed, crawling through two back-to-back intersections. The road expanded to four lanes. Civilian vehicles now approached from side streets, too—side entries always alerted the men to possible Vehicle-Borne-Improvised-Explosive-Devices, what the Army called "VBIEDs." Everybody's eyes fired, looking for threats.

Moose, D24's gunner, traversed his 50-caliber onto an approaching car.

"If only they knew the damage this baby could do," he said over the intercom.

"Some of them might, knucklehead," commented Cooke, always eager to convey the right lesson.

A few minutes passed, then Turnbeck continued, "Car coming in at one o'clock."

"Another coming in at two o'clock. Got three pax in the first one. No problem. Three more in the second one. No problem."

"Another vehicle trying to cross the road."

"They're coming from all around," said Turnbeck, unconcerned. "No worries."

"Awful smell coming from all around, too," someone commented.

"Because the place around stinks."

A dilapidated water treatment plant sat off the north side of the road. The Wolfhound battlespace contained three water treatment plants—two, surprisingly, still in operation.

Moose, up in the open air of the hatch, pulled his do-rag from around his neck up higher over his mouth. The stench still got through.

Past the plant and the next intersection the traffic lightened again. The convoy resumed higher speed.

Several minutes later, D22 slowed suddenly. "Traffic," Turnbeck said on the radio net. Everybody already knew.

"Lots of cars in front."

Abruptly they were standing still again.

Moose and the other gunners looked for targets. "Give me something. Give me something," he muttered under his breath.

"Going swimming," announced Turnbeck. His vehicle jumped the 4-inch center median to the opposite side of the road and drove against traffic, the truck roaring like an angry lion. The other trucks followed. The oncoming traffic jerked to the side of the road, letting the American convoy pass.

About a kilometer later, they crossed back over the median. The road cleared again. Several cars pulled over to let the Wolfhounds pass.

"Ass on the right."

A donkey stood along the roadside. Several men chuckled as they passed it.

"'Ass' has different definitions," Gung said over D21's intercom.

Wynn smiled. Some things never change.

As the Vehicle Commanders—known as VCs—called out pertinent sightings, the Humvee gunners spun from right to left in their turrets. Each gunner was exposed out of the turret above chest level. Gunners took the most injuries, mostly to their upper bodies.

"LN watering his grass."

An Iraqi man worked his garden. The military used the acronym "LN" to identify local nationals.

"Overpass one-hundred-fifty meters front. LN walking across."

The convoy moved along like an accordion, slowing down and closing up, then speeding up and increasing their intervals, always imitating the lead Humvee. Slowing down, the Humvees whined softly, the horsepower held back like an unhappy dog on a stout leash. Drivers tried not to let the gaps between the trucks narrow too much or extend too far. Their Standard Operating Procedure—SOP for short—in dense traffic called for 20-meter intervals so the spacing between them would offer some protection if an IED exploded. If a civilian car got between the Humvees, soldiers would signal those drivers to move away. Most Iraqis already knew better.

"Traffic clearer ahead," Turnbeck announced. The convoy sped up to 40 miles per hour.

"Check out stopped car. Coming up. Two cars," Turnbeck radioed moments later.

Soldiers who could see the cars stared at them. Those who couldn't see thought about how they might look. Seconds later, the Wolfhounds passed two empty vehicles on the roadside, a black BMW and an unrecognized model.

Moose spun his turret around to the rear and watched the two empty cars. Nothing suspicious. Concluding it wasn't a threat, he traversed again to the four o'clock position. In a strange way, the convoying reminded him of riding a roller coaster at night. Everything constantly confused you, and you never knew what might happen next.

Wynn's thoughts drifted in and out of the convoy. No shortage of things to worry about. Iraq had been an education by firehose. His platoon, as they were all aware, had a damn difficult job protecting itself and hunting insurgents—and maybe an impossible one.

By original design, the Wolfhounds were a Tank Platoon, but for the Iraq mission, they had left their four tanks back in America and reconfigured themselves, as had the rest of the battalion. Now they operated from Humvees as an armored mobile security unit, essentially a police-army hybrid thought more appropriate for counterinsurgency.

His platoon's area of responsibility covered nearly 200 square kilometers. "Your area to patrol, understand, and secure," was the way his company commander, Captain Ben Baumann, summed it up. Each of the three platoons in Delta Company had an area comparable to that of the Wolfhounds. Estimates had the Iraqi population in the area at 35,000 to 45,000. That meant 19 Americans responsible for a medium-sized town. By Iraqi standards, much of the population was middle class. The area had electricity three to four hours a day on average. Most of the home construction was densely packed two- and three-story concrete block multi-family units. The far south of their area was lower class, the people scratching a living out of nothing. Their housing was primitive. Mostly dirt roads. No electricity or public water. No sewer. No government services.

Wynn needed to know more about the area than any other American alive in order to conceivably do a first-rate job. It was a common joke in military that by the time you got proficient at your job, you rotated back to the States. Five more months to go.

Rarely did other American forces enter his battlespace other than other military convoys passing through. Sometimes battalion aerial assets, both manned and unmanned, worked over it. When necessary, the platoon called in other special assets, like EOD teams. Since the Wolfhounds had occupied the battlespace, a special operations team had twice conducted unannounced raids. One such operation nabbed a financier identified by Baghdad intelligence assets. The other raid followed up on a residual WMD lead. That was a false alarm. A box dressed up like spent uranium had been nothing more than a box dressed up that way.

His platoon was expected to be as self-sufficient as possible. If other American forces came into the Wolfhounds' area, it meant those assets weren't available elsewhere. If he operated independently and kept the violence down, his superiors were happy. He frequently felt like a town mayor. That was fine; he didn't complain. The independence and responsibility fired his pride. Nevertheless, the burden weighed heavily. A wag commentator had called the whole American-Iraqi enterprise "playing three-dimensional chess in the dark."

The convoy passed an Iraqi government building. An elderly man sat on the entrance steps reading a newspaper. Wynn wondered whether anyone was working inside. Army leaders spoke like the Iraqi government was operational, but that was overstated. What local government did exist was fractious. Traditional sources of authority, like the tribes, were more important than they had been under Saddam. New fiefdoms—like criminal networks of smuggling and extortion—were active. The remaining government offices were corrupt, inactive, or worse. In Bejanas, the Coalition had attempted to set up a governing council with representatives from various Iraqi ethnic groups, more or less a mirror of what was being tried at the national level. But the council operated fitfully, lacked resources, competence, and real authority.

Wynn noticed a green crescent painted on a building, symbolizing a medical facility, similar to the Red Cross. Medical care in Iraq was very poor. Professionals throughout Iraq, including doctors, were leaving the country. Too many had been murdered, kidnapped, or threatened. One hospital on the eastern side of Bejanas was now closed due to damage and looting. Both remaining hospitals were several kilometers east of the Wolfhounds' battlespace.

The remaining Iraqi police, whom the Americans called the IP, were largely ineffective. Many were untrained, crooked, unreliable, or all of the above. Many areas had no police coverage. The Iraqi Army, or IA, was in the early stages of rebuilding.

To his left, he noticed several green flags flying on rooftops, the flags increasingly displayed by Shia as a symbol of religious pride. Or maybe ascendency? Wynn knew his battlespace contained a brew of antagonistic neighborhoods: Sunni Arab, Shiite Arab, Kurds, and Christians. Some neighborhoods were clearly delineated, the locals aware of the important boundaries. In other areas, the ethnic mix was unknown and evolving. Kurds and Shiite Arabs were on the rise. The Sunni declining, retrenching; many openly admitted missing Saddam. The Americans were conducting a door-to-door census, designed by the battalion with each company responsible for their areas. Wynn's platoon had their piece of this census and would be back at it tomorrow, visiting Iraqi households to get basic personal information from the residents. American units were assigned extra interpreters, when they were available, to assist with this work. Another objective was increasing the informant network.

The convoy drove past another small mosque. His platoon's battlespace included three large mosques and dozens of smaller ones. Behind this mosque was an old soccer field. The stadium's bleachers were stolen sometime after the invasion. Only the unkempt field remained.

The Wolfhounds passed a parked fuel truck. The truck had probably driven into the city from one of the refineries. Along the northern edge of the Bajanas ran pipelines from the Iraqi Oil Company and most of the pipelines lay above ground, unprotected. Terrorist pipeline bombings were on the increase, causing huge problems.

Ahead Wynn saw one of the few road signs with English translations next to a school. A group of children were lined up, probably waiting to be released to go home. Several kids carried American-style backpacks. The Iraqi public school system remained in operation in about half the Wolfhound area, but many of the schools were in poor condition. Most had no electricity. Teachers complained about not being paid. Open schools split age groups into morning and afternoon sessions, and the average school kid in the area got two hours of schooling each day.

This was all his, Wynn congratulated himself in silence. He exhaled, extending the breath, letting it drift away like unwanted burdens. Five hundred years ago, given all this, he might have been a small-time emperor. Now he led a small part of the American Army. Nineteen men, counting himself, none who had ever been in the Middle East before. None could speak Arabic. None had more than cursory knowledge of the local customs and traditions. None had been policemen, firemen, government officials, utility operators, lawyers, engineers, doctors, or diplomats. None had prior experience in war. All were young men. Only his platoon sergeant, SFC Raymond Cooke, was older than 30.

With this make-up they fought an insurgency.

The whole thing, he thought, gave real meaning to the phrase "learning on the fly."

"Car parked under the overpass, three-hundred meters front," SSG Turnbeck reported.

The convoy approached rapidly. D22's crew scrutinized the parked car.

"Passenger getting out. Has something in his hand."

Trouble? Anticipation ricocheted inside the convoy as the men focused on the person. It was a man. Middle-aged. Something in his hand? A phone? A book? Less than ten seconds later, the lead Humvee passed him. Still couldn't make out what he held. The Iraqi stood too close to the road to detonate a bomb on the convoy. He got back in his car as the second Humvee passed him. Every Wolfhound looked hard at him. The man looked as if he was talking. On the phone, maybe? The last Humvee passed.

Moose, in the gun turret, watched the Iraqi the longest. Something held to his ear. Must be a phone. A minute passed. Nothing happened.

Turnbeck came back on the radio. Ahead of them, another bridge crossed over the road.

"People sitting under the bridge. Right side. Four-hundred meters; vehicle crossing the bridge left to right."

The car crossed the bridge as they watched. The convoy closed. Five or six men sat in a circle on a large carpet on the ground next to the bridge, some papers and small items assembled between them. Making tea perhaps. The convoy continued past.

Another bridge ahead.

"Man on the bridge," Turnbeck radioed.

"He's shooting me a bird."

"No he's not."

"Maybe he wants to."

"Maybe he doesn't."

"Watch it. Watch it," said Wynn, to end the bullshit chatter.

"Pedestrians on the right side," Turnbeck announced.

"Guys wading in the canal."

A canal now paralleled the right side of the road. One guy stood in the water up to his waist. Further down, a boat with two men inside it floated in the middle of the canal. Probably fishing, Wynn thought. Three people stood next to a concrete slab bridge. No side rails on the bridge.

"Surprisingly deep."

"What's he fishing for?"

"A way out of Iraq." Laughter on the net. This time Wynn laughed too, and ignored it.

The Wolfhounds drove at 45 miles per hour on open road for a couple of minutes. They passed several cars. Then they passed another car. This car drifted about, as if driven by a drunk. Apparently he hadn't noticed the Americans. D23 blew its horn and the Iraqi driver jolted erect. He looked like a thief caught in the act, or a man chastised by an infidel.

"Highway railings left and right."

"Picking up speed."

IEDs had been hung on the side railings. Consequently, over the last year, most of the railings were removed. But the vertical supporting beams remained in the ground. Driving by, several men stared, wondering if the beams were big enough to hide bombs.

Wynn noticed a woman and a small child walking along a freshly cut irrigation ditch that ran from the canal into a field. Other than the concrete and electric pumps used in the canals, he thought the basic irrigation design couldn't have changed much since biblical times. Vegetation growth lined the belly of many canals. From the air, during the dry season, the canals looked like giant green serpents.

When CPT Baumann came on the company radio in a net-wide call, his voice sizzling with anger, Wynn knew instantly that something serious had happened.

Wynn answered first, and the two other platoons just after. But the voice coming from the 3rd platoon was that of the radio operator, not 2LT Ray D'Augostino.

"Get me 'Actual,'" Baumann responded firmly, unsatisfied.

"Wait one, over," came the response.

The company net went quiet for a long moment. The radio operator must have gone looking for D'Augostino.

Baumann rarely talked to the entire command team on the radio. He preferred dealing with them one by one. That was his way: direct and targeted. The last time he radioed everyone, 3rd platoon had been hit by an IED, and one of their men had been killed.

More minutes passed. Everyone hung on their radios, waiting for D'Augostino to get on.

Wynn detected the increased density of buildings as they entered the W3 sector, the most populated area in 2nd platoon's battlespace. Hundreds of people lived inside the housing to his left and right. What did they think of Americans in gun-trucks?

"Dog Six, this is Dobbie One-Alpha."

"This is Dog Six," Baumann responded.

"Dobbie One-Actual is two mikes out, over." D'Augostino would be available on the radio in two minutes.

"Roger, have him come up on the net then. Out."

Wynn saw the message-received indicator flashing on D21's Blue Force Tracker. Wynn clicked the inbox.

"What's up?" said a message from Pit Bull One, 1st platoon leader, 1LT Evan Smith.

Wynn typed a reply, "Don't know," and sent it.

The rest of D21's crew had heard the radio traffic on the company net. They couldn't see the computer texting, but Wynn could sense their anticipation.

"Dog Six, this is Dobbie One, over." D'Augostino finally came on the air.

"Roger, over." The company commander, after pausing a few seconds, said: "All Dog elements, acknowledge readiness to receive the following transmission, over."

All three platoon leaders confirmed they were on the horn. Then Baumann continued.

"At 1422 today, Charlie Company reported a KIA. Subsequent traffic confirmed KIA from sniper fire. Incident took place in the W17 area. Soldier killed while standing outside his Humvee. No other small arms fire. Break."

The radio went silent for several seconds.

"Damn," Wynn muttered. He sensed the crew's sudden gut-check. W17 was about four kilometers away from the Wolfhound's present location.

Baumann continued: "All elements will ensure that all Soldiers dismounted take appropriate evasive actions. Stay mobile when possible. Stay in vehicles when possible. No fucking lollygagging on the street."

Lollygagging? Had the soldier been lollygagging? Regardless, it had been a helluva bad day for that soldier.

Baumann did not identify the KIA. That information would be kept close-hold for a while longer; more details would follow. Baumann ordered all to acknowledge receiving the message. All did.

At first, Wynn said nothing to his truck's crew. Silence seemed the right response.

Somebody back home would be getting that impossible visit, hearing that impossible news, having to deal with something they would have been telling themselves every day would not happen to them. Another terrible day back home for a mother, a father. Wife. Kids.

Wynn didn't tell the rest of the platoon anything over the platoon net, worrying it would affect their concentration. He'd tell them back on the FOB. About a month ago, another soldier was shot through the neck by a sniper. Fortunately, that soldier survived. That shooting, which happened while the soldier was talking to a shopkeeper, took place in another battalion's battlespace, about 40 to 45 kilometers south. Had enemy sniper activity increased?

To his own crew inside D21, he said: "That's why we can never ever let our guard down. It can happen anywhere. All we have is our equipment and our vigilance."

His crew kept quiet, each probably digging in his own mind for impossible solutions. Wynn knew that Specialist Lee, the medic in D21's backseat, would be asking himself whether he could have done anything to save the victim. Singleton would stare harder into the forbidding landscape around them, stroke the big .50 caliber, and want to shoot somebody.

"Bastards!"

Gung spit the word out, shaking his head rapidly side-to-side, as if he'd just resurfaced from underwater.

Arriving at the FOB's entrance, the Wolfhound convoy pulled into another circuitous arrangement of concrete barriers and entered the Bravo gate. Dirt blast-barriers bordered the concrete jersey barriers. From outside the gate you could not see inside the FOB. It looked like the entrance to a mine.

A series of fences enclosed the FOB. The perimeter fencing consisted of an outer belt of triple concertina wire, and inside of that a chain-link fence crowned with another coil of razor wire. This fencing spread out from the gate area like an industrial scar on the ancient land, running 400 meters west before it turned northwest and continued almost a kilometer and a half before turning again southeast and completing the encirclement of the base. More dirt berms shielded the inner camp. These berms prevented a potential car bomber from crashing the fence and penetrating the inner camp.

Wynn saw a dozen Iraqi civilians waiting at the pedestrian gate. On some days, 50 or more waited here. Most wanted work on the FOB. Every day except Friday, Islam's Holy Day, Iraqi laborers entered the FOB to take care of menial work such as cleaning and minor construction projects. Before entering, laborers were thoroughly searched. Those chosen made a few dollars a day, more than most had ever earned.

Today, a half-dozen Iraqis filled sandbags for an upside down U-shaped concrete duck-and-cover bunker designed for mortar and rocket protection. The base was alive with constant construction. A new Dining Facility—called a DFAC by the Army—was nearly complete. On the other side of the camp, a company had started a new detention center.

Other than the Iraqi labor that came daily from town, more than 100 civilian laborers lived and worked on the FOB. Most were foreigners, Indians and Pakistanis and Filipinos, not Iraqis. These workers lived in a special camp on base. They'd been imported by KBR, the big multi-national services provider with the massive contract to support many bases.

All the activity left the impression that America had come to stay.

The Wolfhounds had arrived in the motor pool behind their block of living trailers. While the soldiers did post-operation checks on their equipment, Wynn met with his senior NCOs: Sergeants Cooke, Turnbeck, Pauls, and Singleton.

Wynn knew he looked into the faces of men forged hard in war: men who had seen things that should not be seen, who had by now spent enough time around death to know it from the inside. Yet he saw a strange contentment, an acceptance of the task at hand, and no regrets. Every human being carries burdens and doubts—nevertheless, the men who stood before him were all can-do men: bold, ambitious, wanting to prove something. None of them wanted to be anywhere else than where they were right now.

These NCOs were his platoon's leadership. And all good men. SFC Cooke was senior. Cooke never thought big picture, but possessed all-important street smarts. SSG Turnbeck kept to himself. You had to pry opinions out of him, but he had an unmatched sense for what was important in the field. SSG Pauls, who had been a high-school swimming champion, kept the tightest crew and truck in the platoon. SGT Singleton, reliable and unassuming, provided ballast to Wynn's crew in D21. They were the gears in the motor. Without them, the platoon couldn't function. Before speaking, Wynn paused a little longer than he should have, looking around carefully, locking for a second or two into the eyes of these three men, hoping to reinforce singularity of purpose. Their cooperation and support were crucial to his success.

After Wynn spoke a few minutes, including telling them what he knew about CPT Baumann's sniper report and the KIA, Cooke proceeded to talk the group through the next 24 hours. Wynn added occasional comments. He was glad for Cooke's years of experience to help guide him. Because of his shared enlisted rank and experiences, Cooke was better than Wynn at getting the other NCOs to speak candidly. They would tell him what the soldiers were thinking and offer their interpretations. Just as senior leaders filter what junior leaders needed to know, Wynn knew that juniors filter for their seniors.

Minutes later, SFC Cooke called the rest of the men together out in front of their trucks. Wynn repeated what he had said to the NCOs about the sniper attack. He asked for a moment of silence for the victim, and as each man reverted to himself, a chill of solemnity embraced the group.

"When I get more details, I'll put them out. Let's not let the next one be one of us," he concluded.

Cooke spoke for a few minutes, reviewing the completed patrol, making both positive and negative comments about the platoon's performance. Then he thanked them and encouraged them to talk further among themselves about anything that needed tightening up. Cooke closed by reminding the men to take care of their personal needs in the next 12 hours: laundry, haircuts, writing or calling home. He next told SSG Turnbeck to reiterate the guard duty schedule.

The gym was full of sweaty male bodies and reeked of sweat and clothes that needed washing. The facility was an old Iraqi Air Force gymnasium, now filled with heavily used weightlifting equipment, both free weights and nautilus. All of it had been shipped in from the States.

Moose believed two types of soldiers came to gyms: those who worked their bodies patiently and hard, and those, the majority, who wanted to look as if they did. He definitely considered himself in the first category. Some of the men wore the official grey-shirt-and-black-pants Army PT uniform. Others, like Moose, wore their uniform pants and the brown t-shirts and still had on their boots. Black hard rubber-tile mats covered the floor. A half-size basketball court took up the rear of the gym. The place was noisy. Men shouted and grunted, and the clanging of metal on metal rang with motivational noise.

Moose and his work-out partner, a platoon soldier named Tyson, exercised hard for about an hour. Each looked at the other like a winning gladiator, powerful and dominant.

The two worked out as often as their schedules allowed. Moose typically pulled Tyson along, the way a lead dog pulled a dog sled team, motivating, hot breath panting, legs running, trash-talking when necessary to keep him moving. For Moose the workout was a piece of exertion art, a physical performance. Attentive to all the exercise details, with just the right weight and form, he pushed himself until his body screamed but didn't break. He knew exactly which machines worked what muscles and could make his legs and arms and back perform at their natural peak, but he didn't care about the look as much as he cared about the psychological effect.

Tyson, on the other hand, loved the look. Soldiers regularly saw him make a show in front of mirrors and say, "I love me." He'd twist and turn, showing off his body as well as the 18-inch-long red and yellow lizard tattooed on his right shoulder.

Now Tyson was on an inclined bench, pressing 75-pound barbells in each hand. Noticing his accelerated breathing, Moose leered.

"OK, man?"

"You're killing me."

"Bullshit. Die a little, get stronger, live a little longer."

"I'm working it, man, working it hard. Cut me some slack."

"Yes, you are."

"It's all good, but you're killing me."

National flags of more than 20 Coalition countries hung on the gym walls. Most soldiers noticed these and took some satisfaction in the international teamwork, but few could identify half of the flags. Even Macedonia, a new country, had a flag. All the guys in the room, however, were Americans. No other Coalition members were on this FOB, nor most others.

"You're a beast, Moose. Where'd ya get that stamina?"

"Running from my old man."

"Huh?"

"He's worn out a set of boots every year on my ass."

A couple of civilian KBR employees manned the check-in counter and periodically policed the facilities. Against the wall by the counter stood two large white freezer-type storage units holding hundreds of water bottles. Cardboard signs taped on each of the coolers read: "Take a cold one, put a hot one in." Somebody had scribbled, "That's what she said," on one sign.

Moose and Tyson finished their workout. They signed out and walked outside, heading for their hooches. Outside of the gym, loud electric generators drowned out other sounds. They passed four green and white porta-johns. The plumbing didn't work in the gym.

"What you doing after chow?" Tyson spoke loudly, to cut through the noise.

"Got laundry to do. Machines are less crowded later. Next time I go to war, I'm bringing a maid."

"Want to do mine while you're at it?"

Both men smiled. "Haha. What's the compensation?"

"Compensation? How about I agree to rescue your ass if the shit goes down?"

Tyson laughed at his own proposal. But Moose knew that if the shit hit the fan, Tyson wouldn't hesitate to rescue him. And he'd do the same for Tyson. It had to be that way.

Moose responded. "Who rescued who from those seventy-five-pound barbells?"

"Just testing you, old man. Hey, some of the guys gonna sit around and shoot the shit tonight. Gonna come?"

"Don't think so. I'm on Sergeant Cooke's list for 2200 guard duty. Need to fit some beauty sleep in after dinner," Moose answered.

"What a wuss," Tyson scolded.

Moose, annoyed, said, "We'll see. Maybe I'll take a six-pack of Red Bull from the DFAC and stash them for later. Uncle Sam's contribution to me."

They passed the post office on the corner, then the finance office where they could draw a cash advance on their pay, and proceeded down the road that would take them past the battalion headquarters. The company area with their living trailers was another 400 meters beyond that. Dust as powdery as flour rose up from the road to greet them as they walked. Moose could feel the grit collecting in his saliva.

"Fucked-up about that sniper shooting," Tyson said. "Ain't no place safe. I think I knew that guy. That makes nine KIAs so far in the battalion since we been here, don't it?"

"Think so," Moose answered, without thinking about it.

Shortly after getting back to Apache, everyone learned the identity of the KIA. That kind of bad news passed through the FOB like an arctic wind.

"Hey, what's up with Kale?" Tyson inquired, changing the subject. "The guys are talking about him. He's—I don't know—out there, or something."

"He doesn't talk much, that's for sure," Moose replied, after thinking about it for a second.

"It's like he's lost in his own world or something. The dude is dreamy. No jokes. No more smiles." Tyson added, curious about what Moose thought.

"I don't know, buddy. I do remember him being more alive, more with it, back stateside," Moose said.

"Yeah. Think so too. Remember how that dude could run? He used to run all the time. Never see him doing PT now."

"Combat duty ain't for everybody, Ty," Moose commented, making an evaluation rarely voiced, but obvious to anyone who thought about it. "Does something to you, they say. Trouble is you don't have a way of finding out 'what' until you're in it."

Everything in war was everyone's business. No place to hide. Men stripped each other psychologically. If a man's bowels were loose, people joked about it. If a lady back home was messing with you, it wouldn't stay secret long. If a man was a risk to the platoon, people would know. They might not talk right away. But they would know.

"Yeah, I suppose that's right, Moose. War damn sure ain't for everyone. Since Ramirez, Kale hasn't been the same," Tyson said. Ramirez was the first—and only so far—Wolfhound soldier killed.

Tyson hesitated, wanting to get the words right.

"Certain things you won't know until you're right there in it. No trial run here. Here the race is always on, man! Fuck, you know that, Moose."

"Who talks to him most?" Moose asked.

"Who what?"

"Who talks to him most?" Moose asked again.

"Probably you, don't ya?"

"Don't know."

"He seems to be lugging around a pack of disappointments."

Moose saw the problem, and remembered checking Kale out on the rooftop earlier. Kale was his friend, ever since Army basic training. Something in his head wasn't right anymore. Moose said nothing. Tyson dropped it.

They arrived at the living trailers.

"Meet you in about twenty minutes after showers, and we'll go eat." Moose said.

"I'll knock on your hooch."

"That works. Make sure you use soap!" Moose retaliated for the earlier abuse.

"Fucker. You know it."

Kale sat in his hooch, alone. Earlier, after Cooke released the men from the day's patrol, the platoon sergeant had walked over and commended Kale on his professionalism during the day's missions. He hadn't expected it. Thinking about Cooke's comments now, Kale flushed with pride—but he also felt ashamed. All of his life, pride had both motivated and consumed him. Sometimes, when he felt on top of the world, a tiny voice inside him whispered that the air in high places was thin and the footing treacherous.

Kale stood up abruptly and looked at himself in a small wall mirror. His face resembled one of those you saw in paintings of American Indians: a large upright chin, wide prominent cheekbones, watchful green eyes, square shoulders and a narrow waist, and reddish-brown hair that looked as if its ends were burning when he stood in the sun. Fitness came easily to him. He had the metabolism of a furnace and never gained weight. Naturally reticent, he was the type of guy who talked less than others thought he should.

"Textbook stuff, dude. You're a damn fine soldier," Cooke had said, slapping Kale on the helmet.

That was two hours ago, and Kale's spirits still soared. He loved compliments the way a dog loves attention.

All his life Kale had felt as if he needed to prove something.

Was Moose hungry for praise the same way? Something about Moose made him appear permanently satisfied, as if he didn't seek praise from other men. Kale wanted that kind of independence.

He thought again about what Cooke said, and how he'd said it. Maybe Kale did well today, but others had too. He certainly wasn't one of the top soldiers. Guys like Moose were much better, Kale knew. Something calculating was in Cooke's look. Was he giving genuine compliments, or was it something else?

A feeling of being scrutinized flooded over Kale again. He understood why.

4

Specialist Juan Cuebas, one of the Wolfhound's Soldiers, relaxed in the company orderly room staring gargoyle-like at nothing and everything. He was deciding whether to call home. His aunt would be anxious to hear from him. Even before Iraq, she had spent many an anxious hour worrying about him. As a little boy, he'd hide from her, once for a whole day, making her search everywhere, sometimes bringing her to tears. Cuebas had a distinctly primitive look—a mottled alligator-skin face and dull wet gray eyes, like raw oysters. His tight mouth and thin narrow lips intimated confidentiality and prudence, the look of a man holding secrets. Another side of him was pure jokester. He liked that side best.

Cuebas was Puerto Rican. His remaining family still lived on the island. Both his parents had died before he started school, his father of cancer and his mother in a car accident two years later. His aunt had raised him while caring for her own three children. She became his surrogate mother and father. Her husband had died before Cuebas moved in. Life skills came from living; that's what his aunt always said. Several of his relatives were combat veterans. His grandfather got wounded in the Korean War. Two uncles had served in Vietnam. One got a Purple Heart.

Cuebas fondled the brass memory chain on his wrist, which was a gift from his aunt. His uncles' names were stenciled on it.

He joined the Army three years ago, immediately after graduating from high school. He left for basic training promising his aunt he'd write regularly. He never did. But he did call when he could. Since arriving in Iraq he'd developed the routine of calling her once a week. The calls were mostly one-way conversations; she did most of the talking. They lived in different worlds now. She asked him little. Her job was conveying to him the news of the island, keeping him connected to his home, and this she did meticulously, pausing to ask repetitive questions about his well-being but nothing more. It wasn't her nature to be inquisitive.

Cengo came into the room.

"Ayeee. Hey Cengo," Cuebas started most of his statements with "Ayeee," a sound a man might make when he's sipped scalding coffee.

Cengo nodded, friendly but silent.

Cuebas watched Cengo ready himself to leave the FOB. He got extra time off today, like the Americans. Cengo shed his American uniform and stowed it away, along with his helmet, boots, and body armor, in a footlocker inside the dayroom. Every day, like most of the other terps, Cengo arrived at the FOB and reported to work before the American patrols departed. At day's end he would leave, unless an extended mission required staying on the FOB. The Wolfhounds controlled Cengo's schedule.

After work, the only American-supplied thing Cengo regularly took home was his sunglasses.

He sat on the footlocker and put his sandals on. As an Iraqi Kurd, Cengo was—even before the war—a rebel inside his own country. The Kurds, about 15 percent of the Iraqi population, had fought the powers in Baghdad for centuries. More Kurds lived in the surrounding nations. Kurds were one of the largest ethnic groups in the world without a state to call their own.

Cuebas knew Cengo had a large family, but his mother's family had been killed in one of Saddam's chemical attacks on the Kurds. Second to Kurdistan, a country that did not yet officially exist, Cengo's favorite country was America.

Cengo wanted to leave Iraq. Cuebas understood why. Cengo's family didn't have money. Now, as an interpreter he made $600 a month, royal wages in the local area. If he had a flaw, it was his hostility to the Arabs. The Arabs wouldn't trust him. His accent made it impossible to hide his Kurdish origins. On the other hand, Cengo knew the area, knew who the important families were, and better detected dishonesty in conversations than the other terps. Two of those were older

Americans, immigrants from other Middle Eastern countries. Two others were Iraqis, but their education level was low and their English barely passable. So the platoon felt blessed to have Cengo as their full-time terp.

"Wanna take some soft drinks with you?" Cuebas asked. "Put in your backpack?"

"No can do. Terrorists no like coke."

"Ha. Ha. You don't have to share them."

"They no ask. If they want, they—take."

"OK. Then we make a special coke for them. One that goes BOOM. Like what they do."

"No. I go quick and be invisible."

Be invisible was Cengo's usual parting declaration. Cuebas hoped it would be true.

He walked over to Cuebas to say goodbye. As they shook hands, Cengo's face turned serious.

"Sorry about Soldier killed today," he said.

An hour later Cuebas was finishing dinner in the DFAC when he heard a familiar voice mention the Twin Towers. Curious, he looked over. A few seats away, Halliburton, a lanky Texan with a reputation for having the biggest and dirtiest mouth in the platoon, was talking to Moog, a knotty dark-skinned Asian-Hispanic from New Mexico whom the Wolfhounds called, "Mongrel Moog," or just "Mongrel," and Randell, a New Yorker with three lifetimes worth of acne and habit of making his finger knuckles pop like an Orchestra's percussion practice.

Halliburton said, "When those two towers went down in flames, I knew what I had to do. I made up my mind that fucking day." He bent forward over his plate and spooned up a mouthful of creamed corn. Mongrel Moog, tearing open a plastic packet of salad dressing, looked as if he wanted to respond, but thought better of it.

Everyone knew why everyone else had joined the Army. Or at least their claimed reasons. For most of the youngest guys, it was 9/11. Everybody defended their reasons 24/7. Pretending not to believe each other was a kind of game.

Mongrel, after scratching his crotch, spoke up. "I'd already made up my mind by then, but after 9/11, I didn't have to worry no more about persuading my Mom. It was a done deal, dude. She never said another word."

"Those Fuckers," Halliburton continued, referring to the 9/11 attackers, shaking his head with disgust as he spooned up more corn. "Ain't nobody in this man's Army going to rest until we bury those bastards."

"Sure better not," Cuebas answered.

Mongrel and Halliburton, two of the youngest guys in the platoon, looked at Cuebas. Neither had noticed him until this point. Mongrel reached over and acknowledged him with a fist bump.

"You brothers are still wet behind the ears. Surprised the boys in recruiting took you in," Cuebas jabbed.

"Shit," Randell said.

"I was born a killer," Halliburton protested. "They saw killer in my eyes when I walked in. Now I'm here. We need to get down to business in this place." He hunched back over his food, leaning so low he looked worried someone would steal it.

"We, the few and the brave," Mongrel offered, not sure if he had the line right.

"Shitttt," Halliburton grunted, "that's the Marines you thinking about. The few and the proud."

"You're thinking 'home of the brave,' Mongrel," Cuebas said.

"Tell you one thing, I'd give my left nut to be the guy that puts a bullet in Bin Laden's head." Mongrel smirked and looked around, seeking praise.

Cuebas whistled to get their undivided attention, seeing a perfect opportunity to spring a trap.

To Mongrel, he said, "I'd give your left nut to blow away that bastard, too."

All laughed. Cuebas picked up his tray and got up to leave.

"Eat me," Mongrel replied.

Cuebas looked back. "What? Your boy, Halliburton, not making you happy anymore?"

Mongrel, flustered by Cuebas' retort, dribbled bits of food out of his mouth.

Cuebas walked away, chuckling. Another score by an insult artist. He claimed victory if he left them sputtering.

After 9/11, Cuebas felt vindicated. He'd joined the Army just over a year before the attack. In the early days, he watched his fellow citizens' surge of patriotism with a combination of amusement and a where-you-been-all-this-time bravado. Nonetheless, he didn't begrudge those joining because of 9/11. It was an excellent reason. Yet in his way of thinking, they'd needed an extra push, a push that he didn't require.

He of course wouldn't deny he too got caught up in the post-attack patriotism. Everyone did. Even his aunt, and he'd never heard her say an angry word. She'd called Bin Laden El Cabrona. Son-of-a-Bitch. And the letters! Cuebas had received dozens of "thank you for your service" emails and letters, including from folks he didn't remember. His aunt had distributed his address. One letter had come from his high school English teacher. He'd had a crush on her in school. She wrote to him as if he were a rock star or something, even calling him "hot stuff." Once, four or five months after 9/11 while back in Puerto Rico on leave, he'd thought of looking her up with ideas of her thanking him in another way. He'd decided against that. The mass support made everyone feel proud to be a soldier.

But this was Iraq, not Afghanistan. Few thought they would be putting a bullet in Bin Laden's head here. So why were they here? Cuebas didn't need explanations. He wasn't sure it mattered. The thing was, some Islamic bastards here were fighting us—just like those 9/11 terrorists did. Better here than back home. It made sense to him.

5

Wynn walked over to a new wooden picnic table under a grey tarpaulin near the FOB's mini shoppette. The outside heat sizzled. Even the bugs sought shade. He sat down, hoping for a bit of privacy. The rug and jewelry shop trailers were to his right. The barber shop further up, and beyond that the Burger King and Pizza Hut stands, arranged in trailers like vendors at a county fair. He had just gotten a haircut, and now planned to finish his weekly report for CPT Baumann. Wynn looked around. The FOB used massive quantities of wood. Where did it come from? Someone said that America shipped it in. As far as he knew, Iraq had no forests. New guard towers with four massive telephone pole corner supports. Bus stops. Outdoor furniture. Indoor shelving and partitions and desks. Army engineers were hard at construction, erecting new American-style things on top of the war-damaged Iraqi stuff. It made you think. But those were unimportant thoughts.

What was important for him was understanding this part of the world. Everybody asked the same questions: Do Iraqis want what we want? Can we win this thing?

At Temple University, he'd taken a course on psychology on his way to a political science major. He remembered a discussion on Maslow's hierarchy of needs, the theory that basic physiological needs came first: food, water, shelter, basic survival, things like that. Then came safety. Sophisticated political considerations came much later, if at all. Was there a message in that for a counterinsurgency? Societies developed step by step and what you had at any given time was a Sudoku puzzle, with thousands of big and small imprecise evolving pieces. The ruler, whoever was on top, dealt for better or worse with what he had. In most times and places, retaining power was all-important. Sometimes rulers fiddled benevolently with the pieces. Sometimes they smashed them. Sometimes they didn't care.

Two young soldiers walked over to the Pizza Hut stand, carrying their rifles and wearing their helmets. The security rules required that soldiers stay in this uniform in most places on the FOB. Wynn didn't recognize the men. They had combat patches on their right shoulders, so they'd been in country at least a month. The pizza man slid open the stand's window and Wynn smelled the rich spicy aroma.

Eighteen or nineteen years old maybe. Nations sent their young men to fight wars. Few of them had studied psychology or sociology or Middle East history or anything else like that. Few understood the puzzle pieces: the Sunni and Shia, the Arab and Persian rivalries, the history of confrontation between the Islamic and Western Worlds. Who in America really did? Academics, maybe. But even within that academic community differences were intense. Some political leaders, maybe. But they weren't here. He and these young men, and other men and women like them, were here. They manned the front lines of America's foreign policy, to work and fight—and possibly die—for political ideas. It was ironic, even cruel, that these ideas were imperfectly understood. Could that be enough to motivate men? There had to be something more.

Wynn had five or six years on the soldiers ordering pizza. A few years more of school. Maybe nature had given him better cognitive abilities and a better memory. Probably no difference in drive. Or in ambition. The two soldiers walked to the other side of the break area, holding their pizza slices and their guns.

The talk with Amir today had, again, confirmed the incredible complexity of the whole enterprise. Wynn wanted to think he'd made some progress—despite the great distances between them and us, language obstacles, huge cultural differences. And culture clearly mattered. Basic to everything was information. Information was available all around him, information about the area, the people, about the tactical situation on the ground. The question was how to absorb it and use it.

A sparkle of color on the ground caught Wynn's eye. Curious, he got up from the bench, took a step, and bent down to take a closer look at the colored object. On the ground lay a thin inch-long strip of bright green-and-red plastic foil attached to a broken stick of black plastic the size of a toothpick. A piece of waste blown here by wind perhaps. He picked it up. It looked vaguely like a part of one of his grandfather's old fishing flies.

His grandfather—Paps—had made his own flies. He liked red and green feathers best. "Good fishing requires attention to detail," the old man would say. "That starts with first-class flies." Attention to detail was critical for progress here in Iraq as well.

The other two soldiers got up from their table, their pizza and drinks finished. They glanced at Wynn, probably recognizing him as an officer. Did they wonder what he was thinking about? They would never guess "fishing."

The cabin up in the woods where his grandfather did most of his fishing had a thickly shellacked oak countertop. Paps treated the countertop like an altar. On that countertop, always clean and polished, he did his fly prep. Everything in fishing had to be well thought out. He'd described fishing as an intricate conspiracy of man and water, requiring the smooth blending of delicate motions and an artful lure to secure the strike, make the catch, and get a win for the hunter. Maybe what the Wolfhounds were trying to do in Iraq was not too different.

"Fish are smart, boy. You can't fool a fish with a bad fly," Paps would say.

Across the room from the cabinet where Paps kept his fishing supplies was another small cabinet he called his old war chest, where he kept some other things important to his world—and to Wynn's. Sitting on top of it was a Korean War Chinese Army helmet. The star on the front of the helmet still held flecks of red paint. Paps had taken the helmet as a souvenir during the fierce fighting in January 1951 that finally blunted the Chinese intervention. Too young for World War

II, Paps had joined the Army four months before the North Korean invasion. He'd enlisted to get off the farm. Paps never talked much about the war, said no good came from talking about it. What he didn't say had spoken loudly enough. Even on all those fishing adventures, Wynn had been conscious of the fact that his grandfather had experienced combat. Over the years, Wynn had read books about the Korean War, and other wars. All that reading and thinking and dreaming had surely been stepping stones to where he now was in Iraq.

Also inside the old war chest were a few notebooks documenting Pap's military service and a shoebox full of other memorabilia, such as his service ribbons. And his medals. The Bronze Star meant the most. The accompanying citation and its crowning words—for conspicuous bravery—rung in Wynn's ears all through his adolescent years, and even now. He never understood why Paps hadn't framed any of these things and hung them on the wall. Paps never satisfactorily explained to him why a man shouldn't take maximum pride in the things he deserved. Paps' pat answer was that he was "beyond that" or that it was in the "distant past." Wynn's feelings about that now was that you never got beyond or past certain things.

Paps was done with making fishing flies. He had died of cancer three months after Wynn's last visit to the cabin, four months before the Wolfhounds deployed to Iraq. Arthritic hands had not prevented him from making that last fly. Would Paps be proud of what his grandson was doing in Iraq?

Wynn timed his dinner so he could go straight over to the HQ after chow for his weekly meeting with the battalion S2, the unit's Intelligence staff. So he lingered alone a few minutes more in the DFAC, enjoying a double scoop of Baskin Robbins ice cream. He looked around at the soldiers. Many faces had that youthful, cool, cocky look, a look that shouted "I'm indestructible." That mindset that proved indispensable when old men sent young men to war.

As he waited, he thought about what he would tell the S2. Everyone said Intelligence was the key to this war. The S2 asked him and others to share more about what they saw and heard outside the wire. HQ wanted to cull more than the abbreviated material the platoons sent up through channels in their normal reports. In past S2 debriefs, Wynn had tried to add context to operations in his platoon's battlespace, elaborating on anything the Intel analysts were curious about. He knew the idea was that their info would help build the overall Intel picture. He checked his watch: 1904, time to go. The sun lingered stubbornly, the evening sky the translucent blue of the Caribbean Ocean.

After a short walk, he entered the fenced-off inner compound of the Battalion Tactical Operations Center, passing a guard station at which he had to show his ID card. Pictures of battalion soldiers at work hung on both sides of the center's hallway, shots the Public Affairs guys had taken from all over the unit's battlespace, showing daily soldiering in and outside of the wire. No Iraqis in any of the photos. As Wynn approached the S2's office, Sergeant Rais, an S2 NCO, came out, saw him, and said, "We're running behind, Sir. One of your fellow LTs is still at the dance." Rais suggested Wynn come back at 1930.

Wynn left the building and walked to a quiet area with a view into the distance. To his front lay a mustard-colored landscape. The distant horizon, inexact and obscured by haze, appeared to mirror the turbulence and mystery of the human world. It made him realize how alone he was. After a few moments, he went back inside. Soon the steady rush of the electric noises of equipment around the HQ again flowed over him, and he felt reconnected. The technology-dominated mini-world the Americans had planted here could be reassuring. Millions of dollars' worth of highly sophisticated computer and communications equipment purred, operated by trained soldiers, all installed inside a rudimentary nondescript masonry building, built 30 or more years before by local illiterate labor. Inside, the past was still present. A scent of urine suggested not everything could be erased. Iraqi plumbing, when it existed, was always inadequate.

1LT Nathan Petty, the Battalion's Assistant S2, was Wynn's trailer roommate and friend. Petty's dad was a retired Air Force Master Sergeant and had taken a Korean wife. Now this officer, with 50 percent of his family heritage originating in the coastal Korean villages along the China Sea, tried to help the American Army understand what it faced here in Mesopotamia. Petty had once joked to Wynn that the Army's multi-ethnicity represented a unique form of globalization. Wynn took a seat at a large brown table the size of something out of a Fortune 500 boardroom. Petty and a couple of S2 Analysts sat across from him.

"Hi Christian," opened Petty, "good to see you."

"Always a fine day when I can visit battalion," Wynn responded.

"Glad to know you welcome the assistance we bestow," said Petty, playing along.

Wynn grunted. "Assistance? You staff clowns run me through the wringer and call it assistance."

Petty smiled and proceeded. "I've got a spiel here today that I've got to go over with all you guys." His eyes glowed like a proctologist's.

Wynn listened patiently for several minutes. The gist of Petty's statement was that without good evidence, we can't nail suspects. Wynn felt as if he was watching a TV cop show. Police made mistakes. Bad guys got turned loose because of lack of evidence. The Army role in Iraq was de facto police work. Get information about a crime. Go to the scene. Look at it. Gather physical evidence. Do the questioning. Assess, decide, and then make an apprehension, if possible, based upon the evidence.

"Soldiers make mistakes, too," Petty said after a moment, almost sanctimoniously.

Then he explained that soldiers were constantly screwing up evidence. "Recently a platoon had a mission to pick up a suspected insurgent financier. They knew that finding the suspect's cell phone was crucial to the raid's success. They'd apprehended the target, but left his cell phone at the scene. They also left behind important documents. The papers they did bring in turned out to be nothing more than handwritten copies of a story about boating on the Tigris." A hint of amusement crossed Petty's face. "It turns out that the cell phone had been used to coordinate smuggling weapons, and numbers stored on the phone could have led to a breakthrough."

Wynn sat silent. Although he understood Petty's point, he sympathized in part with that platoon. You had a thousand things on your mind during a raid. In the field your translators didn't have the time to review lots of documents. Details were easily missed. And every operation was dangerous, the men conducting them highly stressed, concerned about IEDs and enemy gunfire. If Iraqis civilians were around, and it sounded as though they probably were, language confusion would abound. Might even be shrieking women in the house. Lighting in Iraqi houses was notoriously bad. The Americans carried flashlights and night-vision devices, but these only illuminated what you pointed at. A small cell phone was easy to hide. The platoon would have been under time pressure and probably had a slew of other worries that night. No time for a leisurely search. The phone should have been found, but he understood how it could have been missed.

Those seeking good Intel from below often have little idea of what it's actually like out there. Most had never done that work.

Petty sensed his growing annoyance. Maybe Wynn's eyes had a "you-fucking-do-it" look.

"I know it's a nearly impossible task that you guys down in the platoons have," Petty said. "Poor Intelligence is fucking us. It boils down to this." He leaned heavily back in his chair, suggesting he was about to sum up the entire war effort.

"We're trying to buy time for an Iraqi government to build credibility. Fuck, nobody in his right mind believes we're here to take over this place. We came here to eliminate a perceived threat of terrorism and extremism. Then things started falling apart on us. Now violence is steadily increasing. Everything we think or do is questioned."

Wynn listened, trying to figure out why Petty leaped from a small search failure to discussing the overall progress of the war.

Petty hesitated, perhaps sensing he'd jumped track, and started speaking more carefully. Then he looked at Wynn the way an attorney might look at a judge, hopeful his arguments were succeeding. "Violence spiraling out of control will make it impossible for the Iraqi government to get better. Don't you agree?"

He didn't wait for Wynn to answer. "So we have to do whatever we can to suppress that violence, suppress the groups that are behind the violence. It's all to buy time—time to give freedom and a better way of life here a real chance."

"Doesn't make the work easier," Wynn said, finally.

They both remained quiet long enough to wonder why the other hadn't spoken.

"At least Sheikh Amir doesn't think it can be easy for us," Wynn added.

"See him again today?"

"Yes. I wasn't sure whether to be thankful or wash after I left."

Hearing that, an amused look returned to Petty's face. "Well, he's certainly in a position to know a lot of stuff," he said.

"He gave me nothing worth salt, really. And even if he did, I wouldn't know whether to trust him," Wynn said. "It reminds me of something my grandfather used to say: 'It ain't just what you don't know that hurts you—it's what you know that ain't so.'"

"Absolutely right. I guess the key is how to connect with a guy like that in a way that it's in his interest to be truthful," Petty said.

"Yep, but how? I know, show him the value of cooperation. Show him better ways. Do some old fashioned win-win horse-trading. But all that's a helluva lot easier to philoso-phize about than execute."

"Sometimes the best efforts fail," Petty said. Now he gazed at Wynn like a fan might watch an athlete. "Doesn't mean we don't keep trying hard as hell."

"For sure. Nothing tried; nothing gained."

The lime-colored tactical lights in the room made their skin look sanitized, as if they were being prepared for surgery.

They were all privileged in a way, privileged to be part of a great effort, even if it failed. Few of them had illusions it would be easy.

Petty finally asked Wynn to summarize his platoon's activities over the last week. He did. None of what Wynn described prompted hard questions.

"Thank your men for me," Petty said.

Wynn looked at him quizzically, surprised.

Petty continued. "What I mean is that those of us up here—up here in the puzzle place—appreciate what your guys are doing. All this is confusing crazy, ugh, hard. But you platoons have to deal in the local realities out there in the shit. And up here..." Petty did a lasso movement with his head, signifying the whole headquarters, and with his voice trailing off, "...well, we watch and study from a distance."

Wynn shook off the compliments, but it was nice to get Petty's praise and concessions.

"It's our job, brother. We all have our roles."

Maybe both of them looked for reassurance. Almost everybody in a war constantly looked for reassurance.

It was 2110. Cooke and Wynn sat alone together in Cooke's trailer. It was a rare opportunity for privacy, and a place to talk about the psychological and physical health of the platoon's men. Wynn was glad for it. Despite being with each other almost constantly, seven days a week, in the thick of their work thousands of distractions intervened, and events of the moment dominated. He worried about overlooking details. Now they could be more relaxed and candid, and he could let his guard down partially and not pretend that he, as a young lieutenant, wasn't still learning.

Overall, Wynn felt satisfied with his men's resiliency. Hard times in a very hard place, and still the platoon's performance pleased him. But he had a specific concern.

"How do you know when one of the guys is not performing at his best?" He asked Cooke.

Cooke, unhurried, his broad caramel-colored face inexpressive, studied Wynn. He was by now a pretty astute judge of his lieutenant. Wynn was nothing if not deliberate, and he didn't like idle chitchat. Cooke waited for him to continue.

"I'm worried about Kale," Wynn said.

Wynn had been watching Kale for a while now. Not constantly, but noticing little things. Kale seemed increasingly detached, maybe depressed. He was quieter and never joked. He rarely interacted with others.

Cooke said, "With every man you do the same. You watch what he's doing, Sir. You laser the man with your eyes so you pick up the changes, how he is different, ya know? Know what his way of doing things is, and they can't hide anything from you."

"Have you noticed anything about him?"

"None of them can hide, Sir." Cooke replied. "They're all naked out here. We're all doing the same thing. Got the same shit to deal with. Working the same way. Same restrictions. Same dangers. Makes it easier for us to tell if something is outta whack. And, yes, I got my eyes on Kale." Cooke paused and glanced down, as if he were looking for answers on the floor, then said, "His self-defenses are thinning."

Wynn admired his stout platoon sergeant. Nothing fazed him. Cooke was not a complicated man, no inner tensions or anguish. He was blunt and honest.

"And by his 'self-defenses,' you mean his self-confidence?" Wynn asked, seeking clarification.

"Yes, Sir. And his smarts. I don't think it's gone too far yet, though. Kale's just scared and confused half the damn time. Hell, all of them are. Who can explain this place? He's young.

You can't send kids not old enough to legally buy a drink and expect him to be Socrates or Superman or something. This stuff we're trying to do is fucking hard. These people been trying to figure it out since before Christ."

Wynn cracked up, laughing hard, harder than he had laughed in weeks. First "thinning," and now "Socrates."

Cooke smiled, inhaled and puffed his chest out a bit, proud he'd impressed Wynn.

"I didn't know you were a student of philosophy, Sergeant Cooke."

"I ain't. But I got to be a student of men to lead them, Sir."

"Absolutely," Wynn replied after a couple of seconds' delay.

A helicopter flew over the trailer park behind them. The trailer shuddered as the whacking of the copter blades violently batted the air. Another flew over. Again the trailer shuddered. They always flew in pairs.

Cooke watched Wynn thoughtfully, like a baseball manager watching a new pitcher. With his lieutenant he needed to strike a careful three-way balance between being a teacher, a confidant, and a subordinate. He had to both mentor and assist this young officer. There was more to the answer he'd given, and Wynn wanted more. He tried to explain further.

"Kale is the softer sort. He takes reinforcement to keep him strong. He took Ramirez death even worse than the rest of us. His buddies and I are watching him, Sir. Best reinforcement is the other men, not me or you. Not yet."

Cooke didn't want Wynn to talk to Kale. This was his business. As the senior NCO in the platoon, he ran the enlisted world. If he did his job well he could keep it like that. Let the officers stay in theirs. No foolproof way existed to help a man deal with combat stress. Nothing was simple about the minds of men.

Wynn remembered Ramirez, then pushed him out of his mind. He glanced around the room. Cooke's trailer was as Spartan as everyone else's. Metal bed. Metal folding table as a desk. Brushed aluminum desk lamp. Thin yellow curtains made in Turkey. Cheap Asian blankets. No unique furnishings. Little to highlight a man's individuality.

"You know the impact the stress here can have. We need everyone operating at full capacity," Wynn said.

"I sure do, Sir. But we also need every man we got. It ain't like there's a bench we can pull from. We need all playing the full game."

Wynn noticed the family picture on Cooke's desk. Cooke seated with his two boys, one on each knee and their mother—Cooke's gregarious and ample wife of nine years—standing behind him with both her hands on his shoulders. A nice family. The pride on Cooke's face radiated from the picture. Also on the desk stood the bottom half of a cylindrical cardboard smoke grenade canister, now used as a pen and pencil holder. The canister held a pair of scissors and a small American flag. Wynn knew that Cooke cut articles out of the Stars and Stripes newspaper to mark events that occurred during this tour. The hard-gut platoon sergeant was making a scrapbook. The men knew nothing about it. Didn't fit the image Cooke wanted to project. Cooke had a green and yellow colored nerf football with Green Bay Packers markings on the table next to another small white ball. The smaller ball looked like a ping pong ball, a little larger and not quite round.

"What's that other ball there?" Wynn asked, tilting his head in that direction to point it out.

"That ain't no ball, Sir. It's an egg."

"An egg?" Wynn asked, incredulous.

"Yes, Sir. An empty egg shell. Keeping it as a souvenir."

Wynn looked perplexed.

"From those Iraqi Egg Ladies. The ones we got the chickens for," Cooke explained.

Wynn smiled. A few months ago the Wolfhounds had helped two middle-aged Iraqi sisters, both widows, obtain six chickens and a rooster. One sister's only son had been killed serving in the new Iraqi Army. The idea was to help them turn the chickens into a business. It worked. Now these ladies had an egg stall in the marketplace. Somebody heard they were up to about 20 birds.

"That an intact egg shell?"

"Yes, Sir."

"How did you get the egg to bleed out?"

"There's a secret to that, young man." Cooke beamed widely, as if he'd pocketed the last piece of candy in the store.

"I think I remember something about water and heat, but I'm not sure."

"Attention to detail, Sir. That's the only way."

Wynn leaned forward and twisted his back left and right. Sixty pounds of body armor each day did not go unnoticed, even for a young man.

"I know Kale has family," Wynn said. "He's got a gal and a little boy. He's not their dad, though. Not sure if she was married previously. I wonder if they're sensing anything about him."

"He ain't married now, Sir. Didn't marry her yet. But they might as well be. They living together. Two years now. I know he says he's got a biiiggg love for her."

"OK," Wynn continued. "Let's keep our eyes on Kale."

"I'm definitely watching him. I watch them all. We got help too, Sir. Moose been watching him. Thinks he's the sensitive type but says he's doing OK. And the Chaplain. I know Kale's been to the Chaplain several times. Just to talk. A lot of them need it, Sir. Need to know they're being listened to. It ain't no good keeping it bottled up inside. Gotta let them talk."

Wynn was pleased with that answer. Handling a man walking the edge wasn't easy. Too much care could backfire, strip a man's self-confidence. But withholding care when needed was like withholding a rope from a drowning man.

6

KALE STIRRED VIOLENTLY, still asleep. Pale people with dark eyes surrounded him, and bright orange light enveloped the horizon. Something unbearably heavy restrained him. He breathed deeply, desperately. He could move nothing but his eyes, which darted, searching, burning with indistinct images. He felt as if he was tied tightly down on a ledge, his physical life stolen. Why? Was he being punished? The pale people pointed at him accusingly, hostile; shouting with so much anger, all shouting the same thing, with an edge of sadness and pain. He strained to listen but could not understand their words. Everything was in slow motion. He watched their mouths annunciate in unison, the pronunciation of words grotesquely magnified. He again struggled to understand, lost and confused and guilty. Yes—their fierce eyes proclaimed him guilty. Guilty of what? Was he in hell, and they the custodians?

He struggled to focus his eyes on the moving mouth of one of the pale people. Follow the mouth. Listen! Kale now felt his own mouth start moving. He tried to say what they were screaming. Was he becoming one of them so he could understand?

Three words. Was that all? Only three words.

Then he recognized the words, and understood. He repeated them. Kale was crying now.

"Ramirez"

"Is"

"Dead!"

Then again:

"Ramirez"

"Is"

"Dead!"

Why tell him this? Why shout at him?

Suddenly one of them leaned forward and touched Kale's forehead with a long gnarled finger of death. Kale's dream turned into memory, vivid and immediate, rushing back, taking him to where the past eats the present, where he had first seen violent death. His body was now free, soaring back to the surface. His memory came alive.

They had been on a humanitarian mission, less than two months after the Wolfhounds' arrival in country. The platoon was led to a family home so they could pay damages to a family for their shop that Americans had destroyed. The shop, destroyed when EOD initiated a controlled detonation of an adjacent vehicle laden with bombs, had been nothing more than a roadside stand selling pirated DVDs and CDs. Financial compensation for damages such as this was available to Iraqis thanks to the American taxpayer. It had taken about three weeks to get the money, $1,000 in this case. The Wolfhounds, assigned to provide security for the Army Civil Affairs team, accompanied them to dispense the money. Headquarters had gotten word to the Iraqi family by phone that the next day the Americans would come to make payment. That call had been a bad mistake.

The family lived in the W13 sector, near an inoperable water fountain. The plan was simple. A family guide would meet the platoon at the fountain at 1400 and guide them to the residence. As the Wolfhounds waited at the fountain, a man drove up on a scooter promptly at 1400, and identified himself as a member of the family. After the link-up, the convoy drove maybe 300 meters, through a couple of intersections, and stopped near the home. Once the house was identified, Wynn deployed the platoon's vehicles tactically, and established security at both ends of the street. The plan called for the Wolfhounds to provide two extra shooters for the dismounted Civil

Affairs team entering the house. Kale was designated one of these men. Specialist Raul Ramirez was the other.

A staff sergeant named Sanders led the Civil Affairs team. Brown and Callicut were his two men. Ramirez entered the home with the Civil Affairs soldiers. Kale remained outside. Sanders' team had been inside the home for less than two minutes, when he came out into the courtyard and signaled Kale to come inside.

Just as Kale took several steps into the courtyard, everything went crazy. He first thought something had crashed into the building, knocking everyone down. He recalled the sensation of flying sideways. Everything was smashed. He landed on his right side, his arm and shoulder taking most of the impact. As he hit the ground, Kale felt his body trembling from shock waves. Everything he was—his mind, his bones and sinews, his whole life-force—was on the verge of breaking into a million pieces.

Yet, slowly, he regained his senses. He could see through the house. Weirdly spacious now, but smoky. He saw a man on the ground. He thought it was SSG Sanders, sitting upright, frozen against what remained of the outer wall. The man focused downward, fixed on something lying between his outstretched legs. His arms hung by his side. Was he hurt? Dead? Kale couldn't tell.

The explosion utterly destroyed the house. Scattered debris—tatters and chunks of furnishings and masonry, bits of broken ceiling—covered everything. For a moment everything in Kale's mind had stayed still, as if the explosion had somehow frozen time. Then things started to move. Bright sunlight glittered off tiny moving particles in the air, and the glistening dust made it seem as if a grand entrance was imminent. He heard a sound like distant rain. Heavy at first, then tapering away. It was the slow collapse of the blast, the settling of millions of particles blown up in the air by the explosion, everything coming back down to rest, unrecognizable, dead. For some reason, his concussion perhaps, Kale thought he was in a slow-motion playback, all going in the wrong direction. Then time caught up with him, and he tried to concentrate. Yes, that was an explosion. The house had blown up. But he was alive.

Kale heard the noise of people frantically talking. At first, all sound except for the rain of debris had been cut off. The blast dulled his hearing, and he struggled to make out what they said.

"Shit! You OK?" someone shouted, exasperated.

Kale didn't think he'd moved. His eyes still worked, and he saw Sanders ahead of him. Kale remained flat on the ground, face turned to the side. Sanders wasn't sitting up, but was lying on his side. Kale's own orientation had confused the view. His eyes started failing him. He forced himself to blink faster, wanting clarity. The sharp light now shining in the room further disoriented him. It shouldn't be light like this inside. More shouting. He moved his left leg. The shouting reconnected him to reality. Slowly, he turned himself chest down on the floor and flattened both hands on the floor, as if he had been arrested. He raised himself unsteadily. His physical senses, now on maximum intensity, raced back, recovering the precious seconds he'd lost between the blast and the present. He felt grit embed in his palms as he pushed up. The extra weight of everything he wore—body armor, bullets, water, his rifle, his helmet—kept him down. He felt no pain, just dizziness. Amazingly, he wasn't hurt badly. He felt wetness on the back of his legs. *Blood?* No, he didn't have time to feel fear right now.

What about the other men? Who had said, 'You OK?' Who were they talking to? With difficulty, he brought his knees up under him. Then, still with his hands open and on the floor, he saw the tan sole of a boot directly in front of him, no more than six to eight feet away. Only a foot. A severed foot. No leg attached to the boot. Light reflected off the dogtag laced in the foot's boot. Kale threw up, the bile landing on his hand. He whipped his hand in the debris.

Then he saw another boot, on the other side of the still-intact interior wall that separated the two rooms. The front wall—the one facing the road—and a portion of the ceiling on that front side, had disintegrated because of the explosion. Kale crept forward on his hands and knees. Stay down. Stay down. Bile burned his mouth. Whose foot was that? He kept pushing ahead, instinctively more than deliberately. Some-one started screaming for him to stay down, to let others do it. An inner voice urged him to let others do it. But he kept moving forward toward the boot and maybe to the man that must have owned it. More loud talk, yelling, most of it unintelligible.

This other boot he saw was toes up, heel down, suggesting the attached owner was knocked down flat on his back. Rubble encircled it. Kale could see the leg attached to it. Something thin brown and flat lay there too. Then he saw it was nothing, just pieces of paper torn in the explosion. He felt a sharp pain in his left hand. He lifted it. A metal shard stuck in the lower center of his hand. He brushed it away, more annoyed than angry. A dry smoky burning odor overwhelmed his sense of smell.

Kale struggled to focus his eyes on what remained of the house's interior, and where the body lay. Part of him wanted to help the person, but another part of him resisted. No involvement meant no blame. Could he avoid being accused of poor performance if he stayed down, stayed out of it? But he wanted to do right, wanted to be the hero. He kept moving but stayed down. He sought to avoid shame more than he wanted to be a hero. He crawled, trying to keep the rest of his body low to the ground.

His eyes glued on the body he thought was Sanders. The man's uniform, or whatever that was, had turned grey from dust and debris, hardly recognizable. Kale reached out with his hands, tentatively exploring with touch and smell. He felt a gritty wetness. Then he saw. A pile of broken masonry chunks mixed with fetid ooze lay on the ruin of what had been a man. A new realization struck him. It wasn't Sanders. It was Ramirez.

"Medic!" Kale screamed, but did not hear his own voice. Did the others hear it? He screamed again. "Medic!!" It was the first time he'd tried to speak.

He remembered a strange raw smell, like a freshly opened can of fish soup. He choked on the smell, and again spit out thin bile. What was below him was an extinguished life, finished, incomprehensible, and it lay beside him. He resisted looking at what remained of Ramirez. He remembered feeling confusion—not revulsion, not panic, more amazement, mystified at the horror of it all. He had never seen anything like this before.

"Anybody hurt?"

Somebody standing above him shouted.

"Shit!" the speaker answered his own question. It was Lee, a Wolfhound medic. Kale saw Lee move around the room looking for bodies.

"Here!" Kale heard himself say.

Lee came to him. "What is it?" Lee asked cautiously, the tone of his voice signaling he'd rather avoid the answer.

"There," Kale answered, cocking his head towards Ramirez.

"Callicut and the other man are dead," Lee told Kale. Lee's eyes spilled tears.

"They're in the back, back there." Lee said, as if he never wanted to go back, and cocked his head in that direction. "Very little left of them," he added softly, as if whispering a secret.

"Ramirez," Kale heard Lee say in a whisper as he looked down at the body Kale lay beside.

Lee went to his knees and brushed away debris that covered Ramirez's body. Lee stopped, exhaled audibly, staggered by what he saw. "Shit," he said, "shit!" like he didn't know where to start. "Shit," he said, again and again. Ramirez's mangled upper body hardly resembled anything human. What could he do? Lee sat back for a second, very still. Then he leaned forward, plucked a small piece of something white, the size of a grape, and tossed it aside. He sat back on his haunches. He grabbed for another piece of debris and tossed it away too. He leaned over, and using the edge of his palm in a flurry of small movements brushed something else off the body, as if he was still trying to find Ramirez underneath the ruble.

Kale, still dazed, watched all this quietly, not moving, fascinated and stupefied, unsure what to do. There was no doubt Ramirez was dead.

Then both noticed Ramirez's open eye. Debris obscured most of his face, but an open eye stared back like a camera lens encircled by a mess of dirty wet pink flesh. The orb, still round and bright, floated in a small pool of sparkling fluid, looking weirdly perfect, alive with the past, framed by hell. Kale—still now—hated the image. It made him shudder. The exposed parts of Ramirez's face had reminded him of bacon, human bacon. Pieces of torn flesh hung in strips from his face. Kale didn't even look at the lower body, between the upper thighs and the stomach. Lee's hands, slippery and wet with blood and various particles stuck on his fingers, looked as if he'd stuck them in red paint. Lee dropped back on his haunches again, exhaling grimly. Kale watched all this, still motionless, stunned, unable to help in any way, and knowing it.

"What do I do?" Lee, frustrated, asked. He sounded like a confused child pleading with a teacher. But Kale had no help to offer.

Kale tried to put himself inside Lee's head. Lee had just turned 20 the previous month, four years younger than Kale. This was the first time either man had seen a severely injured person. As a medic, Lee's job was to save lives and to treat injuries until doctors could take over. His life-saving skill was intended to bridge the ugliness of the battlefield and the hospital. Medics had done incredible things, deserving much credit for saving lives. And Kale knew Lee had always done well in training, had earned the combat medics badge, finishing near the top of his class.

Before him was a man who moments before had been a breathing thinking living person. The whole situation was simultaneously ridiculous and evil. A look of futility rose up in Lee's face. He could do nothing. Suddenly anger seized him. He balled his hands up to his face, as if trying to shield himself from the scene. Maybe he was crying. Kale watched, but didn't cry. Numbness had sealed his emotions.

Then Kale heard noises. Deep sharp piercing noises, increasing in volume.

He woke. The noises were sharp knocks at his trailer door. He shot up and opened the door. Bright orange daylight blazed outside. Cooke stood there looking like a man born to deliver bad news.

"I heard somebody in here thought we had transformed this place into a resort. Well, we haven't," Cooke barked. "Move your ass!"

Kale's dream reliving Ramirez' death was over.

The Wolfhounds found out after the bombing had been investigated that a bomb had been placed under a couch. The insurgents knew the Americans were coming to pay the family. The whole thing had been planned precisely. The family had been pressured to cooperate with the insurgents, on threat of execution, and had given up their home, $1,000, and the lives of three American soldiers. Just after the explosion, a few men were seen running away. The Wolfhounds chased, but to no avail. They found nothing. They never saw the young guide again.

Cooke walked purposefully towards the motor pool. The platoon would be there, getting ready to go. After the short conversation he just had with Kale, Cooke wanted to find SSG Pauls, Kale's truck commander, and reestablish a meeting of the minds. He wanted no daylight between how they viewed the situation. Kale needed to buckle-up. If he didn't, he might go flying out of this war, as a psyche case, a casualty, or a dead man. Pauls was first on the hook to make sure that didn't happen.

Pauls, who had recently been promoted, was a mild-mannered, competent NCO. He looked wistful, as if he couldn't be truly happy until he was a retiree spending mornings in McDonald's with coffee and friends.

Cooke had seen all kinds of soldiers in his 14 years of military service. They came tall and short, rich and poor, smart and stupid, but everyone one of them had a story; some of those stories ended up being a labyrinth of troubles. War was not the place to untangle old troubles. Soldiers ranged from hard asses to candy asses, and about a thousand flavors in between. Men could be like puppy dogs. Too soft and unusable. He believed that self-reliance—his mama simply called it *tying your own shoes*—was an essential attribute of all successful men; yet men, like dogs, performed best in packs. Knock a dog on the head or separate it from the pack and most dogs go submissive, become puppy dogs again. Keep the dog in a well-managed pack and it stays happy and productive. Men were about the same. In a pack, they could be at their best: manly, strong, unbeatable. Running lose, anything could happen. He wanted to keep his men in the pack.

And packs always had leaders. Since his early days in the army he'd been drawn to effective leaders, men that could gather others to them, hold them, earn their respect, then get something good out of them—far more than would be possible by any individual acting alone. Cooke hadn't known his father. That left a hole in him that he was still filling. He now behaved the way he did—at least in part—because he still hated that hole and wanted it filled. The army had supplied fill dirt. The army exposed him to durable men, men that would step forward even when the going was tough. By the time it came for Cooke to reenlist the first time, three years after he'd joined the army, he had decided he wanted to be one of those leaders. He resolved to work harder than anybody else and try to improve himself constantly—and by the sweat of his own ass become a pack leader himself. 1LT Wynn, the platoon's officer, was the sled driver, and might determine when and where they went, but Cooke, as platoon sergeant, led the pack.

Arriving in the motor pool, Cooke spotted Pauls. He made eye contact and gave Pauls one of those recognizable twists of the head, signaling "let's take a walk."

Others in the platoon had percolating issues. It was his job to know them. Halliburton had a child support dispute festering—he'd fathered a kid at sixteen. Ortiz' was divorcing. The poor bastard's wife already living with another man. Singleton's mother was dying of breast cancer. So far, those men's troubles hadn't overly affected their performance in Iraq. But Kale—Cooke wasn't sure.

He and Pauls walked side-by-side away from the platoon. Cooke leaned his shoulder into Pauls'.

"Kale's about to get on my shit list," Cooke began. "The LT asked me about him last night, and a little while ago I had to wake the young gentleman up. When I did, he looked at me like I'd pulled a wildcat off of him. What's your take?"

The two NCOs spent about five minutes talking. Pauls was defensive on Kale's behalf. Cooke appreciated that. Any leader should stand up for his men. Pauls promised he would come to Cooke if anything about Kale worsened.

"I suppose we can't expect men to fight a war without some cracks forming," Cooke said. "Thing is, we don't want no cracks leading to no avalanches."

By the time the Wolfhounds started towards FOB Apache's exit it was 1100, the later-than-usual departure scheduled due to the platoon's shift on FOB guard duty and a few extra hours of scheduled downtime. A short while earlier, Wynn had re-briefed the plan for resuming the census work today.

Now, he finished adjusting D21's computer navigation system, which was mounted with the vehicle radios between him and his driver. The system connected the vehicle with the automated communication and tracking system in widespread use throughout the Iraqi and Afghan theaters. He marveled at the technology which allowed him to select different maps, scroll up and down, magnify, search other locations, see current operations, and even check a location's IED history. By clicking on the respective symbols, he could see more details and even identify types of friendly vehicles. The built-in messaging system reduced reliance on sometimes-problematic radio communication.

Communications were essential. In addition to the standard SINCGARs radio frequencies between the convoy elements and the higher headquarters—such as the battalion—Wynn had access to the Sheriff's Freq, an emergency frequency monitored by AWACs aircraft. And he had a satellite phone, called TACSAT, and his Iraqi cell phone. System redundancy would reduce the communications problems that had plagued previous Armies—or so it was hoped.

A thick nylon cord hung across the ceiling of the Humvee between two anchor points in the top center above the radio set-up. Three handsets for the radios hung on the cord, preset on the necessary frequency. When he needed to talk to someone, he selected a handset. Sometimes he'd switch handsets in quick succession if he needed to communicate with someone on a different radio frequency. He could simultaneously monitor both the platoon and company freqs.

They drove a recently paved road that cut through the guts of the camp. Moose, leaning back comfortably in D24's turret, noted all the supplies and equipment the convoy passed. Was it all intentionally arranged so they would see it and then never say they didn't know what the Army had brought along to support you? Dozens of prefabricated buildings, heaps of gravel ready for foundations of new construction, various diameters of plastic and concrete piping, spools of electric wire, 25 new GMC SUVs—which nobody knew who would own yet—crowded the FOB. One building had been converted into a 24-hour pseudo internet café with ten computers—but no coffee.

Ahead was a new construction site for more living quarters. Safety signs marked this area. Moose saw one sign that said "no parking," and another "beware of moving trucks."

The whole place looked like any large construction site back home. Behind the PsyOps area, a shit-sucker truck cleaned latrines. Several soldiers waited at the bus stop down from the Mayor's cell. Buses, which ran from 0500 to 2300, got most soldiers around on the FOB when they weren't traveling in military vehicles. Another year to two of progress at this rate and the base might become a tourist destination, if you could ignore all the concertina wire and sandbagged trailers.

Moose considered the men in his convoy, as he did every time the Wolfhounds prepared to exit the FOB. They were like cowboys mounted up to ride out of a fort. Most soldiers on the FOB would not go outside the wire today. Most never did; they were support soldiers. That made the Wolfhounds different and special. The rest were pussies.

A hundred meters before the gate, the Wolfhounds pulled into a small parking lot for final pre-combat checks, locked and loaded their weapons, and again checked individual equipment and special equipment like IED jammers.

Moose liked the next thing best: test-firing their weapons. A pit for test firing was just inside the exit. Moose patted his machinegun in anticipation, as if he was waking the gun's latent capacity for violence. All of them had heard stories about machineguns jamming during engagements. No way did he want that happening to him. One by one the crews tested their weapons. When D24 was ready, Moose swiveled his .50 cal slightly to the right and depressed the barrel, aimed at the firing pit, charged the gun, and pulled the trigger for an instant, firing 3-4 rounds. The heavy deep hammering of the gun thrilled him, the almost-sexual vibrations pounding through his body and the truck.

D23 was in front of D24. Moose noticed Kale in D23's turret. Kale must have sensed him, because he turned and made eye contact. Moose smiled. Kale looked like a man waiting for anesthesia. What was he thinking? Moose brought a salute to his helmet, acknowledging Kale's look and hoping to give him a boost.

Time to get serious again. Moose pulled his dark goggles down from his Kevlar. He felt like a welder firing up a blowtorch. His mind now underwent a purposeful change, a conscious separation from insignificant thoughts. External lights only—on whatever he was looking at. No introspection. No silly memories. He put FOB luxuries behind him. Only the gun, his crew, and the platoon were important.

Kale, after exchanging glances with Moose, found himself once again wishing he had the man's single-mindedness. Kale wanted it to feel right. Why was he different? Fuck! How would he react if something went wrong today? Unlike most other Wolfhounds, he had yet to fire a gun in combat. Sometimes, back on the FOB in the evenings, he would check out a machinegun from the arms room and take it to his trailer. After dark, alone in the trailer, he practiced repeatedly disassembling and reassembling the gun with his eyes closed. Assembly and disassembly of the gun would make him more self-assured, maybe bring a spiritual familiarity with the gun. Confidence gained from practice minimizes failure.

Did Moose ever question things? Moose appeared immune to doubts.

Last night's dream hovered around Kale like an insect squadron. Could he handle another attack? Could he kill? Thus far he'd done his duty. He'd survived the bombing that killed Ramirez. He'd gone on every mission. Yet his insides stewed.

The idea that others would know if he failed revolted Kale more than anything else possibly could. Frustrated, he put the gun on safe and rotated the turret so that the gun faced forward. He sat on the seat sling, his upper body already sweat-soaked.

Wynn glanced around at D21's crew: Gung, Lee, Singleton, and Cengo.

Each soldier was making final equipment adjustments. Gung pulled the wrist end of his gloves to tighten them against his fingers. He switched on the truck's Warlock counter-IED system and revved the Humvee's engine twice.

Singleton unlocked the turret and swung it once from side to side, and then pushed the stock of the 240B downward, lifting the barrel skyward. He shuffled his feet to get a comfortable stance, as if he were a batter getting ready for the pitch.

Then Singleton cranked his music loud for a few moments, as he normally did just before the platoon left the FOB, and Wynn heard, as usual, Seal's soulful lyrics to "Crazy."

"We sure is crazy," Lee echoed.

Lee pushed his goggles up higher on his nose with his gloved index finger. He looked left and right once, reflexively, hunting for anything suspicious. Then he did it again, concentrating harder the second time. Whatever was out there was out there. They were ready to roll.

Wynn repositioned his radio earpiece behind the left straps of his helmet, making sure he could hear well. He leaned forward and turned the SINCGARS's volume up and tapped the remote speaker with the knuckle of his right index finger. He checked his rifle and repositioned it, the black barrel down in the floorboards, the stock secure in a holder. *This must be something like what NASCAR drivers feel just before race start*, he thought. He checked his watch a final time before departing. The designated census area was about 25 minutes away.

The convoy paused for a few seconds at the end of the road leaving the FOB, and Wynn called HQ to report the Wolfhounds departure time.

"All right, old mule. Time to move again," Gung said to the truck.

"Let's do it," said Wynn to the crew, then to Singleton up in the turret, "You awake, old man?" At 29, Singleton was older than all but Cooke.

"Always, Sir."

"Sleep more later, old sarge," Gung said, piling on Singleton.

"All right, go," Wynn ordered.

The convoy moved. D22, SSG Turnbeck commanding, pulled out first. Instantly, a civilian car got out of the way too slowly, and Turnbeck jumped on him.

"Fucker. Get your head out of your ass." Then the radio chatter began.

"He should be shot," suggested someone inside D22.

A car approached from a side road.

"Car moving left to right, two o'clock. Don't get complacent," Wynn said, making sure his crew was on its toes. The moving car ahead of them stopped, then accelerated off to the side of the road.

"Shit!" Gung exclaimed, as he maneuvered adroitly around a few goats that scampered across the road.

"You trying to get dinner, man?" Singleton responded.

The platoon's four turret gunners rhythmically swiveled their turrets, looking for potential threats.

"Traffic ahead."

"Move on."

"Warlocking, Mack?" Wynn asked Gung, referring to the electronic counter-IED system mounted in D21.

"Yes, Sir. Everything perfect."

"One on the right, coming behind us. Same speed," Cooke announced from D24, the trail truck. A car had come out of nowhere and followed the convoy.

"He slowed down. Ugh, and now turned off." The car disappeared down a side street.

The men returned to routine talk, both in the trucks and between them by radio. Most recognized every voice on the radio. Their out-loud, gut-instinct mutual thinking made a kind of soldier's symphony. Short clear comments, playful banter, threaded together by an easy but serious teamwork. No other way to communicate while driving through hell.

As they drove, Moose closely observed his surroundings. The platoon passed through several neighborhoods, each one a quiltwork of adobe buildings, often without windows, all with flat roofs, most constructed of rough-cut block or brick. The exterior plaster looked flesh-colored and full of imperfections, like the skin of an aging man. Multiple generations frequently lived together. Because no reliable public water system existed, Iraqis stored water in the metal tanks on rooftops, which fed indoors by gravity.

Doing his duty scanning the surrounding area while the convoy moved, Moose started thinking about what a body would look like if hit by several .50 caliber rounds. That person would be *hurtin'*. So far he had seen three dead soldiers and more than a dozen dead and injured civilians since arriving in country. He remembered most of them clearly. He felt rather clinical about it, like it was research. It wasn't that the deaths and ugliness didn't bother him—perhaps he was just more detached than most people. Two of the dead had been Iraqi civilians, killed instantly when a 120mm mortar round rigged as an IED—probably intended for the Wolfhounds—blew up their car as the platoon convoy passed going the opposite direction.

The Wolfhounds had stopped to investigate. The IED blew marble-to-baseball-sized holes into the lower part of the car's passenger door. The passenger had taken the brunt of the blast and his body was completely disfigured. His buttocks and hips had essentially disappeared, and the lower part of his back was split open, exposing a section of spine that looked like splintered wood. A bloody mess of thousands of particles of flesh was sprayed over what remained of the car's interior. The driver took the rest of the explosion. Due to the direction of the blast, angled from road level through the lower part of the passenger's door and up, the driver's shoulders and head were smashed, but his lower body was largely unscathed. His upper right arm was ripped from the shoulder, and dangled from thin strips of ligaments. His right forearm and hand were sliced off. A chunk of that hand with three fingers still attached lay charred on the smoking remnants of the car's dashboard. What remained of his head was a messy clump of flesh about the size of a pink grapefruit. Moose remembered wondering what the man had originally looked like.

In his mind, for a moment, he put these two dismembered guys on polished metal tables in a well-lit morgue. He pictured them naked and washed, wounds exposed and visible. Imagining this, he recreated all the details of their destruction.

Then Moose remembered a 10-year-old kid who had his left hand blown off when a mortar round that he'd carried home to show his father exploded. The father was unhurt. He carried the boy to the Wolfhound convoy to seek aid.

And there was Ramirez, and the two Civil Affairs soldiers.

Moose reached forward and stroked the big .50 cal.

D24 hit a sharp bump on the road.

"I'm still here!" Moose yelped.

"Ayeee, yep. Passed your flying lessons. Been there. Done that," rejoined Cuebas.

"You didn't pass, buddy."

"The hell I didn't. The next time we come to a bumpy area, I'm undoing your harness. Let you fly out and join Hajji on a pilgrimage."

"You might get away with it, Mex. You could sneak daylight by a rooster."

"Ayeee. Not a Mex. I'm Puerto Rican."

"I'm the Mex, and I like to party," said Ortiz, D24's driver.

"Drop the bullshit," Cooke ordered.

"Slowing down," Turnbeck reported. "More congestion ahead."

"Fucking move," Ortiz said. "Geeeet out of the way!" The car driver couldn't hear this, but he finally crawled to the side of the road.

"Sometimes we must scare these people shitless," Moose said, after a pause.

A car that looked like a taxi came down the wrong side of the street.

"You idiot."

"We're smart and we're doing it."

The Wolfhounds jumped the street median and drove against the civilian traffic. The oncoming cars pulled hurriedly to the side. A man and three children rushed across the street. He grasped two of the children's hands as if he were afraid he might lose them. One was a girl, maybe 12 or 13 years old. The other two were boys, perhaps between six and nine. All wore filthy clothing, clothing probably worn for weeks.

The Wolfhounds approached a bridge.

"Slow mover on the overpass. Left to right," Turnbeck reported.

"And right to left," someone called out, as a second vehicle drove onto the overpass, going in the other direction.

The first car was almost directly above them on the overpass as D22 drove under it.

Seconds later, as D24 drove under, Moose remembered a story he had heard about a VBIED detonating on a bridge and blowing it up.

The platoon merged on a wider highway, and traffic became lighter. A cart full of propane tanks stood on the left side of the road up ahead—a man, probably the dealer, standing beside it.

"Propane. Exactly what I love," said Moose, as the convoy passed.

The tanks, rusty and beaten up, looked as if they had been hauled out of a landfill somewhere. Propane tanks had been used in bomb attacks. The Iraqis used propane for kitchen cooking.

More road bumps, this time potholes. The road looked carpet bombed.

Moose noticed several cots on the roof of one house. In hot weather, some Iraqis slept outside on their roofs. Most neighborhoods had no air conditioners.

"Red stationary vehicle. Single occupant," reported Turnbeck.

Seconds later, he said, "No problem. Think it's a woman. It is a woman."

Two mules strolled off the right median, a large brown one and a smaller white one.

"Rather see horses," said Cruz.

"We ought to make soldiers out of them," Moose suggested.

"Looks like you and your girlfriend," Cuebas ribbed Moose.

"Fuck you."

Ahead, the convoy was channeled by curbs on the side of the road and a concrete median.

"New palm trees in the median."

"Ayeee. They need water," Cuebas said, mournfully. "Maybe a gift from Puerto Rican taxpayers."

"The whole country needs water," Ortiz said. "Let's spit on them."

"Be quiet. Here we go," Cooke said, as more traffic coalesced.

"Obstacle ahead," Turnbeck reported.

Someone had pulled a big piece of bent metal out on the street to constrict traffic. It looked like a section of guardrail or materials torn off a metal building. The convoy slowed down. Next to the piece of metal was a civilian dump truck. The truck was packed with thin twisted strands of something in the back bed. Soldiers looked as they passed. Dried vines? Metal wires? Maybe that metal piece had fallen out of the truck. Nobody knew.

The convoy moved stop-and-go through the slowed civilian traffic. No way to get around. Two- and three-story buildings paralleled the roadside. Moose continued his regular scan and swivel with the .50 caliber. He could see the gunners in the three trucks ahead of him scanning.

"Move. Move!"

Cars inched out of the way.

The Wolfhounds cleared and moved on, the Humvees groaning angrily.

"Yeah. That's it."

"Go baby, go."

A large pool of water filled the road ahead. Probably a leak somewhere. "Water flooding the road," said Turnbeck. Most of the platoon saw it.

"Push through," Wynn commanded.

"A little shit-water never hurt anybody," Singleton commented.

They drove through the water, picking up speed. Ahead, up on the left, a field spotted with clumps of dying grass bordered the road. Two goats and maybe a dozen sheep grazed, tended by a small boy.

Moose felt an urge to snarl at the boy, to let the boy know he was not from here, that he was a mean, powerful American who could do as he wished.

They drove fast again on open road. Even with his head exposed out of the turret, Moose could feel the brutal temperature enveloping him in an insidious cloud. A man could easily fall asleep in this heat. As hot as it was, if he closed his eyes he could pretend he was drunk and home in the States. But the image wouldn't last. He didn't want to be home anyway—he was happy right here.

7

After getting underway, Wynn, needing assurance, did some self-examination. Most men had the same questions about themselves, he believed. They always did. Once basic survival was secure—not a big issue anymore for the typical American—more complex motivations such as personal desires and ambitions became drivers. Wynn's own life had led to the Army. But why?

Arlington National Cemetery had made a big impact on him. All his converging inner impulses and interests, the military readings, the talks with his grandfather, all those had moved him in the direction of the military. So he'd joined ROTC the last two years in college.

A weekend trip to DC had been crucial. He and three or four of his fraternity brothers at Temple used to go down to DC once or twice a quarter during their sophomore year. One of his fraternity brothers' father owned an apartment in

Georgetown. The night before they visited Arlington had been one long party. The bars and girls of Georgetown had kept them up much too late. Wynn and Phil Craven had run track back then, and both loved running along the Potomac River. Morning came too soon, but out they went to run, still half-drunk. Seeing the famous cemetery up on the high ground on the Virginia side of the river while running, they decided to visit Arlington later that day.

After a late breakfast, the four of them walked to Arlington from the Lincoln Memorial, across the Arlington Memorial Bridge. On the way they had talked about the usual things young and virile college men talk about when their worries are little and their responsibilities even less. He remembered passing through the cemetery visitor's gate. Soon the clean rows of white stone markers welcomed them like an audience of honored souls. The boys quieted, each retreating to his thoughts. Wynn felt that he'd suddenly come under intense scrutiny. Each way he turned were hundreds of grave markers. Sleek and silent, uniform and restrained, these markers spoke for thousands and to thousands daily: row after row of thin white stones equally spaced on green lawns and low hills, some shaded by grand trees, some near larger monuments. He was among heroes. He wanted to take that feeling with him the rest of his life. The best response was silent reflection. Silence meant more than words.

Wynn, wondering if his introspection was noticed, glanced around D21. Everyone was quiet; his men, too, were in their own thoughts. After a few bends in the road, he saw a donkey tied to a wall. Wynn looked for the owner. On the other side of the wall a small boy stood behind a makeshift table. The table held three jugs of pink liquid, probably gasoline for sale. Behind him an old man sat on his haunches.

In Arlington, they passed graves with inscriptions like a roll call of America's conflicts: Vietnam, and Korea, and World War II veterans. The order varied because of the dates of death and interment. Young veterans lay side by side with old. Navy Vets next to Army Vets. Some had spouses interred with them.

The great majority of graves had the small standard white markers, their simplicity of line and shape reflecting a call to common purpose and rectitude. The same could be said for most of the inscriptions. Few had flowery rhetoric. Most simply had name and rank, wars served in, and abbreviations of awards received. The majesty of the place spoke for them all.

Wynn knew what the cemetery meant to America. He understood why so many had chosen burial here. Death has been called the loneliest place—but maybe those who have served their country can rest better in the company of those who have likewise served. That way they could never be lonely.

Turnbeck reported civilian cargo trucks parked half a kilometer down the road. It didn't look odd. Probably the truckers had stopped to eat or something.

"Two of them," Turnbeck said as the convoy neared.

Wynn eyed the trucks distrustfully. At first he saw no one.

"Drivers out front," Turnbeck reported.

Wynn noticed a group of three men standing by the lead truck. These trucks, like most in Iraq, came from the European second-hand market. Still emblazoned on their sides were the German names Gasser AG and Nicklaus Bauhaus.

The convoy kept moving at a steady speed, the Humvees growling comfortably. After a while they passed another small canal in which a heavyset woman squatted. She might be relieving herself. Two naked children waited near her.

Wynn and his friends' visit to Arlington had been before 9/11, of course. No new war deaths yet. So they hadn't seen gravesites of anyone they knew personally. Getting the general experience of the place had been their intent. Today it would be different. Today he knew eight people buried there, including Ramirez.

Before leaving they had visited, as most do, President Kennedy's grave. Robert Kennedy, buried next to his brother, had his own memorial. On it was inscribed, "To tame the savageness of man, and make gentle the life of this world."

If that was the aim of service, Wynn thought it worthy. Since that visit to Arlington, he had begun associating military service with service in the broader, nobler sense. Service in arms was perhaps the most respected service. He wanted that respect, too. He didn't know if he had been born with that desire or had caught it like an infection. Either way, he knew that was part of why he was here in Iraq. To be part of that experience—to be in that company.

As the Wolfhounds neared the objective, radio traffic intensified. Ahead, Moose saw the IP scheduled to help them. The convoy slowed and two IP trucks fell in behind them. He heard Wynn call the battalion TOC and report that they were two minutes out from the objective. Then he radioed the platoon, ordering them to report when they had parked in their designated locations and were ready for the teams to dismount.

A few boys, shouting excitedly, ran alongside the Humvees. The kids screamed and jumped. Inside the vehicles—with engines running and headsets on—the soldiers could not hear the children. Seconds later, their numbers doubled, and at least ten kids now ran dangerously close, all shouting—a chorus melee pleading for something: candy, toys, clothes, or even dreams of conquest.

The platoon had done census work in this area several times over the last two weeks. As the convoy made another turn, it approached the main crossroad of Abo Shabi, a primarily Sunni Arab neighborhood on the southwest side of the city on the boundary of the W14 and W15 sectors. Although local Iraqi Police were participating, for security reasons the Americans had not told them the exact location until the night before. Nevertheless, Moose suspected the children had heard from the police that they were coming.

As the platoon positioned, more children assembled, maybe 25 kids now. A couple gave thumbs-up signs. Others shouted, "Mister, mister." A few teenagers looked more cautious, sullen.

The platoon executed the security plan. D22 had already proceeded to the end of the street, about 50 meters ahead. D24 would stay back at the previous t-intersection with one of the Iraqi police vehicles. D23 would tail D21, maintaining security in the center of the street. While the two pre-designated Wolfhound teams conducted census interviews on opposite sides of the street, Wynn and Cengo, with a two-man security team, walked the street, sometimes joining one census team, sometimes engaging residents who appeared to want longer conversations.

The two census teams focused on completing the questionnaires. Wynn dug deeper when necessary. Cooke was in charge of overall security with the remaining members of the platoon. Two men, Cuebas and Mongrel, took dismount positions on the roof of a specified building. This gave the platoon one higher vantage point from which to overwatch the area. Because of the dismounts necessary for this mission, two trucks were manned by only two people: the driver and gunner.

Kale was one of two security escorts accompanying Wynn. He felt uneasy, even more anxious than usual. Maybe Wynn had picked him for a reason, as a kind of test. Kale didn't like that. With them were Cruz and Cengo. Wynn had Kale and Cruz wait by the Humvee while he and Cengo went to talk to the IP. The two census teams had already started visiting residences.

After he finished with the police, Wynn started walking down the street, Kale a few steps ahead of him. Kale scanned the street to their front, scrutinizing any objects on the road, and shifting his gaze side to side, from doors to windows to roofs and entries on either side of the street. He moved like a man walking through a forest full of wolves.

Wynn carried an M4 and a 9mm. The pistol was holstered. Kale and Cruz carried M4s. Cengo had no weapon; the rules prohibited it.

Two Iraqi policemen followed about 20 paces behind Wynn's group. The other IPs remained in their vehicles. Kale could see two civilian cars parked on the right side of the road. Why only two? Shouldn't there be more in a populated neighborhood? His anxiety started pulsing like a ringing phone. His whole body was already damp from perspiration. As he wiped his forehead, Kale noticed a person sitting in one of the parked cars.

Cengo walked over to get beside Wynn, who walked eastward.

"Check why he's in the car," Wynn instructed Cengo, who then walked over to the vehicle. A moment later he came back.

"He waiting on his mother. When she come out from house, he leave, he say."

Finding no reason to be suspicious, Wynn changed his focus, and walked to the other side of the street.

Kale was relieved. Then, a bit further down this side of the street, next to building corner, he noticed two men standing by the road. Other than the man in the car, they were the only adult civilians on the street so far. Wynn noticed the men too, and walked over. The children who had chased the Wolfhounds now jostled around the Humvees, making a lot of noise. They looked like a gang from a Charles Dickens' story. When they got too aggressive, either the IP or soldiers chased them away.

Wynn and Cengo talked to the two Iraqi men at the corner. The older Iraqi did the talking. He was stoop-shouldered, of medium height, and had white hair as fine as a rabbit's pelt and a thin white mustache. Spiderwebs of wrinkles surrounded his eyes. Wynn asked the standard questions. Who were they? Did they live here? Was the area safe? The Iraqis' answers, not surprisingly, were cordial, if not overly friendly. The older man appeared to welcome the attention.

Wynn made small talk, letting the Iraqis do most of the talking to minimize the intimidating impression of an armored man with a weapon talking to an unarmed civilian. He inquired about conditions in the neighborhood and asked about positive or negative trends. The older Iraqi talked for a minute or two, then asked about jobs, saying unemployment was the biggest problem in the area. Jobs and security were topics frequently mentioned. Because unemployment was high, many families pooled their income. Recent job growth was in the various Iraqi security forces, the new army and police. Iraqis knew these were well-paid jobs and often asked for American assistance in getting employment. A new policeman or soldier made approximately $400 a month, more than twice the average income.

Kneading his hands as if he were making bread, the older man spoke. "Jobs very important. Help many problems, he say. Impossible to live without job, he say," Cengo translated.

"I know," said Wynn. "Ask them for suggestions on how we can help."

"He say his younger brother lost his job and have no job for eight months. He himself too old to work again," Cengo answered.

"Where did his brother work?" Wynn asked.

Unemployed men were vulnerable to insurgent recruitment. Transporting or storing weapons or explosives, assisting in surveillance of targeted areas, initiating explosive devices—any of these activities could lead to a payoff of hundreds of dollars, a lot of money in Iraq. Murder for hire was another available trade. The payoff for a simple murder was less, reportedly under $100.

The man with rabbit-hair spoke again. As he waited for translation, Wynn looked up and down the neighborhood street. He noticed the extreme dustiness of the neighborhood, as if someone had sprayed the whole area with fire retardant. Cengo explained to him that this man's brother had worked at a sewer processing station. The sewer company let him go because it could not pay him anymore.

As the group talked, the unemployed brother suddenly walked up, Kale letting him pass when it was clear the other Iraqis knew him. Immediately the brother confirmed he'd lost his job. After Cengo translated this, Wynn repeated politely his recommendation that the man contact the Army or Police, or look for work with Iraqi contractors doing jobs for the Coalition.

Wynn closed his conversation with the three Iraqi men by thanking them for their time and information. He realized they wanted more tangible assistance, but he had nothing more to offer.

Wynn walked around for another 15 minutes, observing the census teams coming in and out of residences, greeting pedestrians, and assessing the surroundings. More adults, having heard the Americans arrive, had come out to the street. Most just stood by their houses and watched, not wanting to get too close or appear too curious.

The radio on Wynn's vest crackled. "D21, this D24, over," called Cooke.

"This is 21, over," Wynn responded.

"All good, 21?" Cooke asked.

Every five minutes or so, Wynn and Cooke exchanged a few words over the radio, confirming everything was OK. Wynn answered affirmatively, as he noticed Pauls' census teams walking towards the next residence. Based on where they had started, Wynn estimated the team on the north side of the street had by now completed maybe seven or eight residences.

He decided to walk over to Pauls' team to check how the work was going. Just as he turned to go, he heard the sharp cry of a woman. Then she cried again, louder—a horrible screeching sound, like that of a threatened bird.

He spun toward the noise, which had come from behind him on the same side of the street. He saw her. She and two other women, now about 50 meters away, hustled toward him. The woman shrieked from deep within her black clothing, her stressed white face glaring out of her *abaya* like a lantern in a cavern. She had come out of nowhere.

Was she attempting to speak between cries? Was she hurt? Screamers had been used to hide insurgent actions and reports described female suicide bombers feigning injury. But others, many others, were terrified witnesses and victims of this war. He washed the three women with his gaze like an antiseptic.

The women had captured everyone's attention, soldiers and civilians. Now many eyes watched them. Wynn hesitated. He didn't want this scene to divert him from noticing other developing threats. He ignored the women for a moment and did a slow visual sweep of the surroundings. This interruption was an ideal time for insurgents to send a VBIED their way, or—like what had happened yesterday—a sniper taking a shot. He looked back at the women, eyeing them suspiciously. They closed with him fast. He saw no signs of physical injury to any of them.

He checked the soldiers close to him. Distraction haunted everyone; tension was ratcheting up. Kale was blanched with apprehension. Both Kale and Cruz had raised their weapons. Any situation making a soldier distrustful of a crying woman was ugly, but war forced different thinking.

She was supported on either side by other women. They, too, were cloaked in *abayas*. The wailing woman, her face glistened with tears, radiated the pain and turmoil of the whole country.

"Should I stop them, Sir?" Kale yelled, over the cries.

Then two IP moved between the women and Wynn. This was positive. The police had responded properly; he wanted to remember to commend them later.

Kale also moved between the women and Wynn. His heavily armored body, helmet, and weapon stood like a shield separating his leader from the distraught women. Wynn, suspicious, again tried to ignore the women and scrutinize the surroundings. He saw his vehicles. Saw nobody suspicious on the road or the roofs. Saw a few other civilians watching the scene, but they didn't seem connected. He checked the men in his view. Nothing yet looked wrong.

Kale, still between Wynn and the women, looked as if he might shatter from tension.

"Stay calm!" Wynn admonished. *Not easy to be calm in a storm of screams,* he knew. Kale gripped and regripped his rifle, as if steadying himself.

"Easy, easy," Wynn said, extending his arm, palm down, as if scolding a dog for jumping.

Somehow the women knew that Wynn was the man to see. The IPs restrained them about 25 meters away from him and their crying moderated a bit. Slowly, Wynn grew less concerned that this incident was a planned diversion.

Kale relaxed a little too. Wynn had yet to move, continuing to assess the situation.

"Find out what's happening," Wynn directed Cengo, who stood beside him.

Maybe the IP and Cengo could sort it out. Wynn now walked over to where Pauls, leading one of the census teams, had exited a residence.

"How goes it, Sergeant Pauls?" He kept an eye on the crying woman. The quality of the census work would hinge on the attentiveness of his soldiers. They had to keep focus.

"Eleven so far on this street, Sir. Eleven houses, I mean, Sir. Think we got...." Pauls paused to recount, and looked at his paperwork. "...sixty-two people so far, supposed to be living in those. No one's given us any trouble with the paperwork, Sir. Don't know, of course, if they're really telling the truth," he said, with an undertone of resignation.

The Iraqi woman's muffled cry continued in the background, now sounding more like an animal whimpering in a cage, as she spoke to Cengo and the IP. Wynn looked again. Cengo was nodding his head rapidly, pleading with her, moving his hands like a traffic cop.

"Make sure to clearly identify the house on the paper," Wynn said to Pauls.

The house numbering had been done properly so far. He handed the forms back to Pauls. Wynn then moved to within ten meters of Cengo and the women and waited on his report.

The women, seeing Wynn approach, again surged towards him, but less aggressively this time. The IP held them back.

Cengo met Wynn halfway.

"They say...," Cengo hesitated, unsure how to summarize what he had heard "...the middle woman is mother. Her son taken by American army, she say. She say he innocent. She say he good boy. She upset about that. Want you help her find him."

It was not an uncommon request. Many Iraqis thought Americans knew where their missing children were.

"You think she is telling the truth?" Wynn asked Cengo.

"I think so, Sir."

"They all claim their boys are good. Ask her what else she knows."

Cengo went to ask.

"Everything OK, 21?" Cooke voice sounded from Wynn's radio.

From where Cooke was, about 150 meters down the street, he likely could see the ongoing commotion. Wynn glanced towards Cooke's truck as he answered.

"OK. We're talking to this woman. She's got an issue with her son."

Cengo came back frazzled. The distraught woman was getting to him.

"She say he 17. That he good boy. That he do good always. No problem. She very sad and she say she sick, Sir. She need help to find him. She begging."

"What was he taken for?" Wynn asked his original question again. He needed more information, if the woman had any.

"She not know. She say he innocent."

"Get his name. Her boy's name. The full name. We can check with the detention folks. We'll see if they have him. So she knows nothing about why or when? Can she at least tell us when he was arrested? Does she know where, or what unit took him?"

She probably didn't know the answer to those questions, but he needed as much information as possible. He would call it in. With the man's name, Wynn might be able to find out if he was in the FOB detention center, or ever had been. But the name might not be enough. Knowing the arrest date would help. Sometimes captives gave false names. Most had little meaningful identification, or what they had was old and illegible. The previous American battalion in this area had tried to establish a new ID card system, but had finally given up when it became impossible to produce anything permanent or get the Iraqi infrastructure in place to manage it.

Cengo came back again, shaking his head. "She not know. She not know unit. She think maybe beginning of the month he arrested. She not sure where or what day."

Little rivulets of sweat streamed down Cengo's face. He continued, "She no news from him. She give name. Mohammed Aziz Alkieri."

"Is she sure we arrested him? If she doesn't know where or when, how's she sure?"

"She say yes. She say Americans take him."

"How does she know?"

"She say people tell her."

"What people?"

"She not say."

"Ask her. You believe her? That Americans did it?"

"Yes, Sir."

Her crying got louder again, as if she could sense Wynn's skepticism. The other women wept now too. Their cries heated the already foul air, flowing into the streets like waves from Hades.

Suddenly, two scrawny dogs ran up to the crying group, yelping. Cruz aimed his gun at them. An IP twisted around and kicked one dog, chasing them away.

Wynn checked their surroundings again. Nothing seemed odd.

After another minute of discussion with Cengo, Wynn had him get the spelling of the name. He then called Cooke on the radio and spelled the name as Cengo stated it. The translations of names into English varied. The woman might even be illiterate. Some estimates were that half of the Iraqi population was. Even common names like Mohammed were spelled several different ways.

Wynn told Cooke to call the battalion HQ and inquire about the name and arrest in the period around the first of the month.

Her story was plausible. Young men of that age were fertile insurgent recruiting targets. Very possibly the arrest was justified. Wynn wanted to trust Coalition decisions, but he knew lots of mistakes were made. Some units arrested first and asked questions later. The pressures of combat bred caution and aggression, leaving little time or inclination for careful deliberation. Security concerns suffocated other considerations. He would, if possible, help the woman. Locals often came to Americans about missing people because they believed that only the Americans could help. This could be true even if the son had been kidnapped by a group for ransom or arrested by rogue IP. Thousands of Iraqis had disappeared. Either way, all he could do was find out what he could.

Several more Iraqi adults had gathered near the IP and the women. A young boy led a blind man by the hand. Wynn, still concerned about suicide bombers, scrutinized their clothing and facial expressions.

"Tell the woman we're sorry," Wynn started. "Tell her we'll check about her son. If he is in detention, we'll try to determine why. Tell her if he is innocent he will be freed. Find out where she lives, and we'll come back if we get information."

He also wanted her to leave them alone. His emotions now bordered on callousness, and he got no satisfaction from it, but without a measure of steel in his spine he couldn't do this job. They needed to get back to the census. Cengo went back to the group and explained. The woman, her face glistening with tears, looked genuinely distressed and probably believed her own story. Thousands were adrift in this harsh and mysterious world. He could spend no more time on this matter. The platoon had higher priorities.

Wynn looked at her. She touched Cengo's hands and arms, thanking him, nodded her head deferentially, then turned and walked away. Assembled Iraqis started dispersing. A few continued watching with sullen black eyes.

For the next 90 minutes, Wynn alternated back and forth between helping the census teams and engaging with other Iraqis on the street. A surly sun hung high in the mid-afternoon sky behind a thin layer of clouds, burning like a bright torch sheaved by thin curtains. An odor like dirty laundry had impregnated the air.

8

By 1710 the Wolfhounds were back on FOB Apache. The drive back had been uneventful. Twenty minutes later, Kale and Moose were alone in the motor pool. While Moose cleaned D24's .50 caliber, Kale waited for him. Everyone else had cleared out, tired from the long frustrating day.

Moose, still up inside D24's turret, closed the feed tray cover of the machinegun, then dismounted the weapon, ducked down inside the Humvee, and came out the open rear door.

Outside, he cradled the .50 cal in his arms as if he was carrying a pregnant hound. Kale watched him as a spectator watches a favorite sports star.

"I'm taking this gun over to the armsroom. Walk with me?"

"OK," Kale answered.

Moose was about four inches taller than Kale, and at least six inches broader at the shoulders. Walking together, Kale wanted to understand what made Moose tick. Comparing Moose to himself was one way to do that.

"How did it go today, buddy?" Moose asked.

Kale hesitated. Two answers came up simultaneously inside him, both arguing for expression. One answer was part of his personal public relations campaign, what he wanted everyone to think about him. The other answer represented all his fears.

Moose looked at him, curious about his silence.

"Fine, fine," Kale blurted, sensing Moose's gaze. He said it the way a man might swat a pesky insect. He avoided Moose's eyes. Moose's question, though completely natural, had spun his mind.

"How're things back home?" Moose looked at Kale over his shoulder the way he might take aim with his gun.

"Going good. No issues."

"They still remember you?"

"Of course." Kale didn't like questions. They required answers. "How about for you?" Maybe he could flip the question and avoid more answering.

"Good, Buddy. My crazy mom still writes weekly. The place isn't going anywhere. I'd rather be here."

"This census work gets old, doesn't it?"

"Seems a waste of time."

"Guess we need to learn what we're dealing with, Moose." Kale said it like he wasn't convinced.

"We know what we're dealing with. Al Qaeda bastards. What about you; what you dealing with?"

Kale felt like Moose had fired a shot. Taking evasive action, he said, "I'm dealing with this trash, just like everyone else."

He looked at Moose. Just then, another platoon's convoy pulled into the motor pool. Their arrival distracted Moose, and the big man watched them, seeing who he might recognize.

"I heard from Baker the other day," Moose said a minute later, moving off the topic.

"Baker?"

"Yeah, remember that crazy dude that was the honor grad at basic training?"

"Oh. Yeah."

Kale remembered Baker. Kale, Moose, and Baker, had all become friends in basic training and graduated together. In training, they'd seen each other sweat and fail, and then sweat and succeed—their friendship grew from shared experiences forged in challenge.

"Baker said he's going to apply for Officer Candidate School."

"Really?"

"Yeah. The fucker wants to grow up to tell dudes like us what to do." Moose said this as if he believed Baker was about to commit heresy.

"Well. Who knows? He might end up an outstanding officer," Kale answered, not sure he believed it.

He was glad the conversation had shifted away from himself. One thing about Moose is that he functioned in his own world. He never considered anything too closely. Maybe that was a crucial part of his success.

By 1815, eight of them—Cuebas, Sims, Tyson, Moose, Mongrel, Halliburton, Randell, and Ortiz—sat out by the Pizza Hut and vendor area. Kale had declined. The gazebo's shade provided modest respite from the still-broiling sun. They shared three large pizzas and two large orders of chicken wings. Aaron Tippin music played from speakers hanging from the gazebo posts. A Harley Davidson advertisement promising a new freedom hung on one wall.

Several minutes into their conversation, Moose asked, "What's the main thing you clowns will remember about this place?"

"Jesus. Don't ask that." Sims replied. Sims, who was 27 and had already been married three times, was one of three Wolfhounds with college degrees.

"Easier to tell you what I wanta forget," Ortiz joked. He put his cigarette between his knees and pointed with both hands at an Iraqi flag under the gazebo.

"Or what do you think you can't forget?" Moose asked, sincerely curious about what war experiences might last.

Seconds passed as each chewed over the question. Forget something and it dies. Of course, forgetting can be good.

"Stupidity," blurted Sims.

"What?" They all laughed. Ortiz almost spat a piece of pizza out of his mouth.

"Ayeee, some stupid bastards here." Cuebas fondled his memory chain.

"No, not what I mean," continued Sims. "I mean, ah, lost opportunity. It's stupid to fight like this. All Hajji has to do is stop fighting, we would leave, and they can have their country back. This stupidity kills. I won't forget that. Americans don't want this country. Now that Saddam is gone, we just want Iraq to be free."

"You really fucking think it would be better if we left?" Ortiz asked, incredulous.

"Bull," Randell said.

"It would be for me!" Sims said.

"It'd be better for us if you left," Halliburton said.

Laughter again. "You know you want some of this stuff," Moose disputed, always ready to defend his claim to a piece of the action.

"I won't forget you ugly bastards," said Cuebas. "Ayeee, been living with you nasty bastards for way too long. No kind of cleaning will rid me of that."

"Shit!" Randell said.

Cuebas sounded half-serious, as if he believed his own joking. The group laughed at this too.

"You'll be crying your whole life from missing us, you Mex."

"Puerto Rican, you ass."

Moose started to speak again, wanting to say something important, knowing that how something is said can be more important than what is said.

"Ayeee. Got too much wisdom," Cuebas injected, interrupting. "Sometimes I'm surprised at all the wisdom I have from all this—being as young as I am. How will we handle this big wisdom for the rest of our lives?" He looked at the group expectantly.

"I know one thing; I don't buy all this combat stress stuff," Moose started. "Hell, what they calling it now? PTSD. Post-Traumatic Stress Disorder. Hell, you just deal with that stuff. Of course it's stressful, but what the fuck, buddy. This is war. What I think, ugh, is that we got something—wisdom you call it—that is very powerful. We can't share it. It's like first learning about your cojones."

"You have to carry it, man," Tyson said. "It's a personal thing."

"Suck it up. It's a mind thing," Ortiz added. "That's the bottom line."

"Wise or not, main thing is being able to look in that mirror and be satisfied—to have pride in your accomplishments. To know you did it," Moose added, "Think of all those clean-assed people back in the world that haven't never scraped a fucking god-damned knee in ten years, never slept in sheep shit, never seen anybody hurt more than a bloody nose, fucking don't know what's up. It's unreal, man. Everything's sugar to them. No pain. You go from one artificial thrill to another. Life as some kind of a fantasy world."

"A big fucking candy shop," Tyson said, concurring.

"History, if you think about it, is one long-ass war. Now, we're the star players in it," said Moose. "Can't ever take that away from us."

Cuebas looked at his uncles names on his memory chain. Mongrel scratched his crotch.

"Why you always pawing your dick?" Halliburton asked him, after spitting out a plug of paper pulp,

"Exercise," he answered.

"Bull," Randell said.

"Ayeee, he's probably got gangrene of the johnson."

"You're all just jealous of the size."

"I'll tell you what I really miss most by being here is partying," Cuebas started. "General Order Number One is for the birds. Plus, in the old armies they brought whores around. Here, women are as rare as sense."

Several cats ran across the gravel, disappearing under the vendor shops chasing mice. Fast little creatures, with long thin legs and slim bodies, like miniature cheetahs. These cats knew their land and how to survive in it, and wanted no scrutiny or attention, wanted only to hunt and eat and be left alone. Outside the wire were feral dogs. Inside the wire were the cats. Feral men operated in both elements.

Kale had returned to his trailer because he wasn't hungry and wanted to be alone. Moose had tried to coax him out, but Kale shook him off by saying he had an appointment with the chaplain. Soon, having had more than enough of this place for a day and now by himself in his curtain-drawn trailer, his thoughts drifted to home. Separation from Serena and Wilson had been hard. He let his mind walk the memories of their last weekend home together. It seemed so long ago. Sometimes he would leak the recollections into his consciousness like a drug.

He exchanged emails with Serena daily if he could, and he tried to call a couple of times a week. He was glad for that. It wasn't lost on him that soldiers of past conflicts left much more behind when they went off to war, losing connection to home almost completely. How could men endure that? True love was a diamond-hard insurance policy, precious, sparkling, clear, and lasting. Could his survive long separation? Many relationships weren't strong enough.

He and Serena had planned to keep everyone happy their final weekend together. They decided to split it. He would spend one night concentrating on her, and the next night with Wilson. And that required a form of trial separation. Each had to give up something.

Kale closed his eyes and remembered. Serena had gotten the first night. They enjoyed a wonderful dinner at Florentine, their favorite Italian place in the older part of town. They ordered the usual: she, Pasta Diablo; he, Veal Masala. Each purposefully avoided distractions, concentrating on each other. Conversation was difficult and they were quieter than usual. Neither could talk about Iraq. They lingered in the restaurant and shared dessert. One piece of coconut cake. One spoon. Two people. Eating that dessert together consummated a merger of hopes and desires and fears, an intimate demonstration of closeness and commitment. Together they licked the dessert spoon clean. She licked first. Some things are always better when the woman goes first. She started seductively, slow and serious, exactly to send a signal. The exhibitionism surprised him. Both were careful, reserved types—she even more than him. She had been flagrantly sexual. Kale loins stirred and he shuffled his feet on the trailer floor. He remembered getting home late and making frantic love, intense and uninhibited.

The next day would be all Wilson.

Kale had bonded with the boy, though he wasn't his father. He felt about him the way it must feel to love your own son. When he met Wilson for the first time, the boy was two years old, barely conscious of the world. In the last three years, Kale had become a surrogate father and watched Wilson grow into a quiet, happy, even-tempered boy; and their relationship had grown close.

For their special last night, Wilson and Kale intended to go camping. A few months before, they had camped for the first time and had a blast. Camping was classic boy's stuff, confronting the outdoors, surrounded by all the mysteries of nature, and he wanted Wilson to grow fond of call-of-the-wild experiences.

Serena agreed. Camping was perfect. Just the two men. She had encouraged his closeness to Wilson. The boy didn't know his biological father and the title "Dad" had been Kale's early on.

Late the preceding night, while Serena and Kale were out, it had unexpectedly started to rain. It rained hard all night. By late morning, the rain had stopped and it looked like it might dry up. But by mid-afternoon the rain returned. While Kale was out shopping, Serena broke the news to Wilson that the camping trip was off. Nature gave and nature took away.

A tank drove by outside, shaking Kale's trailer like a small earth tremor. Somebody outside shouted about going to chow. Kale, not wanting to be disturbed, locked the doors.

His thoughts returned to Wilson. Sometimes you try to do special things, and it doesn't work. A five-year-old kid can't understand nature. It didn't make him feel any better, but Kale told himself that the one redeeming fact about not going camping was that children learn so much from disappointment. Cruel, but true. Disappointments, large or small, form internal scar tissue. You were supposed to get better handling disappointments after dealing with them. Of course, you could not explain this to a little boy.

"I told him that you can't go," Serena had told Kale when he arrived home. He kissed her gently on the cheek and asked where Wilson was.

"He's downstairs, baby."

When Kale got to the bottom landing of the steps, he peered carefully around the corner, hoping he might spy on the boy. Both loved to tussle, and to play hide-and-seek, and surprise each other. A successful sneak attack would guarantee laughter and vanquish, at least for a few seconds, any disappointment. Spotting Wilson over on the far side of the room, Kale stopped. Wilson sat maybe 15 feet away on the floor, looking down, concentrating intently. One of his hands held something small. Kale realized what the boy was doing.

Wilson sat on a large carpet printed with a town map and played in an imaginary world. A life-truth held him—we always look to the future. To the boy, the carpet had a real community, with streets and houses and lakes, green places too, and fire and police stations. Wilson, a toy car in his hand, had transplanted himself into a make-believe town, his future town. By the "Humm Hummm" motor noises, he could tell Wilson drove a car. Suddenly, a road curve was too treacherous. The boy's voice elevated sharply for a second, but then the child driver steadied, continuing safely. Already Wilson, like other children, had attached himself to the actions of adults, to the adult world. Why? Maybe kids wanted their rightful place in our world as soon as possible? Perhaps he figured that in the adult world he, not others, could make rules, and control things, however illusionary that control was.

Maybe it was self-training through imitation. You learn from all you do.

Kale had lost something by being in Iraq. He'd lost, for one thing, a year of watching a child grow up. He closed his eyes and hoped that would be all he would lose.

At 2230 Wynn sat beside the small folding table in Petty's trailer. Petty's papers and periodicals from back home, including the Army's *Military Review*, lay scattered on the table. From somewhere Petty had procured a shabby reclining swivel chair, and Wynn leaned back in it, contemplative, as if he was nearing the end of a session with a therapist. They had been talking privately for nearly half an hour as Wynn decompressed. Petty sat Indian-style on his bunk, with one leg pulled up higher and his arm hooked around his knee. He was relaxed, happy in his element.

"Do you wonder why these people fight us?" Wynn asked. "What we want to offer them is good. Something so much better than they had before, under Saddam. Why fight us?"

Both men were more candid with each other than with anyone else in the unit. They asked each other questions about the war, sounded out ideas, explored theories. True candor meant blunt questions and answers. Both sought to understand the war, understand what could be understood. Wynn respected Petty's intelligence, his access to official analysis, his insight regarding information obtained from both combatants and non-combatants. He also could share doubts and theories with Petty that he was unwilling to share with his subordinates or his superiors. Petty envied the fact that Wynn, as a platoon leader, led young men in combat. Petty, as an Army Intelligence Officer, lived on the edge of war, vicariously, through Wynn's retelling. Both knew their ideas needed to be tightened by reading and talking and thinking more. Was victory achievable or a triumph of faith over reality?

"I'll give you a concrete example of one reason why," Petty continued, "Today I read a report about a shooting in another Brigade's area, about forty-five kilometers from here. The incident had to do with the wife of an Iraqi contractor being shot by a sniper as she got out of a car outside of their home. One of the insurgent groups we've got some Intel on, a group that calls itself Purifiers for Allah or PFA, claimed credit. A couple of months ago they put out some kind of wordy manifesto. The translated summary of that manifesto has PFA claiming that anyone, Iraqi or otherwise, that cooperates with, or takes advantage from, the American occupiers, has defacto 'joined the infidels and is automatically a bad Muslim.' They claim that only pure Muslims can lead Iraq. It goes on to say they'll kill 'bad Muslims and their families' to 'purify Islam' in Iraq. Other insurgent groups have similar ideologies.

"Put the extremism aside for a moment and think about what's at the core here," Petty continued. "What I mean by that is there's an ingredient that's necessary to get things together. Like for bread to rise, it's the yeast, right? What's the yeast here?"

Wynn considered Petty's meaning.

Petty screwed his eyes, hoping to draw gold from confusion, and went on. "I suppose the yeast is legitimacy—the idea that the ruler or rulers have the right to rule. Unless the folks here think they have a legitimate government, they won't come together. That's the yeast."

"Saddam wasn't legitimate. Yet he ruled," Wynn countered, then paused, thinking the comment needed more.

"That might be true. I guess it is. But not sure we can't say Saddam didn't have the right. Now, I'm not saying his rule is right. And I'm not saying he gained power in a respectable way. But for many years he had, however he got them, the reins of power. The populace probably got accustomed to it."

Wynn thought about that, unconvinced. "Sounds like you're near to saying 'might makes right.' That if you're in charge, it gives you some legitimacy, in time."

"No, I don't believe that."

"Aren't you saying that? Doesn't it matter what the nature of the regime is? Whether they are basically decent or tyrants?"

Wynn watched his friend. Petty looked away, struggling for words. Then he hugged his raised knee closer and looked at the ceiling, as if seeking solutions from a higher power. Wynn couldn't get his own head around a concept of government that didn't associate legitimacy with at least the elementary characteristics of good government. His fingers scratched the imperfections on the underside of his chair's plastic armrest, as if he were digging for insight.

"Let's smoke on it," Petty said suddenly.

Wynn smiled. The two of them smoked cigars twice a week or so.

Anticipation creased Petty's face. "I got an order of Thompson cigars in yesterday. Seems like they ought to be tested."

Petty climbed off the bed and reached into his mini-fridge and got the box of cigars. He took a cutter and matches out of a mug with Lacrosse stenciling. They walked outside to a row of T-barriers 50 feet away and sat down, backs to the wall. Petty cut both cigars with the meticulous care and handed one to Wynn. Petty lit his, deftly rotating the cigar, letting the flame catch the full circumference, inhaled deep and smoothly, then handed Wynn the matches.

"I think legitimacy is a rather amorphous concept," Petty continued. "Maybe you have to separate how you get power from the exercise of it. We're dealing with tough things. I guess I'm concerned that the long-term challenge here is that there's a growing feeling among Iraqis that everything we touch loses legitimacy. That, somehow, only if it's all their doing can there be legitimacy."

Wynn started to speak, but Petty brandished his cigar like a wagging finger, cutting him off and continuing, "I'm not saying I agree or disagree with that. I think it's a perception we have to battle." That thought lingered, as if in silent realization that executing good ideas are always far more difficult than just thinking of one.

Wynn drew deeply on his cigar, energizing it. A cigar in hand gave stature to any discussion. And he liked the image it suggested: two serious men, earnest about their work. He let the tobacco mist linger in his mouth and it felt smooth and cool and soothing, then he let it out, first a dribble through his pursed lips, then expelling the rest, signaling his satisfaction. He felt the discussion now hit fundamental points, and said, "Most rulers didn't get power through democratic means. So question number one is can they be legitimate governments without coming to power democratically? In the past, many rulers came to power with outside assistance—meaning foreign powers helped them. Even America. Maybe the key question is: can legitimacy be gained over time?"

"I think it can. Probably the 'how' to that is whether the new government matures over time and builds trust in the people," Petty replied.

Wynn inhaled the rustic cigar aroma. Cigars always made him think of cabins and trees and fishing. He had none of that now, merely memories. His grandfather used to smoke cigars when they fished. Paps would say that by adjusting his flies with a cigar smoke-scented hand, the fish wouldn't be able to detect the presence of humans.

Petty continued. "I don't know. Maybe all this talk of legitimacy is western thinking. We're always looking for reasons for everything. Maybe it doesn't fit here. In the Muslim world, passive acceptance—even acceptance of lots of ugly things—is part of their inheritance."

"Those guys trying to kill us aren't too accepting."

"True. But they're a small group. At least we hope they are. Most locals in counterinsurgency wars sit on the sidelines. It's always like that."

"Maybe so, but even a small number can be deadly," Wynn said.

"Yes, but small numbers are easier to defeat than larger numbers."

After talking another half an hour, they'd solved none of the world's problems. Wynn wanted sleep. Speculation about the legitimacy and forms of government never ceased, and would be available again tomorrow. His cigar half-finished, he abruptly ground it out in the dirt, and stood up.

"OK man, another healthy dose of brain food. I'm outta here. Need some sleep."

In the dark, Wynn lay on his rack thinking about his platoon and his life. He was thankful for his own upbringing. His few short years in the Army had taught him that two-parent stable families were increasingly rare. Most of his soldiers had been buffeted, at one point or other in their lives, by family breakups, or had never experienced what was still called a traditional family. Wynn's early years had been storm-free. His father had a solid insurance career, anchored in the central Pennsylvania town where he'd grown up, and where he eventually met his wife, Wynn's mom, and raised a family.

Wynn's mom, a teacher, and ever the project manager, had taken the lead on his introductions to young ladies. One was Clare Baldwin. Though considered quite handsome, Wynn's courtship skills in college had the finesse of a concrete slab, a deficiency he acknowledged. His mother stepped in periodically to alleviate this, despite his regular protestations. Clare, the daughter of his mother's teacher-friend, was a student at Bryn Mawr while Wynn was at Temple. The mothers had done their thing, and the next he knew, Wynn had Clare's phone number. After light grumbling to his mother about her continuous matchmaking efforts, he'd ended up calling Clare. They'd started dating in the second half of their junior year. Soon they went steady. How easily a good woman could conquer a man. Clare was sophisticated, talented, and attractive, with long full black hair and fine symmetrical features all topped with a champagne personality. And she had cobalt blue eyes the size of shooter marbles. But he had big ambitions and a stubborn streak, and these attributes prevailed late in his senior year. Despite both of them realizing they fit well together, he'd never come close to proposing.

The Army officer commission he got at graduation would take him far away from Pennsylvania. They both knew that. They both knew, too, that neither wanted marriage straight out of college. She knew he wasn't ready for a total commitment. Finally, after stumbling around a bit, he had told her that maybe the time apart would make both of them appreciate how good of a thing they had.

After graduation and commissioning, he went on to Fort Knox, Kentucky, for basic officer training. She took a nursing internship at Penn Presbyterian Hospital in Philadelphia. They tried to date long distance for a while. He saw her probably three times in the first six months after graduation. Each of those times he felt that their relationship was steadily thinning out, slowly starving, like any living thing without regular sustenance. Soon after that, his first permanent Army assignment took him to Fort Riley, Kansas. Before leaving for Kansas he'd come home to Pennsylvania one more time. A week prior, he had called Clare and they had made plans to meet. The day before they were supposed to meet, she called and left a voice message explaining that she couldn't see him, her work schedule at the hospital had changed unexpectedly, and that he should call her if he had time to meet the following evening. He didn't call her back. Soon after that, back at Fort Riley, over a beer—a couple of beers actually—one of his new buddies told him that he had to let it go—that he had to marry the Army for a while before making room for a lady. So that's what he did.

Had he made the right decision? Could they have made it work?

Early one summer, he had accompanied Clare as she shopped for her mother's birthday present. Clare was wearing one of those turn-a-man-on-fire dresses. He had simply been walking beside her in the Lord & Taylor store when she bent over to pick up a purse off a lower shelf. He watched her in profile, from about 10 feet away, mesmerized. She had to be unaware he was looking, but the delicacy of her white neck, the smooth curving lines of her arching back and bottom, the finely shaped muscles of her calves, all came together in a mini-ballet before his eyes. The totality of the movement she made in bending over, so graceful and beautiful, as if she had put the whole story of femininity on the stage, registered inside him in a way nothing else possibly could.

Paps had said one time that men's experience with women had something in common with fish: "Even if they shake it free, they never forget a hook in the mouth." Here in Iraq was the wrong time to think much about serious romance. He tried to shut it down.

A few moments passed before he finally closed down his mind and went to sleep.

DAY THREE

9

AT 0615, CENGO STOOD alone outside the Company CP, reflecting on the many strange things around him as he waited for the Wolfhounds to pick him up. Even after working for the Americans for more than a year, this place, the FOB, still felt like an alien camp, an incredible foreign creation inside his own country. What the American Army had constructed was a miracle. These people were rich, so very rich. And everything organized. Exact rows of olive green tents set on wooden floors. Neatly arranged square metal boxes all over the camp funneled electricity for America's Army. Hundreds of new same-sized rectangular metal living trailers, all with hinged doors in the center and two windows spaced equally on each side of the door. Cengo had never lived in a home with a glass window. Planning and order meant everything to these Americans, these masters of the material world. Allah had blessed them beyond anything Cengo thought possible.

Nothing in Iraq was the same. Everything was different. On this base, at least, the old Iraq seemed irretrievably gone. He'd heard stories—mostly horrible stories—about executions and tortures, including torture of children on this base in Saddam's time. The base had originally been built when Cengo was a small child. His father helped build it, having worked many years as a brick mason until his hands were dry and hard like bread crust and always getting infected. The Americans said that was because the Iraqi brick masons didn't wear gloves, so the cement ate his father's hands.

Whenever he was on FOB Apache, Cengo could feel relentless intensity and change. This was how creation must have felt. Sometimes, inside the base, he would feel strange tremors, little vibrations of power from all that America possessed and did. Because so much was new, and so much activity resulted from it, a mysterious power resided here now, dominant, magnificent, and inscrutable to outsiders like him. Part of him was afraid of its power and part of him envied it.

Yet Cengo ran with the Americans as a dog runs with a shepherd. He was loyal—but not completely. With his job as an interpreter, he supported a family of 13. Collectively, the other 12, including six adults, earned less than what Cengo made with the Americans. This made him proud, made him an important man.

When he'd started English classes eight years ago, his family was elated. They told Cengo that God had chosen him to learn English. But there was a more worldly reason. Later, he learned that he'd been chosen because his father had once saved the life of a senior Peshmerga officer wounded during a fight with Saddam's soldiers. Cengo's father had carried the wounded man on his back for 16 hours to the nearest medical care.

After health, wasn't education God's greatest gift? A basic education in English opened doors for young Kurds. That school was more than an hour's walk from Cengo's home. For four years he went twice a week. He'd quit in the fifth year after Saddam's agents had discovered that the Peshmerga sponsored this school and shut it down. He could still remember the way to the school and the landmarks along the way. People would speak words of encouragement to him. On some days the old woman who ran a date fruit stand in the marketplace would give him a single date. He prized the sweet chewy fruit, and would immediately eat it, as if he was afraid to lose it. She rarely spoke, but would give him a toothless smile, as if she confirmed a private confidence. They knew why he passed their way. This made him a privileged person, so they treated him as such. Sometimes, on the long walk home, he dreamed of being a Dragoman to a great Caliph, an advisor to a supreme ruler.

Now he worked for the Americans. True, they had invaded his country. But it was to remove Iraq's ruler, and Iraqis hated Saddam and the Kurds hated him the most. Cengo's people were accustomed to fighting and knew it would continue.

Wynn neared the motor pool. He could see a few of his men in the distance. He stopped at the entryway of the T-wall separating the living trailers from the parking area and watched them.

The platoon had gathered around D24, Cooke's Humvee. Wynn considered for a moment what he knew about each man, and how each fit into the whole. He knew relatively little about them. As their platoon leader, he was borrowing them for a while. He had fragmentary bits of information about their pasts, their ambitions, their doubts, their fears. What he knew of them he knew from his experience with them as soldiers, and what he'd heard about them from others, and in brief conversations he'd had with them. He had been the Wolfhound platoon leader for just over a year, getting the assignment about six months before they shipped out for Iraq. Several soldiers had come to the unit after he did. His opinions of them were based almost entirely on how they now fit into the platoon, especially how they had contributed since arriving in Iraq. The months in Iraq had been harder on some than on others. Not surprising. Some men were more stable, steadier and more reliable than others. Turnbeck was wonderful. Moose too. Ulricht, like a rock. It was natural: some men, in any circumstances, were just stronger-hearted.

As the platoon's commissioned officer, Wynn knew he was different, not just one of the men. Certain things only he was expected to do. His education, special authorities and privileges, and his unique responsibilities set him apart. They too realized he was different.

He could barely hear their voices, but listened for several minutes. Cooke talked about resuming the census work and its importance. He covered how the platoon would travel, identifying the routes and reviewing recent incidents and common enemy tactics, techniques, and procedures, known as TTPs. He reiterated salient facts about the neighborhood they would be operating in and ended by designating the four men for the two census teams.

SSG Turnbeck asked to speak. He talked about general security and safety concerns and mentioned that a Humvee had flipped over into a nearly dry canal in a neighboring battalion's area the week before. A rear passenger not wearing a seatbelt had broken an arm. On other occasions, soldiers had drowned in vehicle rollovers into canals. Cooke reminded the group about goggles and other personal protective gear.

Wynn, pleased that the men were attentive, watched. After hearing much of the same information day after day, even if it could save your life, it was easy to become numb to the information and less alert.

Cooke talked as if he had a built-in megaphone and was addressing a group of prisoners, his right foot about 12 inches forward, his delivery rapid, looking from side to side frequently. Wynn could hear him clearly, even from 75 meters away. Cooke had a stoic's face, etched by seriousness. He hadn't had an easy life. His father, an alcoholic, had disappeared when Cooke was a baby. Cooke later became a surrogate father for two half-sisters. In the Army, he had made rank fast and earned respect. The platoon sergeant had seen a lot in his 32 years and was accustomed to carrying a heavy load. Fourteen of those years had been Army years, as compared to Wynn's two. Wynn felt lucky to have him.

What did the men think about Cooke? They trusted and respected him, but occasionally felt resentment. They considered Cooke like an overbearing father, interested in what they were thinking and doing down to the smallest details. Cooke didn't believe in privacy, Wynn knew. He had high expectations for each man. He singled out soldiers and asked random questions to keep the men on their toes. He was fond of saying, "I'm riding in your back pocket, son." He'd ask questions a mother might: about their laundry, about hygiene, about friends, about how they were sleeping, about issues back home, even about bowel movements. "I'm making it my business," he'd say if anyone objected. He might ask when a man had last been to the gym. He would eye their chow plates in the DFAC to make sure they ate more than just a dozen chicken wings. Gung once complained that Cooke had stopped him cold when they'd bumped into each other at the post office, grabbing him by the shoulders with both hands. Nose-to-nose, Cooke stared at Gung for at least a ten seconds before speaking, sucking in everything about him. Cooke wasn't a reflective man. He made instant evaluations. That day, Cooke made Gung feel naked and exposed. A merging of consciousness? And after all that focus, Cooke had merely asked Gung when he'd last called his mom.

Wynn hoped Cooke was right in what he'd said about Kale. They needed to watch Kale closely, and Wynn remained concerned. The weakest men always required the most attention.

Cooke knew each man's strengths and weaknesses. It was his objective to know every Wolfhounds better than they knew themselves. Whenever needed, Cooke goaded them, directed them, counseled them, and punished them, fully cognizant that all men move better when motivated. Fancy thinkers talk about the merits of self-motivation and self-direction, of using inner powers and feelings to decide and act. All that was fine, in theory, but not the whole truth. A good push is often necessary. Men respond to other men. They respond to the challenge and chastisement of other men. A proverb Wynn remembered said: "As iron sharpens iron, so one man sharpens another." Cooke was a man sharpener.

Wynn walked up to his men. The group quieted when they saw him, the usual varied but observant expressions on their faces.

"Just drilling the men on their duties, Sir," reported Cooke. He said it as if it was his favorite thing to do. "As you know, we got some knuckleheads in here that need constant retelling."

Many of the men laughed, easily, deeply, happy to be able to laugh.

Wynn went straight into the Patrol Brief: what and how they were going to accomplish today's missions.

"There are three main parts to today's mission," Wynn began. "First, we'll visit the new Bawa Sah school to check the Iraqi contractor's work. A Contracting Officer's representative, Major Alberts, will accompany us to check the school job. He should be here any minute. Second, we'll visit a new police station under construction and check the progress. We'll drop Alberts back here, and go out again to resume the census."

Then Wynn and Cooke covered details of the day's mission and clarified responsibilities.

Cooke reminded them to avoid looking at and talking to Iraqi women during the census taking, unless no men were available.

"I ain't running no dating service here. And another thing. Don't take no goddamn gifts. No time for hanging around for chai. Don't get bit by dogs. A knucklehead in Charlie Company almost had a finger bit off. Many of these Hajis dogs have rabies. And don't be a pig. Just because the place is a shit-hole, it don't mean you contribute your own trash." American trash had been used to hide IEDs.

"Also, watch out for your battle buddy. Will be damn hot again today," Cooke continued. "Make sure your people hydrate. Also, keep in mind that roads in these neighborhoods are fucking narrow. Anybody get a truck stuck and I'm going to make you pull it out with your teeth."

Didn't they already know this stuff? Wynn mused. But he was glad Cooke stressed these points. People generally had to be reminded more than they had to be taught. Lots of injuries came from stupid safety mistakes.

Cooke looked at Wynn to signal that he was finished. Wynn spoke again.

"Security, security, security. Buddy teams everywhere when we dismount. Stay alert. Think like Wolfhounds should think. Be smart."

As the platoon drove to the school, Moose picked out one possible target after another. He ran short scenarios through his mind on how he would respond to certain contingencies or attacks.

Each man prepared silently for the increased street traffic—guts tightened, eyes widened, breathing accelerated, each man became less conscious of the other and more conscious of his own responsibilities.

SSG Turnbeck reported the usual short bursts of information from the lead vehicle, steady and concise. "Pedestrians, left and right. One hundred meters.

"Big bump.

"Motorcycle ahead. Right side.

"The bike's just sitting. Man on it.

"Vehicle stopped. Left side.

"LNs crossing street."

The further the Wolfhounds drove southwest the more the landscape looked as remote as the moon. An oatmeal-textured dust clung to the place like chaff in a feed mill. Anything green and alive had been banished.

After about 30 minutes of driving, they were within five minutes of the objective.

Soon they would turn north again and take the dirt road toward Bawa Sah.

"Kids on the field, left," reported Turnbeck, breaking a couple of minutes of silence.

After another minute of silence, "Rooftop, nine o'clock. Looks like a man."

A man stood on the roof of a two-story building across the street on the far side of the road. The building was supported by two colorful decorative columns on the outer corners. The man on the roof held his hands behind him, watching. He looked like a man staring out at the sea, Moose thought. The Wolfhounds eyed him, wondering why he was up there, but didn't slow down.

In a few seconds, the platoon passed the building. Nothing happened.

The traffic remained moderate. Some cars were so covered with dust they looked as if they'd just driven across open desert. One man wearing big sunglasses and a bandana around his mouth drove a truck loaded with sacks of rice. He ignored the scrutinizing Americans.

"Dirty fuel truck on the roadside," Turnbeck reported.

"Got a couple of vehicles moving slow on the right side of the road. They're slowing.

"Pedestrians near them.

"One's dressed up nice. A lady."

Soldiers looked for the nicely dressed lady, but she'd disappeared behind a building.

Further on, a bongo truck waited on the side of the road. Nobody appeared to be in it. Next to the truck a boy had set up a soda stand. Turnbeck didn't see adults. Passing, he saw a heavyset man lying on the ground underneath the truck. Moose, seeing the man, remembered laying under dozens of trucks back home at Benson's body shop.

Soon the Wolfhounds entered congested traffic again. Initially the vehicles ahead of them moved in orderly fashion off to the roadside. Then one truck didn't move over. D22 moved closer to it, and it still didn't pull over. Turnbeck turned on his siren and light, and D22 weaved sideways on the road to grab the attention of the truck driver.

"Move the fuck over!" Ulricht, making a rare comment, shouted from his gunner position.

Suddenly the truck jerked sideways, as if stung by a giant bee, and moved to the roadside.

Turnbeck stared sharply at the driver as D22 drove by. "Dumb son of a bitch."

The wedge-faced driver glanced back, sullen and angry. He looked like a man expecting violence any minute.

10

When the Wolfhounds arrived at the Bawa Sah School, a dozen or so elementary-school-age children were outside. Two Iraqi women stood among them, presumably staff members. The old school and the new one being constructed adjacent to it sat inside a compound with low walls on three sides. To enter the grounds, the platoon drove around the school to the open side. The compound walls were crumbling, depositing little piles of brick debris at their base, like ash around a dead campfire. From his position as D23's gunner, Kale could look over the courtyard wall into the grounds of the school. When the children noticed the approaching Humvees, their faces registered a mixture of excitement and astonishment, as if they were witnessing the arrival of aliens from another planet. A few kids kicking a soccer ball stopped instantly to stare. Two other children stood next to a huge tree, passing something between them. The kids must be on a recess, Kale figured. Were the children aware of the chaos and violence around them?

The platoon entered the compound on the open side, the moving trucks encasing the school in a cloud of dust. The impression the school made saddened Kale. It had none of the orderliness and presentation wanted in a school, and had the sick sweet smell of decay—the place looked like it could have been a cattle yard. Abandoned trash lay on the grounds. A long piece of thin plastic or tarpaulin hung over one wall. Something that looked like a burning stack of paper smoldered in a corner of the compound. He couldn't initially see the new school under construction—it was located on the other side of the old school.

D21 parked at the rear corner of the yard. Wynn had instructed the platoon to stop once they'd encircled the school. Each truck was to halt near a corner. Now all the Humvees had stopped, D23 remaining at the open side of the compound. Several of the men immediately dismounted. The drivers and gunners of the front and rear vehicles stayed inside the trucks. Two soldiers unloaded a box of toys for the kids. Today, at least, these children would be happy.

As soon as the Humvees stopped, children approached. Wolfhounds began handing out the toys. Nobody cared whether the school staff approved or disapproved. The truck gunners, including Kale, stayed in their turrets, maintaining security.

Most of the men relaxed a bit, feeling more secure inside the partially enclosed compound. The Iraqi kids seemed excited and the number outside had doubled. Two women, probably teachers, their expressions uncertain but not unfriendly, stood back away from the crowd. A few Wolfhounds had waved at them, but neither woman had approached. One little boy was missing his lower right leg. This kid mixed in with the others, hopping around nimbly on the one leg. Kale didn't see a cane or crutch. A barefoot girl of perhaps six, wearing a dirty light pink dress, walked closer to Kale's vehicle. He watched her sympathetically. She raised her arm so that he could see the small doll she held. A gift from another soldier? Kale grinned at her. She smiled back.

Beyond the children, out the one open side of the compound, Kale could see the nearest town buildings, mostly the top stories of two-and three-storied flat-roofed homes, indistinct like hundreds of other neighborhoods. It looked quiet. About 400 meters separated the school from this section of town.

He looked back at the schoolyard scene. Watching the kids, a surge of joy rose in him, and he felt a renewed connection to humanity. Even here, life could be good. Helping with security, building this school, bringing gifts to young children, weren't these indisputably good things? Maybe America was making a difference.

"I'm gonna wolf down an MRE, want one?" Tyson yelled up to Kale, referring to the packaged meals soldiers ate in the field.

"No, thanks. I'm good."

As the kids bantered and played, Kale noticed the large tree in the back of the compound, perhaps the largest he had seen in Iraq, standing majestic and alone in a back corner of the compound, its massive green canopy shading part of the school.

Mongrel popped out of the D24's turret with four or five plastic water bottles in his hands, which he casually tossed out to the kids. If soldiers were giving away bottles of water, they were running out of gifts. The two oldest boys in the group grabbed the water bottles, smiling as if they'd claimed treasure. Kale thought the boys might be brothers, perhaps a year apart. Seeing them, Kale again thought of Wilson as he often did when he saw Iraqi boys. They could be Wilson, but were a thousand years apart. He felt suddenly guilty. Guilty about whom he was, about what he had. Human inequities were life's greatest unfairness. Crazy contrasts like these had a way of ensnaring his mind, depressing him. Why this unfairness?

Wynn gave the green light over the radio for MAJ Alberts who'd been riding in D23 and the security detail. They dismounted and moved to enter the new school building. No adults had yet greeted them. A dusty black BMW, a small beaten-up mini bus, and an old cargo truck were parked outside.

As soon as he and Alberts were side-by-side walking to the building entrance, Alberts muttered, "This is bullshit." The major looked down at his feet as he walked, as if he was starting to regret coming. Tarps hung over parts of the building's exterior. Construction supplies lay everywhere. Forms for concrete sidewalks were erected, but no concrete had been poured.

"If this dude thinks he's getting more money now, he can forget it," Alberts grumbled. "They called us and said they were ready for final inspection. And that was a goddamned week ago. Couldn't get out to this place until now, and they're still not finished," he spit out his accusations like bits of sunflower seeds. "What pipe's this guy been smoking? He must think we're idiots." Anger and disappointment steamed from him like a man exhaling in icy weather.

Wynn said nothing. Security was his job, not contracting projects. MAJ Alberts had been to this site three times, the last visit about six weeks ago. Today's visit was supposed to be the final inspection.

"You know a Sheikh Amir? The dude that got this school job, Balari Manah, is one of the contractor's that Amir referred to us," Alberts continued acidly.

"Yes, Sir. Met him several times," Wynn answered, not surprised that Amir had maneuvered to get a friend another contract.

As they walked to the main door, Wynn saw two men applying stucco to entryway columns. Another laborer used a chisel and hammer to split bricks. The man wasn't wearing protective glasses. Seeing that, Wynn remembered a discussion he'd once been part of with the Brigade Engineering staff, the office assigned to oversee design and completion of small and medium construction projects like these, about efforts by the senior American authorities to require Iraqi contractors to comply with safety standards. One officer had proposed enforcing the use of welding goggles, protective gloves, and hearing protection for Iraqi contractors. Wynn, with his daily interaction with the real Iraq outside the wire, thought this pure fantasy.

The main door to the school was open, and the four Americans and Cengo went inside. The contractor stood inside, waiting for them. He smiled like a man watching his bride walk up the marriage aisle.

"Ashalam al al'Kum," said the lean dark-skinned middle-aged Iraqi, Balari Manah, as he held out his hand to Alberts. The man wore a dark, too-small business suit. He had an over-sized set of teeth, visible enough to count as he smiled, and rings on most of his fingers. Standing next to Manah was the schoolmaster, a distinguished looking, balding man wearing a clean grey *dishdasha* and gold metal-rimmed glasses.

"Ashalma all kean," Alberts replied curtly.

The rest of the party shook hands. Wynn motioned Cengo forward.

Alberts launched right into complaining, not hiding his disappointment.

"I thought you told us that you were finished with the job and were ready for final inspection."

Cengo translated.

"Job finished," Manah protested in English, transfiguring his face into a puppy dog look. Then he spoke to Cengo in Arabic.

"He say job finished," Cengo said.

"How can you say that? Men are still working. Your stuff is still outside. It still looks like a construction site."

The group stood just inside the entrance. The floor tile appeared finished, but uncleaned. The ceiling had been painted, and, based on the sharp smell, more had been painted this morning. The entryway foyer where they stood now opened out into a larger lobby in front of them. Two hallways branched off. Wynn knew that down each hallway were three classrooms, giving the new school a total of six, three times what the old building had. To the left of the lobby were two administration offices. The construction contract for the building, he had heard, was $420,000.

"Job good finished," Manah protested. "Mostly final cleaning left. Let me show you." Then, without hesitation, he led them, with Alberts by his side, through the lobby and down the left hallway. Manah waved his arm grandly, as if he was explaining a spectacular vista. The schoolmaster looked at Wynn sheepishly, smiling softly. Wynn had met the schoolmaster on a previous visit to the old damaged school next door. The two of them followed behind Manah and Alberts.

"All is ready for finishing," Manah continued.

"How can you say that? Everywhere I look, stuff still needs doing," Alberts retorted, frustrated.

Manah launched into an accelerating monologue about why he felt that the building, regardless of today's impressions, was actually finished. Cengo, walking behind them, struggled to keep up with the interpreting, bewildered himself by the tortured logic. One or two days and complete, Manah explained. These were small details. He'd had a problem getting sufficient water and his original window contractor had been scared off because of threats on his life. As the group passed a classroom, Wynn saw empty window frame holes with the sheets hanging over them. Manah explained that he was looking for another window contractor to finish the job. Wynn, trying to follow Manah's extended explanations, pondered whether the evident inability to understand the difference between finished and unfinished was a fitting analogy for why so many things were screwed up in this country.

Kale watched two Iraqi boys playing by the trucks. They were fascinated by the monster Humvees, and the strange and powerful rich Americans who had come into their world. One of the boys touched the heavy towrope secured to the front grill of the D23. Both boys wore soiled clothing. These people lived on life's edge, crudely, without pretense, unencumbered by western sensitivity to hygiene and appearances. Washing clothes in a place like this amounted to a mother stooping over a bucket. Not even a river or canal near here.

The word "soccer" was stenciled on one boy's white shirt. Kale thought about the irony of English words printed on shirts worn in Middle Eastern countries. The other boy, who wore a dark red shirt, was attempting to communicate with SSG Pauls, who sat in the vehicle commander's position. Kale couldn't hear but he saw Pauls gesturing, most likely trying to decipher what the boy was saying.

At the end of the hall, Manah stopped and turned towards Alberts with conclusive finality, the tour finished. As he faced the stout, towering major, Manah clasped his hands together, his face now broadcasting a request for concessions. Alberts looked exasperated, like a child questioning punishment.

"And other problem, Sir," Manah continued, in a low voice, this time in English. "This very important. Big problem," his eyes darted around Alberts' shoulders, and beyond Wynn, as if confirming privacy.

"What is it?" Alberts asked, his voice more acquiescent, sounds of defeat in the words.

"Somebody steal my electrical wires. Maybe two days ago. From generator to here, they steal."

Manah continued in Arabic.

"He say no electricity. No can finish. Need for fixing other things. Like doors," Cengo translated.

"But security is part of your contract!" Alberts complained.

Just as Manah began to reply, the group heard two loud reports, like somebody puncturing balloons. The group fell silent. Wynn's eyes immediately searched the eyes of the others for explanations. *Gunfire?* All of his nerve endings raced alive.

Watching from the truck turret, Kale had a sudden sensation of something flying by super close. Simultaneously he saw what looked like a splash off the red-shirted boy's shirt onto the white shirt of the other boy. Then he heard the crack of gunfire. And a second crack. Before he comprehended the sound, his eyes told him something terrible. Blood gushed down the white-shirted boy, and he tumbled to the ground. *Gunfire! Shit!* The red-shirted boy fell backwards. Halliburton, who had been closest to the boys, stood immobile, his eyes white with incomprehension. Then he, too, dropped to the ground.

"Halliburton!" Kale yelled.

Halliburton lay on the ground, a shocked expression on his face, transfixed by a terrible image he couldn't accept. *What the hell? What the hell?* Finally, Halliburton moved. The white-shirted boy, now on the ground, his arms above his head, had a huge red splatter in the middle of his shirt. The red-shirted boy had collapsed under the front of the truck, where Kale couldn't see him. Kale's body was unresponsive, frozen by the scene before him.

He shouted "Halliburton!" again, expelling his voice. Confusion gripped him like a vise.

The other kids scattered, screaming. Some ran into the school. Others took off towards the village, fleeing out the open side of the compound.

Suddenly D22 opened up with a .50 cal. Ulricht, up in the turret, shot at something beyond the open side of the compound. The slamming thump-thump-thump of the gun, like a knocking on the walls of hell, jarred Kale awake. He swung his turret around too, furiously, without thinking, hoping to see where Ulricht's rounds were hitting. He saw nothing. The chaos had affected his vision. His eyes felt hard and burning, like smoldering steel spheres. He turned to look back at Halliburton and the boys, his mind screaming for answers. *What the fuck? What the fuck?* One boy hadn't moved. The other now sat on the ground upright, crying. His chest looked as if someone had cut meat on it.

"Talk to me. Talk to me!!" Cooke shouted on the radio.

Kale saw Halliburton again. He appeared unhurt, and leaned over the motionless boy, who was largely hidden by the front of the truck

Wynn and the other dismounted soldiers ran back to their vehicles, leaving the schoolmaster and the contractor in the school.

"What happened?" yelled Wynn on his handheld radio.

Cruz leaped from his Humvee and went to the left front of Kale's truck, beside the Iraqi boys.

Sniper, Kale thought. Must have been a sniper.

Ulricht came on the radio, responding to Cooke.

"Think I saw the bastards! Three o'clock. On a roof! In town!"

Wynn came up on the radio again, asking for details.

"We got kids shot!" Turnbeck shouted on the radio, "right next to 23."

"Mount up!" shouted Wynn.

"What did you see?" Cooke asked Ulricht.

Short, enraged comments flooded the radio net.

A lit fuse sputtered in Wynn's mind. Only immediate pursuit stood a chance of catching the shooter. But they had injured Iraqis at the scene that he couldn't just leave. He made a split decision.

"23 and 24, stay here," Wynn ordered. "Take care of the injured. 22, follow me towards that village. Let me know when you're up!"

The shooter had to be in the neighborhood beyond the school compound entrance. Only from that direction could anyone see inside. Walls on the other three sides restricted visibility. And Ulricht claimed to have seen something.

"We've got a kid shot here," crackled the radio. Cooke had been reporting to higher.

"How bad?"

"Bad."

"D24, see anything?" Wynn asked Cooke. Confusion flowed like lava from an erupting volcano.

"No. D22 shot at something."

"Roger. What?"

Too many men talked on the radio at once.

"Clear the net! Clear the net!" Cooke shouted.

"Let D23 backup and use the truck for cover as Lee checks those kids," Cooke ordered. "They'll be ass to front and he can get to them behind them." This would bring the two trucks closer together and better shield the kids and anyone providing medical care from more gunfire.

"D24," Wynn asked again, "see anything else?" He leaned over the vehicle radio, straining to see where D22 had fired.

"Give me an up, 22," Wynn commanded, "when you're ready to move."

"Up," replied 22, almost instantly.

"Sir, need to check those kids!" Turnbeck shouted.

"Roger. 23 and 24 are on that."

Wynn came back on the radio again, speaking faster. "22, take up a position a hundred meters over toward the road.

Move ASAP. Get somewhere you can see that house better. Stop anything trying to leave from the north. Break—I'm going to move over onto the road down to the left." Wynn planned to position his truck on the road coming from Bawa Sah, to be in a position to observe any traffic leaving the village from the south.

"23 and 24, work on those kids. Stay alert," Wynn ordered.

Lee had dismounted to help Cruz. Cruz grabbed the red-shirted boy's arm and pulled him out from under the Humvee. What he'd seen was horrible. A bullet had gone straight through the boy's chest and out his back. Lee went to the other boy. He found no wounds. The blood on his chest must have come from the boy in the red shirt. Lee went back to the boy who'd been shot.

The Humvees blocked the medical scene for most of the Wolfhounds. The gunners stayed low in their truck turrets, watching the town where the shots must have come from. Tense and alert, everyone thought about what had happened, aware that something new and urgent might happen at any moment. Hands gripped weapons. Guts knotted with anxiety, fear, and insecurity. Feet were firm as welds on truck floorboards, fixed by the heavy trauma. Most men strained to look out truck windows, searching for anything that might be important, any new danger.

Vital seconds passed. Neither Cruz nor Lee moved much from their places beside the shot boys.

"Let's go or we'll lose them!" Wynn, pressing, called to D22. D21 started to move toward the exit.

Kale, his eyes scanning the roof lines of the buildings again, traversed his M240B sideways, and mumbled to himself, "mother fucker, mother fucker..."

Cooke barked on the radio.

"Who the fuck they shooting at? Did we have somebody on the ground by the kids?"

"Two shots, Sarge!"

"Any of our guys around there?" Cooke asked again.

Kale figured Cooke was probably wondering whether whoever had shot had been aiming at one of the Wolfhounds.

"Fuck those bastards. You try to help them and they shoot the kids," Moose said.

Radio chatter cluttered the net again. "I don't see anything."

"Come on, come on."

"Come out, you sonofabitch. Come out, you sonofabitch."

"Did you hit anything?"

Ulricht hadn't said anything else.

"How bad are they?"

"Hit anything?"

"We just going to sit here?"

The men focused their anger on Bawa Sah, eyes burning with accusations.

Kale watched Cruz and Lee, who still leaned over the boys. Though only seconds had passed, it felt like forever. Cruz's hands were bloody. Lee shouted something and Mongrel jumped out of his truck. Carrying another CLS bag, he ran toward the boys, stumbled, fell, scrambling the rest of the way on his hands and knees.

The poor kids' parents, Kale thought. The most horrible day imaginable for them. They better not come here now. He looked towards town to see if anyone was coming this way.

Driving toward the houses, time was of the essence. If they didn't immediately seal and search the suspected sniper position, it would be nearly impossible to find the shooter. A hundred thoughts raced through Wynn's mind, registering in pulses, like phones ringing.

Was it a group or an individual? If it was a sniper—snipers usually didn't operate alone. His eyes combed the distant houses. Where were they hiding? Would they keep fighting or had they already run? Where had they fired from? He needed more info from Ulricht. Maybe 500 to 700 people lived in this part of town. Finding the shooter or shooters quickly would be difficult, unless someone helped them. D22 had fired, but did he have a real target? Ulricht hadn't answered. Wynn wasn't sure. Whoever shot at them was no slack shooter.

Suddenly Wynn remembered MAJ Alberts. He'd left him behind with Cooke. What was Alberts thinking?

Wynn told Gung to stop D21 perpendicular to the road. The road was empty. Wynn pulled his binos out of a pocket on his vest, put them to his eyes, and searched rooflines on the housetops.

"D22...21, are you sure you saw someone on the house you fired at?" Wynn asked on the radio.

He saw D22 moving. Soldiers had been constantly warned to only engage legitimate targets. Battlefields here were full of non-combatants. Since the enemy dressed indistinguishably from the population, it was easy to make a mistake. And a weapon like the .50 cal punched right through most houses. Hopefully Ulricht had fired at a real target.

"I know I saw someone," Ulricht shouted on the net finally. Wynn heard defensiveness in his voice.

"How many?"

"Ah, pretty sure one."

Cooke had gotten out of the truck and now stood over the scene. Kale could see Cooke's face. The black man stared fiercely, pupils on fire, clinching his teeth. Halliburton approached Cooke. Streaks of tears stained Halliburton's face.

Cruz turned around and looked up at Kale with a look that said he needed assistance. Without thinking, Kale hopped up and climbed down off the Humvee.

"Take him away from here," Cruz pleaded with Kale, referring to the boy who hadn't been shot, who now lay flat on his back, his mouth wide open in a silent cry. Kale reached behind the boy and grabbed him under the shoulders. He hurriedly carried him to the school entrance. As Kale placed him inside the door, the boy gave him a look as if he was being left with lions. The schoolmaster hustled over and knelt down. Al-badi's face had the look of a man falling off a building. Kale, dashing back to the truck, saw blood on his hands and pants.

Wynn gave more orders on the radio. Neither 23 nor 24 answered. He tried again. He could only spend seconds thinking about the shooting—the urgency of the upcoming search rushed at him like a mountain torrent.

"D24, 21 over." He tried again to reach Cooke.

No answer.

Billows of dust churned up behind 21 as Gung maneuvered the Humvee, crossing the dirt field separating the houses from the road and school.

Wynn tried once more to reach Cooke on the radio. Gung drove without direction, seeming to sense where Wynn wanted to go. He was consumed managing the situation.

"D24, 21—what's the situation?" Still nobody answered. Had something else happened? Maybe more men had dismounted. Still—somebody should be on the radio.

D22 caught up with 21 and crossed the road. Knowing he still had two vehicles back at the school tending to the wounded, his manpower was limited. Putting dismounts inside the houses with so few men would be dangerous and would handicap the ability of the men left in the trucks to react. Precious minutes passed. Chances were high that the shooter had already disappeared. The Wolfhounds hadn't taken any fire since leaving the schoolyard. But he had to at least do a good search, to try to find some evidence of where and who the shooter was, even if he was gone. If the insurgents had taken up a position in one of these houses, maybe they'd have weapons and bomb-making materials stored there. The residents might know something. A resident telling the Wolfhounds about the shooter would be the most likely way they'd find out. He had to get men from the other two trucks up to help. First, he needed to direct his own team. Decisions that needed making pelted him like hail.

"22, 21, over," Wynn radioed Turnbeck.

"22, over."

"Put a man on that balcony to your front, on the house closest to you, on the end. Have him get a visual on the parallel street behind the front row of houses, and provide overwatch. We're going to put guys into these houses soon as we have more men." By putting eyes on the back street, they might be able to see if someone ran.

"Wilco," acknowledged Turnbeck.

D24 still hadn't responded. What was wrong? Wynn turned around and tried to peer out of the back in the direction of the school. Maybe they were in a radio dead spot. "Why aren't they talking?" he said out loud, frustrated. Only his crew heard him.

"Can you see them?" Wynn, unable to see rearward, asked Singleton. From the gunner's position, Singleton could turn around and look back into the school compound.

Wynn noticed movement in his peripheral vision. He turned. D22 drove the remaining 50 meters to the balcony, dust billowing behind the truck like a mini cyclone. Reaching the house, Mongrel immediately got out, did a quick crotch scratch, and climbed on the top of the Humvee so he could get up on the lower roof of the house adjacent to the house with the balcony. He intended to jump over. Seconds later, Wynn watched him jump. Mongrel's initiative pleased him.

"D21, this is D24, over." Finally, Cooke was back on the radio.

"Go ahead, over," replied Wynn.

"Fucked up situation here, sir. Nothing can be done. The one kid didn't make it. The fucking bullet tore a walnut-sized hole out of his back. The other appears unhurt, just scared shitless. We carried him inside the school."

Wynn said nothing, trying to absorb what had happened and determine next steps.

What should he do? Leave the kids? He could do nothing for them. One was dead, the other unhurt, though probably in shock. Wynn needed the rest of his men for the search.

"Want us to follow you?" Cooke asked, as if he'd been reading Wynn's mind. Maybe he was.

"Yes," Wynn said. He had to go with what was most urgent. "Come here—break—is the schoolmaster still there?"

"Ahh. Don't think they ever came out."

"Still inside?"

"Not sure. Haven't seen them outside."

"OK. Do a quick check. Make sure they know what happened."

Wynn again remembered Alberts.

"Is Major Alberts OK?"

"Roger that," Cooke answered.

Now—the next pressing question fell on Wynn—how to conduct the search? He'd seen no Iraqis outside. Mongrel was on the roof, but no longer visible. Wynn needed assets at the rear of these houses. If Mongrel saw someone leave the houses, Wynn needed a Humvee available to pursue. But the more men he had watching different possible escape routes, the fewer men he would have available to search houses.

He needed to send a report of what was happening to headquarters. In the middle of organizing the search, he didn't have time. He told Cooke to report.

Wynn called D22 again. "You go down to the south end. Watch the street. Don't let anyone leave. Put D22 on the other side of me. We'll put our truck on the far north, across the road from you."

How to best search the place? He needed to talk to Ulricht again, to confirm which building he had shot at. He wanted to search that building first, and then go left and right, if needed.

Wynn got on the radio and asked Turnbeck to confirm again which house Ulricht believed held the shooter. After about 30 seconds of silence, Turnbeck came back on the net and explained that Ulricht confirmed a building to the north. The house had a clothesline on the roof with laundry hanging on it.

Wynn looked. He couldn't determine which building it was.

"Back up, and move that way," he pointed and instructed Gung. "See if we can see the house he's talking about." Wynn twisted his head, searching. He saw D23 and 24 coming across the field. It hadn't taken them long.

D21 pulled away and drove northward. The entire crew strained their necks looking for roofs with clotheslines. D23 evidently saw them moving because Pauls came on the radio.

"It's about two houses up from where you are."

Bending forward and looking up out of the front windshield, Wynn saw the clothesline and laundry. Now he had to decide how to get inside this house. He'd seen no people so far. Should they just knock on the door? This was the standard way of letting residents know Americans were looking for information. But they'd been shot at and had shot back. That was different.

In less than a minute, Gung positioned 21 next to the house. Wynn's right leg was shaking. He ignored that and studied the house. Typical block multi-floored house with flat roof. A water tank on the roof. A large palm tree grew on the other side of the house, and the top of the tree towered over the roof. The contrast of the white sheets and green branches made it easier to see the laundry. And this tree as backdrop might have camouflaged a shooter.

He had to get men up on that roof, and fast. They'd search the roof, then the lower floors. If they found residents in the house, they'd interrogate them.

Wynn organized a search team. He would lead it, taking Cengo, Randell, and Singleton. As usual, his team would be called Wolf One. He'd also alerted Cooke to form Wolf Two. The teams would enter and search houses on command. Wynn didn't want Wolf Two to go into the second house until Wolf One had finished with the first. One team in a house at a time. This allowed the other team to support if either had trouble.

The Humvees were in place now, cordoning the area. The Wolf One team rallied at D21. He ordered Gung to pull D21 up to the house, close enough so the men could climb up from the top of the truck, and with the assistance of a buddy, get up on the roof.

Singleton watched the rooflines. So far he'd seen no one. The first man would go up, clear the far side of the roof, and then signal for the other three to follow. Normally there was a way into the house from the roof. They wouldn't know for sure until they got up there. But going in from the roof was the better way to search a house that might have insurgents in it. Going down had tactical advantages: it was safer and less expected. And insurgents couldn't roll grenades down the stairs at them.

Singleton saw the clothesline suddenly vibrate and one of the white garments flutter. He reported it.

"Eyes on!" Wynn yelled up, chopping his arm in the direction of the roof. Every man aimed his gun at the roof. Seconds passed, and he saw nothing. He got up on D21 and climbed to the roof, scratching two fingertips raw clambering up. On the roof he took a knee, weapon up, scanned from left to right, looking for any kind of movement. Bright sun washed the rooftop like a superheated varnish. The roof was maybe 35 by 50 feet. He saw no one. Why had the garments fluttered? Maybe they hadn't. Maybe Singleton misjudged.

Once the team climbed to the roof and secured it, the men found the roof door. They'd seen nothing suspicious on the roof. They looked around for shell casings and saw none. Wynn walked around the roof a second time, looking. Nothing left behind. Maybe the shooter had not been on this roof after all. Maybe Ulricht had been wrong.

Wynn checked again and got confirmation they were on the right roof.

Confident the roof was clear, Wynn signaled that they approach the access door leading to the floor below. Two men went to each side of the door. Randall looked for booby-trap wires and signs that something might be hidden in the door frame. He saw nothing. Wynn signaled and Randall breeched the door with two hard kicks. The door flung open. The stairwell leading down was dark, narrow, and cavernous. It had a dank pungent smell, like urine in an alley. Their eyesight took several seconds to adjust after the bright sunlight outside. Three thin diagonal cylinders of light came out of the wall, shining miniature spotlights on the stairs just above the landing. Singleton, the lead man, aimed his weapon down the stairs. Maybe ten steps lay ahead and then the stairwell made a left onto the next floor.

Wynn could see around Singleton's shoulder. He assumed the landing below led to more rooms, but he wasn't sure. A delay could be dangerous and allow more time for an ambush to get ready. On the other hand, moving too fast might mean making a mistake. He was committed now; they needed to continue.

Wynn patted Singleton on the thigh, signaling him to move, and the big man led the way down the stairwell. Descending, they realized that the light shafts came from holes caused by Ulricht's bullets. Once at the bottom of the stairs, each man rushed to one of four designated places in the first room they entered, rapidly scanning everything with their eyes. Nobody in the room. The room was modestly furnished. Soiled carpet. Two low sofas, several small tables. Nothing on the walls. A door to another room was on the back wall.

Singleton and Wynn moved across the room to the other door. Singleton kicked a table out of the way with his foot. Then he looked under the carpet. Without hesitating, he rolled the carpet up end to end. Randall looked under both sofas. Nothing.

They continued into the back room beyond the door. A bedroom. Lights, desk, and chests. All of them—Wynn, Randell, Singleton—held their guns up, scanning, alert to any movement, all their senses dialed to maximum sensitivity.

Nothing. Nobody in the room.

"The mattress?" Wynn asked, pointing at it with his rifle, signaling Randall to check under it.

Randall moved. He lifted the mattress. Nothing was under it. He dropped it.

Singleton scrutinized the ceiling, looking for a scuttle hole.

They returned to the other room, intending to continue down the next flight of stairs. Wynn studied the walls, looking for any signs of a hiding place. He glanced out a window. The sun, ignoring their predicament, shone bright and fierce, scorching the ground almond white.

The column of four men worked their way slowly but steadily down to the ground floor. Wynn felt like he was physically connected to each of them. One man followed another: four men, working as one. Eyes ahead, slightly hunched posture, extended arms holding gun stocks and hand grips, making the same movements, equidistant and at the same pace, like train cars linked together on a perilous journey.

The bottom floor had more rooms and appeared to be the main living area. Upstairs were bedrooms. Wynn looked around. Still quiet. No strange movement.

It appeared nobody was in the house. What did this mean? Had the occupants been chased out by the sniper? Where they hiding somewhere in the house? Had the house been vacant all along? Wynn was breathing rapidly, the bombarding unanswered questions stealing his oxygen.

The stairwell ended in a hallway which ran the left side of the house with rooms on the right side. Wolf One moved down the hall. The first room to the right was furnished pretty nicely. He and Randall entered, each man swiftly moving to a position in the room, dominating it.

More carpets on the floor, tables, and chairs, and one desk. They looked under all furniture and turned over each pillow.

Randall noticed a stuffed bag under a table. It looked like a laundry bag. He pulled it out. It was lumpy, like a bag of potatoes, but lightweight. A pull cord kept the bag closed. Randall prodded at the bag with his foot. It was soft. He bent down and opened it, reached his hand inside, and pulled out some children's clothes, wadded up as if packed in a hurry. He dumped the contents of the bag on the floor. Randall shifted through the pile of clothes with his foot, saw nothing of interest, and then moved on.

The house appeared evacuated. Yet the furnishings in the house indicated recent occupancy. Clothing, books, plates, and cups remained. Maybe whoever lived here was out. Perhaps they had been chased. Insurgents were known to take over houses and threaten the former occupants with death if they talked.

Was this the right house? All Wynn had to go on was Ulricht's belief he'd seen someone here. So far they had found nothing confirming anyone had shot from this house. Was he wasting time?

Now Singleton moved to a bookshelf. Wynn could see him fingering the tops of books, searching for anything wrong, or hidden. Randall, on the other side of the room, handled a standing lamp. He looked inside the lamp shade, then left it alone to check something else.

To the right was the kitchen. Wynn told Randall and Singleton to go search it. The kitchen had a few cabinets. The men looked inside them. Then Randall looked inside and behind a cold storage box. The box was empty.

Iraqis didn't typically have conventional ovens. Two gas burners stood on a metal table. Randall lifted the burners off, looked under them, but found nothing.

Another door was slightly ajar on the far side of the room.

"Check that room," Wynn told Randall, and then nodded to Singleton to assist.

The two men moved. Randall pushed the door open with the barrel of his rifle. Light from the street window beyond them shone into the dark room. Carpets on the floor. Stuffed pillows. Stacks of blankets. A prayer room.

"Check that stuff," Wynn said loudly, again signaling with his rifle. Even mosques had been used to hide weapons and bomb-making material.

Randell went to his knees, patting down the stack of blankets, feeling for anything hard.

Suddenly Wynn heard a scraping sound. He looked to his left, saw nothing. Then he heard the sound again, from a different direction. He dropped to a knee and raised his rifle. He saw Singleton on his knees by the wall next to the stairway, pushing a chest away from the wall. That was the noise. They found nothing.

This home was furnished better than he expected and they found nothing suspicious. What to do next? Should he go to the next house? Wynn needed to find people, talk to someone; he had to get information in order to have any hope of finding the shooter. Of course, they might have missed the shell casings. Maybe the shooter had picked them up. Or perhaps Ulricht was wrong. Maybe one of the adjacent houses had been used by the shooter. They would need to check those too. The backside of this house, the side towards the school, had no windows. If a shooter had used this house, he must have shot from the roof. Should they go back up again and look for shell casings? No; they needed to move, needed to check other possibilities. If insurgents were still in the area they'd soon move on, or they might be setting up an ambush.

"All right, we're going into the other houses," Wynn told the others.

Wynn called Cooke on the radio. "Nothing here. Let's clamp down on this place. You put a truck watching the front and back street of this area. Then have your team start at the far end—break—think there's about five or six homes between here and there. We come towards each other, and if we have the street covered, we might luck out and catch anything between us."

"Roger," Cooke replied.

"We've got to interrogate anyone we see," Wynn added.

"Roger."

Any optimism Wynn had about finding the shooter was gone. He suppressed a growing sense of ineffectiveness. It felt as if hours had already passed since the shooting, as if time had been flattened and stretched by the devil. Barely 30 minutes had passed. He radioed CPT Baumann and gave him a quick update.

Wolf Two also entered their selected house through the roof. Pauls led the team. They reported entering the house to Wynn on the radio, less than five minutes after Wynn's team had exited the first house. Wolf Two was a three-man team—Pauls, Moose, and Kale—one short of the recommended minimum number for house clearing. Cooke had not given up an additional man for fear of leaving the trucks too lightly manned to be effective.

Moose moved through the rooms in a combination of rapid and slow movements; he felt as if he was surrounded by a series of confinements, forbidding spaces within spaces, each different: small rooms followed by bigger rooms, then small rooms again. Narrow rooms by wider ones, dark by light by dark. Each room presented a new and different danger. Some oddities or abnormalities flashed. Others were detected by intense scrutiny. Closet doors unclosed. A window looked strange. A rug sagged, perhaps covering something. A box looked out of place. Clothing piled on it. He brushed off the clothing and looked inside. Empty.

Checking this. Checking that. Checking. Rechecking. A sizzle of psychological electricity pulsed through each mini environment. The anticipation of violence dominated every thought, every movement exhilarating him, making him feel supercharged, more alive than he had ever felt. What was it? Controlled chaos? No, it wasn't. It was planned. They were trained. Cover. Anticipate. What about the enemy? Put yourself in their shoes. What would they do? Anything out of place? Where would they hide?

Though disciplined and methodical, in each house entry, in each room clearing, Moose had a sensation of flying. His thoughts moved so fast he didn't have enough time to stabilize his mind. Inside he was restless; outside, constant noise and commotion. A continuum of walls, and doors, and alleys, and halls, and windows, and floors, and stairwells, and furnish-ings, flowed around him, passed him. He was flying in it. There, but not there, looking for something but not really knowing what, everything different but everything the same, as if he were a pilot searching for something on the ground.

In a room with long rugs lining both walls, Moose panted. He took a knee. His ballistic goggles fogged, and he wiped them. A mouse darted across the floor ahead of him. He smiled. No bad guys, just a mouse.

Moose disconnected the hose to his camelbak canteen and took a long draw. He heard something on the radio about moving a vehicle.

Wolf One, Wynn leading, stood at the next house's front door. Someone inside was opening it. Wynn stood to the left of the opening, Singleton to the right. Cengo and Randall stood a few feet back on either side of the entry steps. Wynn felt as if some-one was peeling back the covering of his nerves.

A short, elderly man cracked open the door. His hairless gullied skull looked like a brown gourd. His crippled left arm hung in a sling.

Wynn identified himself and the purpose of the visit. Cengo translated. The elderly Iraqi replied rapidly, his nearly toothless mouth yawing side to side like an animal chewing nuts.

Wynn turned to Cengo, waiting for the translation. In his peripheral vision, Wynn saw Singleton shuffling his feet, scan-ning inside the entrance.

"He say no terrorist in this house. He say he hate Al Qaeda. He say no problem we look in house."

Wynn watched the man for hints of lying. He appeared un-afraid and obliging.

"Ask him if he heard any shooting." Wynn directed Cengo.

Cengo did, then translated the response. "Yes, he say he hear loud noises, maybe shooting. But he say he old, and not know what it is."

"Anyone else in the house?"

"He say his son's baby sleeping in the house."

"Where's his son?"

Cengo talked for another half-minute with the Iraqi. Wynn watched the conversation, occasionally glancing over the man's shoulder into the house. Small pathways led around both sides of the house. Wynn preferred not to break up his team, but suddenly suspicious about this man's son, said: "Randall, go look around the sides of this house, down the paths."

Randall moved out without saying anything. Cengo continued talking to the Iraqi.

"He say son in Syria. He visiting uncle in Syria, he say."

"You believe him?"

"I think yes."

"OK. Tell him we'd like him to show us around his house."

The elderly Iraqi led them room to room, and answered questions. The house was sparsely furnished and clean. As the team looked around the house, Randall returned. He hadn't seen anything suspicious. The team looked carefully under and behind whatever they wanted. When finished with the first floor, the group moved upstairs. Two rooms on the second floor were unfurnished. Wynn asked why. The Iraqi explained that the son in Syria took furniture with him when he moved. The baby slept in an upstairs room on a blanket on the floor.

Why would the son take furniture but leave his baby? Wynn wanted more information.

"He say uncle very sick. Have to sell things for money. Mother stay here."

"Where is she?"

"She go to market now."

Wynn wanted to check the roof. The Iraqi had to go back downstairs for a key to unlock the roof door. Wynn had Singleton follow him. Both men came back in a couple of minutes.

The team walked around the top of the house, looking for signs that someone had fired from the roof. It looked clean. A water tank stood atop a concrete block pedestal. A chair was on the street side of the roof, the opposite side from the school. Wynn looked a second time at the water tank. Insurgents had hidden in water tanks.

"Check that," he told Randall, pointing to the tank.

Randall walked over, stepped on top of two concrete blocks at its base, and peered inside.

"Half full," he said.

"Can you see the bottom?"

"Yes, Sir."

Wynn concluded that either nobody had fired from this house or whoever did was gone. He thanked the Iraqi for his cooperation, and had Cengo write down the man's personal information. Wynn called Wolf Two and told them they could enter their next house.

Kale was now inside his second vacant house. Darker inside. Adjust, eyes, he shouted to himself. See, let me see. Absolute self-control he needed now, absolute self-control.

His vision accelerated and didn't rest. He used all his strength to keep from getting dizzy. He looked from place to place, too fast, too fast. Floor first. In the corner, then along the edge of the wall and floor. Far corner. Then mid-wall height, first looking for a threat, a person, bombs, weapons, then for holes, furniture someone could be inside, something on the wall to kill him. Nothing. Then ceiling. Anything up there? No. Next door.

His eyes darted continuously. And his mind raced faster, making his concentration unstable. Senses sharp as a razor. No hesitating. No time for logic. All instinct now. All training. Muscle memory. That's what they called it: muscle memory. He looked for doors. A piece of curtain-like fabric hung in front of him. A doorway? Probably a passage to the next room. Another door. Eyes glanced back around. What was behind this wall? An empty room. No furniture. Was the floor disturbed? He checked. No.

Anxiety pounded his insides like a jackhammer. Settle down, settle down. Look. Focus. Think. Absolute self-control was what he wanted. Take in everything. Did it seem right? Feel right? Thinking through sensing, through instinct. Powers of logic were overwhelmed. No time for careful deliberation. Move, move, move. All the while, he was moving, looking, thinking, working. He was overloaded with tension and fear. It was like a terrible scene from a horror movie that kept restarting at the most suspenseful part, the villain not yet foiled, the climax constantly delaying. No, worse. He was in it. This was the horror scene, and he the victim. No, bullshit. That's not right. He was the aggressor. What was there, if anything, would react to him: the aggressor. He drove the action.

Settle, settle, he pleaded with himself. Won't work to get crazy, to think too much. Too much excitement, too much nervousness kills concentration.

By 1730, the Wolfhounds had searched eight houses. Three of the houses had occupants. None of the residents admitted to knowing anything about the shooting and provided bare bones information, their eyes and body language signaling that all they wanted was to be left alone. No one was home at the other houses, and one house was completely empty, stripped of furnishings, possibly abandoned. Wynn knew the men were frustrated and tired. His body slowed, as if operating on dwindling air. They found absolutely nothing clearly connected to the shooting. MAJ Alberts, who for the first couple of hours had been a mute passenger in D24, now pointed out that he had pressing work back on the FOB. As the sun ate the rest of the afternoon, Alberts grew increasingly persistent in his demands to return. Finally Wynn conceded.

After a discussion with Cooke, Wynn called CPT Baumann on the radio and gave him a more detailed report. They decided to bring MAJ Alberts back to FOB Apache, and then the Wolfhounds would return to investigate further. At 1805, the Wolfhounds departed for the FOB.

Though Cooke and Wynn recognized the platoon was exhausted, both concluded that one more trip to Bawa Sah was justified.

11

By 2100 the Wolfhounds were driving back to the school. A 2100 curfew had been put into place two months ago, part of an effort to reduce the ability of insurgents to emplace roadside bombs during the night. The curfew, now on, was regularly violated, for legitimate reasons or not.

Moose felt good about going out again. He had spoken to Kale back on the FOB, and Kale looked hallowed out. In private, he got in Kale's face, telling him to get his shit together. He revived a bit after that. Wonder what Kale was thinking now?

Much of the platoon had been skeptical when Cooke and Wynn told them about plans to visit Bawa Sah again, in the hopes that someone would reveal information. Not Moose. He wanted to go because it increased the chance of a fight. Maybe if they had a patrol in the neighborhood tonight, Wynn had said, someone friendly would come forward under the cover of darkness. Moose doubted that, but he was OK with trying. Not likely anyone was brave enough to come forward. It would be like signing your own death warrant. The insurgents would kill them and perhaps their families.

Twenty minutes passed. As they neared Bawa Sah, Moose tried to look at every doorway, every window, down every street and alley. But seeing in the dark was difficult. The convoy drove with blackout drive. Cooke had ordered the last three trucks to turn off their headlights. Blackout driving was a new tactic for the platoon, which Cooke started suggesting a week or so ago, proposing that only the first Humvee have its lights on. Wynn had agreed. That way when the convoy approached it might give the illusion of being a lone truck and confuse possible insurgents.

About a mile from the school, the convoy slowed down. It had taken them 44 minutes to get here, the blackout drive slowing them down.

The truck bumped over several potholes.

"Wake everybody up," said Cooke, "in case those bumps didn't."

The truck drove through pools of water and sewage puddles. The street narrowed. The road to the school was on the far side of this block. At the next intersection, several buildings hugged the road and a small strip of concrete sidewalk, four or five inches high.

On the drive back to Bawa Sah, Wynn tried again to determine exactly what had happened. One Iraqi boy was dead. Another boy was surely badly traumatized by what happened. The Wolfhounds were angry and frustrated. They'd chased the single lead they had—the possible sniper's location—but had found nothing. The sniper must have shot from those buildings. No other possibility existed.

On the FOB, after dropping Alberts off, Wynn and Cooke questioned Ulricht again. No one else had seen anything. Ulricht continued to believe he'd had a real target, but couldn't state anything else meaningful about what he'd seen. His big ears were on fire as he reminded them that it had taken over 15 minutes from the time of the shots before Wolf One got in the first house—more than enough time for the shooter to run away. He was right. Wynn had mentally surveyed the school grounds again and again, considering alternatives, but hadn't come up with any. Cooke defended Ulricht. Other buildings as close to the school didn't have as clear a line of sight.

A sense that the sniper must have known about the Wolfhounds' visit nagged at Wynn. The thing must have been planned. Not just anyone could make a shot like that. But an Iraqi boy killed—the Wolfhounds were asking—who was the intended target? At that range, over 400 meters, the enemy snipers so far encountered in Iraq wouldn't likely try to pick off a man in a Humvee turret. A dismounted man was an easier target. What if the sniper was deliberately shooting at the boy? Why? Maybe he believed the Americans would get blamed. Uncertainty buzzed Wynn, like an insect he couldn't kill.

If they came up empty tonight, the Wolfhounds would need to go back to the school during daylight. He wanted to talk to the schoolmaster again and maybe Manah too. Could either have tipped off insurgents? Both probably had advance notice of the Wolfhound trip to the school. Somebody had to know something.

On the last kilometer, the Wolfhounds drove no faster than 5 miles per hour. The night felt deeper and more impenetrable the closer they got, as if Allah himself was camouflaging the surroundings. To Moose it seemed the night colluded with the insurgents. No one in D24 spoke, each man submerged in his own thoughts. The quiet disguised the tension without erasing it. Every Wolfhound knew that the convoy was surrounded by hundreds of civilians in their homes.

Moose concentrated on what he was looking at, what might be out there. Anyone watching them? Was whoever shot the Iraqi boy still in the area?

The convoy crawled on. Nothing happened.

Hard to see anything in this darkness. Rubble littered the street. He saw another reflection, something in the rubble. Maybe a soda can. Soda cans had been made into bombs. In an armored vehicle, the damage caused by such little bombs was usually minor, but few weeks ago an IED consisting of two stacked 130mm artillery shells had been buried in a trash pile.

Suddenly the radio crackled, shattering the night quiet. "The school ahead," Turnbeck announced.

Wynn had earlier directed Turnbeck to proceed to the neighborhood street where they had searched houses.

"Car parked ahead."

Moose tightened his grip on the .50 caliber.

After getting orders from Wynn to investigate, D22 proceeded slowly forward. Another minute passed.

"Somebody's sitting in the car," Turnbeck reported finally.

"Say again?" Wynn asked.

"I believe someone's in the car."

A few seconds later Turnbeck radioed and said it was a false alarm. A shadow. Nobody in the car.

By now it was almost 2205. Wynn radioed the platoon that they would drive a slow circle around the neighborhood prior to stopping by the houses. Then they would knock on the doors of some of the earlier vacant houses. If someone was home this time, they'd interrogate them. Lastly, the platoon would drive slowly twice around the area to see if anyone might approach them with information.

Moose believed Wynn had another reason: to prove to the insurgents that whatever happened, the Wolfhounds would not run away. "Chase you to hell," he mumbled to himself.

The streets and houses remained quiet. No one approached the platoon. No civilians on the street. The dark quietness, so soon after a death, disturbed the men. It was as if a fog of inexplicable strangeness covered the neighborhood, and the memory of what had happened that afternoon had already penetrated into the walls. Questions without answers surged through the men like hot oil.

After circling the area, Wynn dismounted with Cengo and a security team. He started knocking on house doors. When residents answered, he explained what had happened and asked for help. Residents of two of the homes that were vacant earlier had returned. The families were not particularly happy to be visited by American soldiers, especially at night. One family did not realize their home had been searched earlier. Another family, when hearing that, requested compensation. Wynn changed the subject. Both families had plausible reasons for being absent earlier and neither admitted to being aware of insurgent activity in the area. Neither admitted to knowing anything about a shooting. Other houses were still vacant—including the house Ulricht had shot at—or abandoned.

Wynn, tired and frustrated, eventually concluded the platoon could do no more tonight. He walked over to Cooke's truck.

"What do you think, Sergeant Cooke?"

Cooke licked the perspiration off his upper lip delicately, as if he were tasting their options, then answered: "We could move in here. Not go back to the FOB. But if we stay, the CO won't like it. We could leave and come back tomorrow."

"Yeah. We probably should leave. Come back during daylight."

"You're right, Sir. Truth is, if a sniper shot from one of these fucking houses, the residents probably got sent away beforehand and know next to nothing about it. Either that or the residents were threatened to stay quiet if they didn't want a family member's head to show up in a bag at their door. It'll be hard as hell to get them to tell us anything."

He was right, of course. Even if somebody in the neighborhood knew anything, that person might be too scared to talk. Lying was safer. The Wolfhounds couldn't know for sure.

Wynn stared at the dark outlines of the houses. He didn't see a single light on the street. The place was as black as erased memory. The relentless obligations of the Wolfhound's daily work remained and he worried that if his men were too tired tomorrow, the missions could be compromised and the risks would be greater. Weariness augured mistakes.

His hopes for getting helpful information had been yet another triumph of hope over experience.

"OK. Let's leave," Wynn decided.

At 2340 the Wolfhounds departed again for FOB Apache.

Just after 0100, Kale slammed his trailer door shut. His roommates were still out. He flicked the light switch on so hard it hurt his finger.

Damn fools. Damn fools, he muttered to himself. The whole country was a shithole. How in the world they held anything together, how in the world they made anything work, how they lived, how they survived, why the hell anybody stayed, he did not know. He steamed disgust.

Kale jerked his IBA off and threw it on the floor. The clunk of the heavy weight landing on the floor shook the whole trailer. In the process, he ripped the elastic head band of his goggles and they fell to the floor, skittering beside his bed. He slammed his helmet on the desk and kicked the goggles under the bed.

Damn fools. The world is full of fools.

Shooting children! A sniper shooting children! Is there anything more screwed up?

He sat hard on his bed. The Chinese bed frame vibrated noisily, squeaking like a trapped rat.

He put a hand on each leg and looked down again at his blood-stained pants. Blood from the dead boy. The trailer light illuminated the brownish-red of the blood. He looked at his hands and studied the smudges of dried blood and dirt collected in the crevasses of his palms like tiny red footprints.

Had the bastard aimed at a soldier or the boy?

Kale fell backward, swinging his legs up, then lay on the bed staring at the ceiling. White ceilings. White was wrong. He stared straight at the fluorescent lights, defying the discomfort, as if he was seeking purification. He imagined the light was an acetylene torch that could burn his eyes to help him forget, and his eyes started watering, misting over, blurring his vision.

He felt like never using his eyes again.

He ran through the events again, churning every detail in his head, struggling with disbelief.

At a school. The children—smiling children. No guilt or evil in them. Then a boy took a bullet to his chest, killing him. Could they have stopped it? Ulricht, on the gun, had responded quickly. Did he really see anything?

And they couldn't find the fucking bastard. They had searched for hours, and discovered nothing. Of course no one saw anything. Of course. Same shit.

Damn fucking country. Crazy fucking country.

His bed was wedged tightly between the walls. He kicked the wall hard one time, lashing out at the brutal craziness poisoning the world.

He looked again at the light through closed eyes, the acetylene torch burning behind a thin screen. Can't burn it off. Never can.

DAY FOUR

12

AT 0430, THE EARTH HERSELF still asleep, all Wynn could hear was his feet hitting the gravel of the running trail around the perimeter of the FOB and his steady deep breathing. He hadn't run for several weeks. He'd decided to run this morning to help purge the craziness of yesterday. After a day like yesterday, night sunk the whole earth into a suffocating silent pit, and he wondered how ordinary life could ever return. Nonetheless, every 24 hours—an immense achievement—the world turned back from the black, muted, and lethargic night into a living, breathing, buzzing spectacle. He pushed the air out of his lungs. Of course everything wasn't asleep. Bad things happened in the night; things that could hurt his men—people like whoever shot that boy. Wynn's chest heaved and expanded as he ran, sounding like a hospital breathing machine. He'd rounded the back of the FOB a second time. His body-burn felt good, as if every cell was rejuvenating. He couldn't change what was happening around him. Part of him maybe didn't want to. To count when it mattered most was what mattered most.

What does matter and what doesn't? Perhaps there are a few true things, a few large and stable rocks in a cold stream that you could use while crossing, while moving through your life. Life was inevitably a precarious crossing; sometimes the stepping stones were wet and slippery. You had to keep going. That was the main thing.

Some didn't keep going. He had lost one: Ramirez. Wynn hoped, prayed, he would not lose another. Long after the Wolfhounds returned stateside and the war was old history, after the country had moved on to new crises and his men had married beauties and fathered children, and gotten new jobs, and lost jobs, and gotten new jobs again, and gotten divorced, and started again, and kissed grandkids, after they had built a thousand new memories—the one thing they would never forget is that not everyone came home.

After breakfast, Cooke huddled with Sergeants Pauls, Turnbeck, and Singleton. Dawn cracked like a smoldering fire along the horizon. The night's darkness resisted banishment, and bright light from a pole-mounted fixture shined down on them, the four men's bodies casting long lean shadows, like dark fingers pointing impenitent at the day to come.

"We got to shake that mess yesterday off the men," Cooke said. "No man can see kids killed without being affected. Watch your guys. Keep telling them things will be all right. Keep each other safe, that's the main thing." He worried that the men would hold on to that image of the dead boy and thereby degrade their performances in the days to come. He kicked at the ground, grinding the toe of his boot into dirt, trying to squash any such possibility.

"We lost him," Pauls said, his voice sodden with residual frustration.

"Lost what?" Cooke asked.

"The damn shooter. That'll eat the guys."

"True. It's fucked up. But it ain't over. Keep talking to your guys. What's important right now is the men need to be reminded that a man, especially a fighting man, wins some and loses some. Being able to handle both is the definition of maturity."

"We gotta get something to make up for it, kill something, fuck them up. We find the bastards that did this, the guys will put it behind them," Turnbeck said.

"We watch out for each other," Cooke said. "We want to bring everybody home. I don't want to lose anybody else." He thought about Ramirez. He'd lost one of the Wolfhounds already; it couldn't happen again. "You remind your guys about that. Remind each other. If anybody lets me down, I'm gonna deliver a really hard time."

"We got it, Sarge," Pauls answered.

"The LT and I've been talking," Cooke continued. "We'll find these bad guys. We all work hard, and we'll find them. Keep your eyes wide open. Keep your crews alert. We'll dig until we find some clues. Something will break our way."

After talking for a few more minutes, the group broke up. Cooke watched the others walk away. Then he stuck his left hand in his pants pocket and fingered a thin strip of fabric. He touched the familiar embroidered letters on the fabric. The letters spelled a name: Ramirez. After Ramirez had been killed, the platoon had packed up all his personal effects to give to casualty affairs. On a table in the FOB trailer where Ramirez had lived had been a small packet of spare uniform items, including three name tapes for his desert cammies. Cooke, seeing these, had softly run his finger over Ramirez's name and taken one. Ever since then he'd carried Ramirez's name tape in his pants pocket. Inside Cooke's kevlar vest cover was another Ramirez memento, a printed picture of Ramirez that Mongrel had taken during the flight from America. The photograph caught Ramirez in the aisle of the aircraft, horsing around, his mouth twisted insolently, his hands extended like two six-shooters aimed at Mongrel. With the photograph inside Cooke's vest, the dead man remained part of the pack. Whenever the Wolfhounds left the wire, Ramirez still ran with them.

Moose arrived early in the motor pool. Other men, other early arrivals, clambered about their trucks, some with a casual distractedness, privately at work, taking care of business, their minds elsewhere. Their activity suggested purposefulness. Few talked. They were busy, busy in the way of serious men who know their jobs. Each was preparing, checking, rechecking, readying for the day—each alone, yet fulfilling a necessary task for the whole. Moose saw Lee installing a repaired radio.

Gung did maintenance checks under the hood of D21. Cuebas crawled inside the back of his truck, rearranging equipment.

Ulricht stood like a centurion on top of his truck, adjusting the gun turret. In addition to his uniform, Ulricht wore an assortment of the combat soldier's discretionary gear and black gloves. A Leatherman multi-tool hung off his belt. His quick decisive movements—leaning over one second, manipulating the turret the next—made him look vigorous and strong and important. He was all about getting things done. Moose watched him. Ulricht was silhouetted against the sky, his lean body contrasted with the immense blue sky backdrop, as if, in its oddly fragile human form, youth and freshness nevertheless stood up defiantly against the physical world. Maybe his silhouette symbolized how important they each were as individuals. The platoon was a small part of a big Army, yet each man was something big too.

What was Ulricht thinking about yesterday's events? He was probably still wondering whether it was right to fire, and whether he had hit anything. Everyone was frustrated at their inability to find whoever had shot at them, and each felt bad about what had happened to the boy.

Moose contemplated the day ahead. It wasn't about helping the Iraqis. He cared only about helping other Wolfhounds. How could they stay safe? Their training had focused primarily on that. They had spent weeks making sure they understood and could work their equipment. They had repeatedly shot their weapons. They studied military techniques again and again. They'd spent dozens of hours on counter-IED training, trying to master taking care of themselves in combat. Sure, they went out to look for bad guys. Sure, they engaged with the local population. But at least 75 percent of it, especially the outside the wire part, was about protecting themselves. After yesterday, the focus on self-protection would increase.

Wynn looked across the hood of his truck at his men. He would give it to them straight. They knew the cost of war, and the difficulty of operations in Iraq. The death of the Iraqi boy yesterday was a cost of war. With all the fat boiled off, the Wolfhounds' mission was to keep the violence levels in their battlespace as low as possible. After yesterday, his soldiers would be asking whether they had failed. They hadn't failed. They'd been out in it, doing their part, trying to bring a little better life to the Iraq's citizens by helping with a new school. Had the Wolfhounds stayed away, progress, such as the construction of new schools, wouldn't be possible. Whoever attacked them yesterday was attacking Iraq. That attack didn't negate what the Coalition Forces were trying to do. Wynn wanted his men—today and every day—confident that they were trying to do the right thing.

He studied the faces of war-chiseled men, tested men, tired men, men who had seen things that should not be seen, who had by now spent enough time around death to know it from the inside. He detected their resolute acceptance, a kind of readiness to attempt the task at hand. It wasn't so much that they believed fully in the mission but that they ought to try. They were all can-do men focused on getting the mission accomplished.

Wynn laid his notes on the hood of the truck. He had spent time last night before falling asleep—and again this morning on his run—thinking about what to say to the platoon about the sniper attack yesterday and what needed reinforcing. Each night he forced his mind to take perspective of where they had been, look forward, and decide how to articulate his thoughts.

He covered his points in a tight, business-like fashion. Speaking about the sniper shooting yesterday, he chose his words carefully, appreciating the gravity of the event. He concluded: "It was very ugly. Can't hide that. But it shows how ugly our enemy is. There is no blame on us. What we were trying to do is good. Our mission is right. And if it takes a trip to hell to find that sniper, that's where we're going."

Then he paused longer than usual, looked around the group, locking for a second or two on the eyes of several men as if that connection might fix a special confirmation, cement an intimacy. He wanted to see singularity of purpose. They looked back, expectant, receptive.

He told the platoon that orders from higher headquarters required that they continue the census that morning for a few hours. After that, they would go back to Bawa Sah, once again looking for anyone that would give them any information about what had happened.

Wynn saw Cooke ready to speak.

"Listen! You have to toughen yourself. There's no other way. You have to harden your soul so completely that your concentration, no matter what happens, is not distracted and your actions are automatic. One of two things will happen if you don't. One, you'll be paralyzed into inaction, where you can't do anything because your system is shocked silly, and you won't be worth a fuck. Two, you'll be killed, because the bad guy is meaner than you. Dead, or not worth a damn. Two bad options. That's the way it is. Harden the heart. If we don't, we ain't gonna win." Cooke said all these things like he was born to say them.

13

The convoy exited FOB Apache.

"Clear!"

"Roger."

"Loaded .50. Dukes on. Run."

"LNs ahead," Turnbeck reported.

"Kid in a ditch on the right."

Kale remembered the bloody, dead boy. And he remembered Wilson.

"Don't know what he's doing. Fishing or something," Turnbeck added.

"Passing LNs on left."

"Lady with a bunch of sticks."

Kale saw the woman. She was dressed from head to toe in a brown burka and carrying a bushel of sticks on her head as she walked. She looked as if she'd been carrying the load a long way.

The convoy continued their routine.

Minutes later, Turnbeck was on the radio. "Donkey cart with green foliage in the back."

A boy pulled the donkey by a rope. The foliage was stacked so high that it nearly fell off the sides of the cart, and Kale didn't see the boy until he passed.

"Approaching car," Turnbeck reported. The car, with three occupants, passed them going in the other direction.

"Were they waving or flipping us off?"

"Flipping us off? Makes me want to go home."

The convoy continued moving, but soon the traffic slowed. The first Iraqi check-point consisted of a small office made out of a metal shipping container. The road side of the container was covered with a layer of sandbags. Two IP manned the checkpoint. One of them slowed the civilian traffic by waving the cars down with his hand, and the other man walked up to the car window and checked the driver and his identification. As the first Humvee neared, one of the IP removed two orange street cones and a welded triangle of steel that blocked the road.

The policeman, wearing a black ski mask over his face to hide his identity, waved the platoon through. If his identity were known, he and his family—even his extended family— might be threatened or even killed. War had forced the man to hide in his own country.

Passing through the checkpoint, each vehicle sounded off on the radio.

"Two's out."

"Three's out."

"Four's out."

Out on the open road, they picked up speed again, maintaining intervals of about 50 meters.

Moments later they arrived at the location Wynn had chosen.

By the time the census teams had finished a dozen houses, a burning, orange sun stood stark and indomitable in the sky. Though it was still early, heat already swathed the land and the men in what felt like hot, sticky syrup. The soldiers continued from house to house, slogging through the heavy air, uncomfortable in the clamminess of wet, salty, sweat-filled uniforms, the itch of soil, sand and debris coating all exposed skin, burdened by the relentless stress of the tedious work.

A two-man security team of Kale and Tyson was on a rooftop, overwatching the census area. A three-foot-high wall bordered the edge of the roof.

Kale looked south at the people in a small makeshift market below. Shoppers walked the street, mingling with vendors at small stalls. Just below his position, a tall man sold fish and vegetables and flat bread. Other vendors sold electronics. Some offered assorted beverages. Many of the vendor stalls were nothing more than a cart or oversized wheelbarrow. Few had overhead cover. Kale watched people's behavior. Most shoppers were women. Some had small children in tow. Most vendors were males—a few were kids, not much older than the boys yesterday, or Wilson. People moved about purposefully, taking care of their daily tasks. For a moment he imagined himself down in the market, moving through it, mingling with Iraqis. He would be lost in their world. He knew nothing about their lives. What made them happy? What were their worries? No, he didn't fit. The past is a selfish thing, and nothing in his past prepared him to be one of them.

In their pre-deployment briefings this phenomenon was called *culture*. To understand the place they had to understand something of Iraqi culture. The Army called this cultural awareness. Why did it matter? Did culture really have something to do with killing that boy yesterday?

He tried to remember those culture briefings. How did you get a culture? Where did it come from? They'd been told it had to do with long-established characteristics of a society. Things like language, customs, history, and beliefs—a blend of tangible and intangible stuff like that. You didn't get the option of buying in or rejecting it. Life's inevitable baggage. You got born into it—almost like genetics, but not quite. A lot of culture was psychological. To change it took years. The textbooks said that culture was intertwined in everything, that you could not separate it out. Just as you couldn't build a house without a frame, you couldn't have a society without a culture.

Kale heard Tyson mutter something and glanced over at him.

"Cleric," Tyson repeated, and pointed. A tall man with a black turban talked animatedly to a vendor. A small crowd had gathered. Kale had no idea what the conversation was about. Might be everyday talk. Clerics wearing black turbans claimed to be descendants of the prophet Mohammed. Clerics wearing white turbans did not. Was it a scolding for improper behavior?

The man getting the talking-to had a round placid face. If he was receiving a lecture, he absorbed it with suitable humility.

Several other men with cloaks and turbans surrounded the cleric, probably his escort. Some might be bodyguards.

On the far side of the roof, Kale saw flat and sunburnt ground in the distance. They were near the edge of the city—a few more streets of houses separated them from open fields. Further off, several miles away, he saw the tall smoke stacks of the idle brick factory, jabbing up into the sky like angry fingers from the underworld. The platoon had not been out there. He doubted if any units had. Too much space to worry about and too few men. The factory was out of action anyway. It had surely been stripped of anything valuable. Whatever jobs and income it had provided was gone.

Wynn, partly to get his mind off the dead boy and the boy's killer, decided to watch Turnbeck's team conduct a census. Minutes earlier, Turnbeck had reported entering a residence behind a lone eucalyptus tree. Wynn walked the 20 meters to the house.

Moose, now on Wynn's security detail, moved ahead of him and knocked on the door. In less than a minute, a chubby Iraqi boy of nine or ten opened the door. The little fucker would probably grow up to be a terrorist, Moose thought.

The boy's eyes flickered uncertainly and Wynn assumed he was still intimidated by the other soldiers who had entered his home a few minutes earlier. Wynn and Cengo went inside, passing the boy as he stepped out of the way. Wynn didn't wait for an adult escort, since Turnbeck's team was already inside. The hallway was narrow and poorly lit. Wynn smelt bitter Iraqi coffee. Sunlight cascaded brightly through a hall window into the room ahead. He could see people sitting in that room.

Moving forward, he recognized Turnbeck's leg and boot through the doorway ahead, one of two men in the platoon with a red dog tag laced to his boot. Turnbeck was allergic to penicillin. Across from this boot was a giant sandal-clad foot, perhaps twelve inches long. Must be a big man. The worn-out sandal had seen better days. Sometimes little things told the most. A $75 high-top Army boot of tan suede leather, composite parts, custom-designed soles, and nylon laces, confronted a cheap, thin plastic sandal. What must an Iraqi think when a heavily armed and armored man arrives wearing a kit of equipment worth probably more than the contents of his house, sits down across from him and starts speaking to him in a strange foreign language?

Entering the room, Wynn was stunned by the appearance of the sandal-wearer. He looked like a massive scared blowfish: beady small silver eyes, grossly engorged body. Fiftyish, he wore thick rimless glasses, a stained *dishdasha* the size of a tent, and sweated profusely. Turnbeck introduced him as Banah Kassam. Kassam struggled to get up as Cengo translated formal introductions. The effort to rise proved so difficult that Wynn signaled for him to remain seated. Compromising, the fat man nevertheless reached up to shake hands from a seated position. His handshake was soft and unstable, like touching Jello.

The room had no extra chairs. Turnbeck offered to get up so Wynn could sit. Wynn waved him off.

"Continue," Wynn told Turnbeck. "You're doing fine."

"Mr. Kassam completed the questionnaire a minute ago, Sir. Zanac has it, and is reviewing the answers with me," Turnbeck said.

Zanac, the extra terp assigned to the platoon today to help with the census, knelt next to Kassam and held the questionnaire in his hands.

"Thank you for completing the questionnaire. Anything else you would like to add?" Turnbeck asked Kassam.

From where he stood, Wynn could see the Arabic writing, neat and measured, in each section of the questionnaire. He looked at Kassam again, still amazed at the bulk of the man. A man this huge was nearly immobile and surely unhealthy. He appeared perpetually out of breath, heaving like a bellows with air intake. His teeth were yellowish with thick plaque, and he had a large black mole on his ample upper lip that rolled like a bean whenever he moved his mouth. Kassam smiled broadly at Wynn, but was clearly nervous and insecure.

Kassam hadn't answered Turnbeck's last question. He looked hesitant. Wynn suspected he might be unwilling to share more than the bare minimum necessary to get the soldiers out of his home.

"Would he like to add something?" Turnbeck tried again. Kassam remained quiet.

Sensing indecision, Wynn intervened.

"Tell him we are sorry to have come into his home," Wynn said in as non-threatening a manner as he could muster, wanting to reduce any additional tension caused by his arrival on the scene.

"Our purpose here, as he knows from the questionnaire we asked him to fill out, is to collect this information so that we and the Iraqi government better understand the people living here."

Cengo translated. The fat man did not reply, but kept smiling, making no indication he wanted to volunteer anything, nodding his head every few seconds, looking back and forth from Wynn to whoever translated.

"We thank you for your cooperation. We would like to know how you think we can help."

Finally Kassam started to speak, but immediately hesitated again, breathing deeply.

"Can he talk?" Wynn asked Turnbeck.

"Yes Sir, he spoke a few times to us already."

"Ask him if he feels security in the neighborhood is better now or six months ago," Wynn told Cengo, putting a slightly different twist on one of the preprinted questions.

The man finally answered, in a raspy voice, that he felt security conditions were unchanged and still dangerous, but that he was pleased to see growth in the Iraqi Security Forces.

This answer pleased Wynn. It suggested the population was aware of the increased efforts to build up the Iraqi Security Forces. Confidence in those forces would be critical for the new Iraq.

"What did he put down on the questionnaire for profession?" Wynn asked.

"Taxi Driver," Zanac answered, after looking for that answer on the paper.

Wynn was surprised by that answer. The size of the man made it hard to envision him driving a taxi, or even getting into a car without great effort.

"Does he still own a taxi?"

Zanac asked the Iraqi.

"No."

"When did he last drive a taxi?"

"This Friday, going to Mosque," Zanac translated Kassam's answer.

"Whose taxi was it?" Wynn persisted, doubting the taxi story. Did this man really drive taxis?

A shadow passed the hall window. Wynn glanced in that direction, but saw nothing.

"He say he not know. He say he just get in taxi to go to mosque," Zanac said.

"How long was he a taxi driver?"

When this question was translated, the fat man shuffled his feet, and rubbed his wrinkled forehead. Zanac repeated the question.

The fat man answered. "It maybe ten minutes to the mosque."

"No, I mean if he was or is a taxi driver, how long did he drive a taxi? For how many years?" Wynn tried again, putting emphasis in his words in a way to make his question clearer.

Wynn continued to project the warmest smile he could, conscious that the image he represented might be what this man remembered about Americans.

"He say he never drove taxi. He say he ride taxi." Cengo translated.

"Then why did he say he was a taxi driver? I don't understand," Wynn said, unsure.

Cengo spoke with Kassam for maybe a minute. Kassam listened patiently, then responded, his tone of voice unchanged.

"Oh," Cengo said, looking at Wynn, "that mistake. Kassam say that his brother drive taxi. He himself not work. I think he little embarrassed by that. So he mean his brother, when he say that on the paper." Cengo pointed to the census form.

Wynn nodded, understanding.

"Please tell him that we want to be sure all the information is accurate. Only with accurate information can it be helpful to us. Does the brother live in this house?" Wynn turned to Turnbeck. "How many names did he put down as living in this house?"

"He say 'no,'" Cengo reported.

Zanac answered, "Six."

Kassam spoke again, looking at Cengo. He probably sensed now that Cengo was the more important translator.

Cengo grunted and said, "The brother is in Maiarad, he say. The brother is only one in family with paying job right now. That why he put this down on census paper."

Wynn considered the response. He smiled again at Kassam, and nodded his head. Was Kassam's answer suspicious? Probably not. It was plausible. The man, if not entirely candid, might well be correct that the census question—what kind of work does the head of household do for income?—left room for interpretation. That's why his soldiers had to review answers with the home occupants. Americans, too, got confused by legalistic questions. Wynn thought about telling Kassam that he didn't like paperwork either, to put him at greater ease, but decided against it.

"Ask Mr. Kassam if he himself worked in recent years, and if so, what his profession is."

Cengo asked.

Kassam sank even lower, and the mole on his lip rolled around like a marble on a table. He answered slowly, the rasp in his voice more intense.

Cengo asked another question. The fat man responded again, subdued, but with a lengthier answer. Wynn and Turnbeck waited.

Cengo turned to Wynn and explained, "He say his father was partner in business exporting Iraqi dates for many year. The business close down five year ago because big problem with Saddam government. His father now dead. Die two year ago. His mother, she die four months after. The family poor now. Now he poor. He cannot work because his bad health. His brother, the taxi driver, support the six living here."

"OK," Wynn said, appreciating the Iraqi's answer. "Tell him that we have taken enough of his time, and we thank him. And tell him I've enjoyed Iraqi dates. They have excellent flavor."

Cengo translated hastily, and Wynn put his hand on Cengo's arm, signaling him to correctly finish what he had said. It was important that Cengo show due respect to the LNs, since the terps represented the Wolfhounds' public face.

"And tell him that I am sorry for his family business," Wynn continued. "I hope that one day it will recover." Then Wynn pointed to the chunky boy they had met at the entrance, who had been standing in the room doorway listening to the conversation. "Is that your son?"

Kassam, breathing with difficulty, said warily that the boy was his nephew, and that the boy's father had been killed by Saddam during a Shia uprising in the south. Kassam held his folded arms tightly around his chest, as if he was trying to protect his heart.

Wynn started to say something else, but halted, considering whether to explore that story further. He wished to end the visit on an uplifting note if he could. This family, like so many Iraqi families, clearly had many burdens to shoulder. Duty had required the Wolfhounds to enter this man's home and ask personal questions. The Iraqi had cooperated and told them something of his family. Wynn knew that Kassam had no idea what the Americans would do with this information. The most important thing the Americans could ever convey was that they really wanted to help.

"Maybe this boy will one day run a date farming business again," Wynn said.

14

By noon, Wynn decided the platoon had completed enough census work for the day. It had taken three hours to obtain questionnaires from 23 households—not enough, but it probably sufficed to keep headquarters happy. He wanted to get back to Bawa Sah.

As Wynn walked back to his truck, his Iraqi cell phone rang. He reached into a pocket in the vest covering his body armor, pulled the phone out, and answered it. A man spoke rapidly in Arabic.

"Wait, please," Wynn answered.

He called Cengo over. He could still hear the man talking on the phone as he handed it to Cengo.

"Take this call."

Cengo took the phone, grunted something in Arabic, and then fell silent. The man on the other end spoke rapidly, and Cengo looked as if the conversation burned his ear. After a blast of information, he addressed Wynn.

"Sir, he say he have very important information. He know place you need to search." Cengo's voice tempo echoed the man on the phone.

Wynn looked at the terp quizzically.

"Slow down. Who? Who you talking to?"

"This Sheikh Amir," said Cengo. "He say he know place of *Takfiri*."

"What kind of place? What does he know?"

Cengo asked Amir several curt questions, then went silent again, his expression broadcasting Amir's intensity.

"Amir say something make him very, very angry. Something *Takfiri* do to his friend. He say you must go this place. You be happy of it," Cengo reported, his voice lashed by pressure.

"Happy of it?" Wynn asked, seeking clarification.

Again the language was an obstacle. Wynn looked at his watch. It was 1214. A high, white fireball sun burned remorselessly in the sky. He wiped his brow.

"Did this happen since I visited with him? How important is it we go right now?" Wynn asked, concerned about losing another opportunity to visit Bawa Sah.

Cengo, back on the phone, looked as if he was talking to a flamethrower.

Wynn sensed Amir's dominance. Then he suddenly felt uneasy. Was Cengo being bullied to persuade the platoon to do something unnecessarily dangerous? Or was Amir passing on a valuable tip? Powerful men liked to get their way.

"He say he want revenge something. Stop something," Cengo continued. "Something make him very angry."

"Won't say what?"

"No. It *Takfiri*, he say," replied Cengo.

"Let me talk to him."

Cengo handed Wynn the phone as if it was hot. The sheikh would be more respectful of him.

"Sadi, Lieutenant Wynn here, why you want us to go this place?"

"Bad place. *Takfiri* place. Terrorist place. Now there."

"Terrorists there now?" Wynn asked, trying to confirm what Amir meant.

Two black birds flew low and fast across the road towards Wynn, startling him. They looked like miniature jets on a strafing run.

"Yes. Now. Go there now," Amir said again, pleading.

Wynn's nerves sang with anticipation. What awaited them? Should he take the word of this sheikh? Wynn had wanted to tightly manage the days' time schedule. He'd already cut the census short. If they now went off hastily on a fruitless search, they'd lose more time.

"What's there?" Wynn asked.

Amir started speaking in Arabic, and Wynn handed Cengo the phone again.

"Try to find out more about what is going on. I need clear information."

Cengo spoke again with Amir. After another minute or so, he turned to Wynn.

"He say it very important. Must stop *Takfiri*. Bad people at this place. They do very bad thing. You not go, he say, more people hurt. He also say *Takfiri* there killing family to scare Iraqis, so Iraqis no want work with Americans. He say that his friend's son is doctor that sometimes help Americans. He help American teams on medical visits to Iraqis."

Amir was probably referring to the mobile medical clinics that Americans teams periodically set up in Iraqi neighborhoods. Iraqi doctors sometimes assisted with those. Wynn took back the phone again.

From the scratchy edge in Amir's voice, Wynn sensed seriousness. Amir had only called him twice before. Each time Amir had asked about a previous request. Each instance had something to do with possible business opportunities. This time was different, a new side of Amir. The blend of anger and worry in his voice revealed a sincere concern Wynn had not heard before.

"What is this place?" Wynn asked Amir, after taking the phone once more. The sheikh hesitated, unsure of his words, then spoke rapidly in Arabic. Wynn handed Cengo the phone again.

"Find out what he wants us to search and where it is. And ask him: how many *Takfiri*?"

Finding out as much as he could about the place was critical, Wynn knew. He couldn't go in blind. Success required preparation.

Wynn keyed his radio and called Cooke, "Wolfhound Four, this is One, over."

A short pause, then Cooke responded, "This is Four, over."

"Meet me by my vehicle in two mikes, over."

"Wilco."

Cengo spoke with Amir for another minute or so, each communicating in bursts of words and grunts.

"Sir, he say his doctor friend son prisoner there. He know place this happen where *Takfiri* do this. This place he tell us to go now. It old warehouse. He tell me where. He say *Takfiri* stay there. They kill his friend son there."

"OK. Tell him we'll go." Combat leadership required quick decisions. Wynn felt as if he stood on a steep muddy bank, and a swift rocky stream lay before him that he had to get across. Some decisions were made in a crucible so tight that second-guessing had to wait until later. His instincts whispered that Amir was telling him the truth. The Iraqis' strict honor wouldn't let him lie about something like this.

"Where is this warehouse?"

Cengo tried to explain. It was outside the Wolfhound's sector. Wynn calculated that the place was in 1st platoon's AO. Amir had described it as an abandoned warehouse near a cemetery, east of the Wolfhounds' present location. Wynn thought he had heard of the cemetery.

His mind now stretching, Wynn wondered whether this warehouse group was in any way involved with the school shooting.

Wynn hurried over to his vehicle and the computer map. If Cengo had a good description, the location was about a click and a half outside the Wolfhounds' battlespace. Now another choice was necessary. He could request permission to go outside his area from CPT Bauman, or he could call Jeff Smith, the 1st platoon leader, and not let Baumann know. It wasn't much of a choice. Wynn really wanted backup from 1st platoon if he needed it. It would be difficult to secure that without talking to Baumann. But on the other hand, Wynn wanted the mission for the Wolfhounds. He wanted the Wolfhounds to get credit if it was a significant find, and it would also help him in his relationship with Sheikh Amir. But Baumann might refuse. He might give the job to 1st platoon. On the surface, letting 1st platoon do it made sense. The Pit Bulls presumably knew the area. The Wolfhounds did not. But it was his lead, and had come to him because of their connection with Amir.

Wynn called Baumann.

CPT Baumann's radio operator said it would be a few minutes before the commander was available. In the meantime, Cooke had arrived, and Wynn briefed him.

Cooke was all over it. He said he'd put initial instructions out to the team, while Wynn waited to talk to Baumann.

Wynn had another thought, and said to Cooke, "You do that, then call first platoon. Tell them what I'm requesting, that I'm on the radio with the CO, and ask them about what they can tell you about the warehouse. If the CO gives the go ahead, I'll come up on the net and tell the platoon what to do. Come back here after you call first platoon and we'll discuss further."

Time was vital. Any insurgents at the warehouse might soon be gone. Yet Wynn wanted to be deliberate. He could not risk a foolish mistake.

The short conversation with Baumann ended positively. Baumann explained that at the moment Wynn's platoon was actually closer to the warehouse than 1st platoon. Although the warehouse was in 1st platoon's area, today the Pit Bulls were patrolling further north, and could not react as promptly as 2nd platoon. This decided the matter.

Cooke now rehuddled with Wynn by D21. They kept the initial discussion private, wanting to settle on a plan before briefing the rest of the men. Wynn wanted simplicity and clarity, a solid plan they could execute now.

Within minutes they made a plan. They would move the platoon to a more secure place where they could dismount and draw a quick sand table—an illustration sketched on the ground—to explain the plan. Pulling the men together where they were now would be too dangerous.

The Wolfhound convoy pulled into a gravelly field often used for soccer about five clicks south of where they had been. Wynn had chosen this field because it was the largest easily accessible flat and open space distant from any buildings near to where the Wolfhounds had been that morning, and the danger from sniper fire was minimal. He and Cooke felt it safe enough to have a platoon meeting here. Even if locals saw the Wolfhounds here, it would be impossible to determine their plan. Wynn looked at his watch. It had taken about 20 minutes to get here and was now 1255. The warehouse Amir had fingered was about 3.5 kilometers southeast of this field.

With their Humvees in a circular formation, everyone but the vehicle gunners now dismounted. Wynn and Cooke stood inside in the middle, the soldiers forming a half-circle before them. The truck motors were off so the gunners could hear the plan.

Wynn started by explaining Amir's report, then said, "Clearly we have little to go on, but I've got enough confidence in Amir's credibility to think we have to check out this lead."

When Wynn had spoken to CPT Bauman, the CO had offered to request helicopter gunship support. During the Wolfhound's drive down, HQ had confirmed an air team, with a call sign of Sledgehammer, would be on stand-by.

"We don't have much of a description of the location. All we got out of Amir was a general description of the place. And he said it had a bronze-colored painted gate," Wynn added.

Wynn explained that the Wolfhounds' mission would be to conduct a mounted reconnaissance of the location first, then search the place.

"I've been studying the map on the drive down," he continued. "It's some kind of warehouse backed up to a large cemetery. Supposedly, it's next to an abandoned Christian church. If this is right, the map says a road parallels these buildings."

Wynn looked around the group, making sure they were paying attention, then said, "I'd like to approach coming through the cemetery, but I doubt if we'll be able to. We'll probably have to take the main road."

He sensed a feeling of gritty seriousness radiating off the men. When they were together like this, a kind of mind meld took place, a group acclamation, as if they were renewing a psychological contract. Each man, through his presence, in effect re-enlisted in the mission and in the defense of the platoon. Their participation meant they shared something indispensable to success: commitment.

"According to the map and what first platoon shared with Sergeant Cooke," Wynn continued, "a road cuts east to west south of the cemetery, and intersects with the road coming down."

Wynn sketched a map on the ground, using the bail of his knife to draw. He drew the set of buildings, the roads, and the cemetery.

"If Amir's description is accurate, it's one of these buildings." Wynn tapped his knife on the sketches on the ground he'd made to represent the buildings.

"We'll ride by, get a sensing, coming in around the cemetery. If we can't come in via the cemetery, we'll pass again in front of the building, park, then go inside. Any questions?"

Then Cooke spoke for several minutes, detailing the truck and dismount assignments. He explained the search team organizations, and how he wanted them to work.

After Cooke finished, Turnbeck asked, "Is Sledgehammer going to fly over first?"

"No," answered Wynn. "We decided not to risk detection. If the birds look too close right after we go driving by in four Humvees, it might excite any bad guys in there."

That answer satisfied.

Pauls asked about MEDEVAC plans and they discussed that for several minutes, intending to use part of the cemetery if possible.

"Any more questions?"

No one spoke. A ripple of apprehension passed through the group. Perhaps the earth, soundless and watchful, anticipated what was coming.

The platoon found the cemetery without difficulty. They drove slowly along the eastern edge, looking for possible routes to the other side. The only way to pass through the cemetery was by foot. This wouldn't do.

It took a few minutes to wind around to the far side and find the road that passed the church. Moose could see two equally sized little hills in the cemetery, like horns on a slumbering giant. Thousands of various-sized grave markers, silent and remote, stood starkly on these hills, as if they were stadium spectators warily watching a procession of unwanted foreign visitors attending an event.

Soon Turnbeck reported the church spire. When the convoy got to an intersecting road, they turned right, each crew on maximum alert. Moose saw the church ahead, perhaps 250 meters down the road. He knew that the soldiers in the lead vehicles would now be evaluating the buildings on the left and right of the road, trying to identify the warehouse, and looking for a bronze gate.

Two and three-story buildings and small shops lined the road. The platoon continued slowly, Moose combing the surroundings.

Turnbeck reported a red car ahead pulling away from the curb and driving rapidly away.

"He's moving kinda fast," he reported seconds later.

Moose wondered whether that car might be significant. No one said anything else about it. A pursuit of the car would be difficult now and take the platoon away from their plan.

Then the platoon passed the church. It looked abandoned. Graffiti marred its walls. About 10 percent of Iraq's pre-war population was Christian, but the community was under increasing pressure from Islamic extremists, and many Christians had left the country.

The compound following the church was set off the road about 20 meters. The wall around it was the highest one on the street. It had a bronze-colored wrought iron gate.

The warehouse gate was locked. On Wynn's order, D22 pushed the gate open, then the breach team rushed in. Six dismounted men went into the grounds. Two men went left. Two right. Two remained by the gate. Two Humvees rolled into the compound grounds and took up positions on the far sides. The other two trucks stayed on the street. The first dismounted team worked their way behind the building, down a parallel alley.

Moose went down on a knee by the front entrance. Cuebas was on the other side of the door. Pauls moved in a sprint to the far side of the building in order to watch the rear approach. Time clicked methodically on, like the regular swing of a scythe.

The other team moved to the back of the warehouse. Both men positioned themselves on the ground in a prone position beside a small well, about 15 meters from the wall. One man watched the rear exit. The other observed the rear approaches, to prevent anyone from coming in or out.

So far they saw nobody.

A small decorative garden separated the compound wall from the warehouse entrance. Somebody had been watering the plants.

Pauls knelt below an idle window air-conditioning unit on the left side of the house. Something looking like a wire bird-cage housed the air conditioner. Wires dangled from it. At least the owner had tried to secure it. Probably wouldn't be long before the unit was stolen. Must be an office on the other side of this wall, he thought.

He looked across the yard. A pile of trash had collected. Bricks had fallen out of the wall in one section. Pauls was glad they had come through the gate and not climbed the wall. Carrying too much equipment to be climbing tall walls.

Tyson, manning the 240B machine gun in his truck, watched one side of the neighborhood and made sure no one penetrated the security cordon. A metal gate across the street cracked open slightly. Tyson's eyes caught the movement, and he turned toward the noise, lowering his weapon in that direction. A wisp of black hair bent around the gate below the height of the door handle. A small face emerged, like an animal peeking out of a cage. It was a child, a little girl. She wore a bright red dress trimmed by a colorful gold and red collar. She looked at Tyson coyly, her tiny mouth compressed, innocent questions about the complicated world written on her face. He turned away from the distraction and again scanned second floor windows, roof tops, and other doors along the deserted street. Though not a ghost town, Tyson thought, life here stayed hidden.

Pauls, on the side of the building, kept eyeing the empty lot to the rear of the warehouse. The cemetery lay beyond this. Suddenly he heard someone talking. He could not make out what they said or exactly where the sounds came from. From inside the warehouse?

Moose and Cuebas were at the front door. Moose tried the handle. It was unlocked. He opened it and slowly inched inside. Cuebas moved right behind him and had the sensation he'd followed Moose into a snake pit.

The darkness inside disoriented the two men. They moved forward slowly.

Then Moose saw a shadowy figure move. The shadow stopped. It was a man, standing alone on the far side of the room. He and Moose looked at each other. Their glances locked. Moose felt a surge of horrible urgency. Then the man started stepping back. For a brief second, in the darkness of the room, the man stepped past a place illuminated by a shaft of sunlight striking millions of microscopic particles floating in the air. Moose could barely make out the man's features but thought he saw shimmers of tension climbing a white face, and black eyes, like nuggets of coal. The man's tongue stuck out a little between his teeth. He was skinny and had no bulk around his mid-section that might be a suicide vest. But Moose's instinct told him the man was a mortal threat and no further analysis was necessary. The man glanced left. Then glanced left again; a minute signal of some sort rippled across his face. He then looked harshly at Moose, anger rising, now confirming the inevitable exigency of the situation, as if he was finally isolated in the world with the antagonist he had been waiting for all his life. Moose stood ready, gun pointed at this man not more than 20 feet away. Moose knew he could take him. They were alone: two irreconcilable men inside a ruined building in a dry and dirty and inscrutable place. The past didn't matter anymore. Moose saw the man's hand move, the barrel of a rifle rise. Then Moose shot him.

Moose shot twice, double-tapping the man, putting two rounds in him center mass. The man stumbled back, vibrating as if he'd been jolted by electric voltage, and crumpled forward, falling face first to the floor. Silence retook the room. Moose hesitated, stood still, looked hard at the man on the floor, then scanned the room again. Before he'd shot him, the man had glanced twice to his left. Moose now moved forward slowly, looking, listening, feeling, smelling, his senses on fire. Was something else there? What had he been looking at?

He looked at the man he had shot. His body lay face down on the floor, almost still, and Moose knew it would remain that way. But not perfectly still—the shot man's foot twitched, tapping to the rhythm of silent music. The rhythm of his own death. Acutely aware he had taken a life, Moose could not dwell on that, not now. Put it out of his mind. It was done. He had to keep working. *Keep alert. Look for the next thing.* It was as if he'd come up from deep cold water and now had to breath normally again. Moose concentrated on what might be beyond where the man had stood, and whether—whatever it was—could also be a threat.

A half wall covered with deteriorating stucco stuck out into the room. Moose figured the man knew something was hidden. Another insurgent? In the seconds before Moose shot, he thought he saw a flicker of guilt in the man's face, an enigmatic gesture signaling that something was hidden.

Moose called out to Cuebas, then nodded. "Follow that wall up. Look, look!"

Cuebas still reeled from the shots. Though in the same room just behind Moose, he was not instantly sure it was Moose who had shot. Inside the room the report of the rifle was deafening. Seconds later, reoriented after hearing Moose's voice, Cuebas realized what had happened.

The rest of the team was now inside other parts of the building. Cuebas heard them.

Moose became cognizant of chatter on the radio that hung on Cuebas' vest. No one had identified the shots. They were asking. Cuebas spoke hurriedly into his radio, reporting, but still disconcerted, unconvincingly.

"Ayeee—put one down."

A pause, and then, "Say again?" someone questioned, loudly, frantic.

"Moose shot him. Looking further. I'm covering."

"What?"

"Moose shot a dude!"

"Fuck. Need help?"

Moose was now close enough to the corner of the wall stuck out into the room that he could start seeing around it.

"We're OK," Cuebas answered.

They moved into a narrow long room with low ceilings. Moose hugged the edge of the wall. He moved the barrel of his weapon forward around the front, crouched slightly, then rushed into the room, ready to fire again. Cuebas covered. No one there. Like a camera flash, Moose mentally captured the contents of the room with a quick scan. Mostly nothingness stared back. No windows in the room. He saw no one. He was sure. Not much there. No other people. Something big and boxlike sat in the middle of the room. Furniture? Around it were two chairs. No, three chairs. An electric cord dangled from the ceiling and held several small light bulbs. A baseball-sized hole had been punched head-high in the far left wall, through which the electric line ran outside, presumably to a generator. This hole was where the light had come from that briefly illuminated the man he shot. A gritty sandy coating covered the floor, crunching as he inched forward. Now he could make out a closed double metal door on the far wall. Another wafer-thin slice of light framed the left side of the door. No rug on the floor. Nothing on the walls. No signs of regular life. Just that large piece he saw in the middle of the room.

The room was musty. Moose's feet kicked up some papers scattered on the floor. Then he saw splotches of something dark visible on the floor. What was it? More stains on the floor near the big boxlike thing in the middle of the room. Over against the other wall he noticed two stools and a wooden box. He sensed a hint of quick abandonment in the room. His mind started cycling, reliving what had just happened. *Cut it out,* he scolded himself. He had to keep thinking forward. *What had the man he shot been doing?*

Another hall out of this room. Moose couldn't see down it from his current position.

He heard other platoon members coming down the stairs. Sounded like they were finished upstairs. He heard bits of their talk, understanding a few words.

"Beds...nobody...sleeping place...not coming back," and something else he could not make out.

Cuebas darted back to the stairs and looked up as the others came down.

SSG Pauls came out of the stairway first, the others just behind him.

Cuebas looked at Pauls for reassurance.

"What else do we do?" Cuebas queried.

"Watch out!" Moose said firmly.

"Check out anything else down here," Paul ordered. "We'll go out back." He pointed to the warehouse area behind him with his rifle.

"Cuebas—you go with Moose."

"Where's the body?"

Cuebas pointed with his rifle.

Moose gave a thumbs-up. Followed by Cuebas, he went to the far corner of the next room. Both suspected more rooms existed back there. The place had looked bigger from outside. The darkness in the windowless room obscured vision, making it feel as if they were exploring a cave.

Moose moved fast, the gear on his vest shaking noisily as he went. His eyes registered a series of shadowy images. A metal cabinet against the wall, two drawers partially open. A light hanging from the ceiling above it. Two tea glasses on the cabinet. A rack of what looked like folders hung on the side of the cabinet. Moose stepped on more papers scattered on the floor as he moved.

Cuebas knelt by the insurgent's body. "Motherfuckers!"

Moose heard Cuebas curse, hostility in his voice.

Moose could see part of the hall now. A long corridor, sloped floor. Blocked up window on the right side about half way down. This way looked to be the end of the line. He wasn't sure. Even darker there. Halfway down the hall one small unlit light bulb hung loosely on a thin wire like a man hanging from a noose. He'd check it. Moose did a double-cock of his head in that direction, signaling to Cuebas that he intended to proceed down the corridor. His eyes told Cuebas to follow. Soon Moose saw another door at the end of the corridor on the left. A narrow closed door. Moose got to the door. He leaned against the wall outside it and listened. Cuebas stopped halfway down the corridor, and went to a crouch on his right knee, his weapon aimed at the door.

"What the fuck?" Cuebas mouthed soundlessly at Moose.

Motionless, silent, alert to any sign of life coming from inside the room, every fiber in Moose's body listened. All he heard was his own breathing, measured, steady, necessary. He'd just killed an insurgent and felt empowered. No smile, no humor, no peace, but satisfaction surged within him.

The door wasn't fully closed, ajar just enough to get fingers through. *Booby trapped?* Still dead quiet. He smelt piss. The odor might be coming from that room. Maybe it was the bathroom. He scrutinized the thin gap in the door. Just last week he'd heard that the Army was developing mini surveillance devices, small things that could be hand tossed, and would fly and spy inside confined areas. He wished he could pull something like that out of his pocket right now. Wild what was happening with technology. But he didn't have that. He was the only available sensor, Cuebas backing him up. The rest of the platoon could have been a mile away. Moose: the big 22-year-old boy from Virginia, former football player, former car wash attendant, former plumbing apprentice, former body shop mechanic. He would be charging through that door and checking things out. Something as hard and real as cold steel jabbed his soul, and he felt the rush of energy and anger simultaneously; anger as a protective mechanism; energy because, *DAMMIT,* he was on the tip of the spear for the whole U.S. Army!

No signs of booby traps. He slammed forward. Crash! Door flew back violently. Moose moved inside the room.

Too big to be a bathroom. Windowless. Dark. The piss smell stronger. And another sick pungent smell. He had the sensation of having emerged inside the entrails of a large beast. He stumbled and stepped further in. Momentum. Stumbled again. He saw something big and cylindrical on the floor. *Long rolls? Rolled up rugs?* Hard to make out anything in the darkness. He took a knee. He breathed big gulps of foul air. Scents of what had to be rotting body fluids drifted into his mouth and nose and clung to his lungs. He gagged violently, twice.

"Fuck. What is it?" Cuebas asked, from behind him, "Anything?" Cuebas froze in the doorway.

"Get your light on!" Moose shouted. He needed light from Cuebas to see what was on the floor.

With his gloved hands Moose probed the floor. A million nerve endings sizzled, every one of them wanting to be the first to find something important. His weapon hung from its sling. Too dark. He needed his night vision goggles, but had left them in the truck because it was daylight outside. He saw nothing yet. One hand balanced him. The other felt around blindly.

"Light!" he yelled to Cuebas.

Then Moose felt something solid. He patted his hand gingerly over it, as if he was checking on a sick child. It was something substantial, with a thin layer over it, baggy, heavy, and hard inside. Bags of rice?

The terrible stench got worse. More like puke than piss now. The odor hit him like a gas leak and he nearly buckled over, coughing again, several times.

"Ayeee. Jesus Christ!" Cuebas exclaimed. "What a shitty smell!"

Moose knew. By instinct he knew. The singular odor of decaying meat dominated the room.

"Something dead?"

Cuebas had recognized it too.

Cuebas' flashlight came on, a thin silver beam skipping rapidly over round log-like bags. But not bags. People. Once people. Now bodies. Moose saw them clearly now, and counted three bodies.

Moose stood up. Cuebas came closer. Moose grabbed Cuebas' light from his hand.

"Call Sergeant Cooke," Moose said.

He shone the light on each of the bodies, starting at the feet, then up to the heads. Only there were no heads. Feet, legs, torsos, but no heads.

Cuebas hadn't moved further. He hadn't called anyone on the radio either when he realized what the stench was. He retched, spitting, coughing, and hurriedly left the room.

"Call Cooke!" Moose called loudly after him.

Moose bent down and leaned over the corpses. The exposed feet confirmed they were human. With the light he could see the feet. Each body wore a white *dishasha*. The bodies gleamed in the dark. Each was spotted brown in places, like fallen leaves on white sheets. As a boy he had raked up autumn leaves onto old white sheets. He shook that crazy memory out of his head. He looked closer at the brown spots. Blood, maybe? The bodies were flat where the necks should be. Definitely no head. He stepped forward so he could look down at the decapitated necks. It made him think of a split cantaloupe. In disbelief, he waved the light around the edges of the room, half thinking the heads might be lying against the wall.

He had never seen a headless man. The folks back home wouldn't believe it. By now he had seen a couple of dozen dead bodies. Recognizable pieces of bodies, and unrecognizable pieces of bodies. But not headless ones. They had heard about the beheadings going on. He'd seen the snuff videos, even watched them on the web. The insurgents were capturing people and slicing their heads off like so much meat in a butcher shop.

What was this place? An execution center?

Moose stepped out of the room. Cuebas waited at the far end of the corridor, silent, looking down.

The Wolfhounds searched the rest of the warehouse, including a large open bay and two smaller outbuildings looking for more insurgents. Others looked in two adjacent smaller buildings. Security remained tight. After confirming the place was clear, Wynn ordered the men to drag the dead outside. He watched from the side of the room. Cooke stood beside him. When soldiers pulled the bodies across the concrete floor to the outside it sounded like cardboard boxes sliding. The bodies smelt like rotting meat. Wynn followed the last one outside, then walked back to his Humvee to send a report to higher. Outside they didn't smell as noxious.

Cuebas stared at the four bodies laying side by side outside. Three were decapitated, dressed in soiled white *dishdashas* like grotesque morgue creatures. One still oozed blood from the neck stump. The fourth, the one Moose killed, wore black pants and shirt. In the daylight things became clear. The imaginary dead leaves on white sheets were dried blood spots soaked into clothing. Small holes punctuated many of the dried blood spots, as if someone had stabbed the bodies multiple times with an ice pick. Some of the Wolfhounds standing next to the bodies wore bandanas around their faces to filter the stench. Cuebas didn't have his bandana with him, but kept holding his hand over his nose and mouth. Flies swarmed. The exposed hands and feet on the headless corpses were purplish, nearly black. The underside of the feet retained a brownish tint. All three bodies were engorged, unreal, like inflatable headless manikins. The heaviest corpse had his wrists broken, splintered bones like snapped pencils protruding from the surface of his lower forearms. The liquids of death had mostly dried, the sweet heavy redness of fresh blood long gone. Two headless men had been dead for several days. The other looked recent.

"Looks like they broke his hands by pushing them forward over his forearm. Must have held him pretty tight. Hurt like hell, I bet," said Lee, softly, as if he had to say it to believe it.

Cuebas tried to imagine the man's extreme pain.

"Snapped 'em in half like it ain't nothing," Moose injected.

"Jeez," someone said, sighing in disgust.

"Like big infected bee stings on his feet," Pauls conjectured through his bandana. "Whatever it was left ugly welts."

Two of the dead men had the odd marks on their feet.

Lee pulled up the *dishdasha* of the biggest man to above his waist, exposing his lower body. Cuebas looked down at it. Flies scattered. The man's penis had shriveled into what looked like a fat brown slug. More dried blister welts on his legs. Streaks of dried blood ran out of some of the welts. Lee leaned forward and looked closer. "Fuck! Must be eight or ten of these per leg," Lee said.

Cooke walked up and looked.

"Private Halloween party here dudes?" he asked insouciantly, as if nothing would surprise him.

The others said nothing, staring at the bodies.

"You shoot this dude?" Cooke asked Moose, pointing at the recently dead body, blood still pooling around its sternum.

"Yes."

"Good shooting."

"It's what he needed."

"Tell the LT he's going to want to see this," Cooke commented, motioning to Pauls to walk over to Wynn.

Lee still bent over the headless bodies. Cuebas took a knee and looked closer too, simultaneously fascinated and repulsed. Lee probed the welts on the exposed legs of the big man with his gloved hands, tenderly, clinically.

"We're going to do another fucking thorough search of this place," said Cooke.

"No power on it," said Moose.

"Bring us one of those spot lights," Cooke shouted back to no one in particular in his vehicle. "And I wanta yank the fucking doors off this place and take a better look inside."

Moose had shot the insurgent in what had probably once been front offices. At the end of this room double doors exited into a parking area. These doors were locked with a chain. Cooke intended to pull these doors off using a Humvee.

Wynn reassured himself that the platoon had good security of the surrounding area and then gave the TOC an update on the platoon's status, telling them about the four bodies. He left his truck again, taking his portable radio with him, and walked back over to where the dismounted men stood.

Five Wolfhounds stood over the bodies now. Wynn could see Lee on his knees, leaning over one body. Wynn contemplated what to do next, trying to stay ahead of things, remembering the principles of site exploitation. Collect what we can that tells us what's important about this place. Learn what we can about the bodies. This meant search, collect evidence, take pictures. The closest house showing signs of occupation was 50 or 60 meters away. Wynn had already ordered D22 and Cengo to go to those nearby houses and ask if anyone knew anything about what had been happening at this place, and if anyone could identify who had been coming in and out.

After talking to the dismounted men for several minutes, Wynn stared at the dead insurgent. Surely this man hadn't been alone. Somebody else had recently been here. They'd seen that red car drive off as they came up. He'd decided not to stop it. Didn't want to split his force. Probably should have stopped the car, but of course he didn't know then what he knew now.

Something was strange about this deal. They hadn't been fired on. The insurgent killed hadn't fired a shot, though he did have a weapon. The way the man's open eyes were glazed and bright, Wynn wondered whether he'd been drugged. Drugging was not uncommon with insurgents getting ready to fight or blow themselves up.

After thinking another minute about the situation, Wynn said to Cooke, "Let's check it out closely. Leave nothing unopened. Take pictures of everything." He paused. "Be careful looking around in there."

Wynn walked back over to his vehicle and called in another report to the HQ.

A clanging sound signaled that D24 had pulled the doors off the place using their tow rope. This brought daylight inside the bigger room.

Moose, Tyson, and Sims went inside to search more. Most of the rest of the platoon maintained security.

"I'll hold the light," Moose said. He again smelled the filth in the room, rancid, abnormal. Now he could better see the large table in the middle room. The table had a thick wood top with multiple drawers underneath, like an oversized wood carpenter's table. He looked around. He again saw the two-drawer cabinet he saw earlier against the wall. Symmetrical holes in the wall suggested shelves had once been mounted. Nothing on the floor but filth.

If this place had been an old agriculture storage operation you couldn't tell that now. Surely it had been stripped by looters, like everything else. He held the spotlight over the large table while Sims looked in the drawers. Three opened easily. Stacks of papers inside. Another was locked.

"Get the crowbar," Sims called to Tyson, who stood by the door. Tyson in turn shouted to Kale, who still sat in D23.

Cooke walked into the room, coming up to where Moose and Sims were. He kicked something on the floor, then bent down and picked up a long thin strip of something flexible.

"Why are fucking belts on the floor?"

Cooke held a leather belt up.

"Several of them here." He bent down and picked up another belt. He saw two more on the floor, coiled like sleeping snakes, but did not pick them up. Moose watched him.

Cooke held the belts horizontal up in the air, and slowly slid his hands outward in opposite directions, all the way from the buckle to the end tip. Moose turned his light on the belt.

"Hey, I'm still prying at this drawer. Need the light," Sims complained.

Tyson had entered with a crowbar, and moved to help Sims pry open the locked drawer.

"Something strange about these belts," Cooke said. "Rough-finished, as if painted with something."

"Hold on. Sarge is looking at something," Moose to Sims.

Cooke ignored them, and walked closer to the now open door to look at the belts in the sunlight.

"Weird," mumbled Cooke, curious. "That's dried blood on this belt," he said, coming back into the room.

Lee walked into the room, a disgusted look on his face. He'd finished examining the bodies outside.

"Sergeant Cooke, those headless guys all got puncture wounds. Multiple puncture wounds. All over their fucking bodies. It's wild. I don't know what did it. Punctures all the same size. Especially on their feet and legs."

Cooke glanced at him, questions in his stare. He said nothing. Cooke walked outside again with one of the belts, scrutinizing the stains on it.

"Definitely blood." Cooke was fascinated and couldn't understand what had happened.

A smaller clinging sound, like a stuck toaster releasing. Tyson had opened the drawer. He reached in and pulled out a bulky item wrapped in loose fabric. He laid the heavy package on the table, and unwrapped it. Inside was an electric drill.

"An electric drill?" Tyson questioned, perplexed, surprised to see that kind of equipment. The others heard him.

Cooke heard too, and walked back inside. The four men all stared at the table. They looked at the drill, then at each other. Tyson fingered the drill cautiously, as if checking if it was alive. Nobody spoke or moved.

Moose put the light on the table top. The sudden illumination got everyone's attention. The surface of the table looked as if someone had finger painted dark colors on it. The drill lay on the table.

"Jeezzzz," expelled Lee. He cleared his throat by coughing. "Is there a bit in it?"

They were all thinking the same thing.

Cooke put the belt he held on the table. He reached for the drill, pulling it towards him. Moose shone the light. The drill chuck held a bit.

Cooke looked back at the surface of the table. "Blood," he mumbled.

"I bet they drilled those fucking bastards," said Lee.

"Fucking A," Moose agreed.

"Shitttt," said Tyson.

For several seconds, nothing else was said. They all imagined it. The contemplation of brutality iced over the room.

"Lemme look at those bodies again," Cooke said. He went outside, followed by the others. He knelt beside one of the bodies. Lee had carried the electric drill outside. Cooke snatched the drill from Lee's hands, held it up above the corpse, looked at the drill, at the bit, then back at the corpse, several times, and then handed the drill back to Lee.

"Bet they used those belts to tie the men down. Maybe their own belts," Cooke said. "Go get the LT again."

"One fucked up way to send a message," cursed Lee.

Cuebas couldn't believe it. Before the Wolfhounds left the warehouse, everyone in the platoon knew they found three headless bodies. All three of them had apparently been tortured with an electric drill. No heads had been found. The Wolfhounds were subdued, absorbed in introspection.

An electric drill? He tried to picture the act. How sick is that? Unbelievable. If he closed his eyes he could almost hear it: sharp spiraling steel plunging into soft human bodies, spitting bits of skin, meat, and bone. No mercy. Certainly would inflict devastating damage. Didn't take much work on the part of the torturer. No way a human body could resist it, stop it. Thin shaft of spinning steel versus human flesh. The bit would go in so easy, penetrating smooth and quick. It would surely amaze everyone, the torturer and the victim. Just a small hole, immediate.

Cuebas had done carpentry work on the Island. Several of his extended family were contractors or worked for contractors. He'd used a drill many times himself. On wood. Maybe on plastic once or twice. He could hear the high-pitched business-like sound. Zizpp. Zizpp. Always quick. Then it would stop. The drill would come back out of the wood. Clean round hole. Maybe a little volcano of wood powder left around the hole.

But in human flesh? Completely vulnerable. The victim must have been screaming, horrified, pleading. The beheading must have been afterwards. For the victim, the beheading might even have been a relief.

Cuebas looked away. For a second he thought he heard echoes of the screams.

Even in the terrible game of war, this was outside bounds.

And the missing heads—where were they?

Maybe the heads had been delivered to the families. Other heads had been dumped on the roadside like routine garbage.

The whole thing appalled him. Were there no rules in war? Rifles, bombs, jets, mortars, gunfire. But electric drills? The other things were intended for fighting, technology built for war. But using carpentry tools to mutilate human bodies?

And beheading—wasn't that the ultimate way to die? Cuebas closed his eyes and pictured a victim: the frenzy, the screaming; then the act itself, the sharp blade slicing right through the center of it all: neck, nerves, throat, spine. Death rushed in—inevitable. He knew that beheading wasn't something new. It had been done pretty much since the beginning of time. The guillotine was even considered a clean, quick execution, he'd read somewhere. But brutal with a knife, no doubt; not as predictable or clean. And so primitive, even savage. Did that make the terrorists savages?

Cuebas pressed his lips together and outward, as if expelling something. Then he took in a breath of air and exhaled slowly, extending it like an unvoiced commentary on the depravity of man.

The platoon had finished searching and prepared to return to the FOB. Moose, now back in the gun turret of D24, looked down the street warily. After examining the large table they'd found in the room, the Wolfhounds had concluded that the victims had been tied down on that table, perhaps with the belts found on the floor, and tortured. In addition to blood stains, the table had small puncture holes caused by the drill bit. Blood was splattered on the walls and the floor too. The place was a slaughterhouse.

Moose was even happier he'd killed that man. He wanted to do it again. During the urgency of the moment he hadn't thought much about it. Now he revisited all the details and felt no remorse. He had no doubt the dead man was connected to, even responsible for, much of what had occurred in the torture house. Only a mad dog would do something so terrible, so as far as Moose was concerned he'd put down a mad dog. That's a good thing. It didn't matter that he knew nothing about the man. Inside the warehouse, adrenaline had turbocharged him, readying him to challenge hell itself. His actions were almost a work of beauty. After the many hours of patrolling, the furious heat, all the complex and terribly inadequate conversations with these foreigners, and the apparent worthlessness of the information obtained, it felt as if he had just finished an obscene triathlon. He'd sweated gallons. His shirt was drenched, the heavy body armor pressed hot against his torso like a super-sized iron.

Before leaving the warehouse, Wynn called higher headquarters and organized for the Iraqi Police to come. While waiting for the IP, Wynn leafed through the papers the men found on the premises. All seemed to be in Arabic, so they were gibberish to him. The Intel guys would translate these and check them for valuable information. Every few minutes, one of the Wolfhounds would walk up and look at the headless bodies. None had seen a headless body before.

When the IP arrived, Wynn showed them the bodies. Cengo translated. The Iraqis appeared nonplussed. Whatever thoughts they had they kept to themselves. Wynn asked what morgue the bodies would be taken to.

The platoon departed at 1830.

15

Back on the FOB, Wynn briefed Baumann. Baumann was pleased. After discussing the find at the warehouse for 45 minutes, Baumann shook his head. "This is one fucked up country."

It was now 2110. The heat broke against the coming night, and gradually retreated.

Half of the Wolfhounds sat outside around the trailer area on the folding chairs they took outside. The men had un-wound, temporarily shaking off the horrors and exertions of the day. But sleep had to wait—the platoon was scheduled to depart the FOB again at 2330 for a night patrol.

Wynn, after consulting with Cooke, had decided to visit the Bawa Sah neighborhood again tonight, to make another attempt to engage with residents since they hadn't been able to go during the day. He still held out hope that their repeated presence in the area might encourage an Iraqi to come forward with information on the sniper.

Before departing, Wynn wanted to tell Amir about what they found at the warehouse. He called Cengo over.

"Let's get Sheikh Amir on the phone."

"Yes, Sir."

While Cengo dialed the number, Wynn wondered whether the materials the Wolfhounds had brought back from the warehouse would be helpful. Clearly some kind of insurgent cell had used the building for torturing people. Who were they? Criminal groups had set up shop for purposes of kidnapping and bribery. But this horrible torture was definitely different. It had to be an extremist group.

Cengo was now talking on the phone in Arabic. He paused, and looked at Wynn.

"This his brother. They get him," said Cengo, referring to Amir.

Wynn didn't know if the beheaded corpses could be identified. The bodies were now at an Iraqi morgue. Many families with missing relatives regularly visited morgues, hoping to resolve mysteries. Sometimes hundreds of people came to look at a single unknown body.

Cengo said, "It's him," and handed Wynn the phone.

Wynn took it and said loudly, "Hello Sadi. I want to tell you about what we found at the warehouse. It was ugly. Very bad people there. Cengo will explain."

"You find prisoners?" Amir asked.

"No."

Wynn gave the phone back to Cengo and told him to translate. Wynn explained what they found at the warehouse. Amir said little, but asked where the bodies were taken.

"Sheikh Amir will tell his doctor-friend where to look for son," Cengo explained.

Wynn, remembering that MAJ Alberts had told him that Amir had recommended Manah for the Bawa Saw School project, asked if Amir had heard about the sniper shooting.

Cengo asked the question. Amir replied that he would talk to Manah.

By 0015 the platoon was back in Bawa Sah. Wynn directed one truck to both ends of the street, about 125 meters apart, and kept the other two near the dismounted patrol. He had two of the trucks park. The other two positioned at the opposite ends of the street. Wynn had decided on the split in order to increase places and opportunities for the locals to approach.

SSG Pauls led a small team that walked the ground. About halfway down the street, Pauls signaled for Kale to climb to the roof of a home. Kale knew Pauls wanted one of the men to be able to see all four of the Humvees and watch the street. "And don't lose sight of us," Pauls ordered.

Kale climbed a low wall, and then scaled another to climb up on the roof. Once there, he looked around. He could see all four Humvees. He sat down, momentarily winded from the climb. He got up on a knee, but it was all he could do to keep his nerves from extinguishing his ability to think.

Pauls' team moved on, 25 meters down the road. For several minutes, Kale watched and listened to his surroundings. Nothing appeared to move, or even be alive. Despite the others being near him, he felt incredibly alone. All the horrible events of the previous days climbed on him like maggots on a dead animal. Seconds slipped by and he felt increasingly disconnected. Darkness obscured everything and he heard nothing. Silence, a deep, dead silence, had enveloped the landscape, as if leaving the restless world to contemplate in isolation the next. It was anything but quiet inside him. Then he heard the muffled singing of night insects. He welcomed the outside noise as confirmation of life. Pressure grew in his stomach. He couldn't be still. He kept touching his stomach, scratching it as if he had an irrepressible itch. If only he could push a release button to make all these unwanted feelings disappear.

To regain control he tried concentrating on a distracting detail, on the toes of his feet curling inward and downward inside his boots. Then, deciding no one could see him anyway, he plopped down, emotionally exhausted, and leaned against the wall along the edge of the roof. He no longer watched his surroundings. He became a beaten animal and hugged his knees. Fear invaded him, taunting his soul.

All his life he had admired courage above all things. He despised himself because that which he most wanted chose this time to abandon him. It was as if his greatest wish mocked him. *No. Not you. You shall not have it; you are not worthy.* Courage was like a god to him, and because he worshiped it, its absence now hung as heavy as a tombstone on his heart

Another immensely heavy minute passed. Finally, overwhelmed by an accumulation of personal pressures, Kale cried, the tears burning his face like acid. *Why was this happening? Why could he not be what he most wanted?*

A reflexive survival instinct smacked him and he kicked both feet out. He seized the hard plastic stock and hand guard of his M4 rifle and gripped it like an escape ladder. He tightened both hands around the weapon, angry and desperate—making hatred of his own self-pity a physical thing he wished to crush. He closed his eyes so hard his cheek muscles swelled. If he wanted to rebound, wanted to prove himself and claim a piece of that true courage that he aspired for, he had to do it now.

Then he heard voices. Kale jumped up on one knee, back in his position, looking over the wall down the street for the other dismounts. In that instant, pulling himself together, he thought he had avoided the abyss, giving himself another chance to claim his right to courage. Ambition pushed fear out of the way, at least for now.

He had another opportunity.

Two hours later, Wynn saw the lights of FOB Apache ahead, the bright glow making it look like an airport back home. It had clearly been another difficult day and he knew his men would be bone tired, aggravated because it would be hard to call the day a success. The Wolfhounds hadn't made progress in finding the boy's killer. The last trip back to Bawa Sah had turned up nothing, and Wynn had conflicting emotions about the warehouse. He was proud of his platoon for having taken the place down, but since they had captured no one alive, part of him now questioned whether they'd acted too hastily. Perhaps if they had put the building under surveillance rather than searching it immediately, they could have detained someone. Of course putting a surveillance team quickly in place would have been hard to organize; not enough Coalition assets were available. He had made the decision. CPT Baumann approved it. Here, no decision ever seemed completely right or wrong.

He had not heard back from Amir. Had the sheikh's friend identified his son?

DAY FIVE

16

MOOSE WOKE TO A bright blue morning and an electric alarm clock that read 0730. Cooke had told the men they didn't need to be in the motor pool until 0900. More census work was scheduled, but Cooke, because of the late night, wanted his men to get enough rest.

Moose felt good, strong, vindicated. He had replayed yesterday's action multiple times overnight and he believed he'd done everything right. It was bizarre: he'd killed a man and was satisfied with it. The violence was right and necessary. Pulling the trigger was merely the climax of an inevitable chain of events. It put him in a special club. He was now somebody who had killed in combat and people back home would think he was a bad-ass son-of-a-bitch. It felt great.

Similar thrills came during football. When as a linebacker—in the heat of a competitive game back at Mountain View High—he would lunge off the line after the snap, breathing hard, adrenaline pounding, hands reaching out to clinch the ball carrier, and, if he made the tackle, he'd feel exhilarated and totally unconstrained. Then, if another play followed, it would start all over again.

Yesterday's killing was hardly like that. Killing wasn't a game. For his opponent yesterday, play was over—forever. Still, he felt damn good.

Before heading to their trailers the night before, Wynn and Cooke had reviewed plans for today. Orders from higher headquarters required continued census work. After that they planned to visit the northwest of their battlespace. A week had passed since the platoon was last there. Generally, they tried to visit each major part of their battlespace weekly. Nobody knew whether this really made a difference, and they had no specific leads prompting a patrol, but counterinsurgency theory stressed the importance of frequent presence.

Although Wynn initially intended to continue investigating homes around Bawa Sah near the school, Cooke had persuaded him to let it rest for a day. So after the morning census work, the Wolfhounds would patrol the northwest, and then follow that with a visit to Sheikh Jassim. CPT Baumann had reminded Wynn about Sheikh Jassim, reportedly an influential figure around Bawa Sah. He might have information on the attack and might know the families of the slain boy, Baumann speculated.

At the school, Wynn wanted to talk more with Schoolmaster Albadi to see what he had heard from the families, and whether he had learned anything new about the shooting. Jassim would send a representative to meet the Wolfhounds at the school and guide them to his home. At the very least, Wynn hoped Jassim could assist finding the family. Late in the afternoon, Wynn planned to attend a meeting the S2 had scheduled with Mr. Manah, the school contractor, on FOB Apache. They hoped Manah might now be more forthcoming with any information he had about the shooting.

Another day of tight schedules was inevitable. 24 hours in a day weren't enough.

"We're moving," shouted Turnbeck from D22.

The lead vehicle pulled out into the road in front of FOB Apache and immediately drove over a bumpy patch of holes, rattling everything inside the vehicle, the radio handset cables swinging back and forth and, Ulricht, the gunner, seesawing in the turret's seat.

The time was 0938. Radio chatter started immediately.

"Pedestrians on right."

Two high school age girls wearing western clothes walked ahead on the side of the road. "I want some of that," Halliburton snorted, and shuffled his paper wad to the other side of his mouth.

"Let's ask them if they want to build a Walmart here," Ulricht responded.

"I'll take them shopping," Halliburton said.

Into the city the Wolfhounds plunged, navigating the arteries and veins of this steaming habitat of Mesopotamian humanity like a miniature robotic machine exploring the vascular system of a giant behemoth.

"Lots of vehicles ahead," reported Turnbeck over the radio.

"Oh, how I love to hear that," Ortiz said.

"Bullshit," said Cooke, "the only thing you love is your momma."

The traffic thickened as the platoon approached the first IP checkpoint. Up ahead they could see the police checking IDs and a line of civilian cars waiting to pass. The platoon slowed and moved to the left around the queue.

"Ayeee, might be a shaaake down," Cuebas speculated.

"Toll collection," Ortiz offered facetiously. "Looks like Haji's going to lose his pocket money."

The IP at these checkpoints sometimes required small bribes to allow passage.

"Balcony—9 o'clock,' Turnbeck barked.

Eyes looked that way immediately, hungry and searching, like skeet shooters hunting clay pigeons.

But seconds later Turnbeck came back on the radio and reported what he'd seen was clothing hung out of a window.

"That's only mommy working," Ortiz commented.

A few minutes later, Turnbeck reported an Iraqi car stopped in the median about 300 meters ahead with its hood up. The convoy closed rapidly with it. No occupant visible. Then, spotting someone bent over the engine compartment, Turnbeck reported it. "LN next to car on the road."

As the convoy passed this car, each gunner swiveled his machinegun towards it, then returned to his original position. The face of the man bent over the engine was smeared with grime.

"Ayeee. Fucker probably shit his pants seeing all those guns trained on him," Cuebas said.

The traffic thickened again on their side of the road. A sputtering green Kia caused a slowdown. "Kimchee car," said Ortiz.

Ortiz pressed hard on D24's horn. The traffic jammed sharply, and the convoy nearly stopped.

"Swimming," commanded Turnbeck again.

The convoy followed D22 over the dirt median, cutting through a gap in partially crushed curb, and drove against traffic.

"Four through," announced Cooke as D24, the trail truck, crossed over.

The traffic was lighter on this side of the road. The oncoming civilian cars moved hastily to the side to avoid the American convoy. Minutes later, the Wolfhounds switched back to the correct side of the road.

17

As the Wolfhounds neared the designated census area, about two kilometers away a white car pulled up in line at an IA checkpoint. The white car waited behind a red van that waited behind a brown car being checked by an Iraqi soldier. Only one of the Iraqi soldiers at this checkpoint noticed the white car, but paid it no attention. A few others standing by the guard shack chatted eagerly with each other about soccer, a sport Iraqis adored. One kicked a small stone, pretending it was a ball. The others made fun of him.

An Iraqi soldier named Akmed casually checked the driver of the brown car's identification papers. The driver of the red van waited impatiently, anxious to pass. The driver of the white car did not want to pass. He was nervous, but not impatient. He had no intention of passing the checkpoint.

Just then an Iraqi soldier named Khuder walked out of the guard hut. He wore sunglasses and glared blankly at the waiting traffic, unconcerned about the growing line of cars. Khuder's mind drifted back and forth between the cars at the checkpoint and whether or not the girl he loved would ever notice him. So far she had not. Khuder, 18 years old, was trying to convince his parents to set up something with the girl's family. He worried her family would think him too young and unestablished.

Khuder hadn't noticed the white car. He wasn't concentrating on the scene in front of him. In 15 minutes he would switch positions with Akmed. He had time to smoke another cigarette and called out to one of the others for a light.

Akmed was still questioning the driver of the brown car. He didn't like the driver's tribe, and this animosity had caused the excessive delay. More than ten cars now waited to get through the checkpoint. None of the other Iraqis took special notice. Khuder remained preoccupied with thoughts of his girl. No one had any idea that the driver of the white car had just made his last fateful decision. That driver said a final prayer, then blew himself up—along with his car, which had been prepared as a VBIED.

The terrible explosion sent large and small pieces of metal, plastic, dirt, road asphalt, and human flesh and bone flying in a 360-degree direction. Particles of all these shattered pieces rained down for several seconds, some landing over 200 meters away. The loud crack-boom temporarily deafened and stunned every nearby living thing. The rain of wreckage and debris made the street look as if a gigantic evil vacuum cleaner had backfired, coughing its unrecognizable contents all over the immediate area. Thick brown haze rose slowly up into the sky, expanding and rolling through the gray black smoke spewing from the center.

Amazingly, Khuder survived, hammer-slammed more than 20 meters away, sliding headfirst on the road as if he were on ice. A big piece of thin aluminum that had sheared off a car skidded along beside him. The blast blinded him, shattered both his legs, severed his right foot, and stripped off his clothes. Half his body was badly burned.

A smell of heavy smoke and scorched metal instantly infused the air. Everything had been blackened, charred, distorted. Three Iraqi soldiers, Akmed among them, and eight civilians were killed instantly. Many more were wounded. The homicidal driver had succeeded, and he met his maker milliseconds before those he so willingly took with him. The red van was blown to the other side of the checkpoint, looking as if it had been dropped on its end from 50 stories. The explosion smashed other waiting cars, some beyond recognition. One car's axle was thrown at least 75 meters away, beyond the guard house. All nearby windows shattered. Four streetlights within 50 meters of the blast, hit by pieces of debris, bent over like trees after a hurricane. Yet cars and trucks about 100 meters beyond the blast center only got showered with dirt and trash.

For several minutes the sky remained a gloomy grey-brown from the residual dirt and explosion mist in the air.

It didn't take long for the first people to walk up cautiously and look around, shocked and in disbelief. Most said nothing, as if the concussion from the explosion had destroyed their powers of speech. Soon people searched frantically for family members. The cries and screams started softly, then rose in intensity, as if the earth itself was shouting recriminations. Several minutes later the pitiful wail of a police siren sounded.

The Wolfhounds, as the closest unit to the explosion, were directed to investigate, despite the fact that the suspected location was, once again, outside their area. They hadn't even started the census.

What the hell happened? Wynn wondered.

He quickly put out new instructions to the platoon. He felt as if someone had tossed the day's plans into a blender. Nevertheless, he hoped to keep the meeting with Sheikh Jassim, if possible. The census had to wait. Wynn also wanted to make the later meeting with Manah. He wanted to refocus on the school shooting.

Moving towards this IED site was like moving towards a mining disaster. Wynn didn't know what to expect. Headquarters could only tell them a large explosion had occurred.

While on the move, he tried to learn what he could. He studied the computer map, looking at unnamed roads, and magnifying the available satellite images. He determined the route after considering the distance, available roads, and urban density. Cooke took the lead finalizing the plan as Wynn navigated to the site. As always, the first task after arrival would be setting up security. They'd do this by SOP—starting with placing their trucks in the 90, 180, 270, and 360 positions around the perimeter, with D22 leading the platoon.

Wynn couldn't be sure what else the platoon could do until actually arriving at the scene. Most likely they could do little. The damage was done. His mind ticked off the items the platoon would need to check. Could they help any casualties? Were any Iraqi security forces and medical capabilities there, or coming soon? Poor communication systems hampered any coordination with them. Determine what had happened with the explosion? They would need to start questioning bystanders to see if anyone had information on what had happened. Wynn glanced back at Cengo; this questioning would not be possible without the terp. After initial assessments, starting with the Wolfhounds' report, headquarters would decide whether a bomb analysis team would subsequently be sent out. If so, that team should, after several days of study, be able to determine technical details about the explosion. Those special assets, limited in number, investigated approximately three out of ten major explosions. He'd seen some of their reports and was impressed with their thoroughness.

Only enroute did the Wolfhounds hear from headquarters that an IA checkpoint had been attacked.

The Wolfhounds arrived at 1041.

"Like a fucking plane crash site," Gung declared.

Unrecognizable debris covered the street. A heavy mist of microscopic trash, dust, and petroleum products still hung in the air. Wynn could see at least a dozen damaged cars. He grimly took stock of the situation. Iraqis started noticing the arriving Americans. He saw injured people and pools of blood on the street. Locals stood around as if lost on a different planet: some cried, some were stunned into silence, others looked anxiously for someone to blame. While the platoon maneuvered into position, Wynn made a ten-second call to headquarters to let them know they'd arrived and describe his initial impressions.

"Roger that. Report again shortly," the TOC instructed.

It took five minutes for the Wolfhound trucks to weave through the ruins to their initial perimeter positions. The men stared at the destruction. Angry Iraqis shouted at some of the crews. Once in position, each truck came up on the radio and reported. Cooke recommended dismounting a few men to take a closer look. Wynn approved.

"They need to be in sight of their trucks at all time. Be careful," he added.

While Wynn stayed close to the truck radio and updated headquarters, Cooke dismounted to talk to some Iraqis with Cengo and a security team following him. Dozens of people approached them, trying frantically to explain what had happened. Within minutes, several wounded civilians had been identified, and the Wolfhound medics assisted with their care. One man held his flayed face together. Cooke walked to what remained of the checkpoint. He stared quietly at what looked like the center point of the blast and shook his head in disgust. The road was pitted and scarred and little tails of smoke still rose from the burnt asphalt between chunks of debris. Heat from the explosion had melted several cars into unrecognizable skeletons.

Cooke stayed in radio contact with other dismounts and Wynn. If whoever planned this thing saw the Americans arrive, they might attack again.

Three dismounts, Moose, Cuebas, and Zanac—ordered to take a position at the corner of two buildings on the perimeter not far from the shattered checkpoint—rushed into place. Here all the roads connected. Their orders were to prevent more cars from entering the perimeter.

They did not see a tall Iraqi in a dark blue shirt come out of a house near the road. The man started running, rounded the corner, and ran full force into Zanac, knocking him to the ground.

"Ayeee—what the fuck?" Cuebas shouted, waving his gun at the man.

Moose charged the strange man, knocking him to the ground with his elbow and shoulder. Moose felt something hard was on the man's chest when he knocked him down.

Bombvest?

Cuebas scrambled towards them, circling the strange Iraqi as he lay on the street. The man might have been 20 years old.

"Watch his hands! Watch his hands!" Cuebas shouted.

Moose glanced at Zanac, needing him to translate. Zanac was squatting on his haunches over by the wall, head hidden between his knees. Moose visually inspected him for obvious injuries. He saw none. The shock of the strange man running into him, and the blood and destruction at the blast site, might have temporarily incapacitated the terp, Moose concluded.

"Zanac!" Moose called.

Zanac didn't move or speak.

Moose reoriented the side of his body towards the Iraqi he'd knocked down, minimizing his own profile, and kept his gun pointed at him. *Who was this guy?* Was he connected to the attack? Suicide vests had been used in secondary attacks following IEDs. Something hard on his chest. Could it be a suicide vest? Had to immediately communicate with him. Search him. Moose then scanned his surroundings, wanting to make sure this wasn't a diversion. Cuebas moved closer to Zanac.

The suspicious Iraqi lay on his back on the street, holding his hands and arms up over his chest as if blocking body punches. Denial and confusion radiated from his face. His eyes were a dull slate gray, like river stones. He mumbled something in a voice laced with either fear or fanaticism.

Moose couldn't see anything bulky under the man's shirt. But he'd seen remarkably thin bomb vests, neatly constructed by hand from slivers of plastic explosives and a layer of nails and ball bearings: a devil-tailored vest. He watched the man closely, alert to any movement of his hands that might suggest he was reaching for a detonator or a weapon.

"How's Zanac?" Moose yelled to Cuebas, without taking his eyes off the man who had run into him.

Cuebas looked back at Zanac, who still hadn't moved. *Fuck!* Couldn't use him to translate. Anger steamed inside Cuebas. They had to immediately search this man somehow.

"Ayeee. Demo it," Cuebas shouted an idea that came to his mind, suggesting Moose demonstrate the necessary searching and get the Iraqi to mimic him.

"OK."

Moose reached down and grabbed the man's shirt and pulled him up to the standing position. He then pointed at the detainee, his fingers nearly in the man's face.

"You watch me. Do what I do!" Moose shouted, aware that it was unlikely the man understood what he said. Perhaps the visual demonstration would penetrate the man somehow.

Moose suddenly realized that if this man had a suicide vest they urgently needed more distance between him and them.

"Get space. Get space!" Moose shouted, and began running backwards. "Might have a bomb!"

He cursed himself under his breath. He should have realized this earlier.

The Americans backed off, 20 feet, then 30, then more, keeping their guns pointed at the Iraqi. Seeing them move, the man started mumbling faster. Cuebas took a kneeling position inside a doorway jutting out slightly, shielding himself against the wall. Moose continued standing in the middle of the road, facing the Iraqi, maybe 50 feet now separating them.

"You! Look at me. Follow me!" Moose shouted at the Iraqi. Between the shouts Moose clinched his teeth so hard he thought he might crack one.

The man in the blue shirt still didn't move. He stood frozen, his hands fixed several inches from his chest as if he was studying his fingernails. His mouth quivered.

Moose demonstrated exactly what he wanted the man to do. First, he raised both his arms outward, away from the body, as if he would fly. The Iraqi copied Moose's moves compliantly. Moose had a feeling that this man had been searched like this before. He followed along almost too easily. Next Moose put both hands on top of his head. Then, with his right hand and arm, Moose reached inward across his chest, opened a pocket with that hand, imitated taking contents out of the pocket, and dropping them to the ground. The Iraqi appeared to understand, and promptly did the same with his front shirt pocket. He dropped a folded paper and a pen to the ground, then, from the other pocket, a small hard piece of plastic fell out.

Moose, from 50 feet away, stared at the piece of plastic. A cell phone.

The man followed Moose's movements nervously, imitating, conducting a self-search as Moose led him through it. Once the self-search was finished, Moose signaled for the man to put his hands back on his head. Was the cell phone what he had felt when he pushed the man? He had contacted something hard. It may have been small. The phone had been in a chest pocket about where Moose's forearm made contact. But why was he running?

"Looks clean so far," Cuebas commented, residual suspicion riding his voice.

"Check around us. Anything going on?"

"Ayeee." Cuebas quickly scanned the nearby buildings.

Moose wanted a closer search of this man. He had to be sure. A small crowd of Iraqis had assembled near them and watched cautiously. Moose eyed them but continued what he was doing. He checked Zanac, who hadn't moved.

"Watch him close. I'm going to put 'hands on' now!"

Moose hurried over to the Iraqi, positioning himself 45 degrees away from the detainee. If the man did have a bomb, he could blow both of them to Kingdom Come. Moose ignored this thought.

He needed to make physical contact again to prove it one way or the other. Putting his hands on the Iraqi, he spun the man around so his back was to Moose's front. Cuebas moved away from the wall, moving around the action, ensuring that Moose's body never got between him and the detainee.

Moose began sweeping the Iraqi's body with a flat hand, beginning at his head. "Like this. Like this," Moose said loudly, showing the man how he wanted his hands interlaced on his head.

Then Moose checked around the man's shirt collar, sweeping his hands down the man's chest and around his back, feeling for anything hard and hidden, like wires. He felt nothing strange. Moose ran his hands down over the man's waist and around his hips. He kicked the man's foot, signaling for the Iraqi to spread his feet apart. Moose put his hand between the man's buttocks and legs, reaching in front, and dragging the back of his hand back through the Iraqi's spread legs, checking for anything hidden in the groin area. Moose felt the ridged zipper, the baggy material folding in as he identified the man's privates. Then Moose checked the man's legs. Using both his hands he walked them down the length of the man's legs. First the right, then the left.

Nothing. The man still seemed clean. Moose crouched, patting down the man's lower legs and ankles. Then Moose stood up and backed away. He made a motion to remove his boot, tilting his head toward the Iraqi, signaling to him to remove his shoes. *A bomb in his shoe?* The man complied without hesitation. Moose kicked one shoe and bent forward to look at the other. Nothing in the shoes. Nothing strange.

Why did this man run? Nothing on him. Fear? Just trying to leave the scene?

No way to be sure. Had they overreacted?

Suddenly Cooke appeared at the street end.

"Let's go! We're leaving," Cooke shouted, waving for them to come back.

Cuebas and Moose had to make a split-second decision.

"Zanac!" Moose shouted. "Zanac!"

The terp finally bolted up from the street, as if he was scared of being left behind. A mixture of fear and embarrassment shadowed his face. Maybe he'd now do what Moose wanted.

Cooke disappeared around the corner of the building again.

"Get his name and address! Right now. Get it! Then we go," Moose yelled at Zanac.

"We can't take him. No shit on him," Cuebas declared.

"I know. We get his info. At least we'll have that."

Cooke was at the end of the street again and now jogged towards them. He stopped about 30 feet away. "What you got?" He saw their guns pointed at the Iraqi.

"Nothing," said Cuebas. "We're coming."

"OK. Do it!" Cooke turned and left.

Zanac got the man's name and address. Then they let him go. They had nothing on him—apparently a false alarm.

"What the fuck was he doing?" Moose asked Zanac about the suspect, as they hustled back to the rest of the platoon.

Zanac answered softly, like a man preferring to be unnoticed.

"He say he running to tell mother about bomb."

The platoon had done what it could at the bombing site. They'd assessed the damage, determined roughly where the center of the blast had been, and taken a number of pictures. Wynn would do a full report later. HQ would decide whether more study was useful. An Iraqi ambulance had arrived. Other injured left in family cars—all departed for the nearest Iraqi

Hospital. Families continue to sort through body parts on the street. The crowd steadily increased, and the Wolfhounds had difficulty keeping Iraqis away from their Humvees.

Wynn called CPT Baumann, filled him in on the situation, and got permission to continue other missions. Baumann also informed him of a company leaders meeting tonight at 1930. After consulting with Cooke and agreeing on next steps, the Wolfhounds departed for the school and the meeting with Sheikh Jassim. No time for census work today.

Cengo phoned Jassim to confirm everything. Driving away, Wynn felt like he was departing hell.

Nobody was at the school when the Wolfhounds arrived. No Albadi. No students. Soon Jassim's man arrived in an older BMW. As a precaution, Wynn told Cengo to have the guide explain the route to the house, so he could observe the man for a few minutes in order to assess whether he might be deceiving them. The man described the route without evident dissimulation, so the platoon followed him.

By the time the Wolfhounds reached Jassim's place, it was 1500. Wynn decided he could spend a maximum of 45 minutes there. If the platoon stayed longer, he risked missing his appointment back with the S2 and Manah. He needed to lock eyes with Manah again to determine whether there'd been any collusion between the contractor and whoever shot the boy. However, after two days of considering the matter, he doubted that Manah was involved. Manah had too much to lose. Nevertheless, double-dealing could offer a prosperous life, Wynn knew; perhaps Manah had been threatened and forced to cooperate. Something about the contractor bothered him. Anybody who wore silk suits as Manah did was doing well. He dressed nothing like the small-time contractors Wynn knew back home. The man, at a minimum, must be affiliated with what the Iraqis had for Mafia. But first Wynn had to deal with Sheikh Jassim, another special character.

Wynn was bothered by the insufficient time. Iraqis never worked fast, especially Iraqis who thought highly of themselves. He had met Jassim once before, about three months earlier at a tribal sheikh conference. Jassim had a reputation for being a big talker. Someone had described him as "thinking he had a natural right to dominate people." No conversation with such a man could be short. Wynn would have to think of ways to accelerate the talk, to get to the point. He wasn't sure—nobody was sure—whether Jassim was a legitimate tribal sheikh, or an up-and-coming businessman who had taken on the aura of an influential person. Jassim, too, had more than a touch of Mafia about him. His thriving trucking business was known to control a substantial part of the transport business running kerosene and other fuels from area distribution points. Much of the product he ran was probably illegally obtained. Jassim supposedly had numerous property holdings in the city and had acquired considerable power, reputation, and resources—what the Iraqis called *wasta*, or clout.

Perhaps Jassim could help. Living barely three kilometers from where the sniper attack happened, he might conclude he'd be well served to cooperate with the Americans, if only to get attention off the neighborhood. If the sheikh was operating an illegal smuggling business, he wouldn't want Americans nosing about. Even if he didn't know where the family was, he might know who would or could find out. Wynn suspected that Jassim—like many of the sheikhs—illicitly balanced cooperation with both the Americans and insurgency groups. For an Iraqi of means, it was just too damn hazardous to stand firmly with any one group. Nobody liked to walk the edge of fire. Survival always trumped.

Jassim lived in an ornately walled compound masked with a look of heavy formality, like what might pass for a mausoleum back in the States. Wynn saw Arabic words black spray-painted on the wall. It looked like punk vandalism. Cengo told him it said: "Vote."

The election had been months ago. Since the graffiti was still on the walls of the sheikh's compound, he either didn't care about it, or supported the sentiment. It didn't seem right.

Reports said many sheikhs, particularly the Sunnis, had not supported the recent election. Sunnis believed they had a natural right to rule, and since they were a minority, worried that elections undermined their rights. Many sheikhs boycotted the elections because they feared a loss of traditional privilege. Even Saddam had struggled with the sheikhs. He had bribed some and persecuted others. America's invasion, and the consequent collapse of government authority, had increased the sheikhs' influence.

Barbed wire, probably stolen Coalition wire, lined the top of Jassim's compound wall. A shiny green wrought-iron gate barred the main entrance. Jassim's security guards milled about, unconcerned, looking more as if they were high in the stands of an uncompetitive sports event than guarding an important man's property. A balding burly man with glasses and a large birthmark on his cheek promptly opened the gate for Wynn and his security escort. No delay. No questions.

Once inside, Wynn's party was taken through a small clean foyer that smelled like fresh oranges, and on into a sitting room. Seated, Wynn noticed elegant inlaid tile work on the floor and walls. Jassim was clearly not afraid of being labeled ostentatious. Wynn could see his own reflection in the polished tile to his front: his hair slicked from perspiration and the corrosion around his eyes evidence of weariness or stoicism or both.

After two minutes, Jassim rushed in. "Sorry, sorry," he apologized. "I very busy. My business dealings are many, and have many friends," he said, with artificial shame, a patriarchal smile splitting his face.

The men shook hands vigorously.

Conversation started immediately. Jassim's English, Wynn had forgotten, was articulate and crisp. He'd also forgotten Jassim's mutilated ear. The Iraqis' left earlobe hung from his head like a bizarre Christmas ornament: a knot of flesh the size of a cherry dangled from a shriveled pink strip of skin. As a young Army officer in the Iran-Iraq war, Jassim was wounded and nearly died in a hospital due to poor medical care. He then vocally criticized the Saddam regime for the poor care. Jassim was imprisoned, accused of being a spy, and tortured. His imprisoners, in a masochistic rage one day, took wire clippers to his ear. He wore the scarred ear now like a badge of honor.

"Thank you for seeing me, Sadi," Wynn said.

"How may I help you, Sir?" Jassim asked Wynn ceremoniously. This pleased Wynn, sounding as if Jassim would get right down to business.

Wynn, not wanting to appear disrespectful, replied by first asking Jassim about his business. They spoke about ordinary topics for a few minutes, and Jassim grew excited explaining the difficulties of the Iraqi economy. After a couple more minutes had passed listening to a Jassim commentary on fuel markets, Wynn finally held up his hand, signaling that the Iraqi should stop talking.

Jassim complied, then reconsidered and pleaded, "But, please, first I must show you very special gift I received."

Before Wynn acceded, Jassim stood up to retrieve whatever it was and walked purposefully to the far side of the room. He picked up a lacquered wooden container about the size of a shoe box and brought it back to where Wynn sat. Without delay Jassim opened the box. It contained a black 9mm Beretta pistol resting on a red velvet pillow. The pistol was the model American soldiers carried.

"A gift from a friend," Jassim said, a hint of confidentiality in his voice, delight on his face.

Had this pistol had come from an American soldier? Wynn was aware of two American soldiers missing in action in Iraq. Should he ask Jassim? The question might insult the Iraqi and delay things. If this pistol had in fact belonged to an American soldier, and Jassim knew that, he surely wouldn't admit it. Maybe a soldier had lost it. Maybe this pistol was manufactured by Beretta, but not the US Army model at all.

As Wynn reached for the pistol, to see if it had a serial number, Jassim closed the box and carried it away. He must have noticed Wynn reaching for it. Should he ask Jassim to bring it back?

No. Only if he avoided going down that path could he hope to get the conversation on the family and move things forward.

"Very nice, Sadi," Wynn responded. "Like my pistol."

"Yes. I like American pistol," Jassim continued, his eyes amused.

Wynn wished he could pursue talk about the pistol, but now was not the time.

"Sadi, I need your help."

The amusement left Jassim's face. He looked interested, receptive, and folded his hands like a priest waiting for confession. "Yes, my brother."

The split between Jassim's thin lips cracked, exposing small, bright teeth.

Had he had his teeth whitened? It would be very expensive for an Iraqi to do that.

Wynn continued, "You surely know about the boy shot by a sniper in the schoolyard very close to here. Perhaps you know my platoon was there when the shooting took place. We've been looking for the criminals. I am sure that every Iraqi wants to help us catch these terrorists that shoot innocent children. This is a great tragedy, and I want to help the parents. I would like to visit these families to talk. I want to express the regrets of the America for their loss." Wynn let Cengo translate this statement.

Jassim remained quiet, thinking, non-committal.

Then Wynn asked Jassim if he'd heard anything about who might have done the shooting. He scrutinized Jassim, unsure how he'd respond.

"This important," Jassim answered, finality in his voice. He then spoke in Arabic to an attendant standing behind him.

Cengo told Wynn that Jassim had asked the attendant for a phone.

The attendant brought a cell phone. The sheikh scrolled meticulously through the contact list, then pressed the call button. In seconds someone answered. The men spoke in Arabic about a minute, then Jassim hung up.

"I asked a friend to see about family, Lieutenant," Jassim explained.

Wynn was unsure what Jassim meant. "To see?"

"To find out, Sir, if family is available," Cengo answered.

Then Jassim spoke rapidly to Cengo in Arabic. The sheikh's little white teeth flashed like a dog growling.

A few seconds later Cengo translated. "He making investigation about the family, Sheikh Jassim say. He find if they here and whether it possible see them."

They spoke for several more minutes. Jassim asked a couple of questions about the shooting. Wynn answered circumspectly, and based on Jassim's questions and his answers to Wynn's questions, it seemed he was not aware of what had happened at the school. Either that or he was a good liar. Jassim expressed sympathy for the family. Wynn then explained the casualty assistance pay program and that it might be possible to obtain some compensation for the family. He made no promises. Iraqi families that lost relatives working for the various security services were eligible for condolence payments from the Coalition. The boy's death did not fit that category, but because of its egregious nature, and the hope that it might encourage the neighborhood to be more forthcoming with any information about the killers, Wynn hoped to get an exception. He intended to tell the family that he was trying, but would make no commitments. Such a revelation was risky. But Wynn had spoken to Baumann about it, and the commander had confidence he could get the special condolence payment.

Jassim replied again that he would see what he could do. "I will call you if I get information on family," he said.

After a few more minutes of conversation, the Americans bade their leave. Wynn looked at his watch. They'd spent 50 minutes with Jassim, five minutes more than he wanted, but not bad.

During the hurried drive back to the FOB, the talk about financial compensation returned to Wynn in the form of a mental knife. He thought about Ramirez, their last trip to pay a family, and it hurt. War, regardless of its purposes, had a terrible cost.

18

After rushing back for the meeting with Manah, now, following that meeting, Wynn was disappointed. It hadn't been productive. The contractor either knew nothing or played dumb perfectly. The Iraqi insisted that he had no information on who did the shooting. He claimed to be an honest businessman. He assured them he hadn't been threatened and would have reported anything helpful. Manah expressed mild remorse, but protested any hint of complicity.

MAJ Alberts had joined the meeting about halfway through. He'd remained quiet until the end. With the meeting on the verge of finishing, Alberts stated forcefully that the school construction contract remained in place. He reminded Manah that he expected the school job to be completely finished within two weeks, and then would visit again. At that point, Manah again ask for an additional payment. His workers would now be fearful of returning, he argued, and he'd have to pay them more. Alberts flatly refused, and threatened that the performance of Manah's company on this contract would directly affect the likelihood of additional business.

The meeting ended with neither party happy. Manah left hastily.

After MAJ Alberts left, Wynn turned to Petty and said, "At the school that day, I heard from Alberts that Manah had actually gotten a referral from Sheikh Amir. Manah hasn't been helpful. If he knows anything, he's not talking. Makes you wonder, once again, whether any of these guys is dealing straight."

"That reminds me, speaking of that shooting," Petty said. "We did more research on sniper activity. We've got limited information, since most of them involve Iraqi killings, but it appears that several Iraqis, or their family members, may have been killed in the last few weeks by sniper activity. Our analysts looked at some of the local news reporting and made a few calls. One report indicates that ten days ago an Iraqi electrician, hired by an American contractor, was shot about twenty-five kilometers south of here while he was hooking up a power generator we supplied a village. And last week it looks like an Iraqi government official, a kind of a mayor in an adjacent battalion's battlespace, was shot and killed at a ribbon-cutting ceremony for a medical clinic. Of course we know that some of these insurgent groups are targeting family members of people working with us. That PFA group is claiming responsibility for both these attacks, as part of their 'purification' campaign. But other insurgent groups are also claiming responsibility for one or more of the attacks. Even a group we've identified as Baathist, and pro-Saddam, claims responsibility. The usual confusion." Petty relayed this information coolly, like he was intrigued by yet more complexity, but baffled about how to take it.

"Looks like a trend," Wynn said.

"Maybe. We have to keep watching it. And I know your boss, Captain Baumann, and my boss are meeting to talk about some of the stuff you guys found at the warehouse. You'll probably hear more from him shortly."

"I hope so," Wynn said. "No one claimed responsibility for the school shooting so far, right?"

"Not that I've seen anything on."

Wynn tried to get his mind around why anyone would shoot the kid. Had the shots been intended for a Wolfhound? None of his men had been within 10 feet. But the shooter had fired twice. Where the other round went, nobody knew.

Moose and Kale sat alone in the messhall. Kale felt the funny feeling rise, again, this gnawing thing inside that disguised itself as anxiety and made him question everything about himself. He didn't have a name for it and didn't know if it was fear or tension or a sickness of some sort. He wanted it to remain nameless—easier to ignore it that way. Why did he sense it now, with Moose here? Why couldn't he be more like Moose, more resolute and confident? Moose had a kind of hot-shit attitude that perfectly fit the image of soldiering. Kale wanted that.

Now, as he was alone with Moose, something inside him clicked like an engaged timer, and he felt a growing pressure to confide his inner fears. Everything they'd been told about mental stress said you had to talk to someone. But he didn't want to talk about it; not now, and he promised himself he wouldn't.

"How come I don't see you in the gym anymore, buddy?" Moose suddenly asked.

It was a Trojan horse subject, Kale recognized.

"Doc says I got a pinched nerve in my shoulder," Kale lied, but went through the motions of signaling where the phantom pain was, patting his right upper back.

"Treatment?"

"Nope. Got some pills. Rest."

"What's he got you taking?"

The medicine question stumped Kale temporarily. He wasn't on any medicine, so what should he tell Moose? Other than common aspirin names, he couldn't think of the names of any painkillers. Then, averting his eyes, he squeezed out a halfway plausible response.

"Don't know. Some long word. Too hard to pronounce."

Moose let it go.

"Tyson's talking about you," Moose started back up after a short silence.

"Oh. What about?"

"Says it's noticeable."

"What's noticeable?"

Kale returned the questions like a man returning a tennis volley. His gut tightened. If people were talking about him negatively, he'd be trying for days to suppress the idea.

"I'm...ahhh," Moose stuttered briefly, and didn't deliver the thought.

"What?" Kale asked, approaching the net again, but was suddenly afraid he'd behaved too anxious to hear the answer. *Don't let them know you care.* Of course, inside, caring about what others thought was what drove him.

"Ah, just wants to make sure no bullshit's going on," Moose finally blurted out.

"No bullshit?"

The big man's jaw churned, and Kale sensed Moose wanted to protect his feelings. Moose knew Kale's sensitive spots. Criticism was one. Moose continued, "Yeah, man, like...ahhh...like you're off somewhere. Not all here anymore."

"Huh? Where's he getting that?" Kale retorted, feigning anger. He needed to think about what he should answer. Maybe simple denial would keep working.

"Others see it too, man. Anybody say anything to you?" Moose had served the ball hard.

"Say what?"

"Well, like you're distracted or whatever. Depressed, maybe. That's dangerous in our profession, man."

Moose paused for effect, then added, "Anything up?"

Kale hated this question. It meant somebody else finding the key for a door you never wanted opened. He'd kept it all inside. His secret bad feelings locked inside. He'd always thought that if he could keep the feelings in the dark, hidden deep inside, he could contain their impact. Now what?

He said nothing. Had Moose sensed his inner contortions? Kale looked away. Obfuscate time.

The messhall was almost empty now. A worker sprayed the table next to them with a cleaner that smelled like vinegar.

Moose stared at the side of Kale's face like a man studying the profile of a marble statue.

"Hey buddy, that's what I'm talking about. You listening?"

Moose hadn't dropped it. Kale turned back towards him and Moose's deep-set walnut eyes studied him with an interrogator's intensity.

"Nothing, Moose," Kale asserted, apprehensive and insolent. "Just tired."

Moose kept staring at him, as if trying to drill into Kale's soul. Moose was about to probe more, Kale suspected, but he couldn't put it into words. Kale wanted the conversation over. He glanced to his right and looked at the different drink dispensers: various types of soda, Kool-aid, Gatorade, iced tea, milk, bottled water, and Red Bull, lining the long counter against the wall. He wished he were elsewhere.

Neither spoke for at least a minute.

"Can't keep it bottled up, buddy," Moose finally said.

Yes, you can, Kale said to himself.

"You know how if you shake a can of soda and open it up, it fizzes all over. You don't want that, man," Moose continued. "That could be your brain."

"It won't fizz over if you don't open it up," Kale answered meekly.

Then, with a chuckle, Moose suggested an escape. "Let's go play cards. Shiiiit! Relax."

"A description of your game?" Kale challenged him, seeing the opening.

Moose laughed. Kale had gotten him off the scent, he thought. He was good at that. It had worked many times before, in other places. How could a man explain his inner fears if he didn't understand them himself?

19

It was nearly 2000 when CPT Baumann started the meeting. The Platoon Leaders, Wynn, D'Augostino, and Smith, and Vallison, the Executive Officer, sat with Baumann in his office. They sat in four salmon-colored deep-pillow chairs facing the commander's desk. Wynn had long since stopped wondering how and why they shipped living room chairs like this into the FOB. The door was closed. Baumann looked even more tired than normal. His hair was longer than usual too and made Wynn think of a young Marlon Brando.

As a group, the company officers met like this at least twice a week, sometimes more often, situation allowing. Baumann's normal approach was to divide the meeting into three parts. During the first part, Vallison would facilitate a discussion of lessons learned in the previous days. Then he'd cover his additional responsibilities as the company supply and maintenance officer, discussing any supply and logistics issues. In the second part of the meeting, Baumann would get a dialog going within the group on their respective platoon operations, since each platoon's experiences and findings might be relevant to the whole company area. This talk might cover enemy activity trends, meetings with key Iraqi leaders, tribal relations, visits to Iraqi security forces, and other such topics. The last part of the meeting Baumann reserved for describing new plans and operations approved by battalion. Since the platoons operated fairly independently in their respective geographical areas, few operations required coordinating movements of the entire company. Occasionally two platoons worked together. Rarely did the company conduct a special mission using all three platoons. So Baumann spent a few minutes giving each platoon leader specific missions or tasks to focus on in the coming days. Then he would conclude by explaining his own planned activities. As a rule, he accompanied each platoon at least once a week, to observe their actions, assess their performance, and demonstrate command presence. Occasionally he would do independent operations with his own three-vehicle element. Because of the unrelenting high tempo of operations, most of Baumann's interaction with the platoon leaders was on a one-on-one basis. They'd talk on the radio or meet face-to-face in the FOB, or out in the red zone, whenever and wherever was possible.

Today's meeting started as usual. Vallison reviewed some of the company's recent operations, including the bombing to which the Wolfhounds had responded. Baumann interjected some questions to the lieutenants. Vallison next discussed the upcoming armor upgrade schedule for the Humvees, which was expected to start in two weeks. The timing had already been rescheduled twice. The Humvee doors were being replaced with more heavily armored doors, because better protection was needed from IEDs. Each vehicle, on a rotational schedule, would be out of action for 48 hours.

The group discussed a reoccurrence of radio fill problems. Across the battalion over the last couple of weeks, several units had lost secure radio contact because of a technical malfunction with the encryption loaded into their radios. Fortunately this hadn't happened to Wynn's platoon. But 1st platoon had been affected for one day. Then Vallison reviewed new facts on the sniper killing of PFC Dwayne Holden four days ago. When shot, Holden had been standing in his Humvee's turret during a routine stop at a checkpoint, and was not dismounted as originally reported. The bullet had entered the base of his neck and clipped his spine. He'd died instantly. When standing in a Humvee turret, the upper body of the average man would extend above the armored cupola. Standard operating procedures required that turret gunners remain seated when possible. When standing up, they exposed their upper bodies. But this posed a classic dilemma for leaders. If a turret gunner was seated, he couldn't adequately see his surroundings, moving or stationary. If a gunner could not see properly, he couldn't contribute quickly and effectively to the fight. Self-protection could not be the sole consideration in a combat zone. Easy answers were nonexistent.

Baumann spoke up, exasperation in his voice. "Do it like this. Have your gunners sit down at halts. Direct them to get up when necessary, like when moving through a busy urban area, so they can see. But, if you're stopped, have them sit down. Damn. This is fucking serious. From what I understand, four soldiers have been killed by snipers in similar circum-stances across the theater over the last three months. We've got to do better taking care of our gunners."

"Roger, Sir," Vallison responded, "I wanted to add that there's discussion going about a new turret kit coming that would offer higher and thicker armor, and overhead protec-tion and camouflage for the gunner's position. The idea being if they can't see the guy clearly, they can't aim at him."

"Speaking of snipers," Baumann continued, turning to look at Wynn, "we got interesting information out of those documents you guys seized in that torture warehouse, Chris-tian. The Intel boys translated stuff saying the bad guys have a female sniper working in the area. A Chechen female to top it off. Can you believe it?"

The lieutenants winced simultaneously, surprised. A chill of disbelief circulated inside the room. Could that be true? A female sniper? From Chechnya?

Baumann paused, waiting for a reaction from Wynn. Wynn was mute.

"This may be what we're dealing with," the commander said. Everyone in the room realized Baumann was also con-sidering the dead Iraqi schoolboy.

"Seriously?" D'Augostino hung the question out there as if he hoped somebody would say it wasn't so.

"They say the warehouse documents confirmed it—ah, that she's here. Documents said they waited on her arrival here, and confirmed it. Also the Chechen connection," Bau-mann explained. "Reports for months have said that Chech-nya opened a pipeline of jihad fighters to Iraq. Also, other documents seem to confirm that this warehouse gang is part of Purifiers for Allah, the group we call PFA. This information would be the first confirmation that PFA has a constant pres-ence in our area."

Wynn remembered Petty bringing up PFA. Now his mind buzzed with speculation, rewinding through the events at the school. Was this group behind the school shooting? Was it plausible that a female was killing kids? Chechnya was a long ways away. Yeah, they had problems with Muslim extremists too. But a female?

"Fucking A!" exploded Vallison, "this is unbelievable." He said what everybody else was thinking and mumbled more expletives under his breath.

"I was going to bring it up in a few minutes anyway," Baumann continued, "when reviewing pending operations with you guys. But with Vallison discussing the Holden shooting, I decided to tell you now."

"Do we think it was this bitch that shot Holden?" D'Augostino blurted.

"We don't know. Perhaps."

Holden's killer had not been captured or killed, to the best of their knowledge.

"Multiple groups have claimed responsibility, but we have no reports confirming anything. As far as I know, no one has claimed credit for the Iraqi boy so far," Baumann added.

In addition to official channels, the headquarters monitored open net sources, including extremist web sites. Often groups like Al Qaeda took credit for attacks. Sometimes more than one group took credit for the same attack.

"Could it have been the same shooter? It was certainly possible."

"We get the war with the multiple enemies," Wynn said, the first comment he'd made since Baumann broke the news.

"Yes, congratulations."

"What the fuck does Chechnya have to do with Iraq anyway?" Smith entered the conversation abruptly, as if emerging from a trance.

No one spoke for several seconds, the silence like a wave of cold water. Minds searched.

Wynn, like the others, tried to get his mind around the incredible strangeness of the story. *Her* story. He would have liked to read these documents himself. He would ask Petty about it later tonight if he could; if he was still awake.

Baumann said, "Bottomline—she's a sniper. From Chechnya. A sniper working with the insurgents. And, according to those documents, a well-regarded one at that. Part of the whole international jihad team, I suppose. It's become almost an international business. The protective measures we need don't change."

"She's come a long way looking for work," D'Augostino offered.

"Coming to where the business is," Wynn cracked.

Baumann added, "More will come to the surface about her. I'm sure battalion and brigade will be digging for info. It will be interesting to see how the Arab culture takes it. In this part of the world she must cut a highly unusual figure. Put it out to your people. Take care of your gunners."

Then the commander changed subject. "Need you guys to really emphasize your census work. We need better progress. Battalion is pressuring to get the population map finished, and our company is behind. Brigade's on our ass. Like I've said before, they're anxious to splice together all the family and tribal names, thinking that with that they can more readily determine who to engage with, depending on the need." *Or who not to engage with*, Wynn thought.

"Let's do our best."

Baumann opened the floor for questions and comments. Smith reviewed the upcoming Pit Bulls' trip to the Iraqi hospital with an American medical team from Baghdad, scheduled for next week. D'Augustino asked about an upcoming prison release. Hearing prison mentioned, Wynn suddenly remembered that they hadn't answered the Iraqi mother's question about her missing son during the census work a few days ago. Wynn asked Vallison to follow-up with the prison, and he agreed. Wynn gave him the name. There was more work than hours.

By the time the meeting ended, Wynn felt as if his brain was slowly dissolving. Maybe back outside he could think more clearly. His thoughts went back to the dead boy. This news about a female sniper had further complicated things.

When he came out of the meeting, Wynn noticed a missed call on his Iraqi phone. Walking back to the platoon area he checked the time, 2205, and called the number. After several rings, Jassim answered. Understanding him was difficult. His English sounded slurry, as if he'd been drinking. Perhaps he had. It was a myth that Muslims didn't drink.

Jassim claimed he'd located the dead boy's parents, and he promised he could make it possible for the Wolfhounds to see them tomorrow. The boy's family lived near the school, he said, and they would return home tomorrow at Jassim's request. Wynn asked where he could visit the parents. Jassim said he could have someone guide the platoon to the parents' home, and he would participate in the meeting himself. This would make the family more comfortable.

While Jassim talked, Wynn pondered concerns. Apprehension scratched at him like a rat behind a thin wall. He remembered the trip with the Civil Affairs team and Ramirez' death. Other Americans had died. Could he trust Jassim? He hardly knew the man, and what he did know about him was shady. Could he again risk the lives of his men following leads like this? It could be another ambush. Yet he'd asked Jassim for help. Now he offered help. And yesterday's visit to Jassim's had been uneventful. Risks were unavoidable, especially in the perilous atmosphere of Iraq. But the rat kept scratching.

Since Jassim offered to participate in the visit, he appeared interested in staying involved. That was a positive. Wynn made his decision. They would go.

Wynn thanked Jassim, and asked him to again have someone meet the platoon at the school at 1030 tomorrow.

"OK. This very good. But I need something from my brother," Jassim replied, an imploring tone to his voice, like a street vendor haggling with a prospective customer.

Wynn wasn't surprised. This man would do business in hell.

"What?" Wynn said, after a pause.

"Please you not interfere with our benzene sales." *Benzene* was the word Iraqis used for gasoline.

"What do you mean?" Wynn asked, genuinely unsure what Jassim was asking.

Jassim reminded Wynn that in some areas the Americans were suppressing the roadside gasoline stands. Both men knew official policy protected the established government gas stations and prohibited setting up new privately owned stations. Wynn didn't care about these roadside stands. This was one of those dilemmas where the Coalition was stuck between supporting existing Iraqi Government Policy and supporting the development of private gas sales. So much for free enterprise. Of course Jassim must have an angle to protect, otherwise he wouldn't bring this up. Officially, all petroleum products and infrastructure in Iraq were state-owned.

"Not my decision," Wynn finally answered. Jassim must realize that an American lieutenant would not make policy on benzene.

"But you have platoon and you must decide how to use them, Lieutenant Wynn," Jassim added.

The Iraqi wasn't wrong. He knew what he was talking about and Wynn knew what he meant. Just because something was official policy didn't mean that he had to rigorously enforce it in his platoon's area. He smiled. Nothing came free in this world.

Momentarily he considered asking Jassim to help the Wolfhounds find the female sniper. But something whispered against it, and he didn't want to muddy the waters with a specific request like that before the relationship with Jassim had leavened further. He thought about Sheikh Amir for a few seconds, and whether he'd been able to conclusively determine anything with his friend and the torture warehouse. Wynn answered Jassim.

"Perhaps, Sadi. I don't worry about benzene."

Jassim acted satisfied with that answer. Wynn hadn't firmly committed, and hadn't said he would. He left it gray. Gray was good enough in Iraq.

20

Wynn headed for the motor pool, where he'd planned to brief the platoon at 2200. It was 2220 now. Baumann's meeting had taken slightly longer than expected, and the call from Jassim had delayed him further. This late in the evening the heat was a light caress. The sky was clear, luminous in half-light, filled with thousands of stars dominating the night.

He had interesting news for the platoon. It was amazing how these Islamic terrorist organizations stuck together, complex and far-reaching, like a human spider web strung between shadowy branches. He was certain all the Wolfhounds would be astounded when he broke this news of the female sniper. He knew that the men felt, as he often did, like the whole mission here was constantly assaulted by hundreds of unbelievable things, as if they were participants in a theatre of the absurd. Nothing was simple or straightforward.

Wynn passed through the gap in the concrete T-wall barrier. He looked, once again, at the elaborate graffiti that soldiers had painted on the wall. He couldn't see the images clearly now because of low light, but knew them by heart. One wannabe artist had celebrated Midwestern pride, nicely sketching the Chicago skyline, illustrating the city of broad shoulders, the great lakes, and the bountiful farm fields far into the horizon. Above the scene was emblazoned: "This is worth fighting for." Another graffiti artist had transformed the opening in the T-wall into a painting of a skyscraper. Eight painted American flags hung out of the windows. Whoever painted these had taken a lot of pride in the grand old flag.

The platoon had much to talk about. He tried putting it all together neatly in his mind, but it didn't work that way. Their work left minimal time for detailed reflection. Much of the thinking Wynn did, he did on the go. He never did only one thing. The Army called it multi-tasking. If he took too much time thinking over past things, he'd get the sense he neglected something emergent, or wasted time, and it left him feeling unprepared.

Undoubtedly, the recent days had been particularly difficult. No way around that. The best thing so far—probably the most important thing—was that none of his men had been hurt. The reaper stalked. Ramirez's death still felt like yesterday and each man knew other soldiers who had died or been badly wounded. He owed it to his men that they hear from him in a little more formal setting, something unhurried and serious, where communication of the essentials was the core message: the mission and their protection of each other, as opposed to the usual businesslike discussions and orders. Where to start this time? The car bomb today. The sniper threat. The warehouse. The dead Iraqi boy. The census.

He had to do what he could to keep the men confident about themselves and their mission. That was basic leadership. He remembered classes back at the Tank School Officer Basic at Fort Knox. One instructor had called it Buffer and Boost. The two Bs. *Buffer* his men, as in protect them from unnecessary stresses, things he could deflect, like shielding them from the higher headquarters pressures. *Boost* was all about building morale and personal pride, keeping his soldiers positive about their jobs and mission. In theory, a well-led man with sturdy pride could stay resilient in all kinds of circumstances.

Cooke had already assembled the men in the usual semicircle, with the T-wall behind them. Most sat or knelt on the ground. Several sat with their backs to the T-wall, hats cocked at weird angles. Although it was dark, in the night light Wynn still caught the range of looks in many of their faces as he walked up. He noted the weariness, but also the defiance and stubbornness. Cooke signaled for the men to get up on their feet as Wynn approached, the traditional respect due an officer. But Wynn raised his hand, indicating they should stay seated. He was long past being concerned about such courtesies. He stared at his men like a coach admiring a winning team.

All of his men wrestled in their own way with difficult circumstances. Moose had that deceitful passivity, like a watchful bobcat resting on the branch of a tree. Turnbeck, edgy and distracted, but still alert and ready to execute any order without complaint. Kale, stamped with a worried longing look, unsure of himself, like a dog begging for petting. Wynn made a mental note to ask Cooke for an update on Kale. Cuebas stood against the wall, nearly invisible, surly, rustling with something in his hand. A cigarette? He didn't remember whether Cuebas smoked.

"Steak and Lobster for chow tonight?" Wynn started with a light question, trying to break the ice.

Soft chuckles all around. The men would have eaten already. Wynn had not had time.

Cooke commented, "Sims here tells me he means to have the big Filipino gal behind the messhall counter. The one with the dimple on her cheek and thunder thighs."

"Naw," hollered Sims.

More laughter tumbled around the group. There was no shortage of food or of thoughts about women.

"Saw something the other day," Wynn said, "saying that it's shocking how many guys go home from deployments having gained weight. We're eating too well!"

Chuckles translated as it "ain't gonna happen to me" rumbled between the men.

Again Cooke followed, "Sir, that's true. But some of these jokers are gaining muscle. Getting much too much time in the gym."

A low boo of dispute came from a few in the crowd. Cooke wasn't serious. Not about the too much time, anyway.

Wynn, never one to consume time unnecessarily, moved to the more serious matters. Afterwards, he asked himself whether he'd dropped the small talk too abruptly. It was not that he didn't know it was important in human relations to personalize things, to try to convey empathy, but at the same time he couldn't quite bring himself to let his guard down.

He'd always had trouble with that. That cloudy distance between natural self-protection and building firm connections to others wasn't easy to navigate. Many stayed lost in the gap.

Moose watched Wynn talk. The lieutenant stood erect, straight-backed, right thumb in right pocket, left hand on left hip, one foot slightly ahead the other. Moose thought Wynn stood somewhat stiffly, like a referee after a questionable call at a ball game. Nevertheless, Wynn could talk in a way that made himself heard. The men admired that. The young officer was not afraid to speak his mind, or to act. Moose respected that. Wynn had demonstrated that many times in the last few months. The action part was the more important. Talk meant nothing in the end. There was another interesting thing about Wynn. He had a way of conveying much with little, and a steadiness when steadiness was the main thing needed.

Why is it we are who we are? Moose asked. He weighed maybe 50 percent more than Wynn, and could probably bench press twice as much. Yet it was the young officer who stood before them right now who could and would say what he wanted. Somehow, officers were different. That Moose knew. Not better or worse, but different. Moose, especially after this week, felt he could fight with the best of them. He'd earned his right. Nobody could take that from him. If they could measure guts, his would be as tough as anyone's. Yesterday he'd shot and killed that man without flinching. But Wynn had something extra too. Whether it was talent or good fortune, Moose wasn't sure. The heavy responsibility of leadership, more than anything else perhaps, set Wynn apart.

After the introductory comments, Wynn reviewed the platoon's actions over the last few days and talked about the progress of the census. Estimates indicated they had visited 15 to 20 percent of the homes in the W14 & W15 areas. He spoke shortly about Iraqi perceptions. The people here are different, Wynn said. The same, but different. How we value or emphasize certain things is heavily influenced by culture and experience. Soon, he believed, they would increasingly work with the new Iraqi Forces as time and situation allowed. Eventually local forces would have to do the heavy lifting, if the mission was to be successful.

Moose listened and remained watchful, attentive, fixed by all that had transpired, spoken and unspoken, between the men in the platoon and their leader. He felt the inspiring warmth that came from being part of a team. And he felt satisfied with his role.

Wynn continued. "OK—now to the last few days. It's been a damn rollercoaster. You guys have been doing great work. I'm proud of your efforts."

He shifted hands. Left thumb in left pocket. Right hand on hip. "I know you are tired and beaten up. When you see the things that we've seen, day after day, it's not easy. I know that. Each of you never stops asking the permanent question: why?

"How can someone use an electric drill on another human beings' legs? Why is it that children cannot even be safe at play?

"I don't know. I wish I did. But what I do know is there's evil in the minds of some men here. Our job remains what it has been—not to figure out why, but to stop the bad things we can stop.

"I'm convinced the average Iraqi doesn't support that kind of behavior. To the average Iraqi, just like an American, that kind of behavior is barbarous. I'm sure of that. Extremist behavior will convince more of the Iraqi population to help us help them.

"And that is what is happening. The calls coming in to HQ with tips are increasing. During the censuses, Iraqis are talking. We're gaining more informants. Weapons cache discoveries are up. As I've told some of you, the tip on the warehouse came to us by cell phone. I feel, as does the CO, that our efforts are paying off.

"Now," Wynn paused briefly and glanced at his feet. Then, looking at the men, he let another long moment of silence hang, as if judging his audience. "I heard something this evening from the CO about the information we seized from the warehouse. Folks have been going through that stuff, translating it, looking for important information in the documents we found. And guess what they found?"

Wynn let this question penetrate. He watched the men for reactions.

For a second, Moose thought Wynn was preparing a joke. Then he saw something like an apology come up on Wynn's face. Wynn went down on one knee. Both hands rested on his horizontal thigh.

Wynn continued, "Believe it or not, some of the documents suggest that there is a female sniper from Chechnya operating in the area. And if so, she may be the one who shot that Iraqi boy. Supposedly she's working with a group known as PFA, short for Purifiers for Allah."

Heads lifted. Moose heard grunts of disgust, and men exchanged disbelieving glances.

"No shit," someone said.

"Ayeee!"

"Turning things on its head," another commented.

"Doesn't matter whose head," Cooke said, "we want it."

Tyson, Moose, Cuebas, and Gung sat talking on the deck of the company orderly room. Now almost midnight, the night air remained warm and stagnant, enduring evidence of the sun's assault earlier in the day. Stars salted the black sky. Power generators hummed monotonously in the background, oddly reassuringly. A few minutes earlier they'd finished watching a *Seinfeld* episode on the DVD player inside the orderly room. After getting a dose of comedy, the group agreed to go outside and return to the questioning, blustering, and speculating that filled up most of their idle time.

Intermittently during the *Seinfeld* episode, and now during the conversation, each man's mind returned to the female sniper. Incomprehensible events can crush like a python, and no one could shake this off. The idea that a woman had traveled 1,000 miles to kill for a dream was a fundamental violation of rationality somehow.

"You know, they won't believe this back home," Tyson said, after a long silence. "They won't fucking believe it. Don't make no sense."

Gung commented: "They don't believe any of this shit, man. None of it. This is just one more thing."

"Ayeee, they believe people die," Cuebas said. "Our people; their people."

"I don't get how she got here." Tyson said, not understanding it. None of them did.

"Ayeee, that's a different country, ain't it. Part of Russia or something fucking far away."

"They all work together," Moose said. "They want to kill us. So they come from all over the world to take their chances."

"That's true," Gung said. "The bastards want a piece of us."

Moose adjusted his hand on the butt stock of his M4. The barrel rested, muzzle-down, on the floor. He leaned the rifle back and forth like the stick shift of a manual transmission. He wanted to accelerate.

"Like a terrorist club," asserted Gung. "Like a goddammed club!"

Cuebas spoke up again. "Just face it, man, some people around the world definitely don't like us. Can't everybody—except me—be liked. Just the way it is. And if you're on top of the hill, somebody's trying to knock you down. Not much room on top." He paused, then, "Suppose it's always been that way."

"Mexs are easy to knock down," Moose swung.

"Puerto Ricans aren't, fucker."

"I'd like to meet this woman," Gung said, imagining her.

They all wondered what she might look like. The flitting image in Cuebas' mind was of a slender dark-haired woman, moderately attractive. She would not be overweight. That wouldn't work. As a sniper she would have sharp eyes and steady hands.

"Wynn didn't say they were sure. Didn't say it was definite this woman shot that kid," Moose said, as if he wanted to believe, but couldn't.

"True. True," Gung cut him off. "But I got a bad feeling about it, man."

"That was done professionally, man—ain't no fucking new shooter make a shot like that," Tyson said, with a bitterness framed in respect.

"Ayeee. We don't know for sure it was a good shoot," asserted Cuebas. "She might just be a lucky bitch or might have missed one of us and hit the kid."

"Naw man, the closest one of us was too far away from the boy," Tyson countered.

"I hope we find out," Moose murmured.

He had killed a man, Moose reminded himself. Would he kill a woman? Yes, he would. Holding his M4 vertical with one had on the hand grip and the other on the butt, he spun the weapon several times, muzzle rotating on the floor like a drill to emphasize the point to himself.

"Don't matter either way. Both is fucked up!" Tyson exclaimed.

"Ayeee, somebody will talk," Cuebas spoke louder than he needed to. He had a feeling about this. "You couldn't hide it long. Too many won't like it. Ugh, the average Hajji may not like foreigners here, but that don't mean it's only Americans they're talking about. I'm pretty damn sure they don't like no fucking foreigners shooting their children."

Wynn sat in the dark at the desk in his trailer. For some reason Clare Baldwin drifted back into his consciousness. Why now? Maybe a smell or an image or a memory had coalesced in his mind. Maybe it was the craziness of a female sniper. Things were difficult enough without constantly reanalyzing past relationships. Sometimes it simply didn't work. He pondered what Clare might be doing that moment. Had she found the right man? He could write her. But that would be crazy now, wouldn't it, after all this time? He could ask his mother about her. No, he wouldn't. Now was not the time to dig around in that. He was due to email his parents, but hadn't been able. The timing wasn't right, his mind full of other things. Perhaps later. At times he felt guilty for not communicating home more often. Maybe keeping the homefront distant was another form of self-protection.

The present clamped down on his mind again. The idea of a female sniper from another country operating in Iraq was nearly impossible to let go. It was plain crazy, something twisted beyond recognition. Could a woman really have killed that boy? Still, at some academic level it fascinated him, adding mystery to mystery, another confirmation of the innumerable complexities and irrationalities in this place. Essentially, this was not a question about war, but a question about culture and human psychology.

What was inside this woman's mind? As a potential mother, a home provider, she should be a giver of life, not a taker. Yet she was one with the fighters, sharing as a dispenser of violence in a man's world. Not only that. She was a foreigner. This was not her place, nor her people. If she spoke any Arabic, it was probably minimal.

Yet she came to Iraq, a place a thousand miles from her home. That surely was no easy task, probably following a tenuous ratline strung from her place to this one, guided by fanatics operating on the edge of the world, most likely knowing little of the places she passed through or where she was going. But she had come.

Wynn knew the elementary facts about Chechnya, about the wars fought there, about the Islamic terrorists. There was one thing—an idea of Radical Islam—which these places had in common. Because of that, jihad had found a home. Like all the foreign jihadists, this female would have had to have come to Iraq more *for* something than *to* something. This purpose must be her life.

Thinking about it now as objectively as he could, she probably had at least two things working in her favor. One, she would initially be above suspicion, because she was a woman.

Two, she had to be an exceptional shooter. These two facts about her, probably combined with an extraordinary mental focus, had caught the eye of someone. Or perhaps she had been picked out as a child, designated early as a future weapon of Islam, and enrolled in a special school and trained as a terrorist. Either way, she had to have had partners, collaborators in this journey, others who accepted and furthered the cause of a very special female.

Still, it didn't seem possible. Everything he had seen here or read about this place confirmed the secondary role of women in a Muslim country. Not that women weren't considered important, but they were, by their laws of God, far more subservient than western women were. Rarely did women in Muslim countries play leading roles.

Perhaps she could have been a suicide bomber instead. Women had done that. A talent for delivering death would always find admirers. Wynn didn't think the American Army allowed female snipers. In fact, other than a few special exceptions like helicopter pilots, the American Army still tried to keep women out of a direct combat role. But as a sniper? No. Finding out your enemy was a woman cheated your pride somehow. If you thought the world was supposed to be a rational, if cruel, place—that things happened for a reason and that reason was discernible to man—this kind of discovery would make you question all internal logic.

Wynn closed his eyes. His mind thirsted for different thoughts and to push away what he didn't understand. Maybe he should quit trying.

Soon sleep ensnared him, and he drifted into an ephemeral world of wanted and unwanted recollections. Speculations danced within his restless mind. Eventually, after struggling for some time, he descended into the refuge of deep sleep, like a fish down deep between rocks in swift water.

DAY SIX

21

AT 0730, WYNN BEGAN his morning brief to the platoon.

"Our first mission today is another trip to the school. We'll talk to the schoolmaster and see if he'll give us more information. Then we plan to visit the dead boy's family. Sheikh Jassim will meet us there. Later, we'll tackle more census work. Probably this afternoon. We also plan to patrol the Houdoud Al'dena market." He and Cooke had decided to postpone the northwest patrol again. "I don't have anything new to tell you about what we talked about last night. I'm sure everybody's been thinking about it."

Wynn covered other points, then said: "Sergeant Cooke will go over the plan details."

Cooke put out the truck assignments, dismount teams, and convoy routes.

By 0750, the Wolfhounds were headed back to Bawa Sah. Wynn felt sure Albadi was back at work. They didn't have an appointment. Wynn didn't want to forewarn the schoolmaster, as he might decide he didn't want to see them and skip out. The school didn't have a phone, and he didn't know if Albadi had a cell phone. This wasn't unusual. Cell phones became available to the average Iraqi only over the last year or so, after the fall of Saddam. They'd visit unannounced.

He doubted that Albadi was involved in the shooting. He didn't seem the type and probably wouldn't risk it. Perhaps after a couple of days to reflect on things and talk, the schoolmaster might tell them something important.

Fifteen minutes after the convoy got underway, CPT Baumann came up on the radio calling all platoon leaders. Wynn and the others answered. All three platoons were out on patrol.

"I got some new information from headquarters a short while ago that I thought was important enough to put out right away," Baumann began. "First, additional documents seized at the warehouse raid were translated overnight. Those docs confirm that the PFA group and their female sniper are targeting family members of anyone cooperating with the Coalition. The Intel analysts are concluding that a number of the recent sniper killings are the responsibility of this group. Make sure you emphasize these concerns with any prominent Iraqis you engage. However, a separate report came in saying credit for the checkpoint bombing that Wolfhounds responded to yesterday belongs to a different group. Supposedly that group focuses on attacking Iraqi security forces. Given the serious sniper threat, and the obvious IED threat, make extra sure all your countermeasures are in place, especially when engaging with Iraqis."

The platoon leaders acknowledged the information, and Baumann signed off. Wynn massaged his neck and wished he could unknot all this tangled information. He again reviewed what he knew. The PFA group was operating in the warehouse. That group and their sniper were killing Iraqis, but nothing they had so far proved one way or the other that that sniper had shot the boy. Maybe more documents would reveal that or maybe new information will come out. He had second thoughts on how the warehouse operation had been handled. Perhaps if they had handled it differently more insurgents could have been killed or captured, perhaps even the female. But he couldn't turn the clock back. He had to find a new opportunity.

Wynn got on the platoon net and put out a short report of what he had just heard.

It wasn't yet 0830 and the angry sun already breathed down with open fangs, turning the surroundings a hazy, pale mustard, and intimidating all living things. Moose felt hot metal all around as the heat and stench of cooked air washed over the moving Humvee. But he cared little about physical sensations, and as the platoon neared the school and moved past the usual activities and places, he noticed the typical struggling businesses, the ramshackle homes, the wary people. He stayed largely oblivious to it all—his mind was insulated by an idea: the idea of revenge. Wynn's latest radio traffic powered that idea.

Prospects for revenge exited Moose. Why? A primeval urge to make something broken whole? Or was it about tearing down, about destroying? To him the idea of revenge was sweet. Would they get it from this bumbling Schoolmaster? Or would he claim, as Moose believed all Iraqis did, to know nothing? Even if they knew something, they admitted nothing. No knowledge. No culpability. No help. Fuck them.

Ahead, two Iraqi men used shovels to clear a sewer. A small curly-headed boy sat on a concrete block watching them. The boy turned and watched the Wolfhound convoy suspiciously. An older man said something to the boy and the boy looked away. Fuck them. Passing, Moose stuck out his tongue.

When the convoy pulled up to the school this time, no children were outside. Maybe it was still closed. Some of the brick stacks were now gone. It was unclear whether anyone was inside.

"Take all four corners," Wynn directed over the radio as the platoon pulled in, "maintain three-sixty security. Security team meet me at D21."

The platoon positioned. Three personnel, Moose one of them, would dismount to go inside the school, providing security for Wynn and Cengo. Moose was glad to get out of the truck. The revenge idea was sweetening. The Wolfhounds remaining outside had orders to stay in their trucks, even if school kids came back outside.

D22 stayed at the entrance of the school compound. Turn-beck's crew was tasked to keep a close watch on the houses where they'd searched for the sniper.

At 0910, Wynn and team walked inside the school. Once inside, Moose glanced around like a hungry dog looking for food. The children were back, but this time they remained in their classrooms. Albadi met the group at the door. He was alone, looking like he hadn't slept and was clearly nervous, his long gray *dishdasha* blending with his placid pastel skin. Sunlight from a window shone on the man's bald head, illuminating shiny tiny drops of perspiration. His clasped hands rested submissively on his abdomen. He acted as if he waited on a court verdict.

Albadi and Wynn exchanged perfunctory greetings.

"Ask him about the other children." Wynn instructed Cengo

"Sir?"

"Ask if the rest of the kids are OK."

Cengo translated, repeating a couple of Arabic words, presumably for greater emphasis. They were OK, Albadi answered. The school had closed for two days. Everyone was worried.

Albadi asked if the group should sit down in his office.

Wynn's replied yes, and they walked around the corner to Albadi's office.

As they walked through the lobby, Moose noticed that bed sheets covered a 12-foot section of damaged wall at the back of the school. The sheets didn't fully cover the opening, exposing the room to the outside. A large dirty stain covered the floor where water had leaked inside.

Out of the corner of his eye, Moose caught movement, and saw a small bird hopping around inside. The bird appeared as lost as the rest of them.

Albadi's office was small, about the size of a department store changing room. The desk and chair only left room for two other people. Wynn and Cengo followed the schoolmaster inside. Moose stood at the door and looked inside. The office was dark, lit only by sunlight coming through a cracked windowpane. A tea kettle simmered on a small gas burner. Albadi did not offer them tea.

Sims, the other member of the security team, walked back and stood guard by the school entrance. Moose remained by the Schoolmaster's office door, oriented out. He could hear the conversation going on inside.

Moose didn't trust Albadi and didn't like him. Albadi was one of those men born with a guilty look. His face was long, lean, and serious, like a Doberman's. And he was too quiet, too worried, too careful. All these attributes meant a guilty conscience. Where Moose came from, if a man wouldn't look at you while talking, you couldn't trust him. Besides, he trusted only the people wearing the same uniform he wore. But Wynn was determined to hear the man out. So Moose would do his job: stand guard and remain ready to—in the sanitized words of military tactics—engage the enemy.

Wynn asked whether Albadi knew the contractor before the school construction job had started.

No.

Wynn asked whether, on the day of the attack, Manah had told Albadi that the Wolfhounds planned to visit the school.

Yes, Manah had told him.

"After hearing we were coming, did you discuss that with anyone?" Wynn asked.

A long pause lay in the room like a corpse.

Moose could not see the facial expressions inside the room. Nobody said anything. A foot shuffled on the floor.

Wynn spoke. "Tell Mr. Albadi that I must know who he talked to. Anybody that he thinks may have heard in advance that we were coming, I must know." Wynn added firmly, "As I think Mr. Albadi must know, that kind of attack was planned. Ninety percent of the time a sniper attack is planned, rehearsed. That takes time."

Another pause. Cengo had not yet translated, sensing, Moose assumed, that Wynn had more to say.

Then Wynn continued. "Tell him that. Tell him that Iraqis and Americans both want to find out who did this shooting. Tell me when you are finished."

"I understand everything. No need for translate," Albadi said abruptly, in a distinctly British accent. "I believe, Sir, that I only..."

Albadi's change to English surprised everyone. His English was as good as Cengo's.

"...that I only talked to workers," Albadi finished.

Another pause. Moose took a step across the doorway and cast a lingering glance inside the room. Albadi's eyes misted, as if he was in severe pain. His hands were hidden under the desk.

"Go on," Wynn urged. "It's very important that if you know anything, you help us."

Albadi stopped talking. Cengo translated. Then Wynn continued again.

"A murder occurred in your schoolyard, Sadi. If you know anything, you must help us avenge that child."

Cengo did not translate that. The room was quiet again for several seconds.

I can get that man to talk, Moose said to himself. He knows something, the bastard.

Wynn, unexpectedly, spoke loud and fast. "Sadi, if I think you are not being truthful, I will take you into custody. One way or the other, you will tell us the truth."

Then Albadi spoke in Arabic again, rapidly, as if a spell had been broken. He spoke for about a minute. When Albadi had finished, Cengo translated.

"He say he only discuss visit coming with his own family, and with school children. He tell children because some families no want their kids near soldiers. If soldiers come, and parents find out they come, and that he not tell them, they be upset with him."

Shit, Moose thought. Everybody knows. If the kids told their parents then the whole damn town knew they were coming.

Then Albadi spoke. "Yes. I must tell them. Some families hate you Americans. They believe Americans should leave Iraq. Should not be in Iraq. Some families have been threatened by Al Qaeda. And because you coming—some parents not let their children come to school."

Again silence filled the room. Wynn must be thinking. Is this man telling the truth? Did it make sense in Albadi's world to protect himself by alerting the parents?

Moose looked at Sims. Stoic face. Mistrustful eyes. Loaded weapons. Moose thought he probably looked the same. Each man a warrior for his country wearing 60 pounds of body armor and carrying a gun permit from Uncle Sam. No talk. Yet the unspoken communication between them was remarkable.

"Do you think any of the children's families are Al Qaeda?" Wynn asked.

"No. They scared of Al Qaeda," Albadi answered, fear now radiating from him like heat from a stove.

"Should the Americans leave Iraq, Sadi?"

"I want Iraq to be free."

"Free for Al Qaeda?"

"No. Al Qaeda are murderers."

"Who in your family knew?"

"Only my family," Albadi responded, his voice cracking.

"Who?"

Rising tension filled the office. Moose thought Albadi might explode if you thumped him.

"Who?" Wynn asked again. "Tell me about your family. Do you have sons?"

Albadi said something, but Moose didn't hear it. Moose again stepped across doorway and glanced inside. Albadi, near tears, nibbled the inside of his lips.

"Do you have sons, Sadi?" Wynn asked again.

"No, daughters."

"Only daughters?"

"Yes."

"How old are they?"

"13 and 15. Good girls, Sir. Good girls."

"Ask him point blank whether he knows anything about the shooter," Wynn told Cengo, putting the conversation between the Iraqis back in Arabic.

Wynn might be doing this to give himself more time to think, to watch Albadi, or to see if putting the discussion back into Arabic would cause Albadi to adjust his story.

Cengo asked Albadi. The two spoke back and forth in Arabic for a minute. Frustration lacquered Albadi's manners.

Moose had been watching the three men in the office. Now he turned and looked at Sims again. Sims looked towards the classroom with the kind of expression a man has when he's seen something good turned ugly. Maybe some of the school children had seen Sims. Whether they had or hadn't, the kids inside the classrooms were as quiet as death.

"Sure there is nothing you can tell us about that day that might help us find the shooter?" Wynn asked Albadi.

"I know nothing. I am afraid for children. It terrible thing."

"It is a terrible thing, Sadi," Wynn said. "The fact that such a thing can happen and nobody knows anything about who did it is also a terrible thing."

"And a boy is dead." Albadi said that as if he still couldn't believe it.

"Mr. Albadi, I want to believe you. But you are here and you have surely been talking to the parents of these children. If somebody said something to you that might help us find the killer, I plead with you to tell us."

"Yes. I will," Albadi answered. He said nothing more.

Wynn gave Albadi another one of his contact cards. "You also must know, Sadi, that if I receive information suggesting you know something and are not telling us, I will not hesitate to take you in for more questioning."

"If I hear anything helpful I of course tell you, Lieutenant."

Wynn stared at Albadi. He hadn't told Albadi the platoon was about to visit the family. Moose, still watching from the office door, questioned whether or not Wynn believed the schoolmaster.

22

Sheikh Jassim's man arrived at the school. Wynn had instructed Cengo to call Jassim when the Wolfhounds arrived at the school, and tell him to have the guide meet them there again.

Wynn asked the guide whether Jassim was already at the family home, and the man explained that Jassim would be waiting.

Now Wynn had Cengo call Jassim and ask him to describe his guide. This was done, satisfactorily, and they prepared to depart.

On the way to the family home, Wynn chewed over the Albadi meeting. Was he telling the truth? Perhaps not fully, but was he involved in a culpable way? The schoolmaster could be squeezed by opposing pressures. It was impossible to be sure. The whole truth was never available in this country, perhaps not in any country.

He doubted Albadi was lying. He probably just hadn't told them everything. Maybe a parent had told Albadi something. Some of the parents lived near where the shots were fired from. Maybe someone in the neighborhood had talked. Perhaps Albadi had been threatened with retaliation. Surely someone would have seen the shooter. That information could have come back to the school, from a parent, or a maybe even a child.

But if he knew something, Albadi wasn't talking.

Wynn turned his mind to the dead boy's family. He dreaded the meeting.

The extended family of the slain boy had assembled for the meeting in a third-party house. It was 1022 when the Wolfhound team and Sheikh Jassim went inside. They passed through a small colorless room into a larger one in the back where the family waited somberly, crowded together on a thin faded carpet on the floor. Wynn counted eleven. Seven men. He immediately noticed one elderly blind man, surely over 80. The youngest person in the room was a child of perhaps ten. The men, all unshaven, in the Iraqi mourning tradition, looked bone-tired, hollowed out by grief. Suspicion and fear hung between them like a heavy curtain, dividing the room between foreigner and local. No one cried. Were all their tears exhausted? No one made eye contact with him. A sour odor of perspiration lingering in the room made it obvious that many of them had not bathed in several days, another traditional demonstration of respect to the dead. He was a little surprised to see women present, huddling behind the men.

Wynn, Cengo, Sheikh Jassim, and Turnbeck took seats on the floor across from the family. Wynn expected introductions. None came. No handshaking either. The atmosphere was freezer cold, and Wynn sensed the inevitable helplessness and burden of the tragedy weighing heavily on the entire group. How could he handle this? He maintained a grim expression, maybe too grim. He felt awkward, ineffective. He couldn't make what had happened go away, but now the blunt realization of this, with the family sitting across from him, made it hard for him to function. He wanted to appear compassionate, to understand what they were thinking, and demonstrate the proper solemnity. How could he start? He took another look around the room. Collective apprehension dripped off the walls.

Then Jassim lit a cigarette, as if he'd started a timer.

Once the sheikh had situated himself, and taken a second full draw on his cigarette, he blew smoke in a vertical plume like a miniature steam engine. Then he started talking to the family authoritatively, as if he was narrating a ceremony. He spoke in Arabic, and of course Wynn couldn't understand.

With every movement of Jassim's head, his mutilated ear swung like a soundless bell. Wynn waited for Cengo. Uncharacteristically, Cengo didn't start translating immediately. The weight of the situation stunned the terp, and he hesitated.

Jassim's preemptive talk with the family had the effect of binding Wynn. He waited and watched Jassim's body movements and facial expressions. The sheikh spoke unhurriedly. After a minute or so, the sheikh's delivery sounded pedantic, rehearsed, and without empathy. Had he prepared a speech? Wynn and Jassim had discussed in advance the purpose of the meeting and the approach they would take. Beyond the obvious expressions of deep regret, Wynn's main intent was to tell the family that their loss would not go unavenged. The Coalition would hunt down the perpetrators. At the end, he planned to tell the family about the financial compensation he was requesting for their loss.

As they listened, the family rarely looked directly at the sheikh, or at Wynn, nor the sheikh at them. Wynn, on the other hand, looked directly at each of the adults in turn—not knowing how to convey his sincerity, but wanting to, hoping that the attempt by itself might signify something valuable.

Wynn did not want to seem guilty. He'd repeatedly pondered whether this visit might look that way and hoped not. If questioned, he would definitely not accept responsibility for the attack. The Americans hadn't killed the boy; presumably an insurgent had.

Jassim talked nonstop for several more minutes. Wynn waited. The families remained mostly quiet, other than occasional grunts from a man wearing dark glasses, who Wynn assumed was the father. Cengo remained quiet.

Finally tired of waiting, Wynn turned to Cengo and said, "I need to hear this."

Cengo leaned towards Wynn and began quietly translating. He struggled to talk, stuttered and didn't make sense.

"Come on," Wynn prodded.

Cengo hesitated before regaining his composure, then said, "He explain first that he," Cengo nodded over his shoulder in the direction of Jassim, "want the family to know that their loss is tragedy for whole community. And that he, Sheikh Jassim, will help. He apologize. He say sorry about what happened. He say he make sure family get justice. He say this terrible thing that happen. Terrible thing."

The look in Cengo's face said he wanted to be somewhere else, but he continued. "He talk about the terrible situation exist now in Iraq. But he want family know that he care about their loss."

Wynn listened, not surprised by Jassim's self-serving tactics. If Cengo's translation was accurate, Jassim had yet to mention the Americans. Wynn had assumed the sheikh might try to position himself to take substantial credit for whatever restitution might come to the families. It was part of the cost of doing this business. Americans were glad to give credit to Iraqi leaders when due. Of course Jassim wasn't the Iraqi Government and shouldn't get credit for anything other than locating the family. The family needed to see that the Americans would not just walk away, forgetting this had ever happened.

One of the other family men said a few words to Jassim. Wynn heard the man use the word *shukran*, Arabic for thank you, several times.

"What else?" Wynn asked Cengo softly.

Before Cengo could answer, Jassim turned and spoke to Wynn in English. "The family asked what amount money they to get?"

Wynn didn't answer and gazed earnestly at Jassim. Jassim and he had spoken about the possible condolence payment, but Wynn had clearly explained that no amount could be stated, only that Wynn would pursue something for them. He hadn't intended for Jassim to raise this topic. Jassim, his face broadcasting superiority, watched Wynn. "Tell them," Wynn began slowly, directing his comments to Cengo, "that we cannot promise them money. But we will try—try hard." Wynn realized he had an edge in his voice. He tried to soften it. He felt exposed, as if he was walking a tightrope. He had clarified the condolence payment matter with Jassim in advance. Now Jassim was putting Wynn on the spot anyway.

"And tell them that the American Government—and the Iraqi Government—condemn that cowardly attack," Wynn continued, his words faltering a bit, "and we reject one-hundred percent that this is a right way to fight."

Jassim and one of the family men started conversing in Arabic. The sheikh responded promptly, but in a more measured way, lifting his cigarette hand in the air in a grand circuitous movement, as if to convey officiousness.

"What are they saying?" Wynn asked Cengo, frustrated at not being aware of the conversation's details.

"He say...I mean, Jassim, he say, you no can promise. No can promise money."

Wynn tightened, unhappy with the way the meeting was transpiring. The possible financial compensation was dominating the discussion. Should he interrupt, to silence Jassim? Wynn wanted to make his specific points.

He didn't wait longer. "Sheikh Jassim," Wynn interrupted, "I would like to speak."

Jassim paused. A hint of irritation at being interrupted flashed across his face. He took another deep drag on his cigarette, deliberately inserting a slice of time between the interruption and his response, not wanting to give up his dominant position. Then Jassim finally gave way. He moistened his lips and stared at his cigarette like a man studying an artifact.

"Lieutenant Wynn," Jassim announced to the family, nodding to Wynn deferentially.

"Did Sheikh Jassim convey my regrets, along with those of my country?" Wynn asked, failing to direct the question specifically at Jassim or Cengo.

Before either could answer, Wynn continued. "I would like to say, ahh..." Then, realizing his first statement hadn't been translated, said, "Cengo, tell them that."

When Cengo had finished, Wynn started again: "Tell them again that we do not accept this kind of violence. Our government, and the US Army, is fundamentally here to protect the Iraqi people." Wynn paused. He didn't want to come across too formally. The most important emotion to show was sympathy. He looked at Cengo. Then Cengo spoke, his voice unsteady.

Wynn added, "And tell them that we have been looking hard to find whoever did this."

Most of the family looked at Cengo now. When Jassim had spoken, the family members had mostly avoided eye contact. Now they looked at Cengo attentively, but cautiously, perhaps more curious about who this man really was than about what he said.

When Cengo finished, Wynn asked him to confirm which man was the father of the boys.

Cengo signaled the answer with almost imperceptible hand gestures, not wanting to communicate any disrespect. It was the man with glasses who had spoken to Jassim.

"The man sitting next to him is uncle," Cengo added.

Wynn moved a few inches forward to be nearer to the father. He was a bantam-sized man, with stooped shoulders and a dark crescent-shaped birthmark on his left cheek. His long disheveled hair and moustache made him look like a gaunter version of Albert Einstein. He wore an open-collar grey shirt, sat motionless and fragile, his eyes oriented on the floor, as if he stood before a judge. Tears now wicked into his eyelashes.

"What is his name?" Wynn asked, suddenly embarrassed he didn't know. An Iraqi boy killed three days ago and he wasn't even sure of the parents' names. Cengo said the name. Wynn, thinking it might convey respect, wanted to hear it from the man himself. "Can you ask the father to state his name?" Cengo asked.

The man quietly said his name. Wynn continued, delicately.

"Tell the man who I am: Lieutenant Chris Wynn. And tell him that in my capacity as an officer in the United States Army,

I want him to understand, on behalf of my country, how very sorry we are." Wynn looked squarely at the father as Cengo translated. The father did not look up.

"Tell him we will do everything possible to bring the killers to justice. And tell him that if there is anything he and his friends can do to help us locate the killers, we will be very grateful."

Cengo translated. Wynn waited patiently. The father remained silent, his grief and anger gripping him in a quicksand of emotion.

"And this man is the father's brother?" Wynn asked Cengo, pointing to the man next to the father.

"Uncle?"

"Yes, Uncle."

Wynn heard the metallic click of Jassim lighting another cigarette behind him. The sheikh had been quiet for several minutes, no longer involved in the discussion. Wynn avoided thinking about that now.

"Please ask him the same. Ask him to state his name."

The uncle was larger, older, perhaps 40, clearly nervous. He stared downward and twiddled with his pant legs. A young girl moved forward from the rear of the group and huddled against the Uncle's back. Perhaps his daughter.

Wynn made his same formal statements. Cengo translated. None of the Iraqis had yet asked Wynn anything.

Wynn briefly explained to the group what the Wolfhounds had been doing at the school, then, struggling to get any conversation going, he asked the family to tell him something personal about the dead boy. That might prove he cared. But immediately he worried he might have breached an intimacy, and they would not want to talk about it. He was right. They didn't. The father remained quiet, as did the other males in the family. His eyes bled grief. The women murmured quietly in the background. Feeling as if the oxygen was leaking steadily out of the room, Wynn's mind writhed about, looking for the right words. There were none. Grasping for something to resonate, he said that this happening at a school was particularly sad. No one replied.

He needed someone to help him, but no one could. Jassim too remained quiet. Wynn was grateful for that. Soon he felt as if he'd reached the end of a long run uphill, only to see around a bend that the hill continued farther than he could see.

So he spent a couple of minutes explaining what America hoped to achieve In Iraq, how we were without territorial ambitions, had goals to help modernize Iraq, had come as friends of the people, not as conquerors. Cengo labored to translate. There was no response.

Finally, exhausted by futility, Wynn had Cengo ask again if there were questions.

At this the uncle finally spoke up. A long statement came out of him like a stream of hate, bitterness lacing every word.

For more than a minute, Cengo made no attempt to translate, apparently taken aback by the animosity. He let the uncle complete his statement, then, tenderly, summarized it for Wynn.

"Sir—he talk about boy's father and he say his son is everything to him. His son was reason of all that come before. All his family, all history of his village, everything to him. He say the work and living of his people—all that was for the future. The future was his son. He very sad, he say, Sir. He say he no can think of future without thinking of son. Think his son was tomorrow. He say tomorrow, he mean the future. He say only when son is alive can his family name live."

Wynn let Cengo go on explaining without interruption. When Cengo finally finished, Wynn, battered by the tragedy and unable to think of an appropriate response, gritted his teeth and said nothing.

"And he want know about the money?" Cengo added, relaying that question cautiously, his eyes saying he knew Wynn wouldn't like readdressing that subject.

Wynn breathed deeply, but suppressed any change of expression.

"Tell the father that we realize his great loss. The family's great loss. His family has been a victim in this war, and we understand that. We want to help the family in these hard times."

Cengo translated. Wynn watched the father as a man might watch a parent at a child's funeral. He saw a glint of ruin in his eyes.

"I will speak to my superiors," Wynn continued. "I will ask them to help. We will be in touch again soon. How can we contact you?"

Cengo translated.

One of the women began sobbing. Others joined her. Tears that had been held behind a dike of unity now overflowed. The women leaned together, comforting each other. One spoke, almost inaudible. Then she tried again, fighting tears. A bearded man turned to the woman and spoke to her, not unkindly. Wynn thought this man might be a Mullah.

"Do you know what she is saying?" Wynn asked Cengo. He thought he'd heard the woman say the same thing several times.

Tears now streaked the father's face, the wet lines like knife cuts.

Cengo looked at the woman again and cleared his voice. "She say," he began, near tears himself. "This is boy's mother. She say she want her son back. She say he not dead. America must bring her son back, she say. I think she not want to believe he dead. She very sad about this."

The women suddenly got to their feet and walked out of the room. Several of the men spoke quietly to one another.

Wynn thought everything that could be said had been said, but he lingered for a long minute, wishing life weren't so inscrutable, wishing that bad things didn't have to happen, wishing, or at least hoping, that his delaying a little longer might make evident to the family his own sorrow and humility.

On the way back to the W14 area for more census work, Wynn thought about what it must be like to lose a child. He'd seen the parents of injured children several times before, like at the destroyed checkpoint yesterday. Today was the first time he'd met the family of a child killed during a Wolfhound mission. Though the language barrier had shielded him somewhat, emotions did plenty of talking all by themselves. In an odd way, he felt as if he'd been present during a relative's open heart surgery, and then watched as the physician came into the room to deliver bad news.

He thought about the parents of some of the dead soldiers, like Ramirez and Sanders and Casey and Ayami and Holden. Wynn had exchanged emails with Ramirez's mother. He'd sent her one written letter. But he hadn't had to look her in the face.

He looked at the map, tracing part of it with his finger. Ramirez was killed just over a mile from where they were. He thought about saying something on the radio to the platoon, but didn't.

The war had taken many others, both American and Iraqi. Each parent had faced the permanent removal of a part of their soul. He imagined trying to deal with such a loss.

He looked out the ballistic glass of the Humvee window. He felt like he was inside a submarine racing away from a black and foreign world.

For the first hour of the resumed census work, Moose manned D24's machinegun. D24 took up position by a road intersection, providing perimeter security, while the dismounted census teams went house to house. In the second hour, Cooke assigned Moose to a dismounted security role. Cooke often rotated the duties of the men, to minimize complacency and broaden experience. From the place he was positioned, Moose could provide close overwatch of the houses the census teams visited.

An IA patrol, coordinated by headquarters, had joined the Wolfhounds to help secure the neighborhood. Moose waited and watched from the shade under a concrete overhang jutting out from the second floor of the building, drumming his fingers on the handgrip of his M4 rifle, looking from side to side regularly, without haste, surveying the street and intersecting alleys as if his mind was a movie camera. A flush of satisfaction rose within him. He was providing good cover, he thought. He had superior visibility up and down the street.

The façade of the building where he stood had been damaged during the war. Perhaps it was a former government building, Moose thought. Pockmarks from bullet shots marred the once pretty masonry tiles inlaid in an oasis scene on the wall above the main entryway. Patterned inside the oasis scene had once been a number of square window panes, probably to bring more sunlight into of the building. Now most of these spaces had been roughly patched with concrete, probably because the glass had been shot out. The thick overhang above him had also been damaged and the ragged edge of the concrete cast a shade line on the street that reminded him of ridges in the mountains. Appropriate. No straight lines existed in Iraq.

Had anyone been killed here? People live. People die. Whatever remained was easily swept away, quickly forgotten. Had it been a car bomb? Or a rocket strike? He couldn't tell. It might have been more than a year ago. The residents would probably remember. But the census takers were not thinking about that as they asked the official questions for the hundredth time, thinking of their duties here and now; mostly oblivious to what occurred before. And Moose wasn't one to dwell on the past. His time was now. He would master the present.

Suddenly he heard a light thudding sound, followed immediately by a fast spinning sound. He turned to his right. A soccer ball rolled into the road from the alley beside him. The teenage boy running after it froze when he saw Moose. The boy wore a blue Nike T-shirt and had a wild look, his eyes dark and small like crab holes in sand. He stood perfectly still in the sweltering sun about 30 feet from Moose.

Moose watched him warily. A child appearing suddenly out of nowhere was common. Iraqi adults came out and watched the soldiers all the time, and curious kids were eve-rywhere. This one was different. More focused. Too serious.

Moose scrutinized the boy's appearance. Kids in this country had killed American soldiers. The boy looked mal-nourished and sunburnt. Big elbow joints swelled inside little arms. He didn't seem to be hiding anything. No indications of a suicide vest strapped under his shirt. Moose had been mis-taken about something dangerous under the shirt of that man yesterday. Didn't want to make the same mistake twice. No bulging pockets on this boy. Nothing visible in his hands. Too long, dirty pants. Cheap sneakers. *What was it?*

The boy remained motionless. Was he looking some-where? No. His small eyes blazed apprehension. Was he sig-naling? How? No motion. Hmmm. Did his lack of motion signal someone?

Moose hadn't moved his weapon. His rifle was still aimed out towards the road in the direction of the census teams. The suddenness of the boy's arrival had stunned him. Now he ad-justed his stance and lifted his weapon towards the boy, not aiming at him yet, more just to let the kid know Moose was communicating with him, cautioning him. The boy was no youngster, maybe 13 or 14. He could be a killer at that age.

The rifle reorientation broke the kid's trance.

Moose finally saw movement. The boy's right cheek shud-dered, inflating and deflating in tiny bursts. *Something in his mouth? Was he doing something with his tongue?* Just nerves, maybe.

"You Army, mister?" the boy asked cautiously, breaking the silence.

Moose didn't answer right away, glancing first one more time back in the direction of the census teams. Team One, now back on the street, having finished in a residence, was walking to the next house. Team Two was still inside its house. Moose had to limit his dialog. He didn't want to take his eyes and concentration off his security responsibility. Maybe this kid was a distraction.

Moose turned back to the boy, curious. "Yes. You know that," Moose replied, impatient.

Out of the corner of his eye, Moose saw a car driving slowly down the street towards the north. He kept one eye on the boy. With his peripheral vision he could tell the car drove past the census teams' houses. In order to be on this street, this Iraqi car must have gotten through the temporary Iraqi Army checkpoint on the south end of the street. That didn't seem right, but D23, also stationed there, must have allowed it.

"You live here?" Moose asked.

Moose watched the boy, waiting for an answer. The boy probed the inside of his cheek with his tongue, his crab hole eyes glued to Moose.

POP! POP! Just as the boy opened his mouth again, Moose heard two shots. POP! POP! Two more. Not real close. Sounded like AK fire. He looked around. He couldn't tell where the shots came from.

Moose instinctively went down on a knee, weapon raised to eye level. The boy darted back down the alley. Moose's eyes clawed the surrounding area for information: a shooter? Where? He didn't see a threat. He could hear and feel his hard plastic kneepads crumbling bits of concrete.

Then five or six more shots, on automatic, closer. A different weapon. Across the street maybe. Moose looked that way. An Iraqi soldier beside an IA vehicle on the other side of the road had fired. Moose watched him, but couldn't tell where he had fired. Moose looked away, down the street, to see if he could see any evidence of the previous firing. Nothing strange. Buildings with windows. Parked cars. Doors. Laundry hanging from windows and on wires. Satellite dishes on roofs. Palm trees. Few people on the street. He scanned down the street, hesitating a brief second on one thing after another, his eyes gliding smoothly from object to object, not rushed, seeing nothing unordinary. He didn't see anyone who looked as if he'd fired the first shots. Who was the first shooter? Where? Moose didn't know. He looked back at the Iraqi soldiers across the street.

Moose's blood heated up. He could feel it, hot and ravenous, anticipating. He knew its call, its purpose. But he didn't worry about it. He was his own master.

On his left, about 200 meters down the street, on the other side of the far census team, Moose saw two Iraqi civilians running. *Why did they run?*

The Iraqi soldiers huddled next to their comrade that had fired. They appeared fine. Nobody looked wounded. They showed no sense of urgency and hadn't taken cover. Was there no threat? No target? Their inactivity probably meant they didn't think anyone had shot at them. Three of them looked at the man who had fired. Then all looked away, as if they'd heard something else. Not all looked in the same direction. Moose looked around too. He saw nothing suspect. Then the Iraqi soldiers assembled closer, talking together, perplexed expressions on their faces. Moose wished he knew what they were talking about. One made a dismissive hand movement. Moose took all this as further confirmation that they didn't have a specific target. Moose was still down on one knee, weapon up, ready.

"What's the shooting about?" came Wynn's question on the radio hooked on Moose's vest webbing. The crackling of the radio cut the statement short.

Nobody answered.

Turnbeck came up on the radio. "Saw some Iraqi soldiers up there shooting."

Moose assumed that radio communication referred to those Iraqi soldiers across the street from him.

"Maintain your positions. Give me a status check," Wynn directed, curiosity in his voice.

Why had two Iraqis run? Moose still had no idea what the shots were about. Nobody had yet reported anything serious. He rose slowly, keeping his body hunched over, and took the three quick steps necessary to get to the edge of the building so he could look down the alley. No sign of the boy. Nobody in the alley. The sewer gutter bisecting the alley reeked in the sunlight. A wall poster had come unglued at the top edge and flipped down, hanging on the side of a wall like a menu. Moose turned around and looked back out at the main street. The Iraqi soldiers stayed together, talking.

Moose looked down the alley again. He didn't know if the shots had come from that direction. The sound had been muffled because he'd been by the building and under an overhang. Sounds did funny things. The firing could have been anywhere.

All Wolfhound Humvees came up on the radio one after another, reporting: "OK." No Americans had been hit. No one had identified a target. Moose stood back up erect.

Then an Iraqi soldier opened up again. At least half a clip this time. AK47 popping stitched the air. Moose went back down on a knee, focusing on the Iraqi soldiers at the vehicle across from him. Now he thought he could identify which Iraqi had fired. He still pointed his weapon skyward. Still none of the Iraqis had taken cover. One Iraqi soldier pushed another. Maybe they argued. One man looked amused. No one aiming at anything. Two of them held AK47s in one hand, hanging down, muzzles almost in the dirt. None focused on an imminent threat. Must be nothing.

Cooke radioed Wynn: "Sir, we got good observation down the street on the north side here. The IA fired some rounds up in the air. Other than that, don't see anything. The first shots might have come from a couple of streets over. A few LNs looking around up here, looking confused. Can't tell where anything or anybody got shot at."

Moose thought Cooke was inside D24, down at the far end of the street, near the intersection. He would be able to see the Iraqis Moose saw.

"Roger," replied Wynn. "Let's keep our guard up."

Cooke again. "Probably just that crazy celebratory stuff they do. Don't see them doing much, just standing around. Their two vehicles up here are still sitting where they were. Don't think they got shot at."

Iraqis, whether because of stress and excitement, or an urge to communicate by gunfire, often sprayed bullets—

sometimes many bullets—into the sky. So-called "celebratory fire." Maybe the Iraqis believed that wild noise and commotion would win the day somehow. Moose had never seen an Iraqi aim a weapon. Then he remembered the sniper. But supposedly this sniper wasn't Iraqi. Chechen. Different breed.

"I'll send Cengo over to ask them," Wynn told Cooke on the radio. "Let's be sure the Iraqis haven't seen anything. Don't want to get even further behind on this census work if no one's identified a possible hostile shooter, break...If the Iraqis' think it's anything, we'll talk. If not, we'll stay here. Probably just neighborhood nonsense."

Moose looked back down the alley. Quiet. No sign of the boy. The soccer ball remained in the street.

Hearing erratic gunfire was common. Almost every Iraqi seemed to own an AK47. Moose figured the platoon leader and platoon sergeant suspected that whoever had fired was not firing at the platoon. No way could the Americans chase down every weapon discharge.

Just as Moose realized that few pedestrians had been out, a man wearing glasses came out of a building across the street and dumped a bucket of liquid. Then he went back inside his house.

Moose watched Cengo jog up the street to the Iraqi soldiers.

Moose walked over to the corner of the building and took another look down the alley. Still nothing. About 50 meters down the alley a piece of trash fell away from the wall. Moose looked that way. A scrawny cat darted across the passage.

Moose turned back around. Across the street, Cengo was talking. One Iraqi soldier pointed, bending his arm and pointing upwards, towards where Moose was. Maybe he was explaining where the bullets came from. Or where their bullets went. One Iraqi soldier walked over to Cengo and shook his AK violently, holding it in both hands, as if claiming it was too heavy. Cengo bit at the man about something, then walked away. "Said something stupid, I bet," Moose muttered to himself about the Iraqi soldier. "Asshole."

He looked again at the soccer ball. A white ball, normal size, scratched and dirty.

Then he heard talking, and twisted around to see what it was. He faced back in the other direction, southward. Two boys had emerged from another alley, 20 or 30 feet down the street, and started walking in the other direction, their backs to Moose. He watched them carefully. Neither was the boy Moose had seen earlier. Moose thought he heard laughter. One boy carried a loaded plastic bag. Neither appeared to notice the military trucks on the street, and looked unaffected by the recent shooting.

Wynn was back on the radio.

"Cengo said the Iraqis didn't see any one shoot. They don't know what happened, but think it was a couple of blocks over—also seems one of the geniuses thought he could scare off any potential threats by firing some rounds in the sky," Wynn added on the radio, his voice balanced between resignation and ridicule. "Keep a good lookout," Wynn concluded. "We got about another hour here."

Cooke acknowledged Wynn's message.

Moose continued to watch the scene. The two boys who had come out of the second alley disappeared farther down the street. No further sign of the kid who had kicked the soccer ball. The Iraqi soldiers across the street kept chatting amongst themselves unconcernedly. *Ensha Allah*. God Willing. Everything was fate, they believed. What comes would come.

Moose walked back to the corner of the building and took another look down the alley. It was all about nothing.

Three hours into the census work, Wynn was ready for a change. And it remained too dangerous to stay anywhere long. His men were drained, and so was he. The frustrating and stressful meeting with Jassim and the dead boy's family eroded his energy. Maybe they should cut things shorter today, and get back to the FOB. He decided to talk things over with Cooke face-to-face and walked the 50 meters to D24.

"What ya thinking, Sir?" Cooke asked, as Wynn stepped up to the door.

"Based on my count, we've done close to forty more houses. That's good progress. I'm thinking of dittimauwing."

"Headquarters has been quiet," Cooke said, remarking on the lack of radio traffic on the higher net.

"The men are dogged-out. Maybe we ought to make it an early day," Wynn said, trying to avoid appearing too tired himself, while wanting Cooke's affirmation that they should finish for the day.

Cooke looked at his watch like a man searching time for answers. It was 1540. "That was tough in there with the family, wasn't it, Sir?"

Wynn didn't expect that question. Maybe he had accrued respect by sitting down with the family. He nodded, and looked away. Maybe if he didn't talk about it he wouldn't think about it too much.

A small battery-powered radio played music inside Cooke's truck. Wynn didn't recognize the female artist. Cooke reached over and turned the radio volume down, then he stepped out of the truck and walked with Wynn a few feet away. When they stopped, they looked at each other, both assessing.

"We'd planned to do the market. I say we do it. Been a week at least since we've been," Cooke proposed.

Wynn looked at Cooke, expecting another comment.

He must have read Wynn's thinking, because he said, "I ain't heard no grumbling. And even if I had, fuck it. I think we should walk the market. The men will hang tough." Cooke paused, adding, "Anyways, I need to stretch my legs. You been the one out."

Wynn smiled. Cooke did likewise. Wynn hadn't seen another smile all day. He said nothing.

"Sir, once you learn to quit, it becomes a habit."

Wynn's smile faded as Cooke's words sunk in. He stared at his own reflection in Cooke's protective glasses and saw what looked like a sea creature.

"I like that quote," Wynn answered, compressing his lips in confirmation. "Good way of putting it."

"Coach Lombardi." Cooke replied.

23

Six Wolfhound soldiers walked slowly through the Houdoud Al'dena market, which stretched roughly 300 meters, meandered roughly parallel with Route Strawberry, and intersected with several side streets. D21 and D22 were positioned on the north end of the street over-watching Route Strawberry, preventing further vehicle access into the market area. D23 and D24 slowly followed behind the dismounted soldiers, driving in as far as they could from the southeast entrance.

Cooke led the foot patrol, and kept contact with the security vehicles by radio.

Kale was on Cooke's team. Before departing on foot, the platoon sergeant had brushed up against Kale and mouthed a message: "Rock steady, soldier." Then he winked in lieu of a shoulder smack.

Kale tightened his stomach. *Circulation*, he told himself, in order to get his mind on the mission, was what headquarters officially called these walkabouts, whether it was in a neighborhood, along a street, in a market, any place where they might be seen by Iraqis. The leaders were always saying that keeping the American forces visible in the community would somehow help the Iraqi government gain credibility. So they circulated. Kale didn't think equating the presence of American soldiers with an acceptable Iraqi political system was straightforward rational thinking. Then again, was rational thinking possible during war? How, without being out in the shit, could you ever know what was going on? Being there gave them a chance to influence the situation, or "shape" the battlefield, as headquarters often called it.

Kale noticed a large woman dressed head-to-toe in a black burka at the edge of the market. She sauntered, her cloak-like garment sweeping around her, the fabric rolling open and closed, buffeted by her movement, as if the changing shape of the burka illustrated a woman's uncertain place in Arabic society. She appeared to greet a familiar vendor, then continued walking. Other civilians, mostly male, young and old, noisily made deals at the various vendor stalls, all parts and pieces of Iraqi mercantile culture.

The market looked busy today. Still, each of the many small businesses were entirely portable, provisional—no permanent stores had been opened. The vendors set up their tables and wares, some separating themselves with partitions, others rolling their merchandise in on carts. Some of these vendors had been helped in the past by the Wolfhounds. The platoon had once helped a farmer by arranging for an Army Engineer unit to repair a dirt road that provided access to a grove of date palms. Now the man sold the dates in this market. The egg ladies were probably here, the ones the Wolfhounds had given chickens. Cooke called these women the hardest workers in the market. By organizing the concrete barriers that now shielded parts of the marketplace, the Wolfhounds had made the vendors more secure. Activity in the market had steadily increased. No reasonable person could claim the Americans didn't try to help.

As the team walked slowly, Kale's painted the roof lines with his eyes. He thought about the sniper in Bawa Sah. A sniper here would probably be on the roof, or behind windows, in an alley, or even the trunk of a car. One case he'd heard about involved a sniper shooting out of a flap in a closed car trunk. The other major threat was, of course, bombs. Bombs had destroyed markets in other parts of Iraq. So far, this market hadn't been bombed.

Marketplace noises of all sorts clattered and screeched: raised voices, metal on metal, wood scraping, living things and dead things being moved around. Shoppers came in and out between the stands. Most of the stands could disappear in a matter of minutes if they had to. The whole market lived a precarious existence. It reminded Kale of local realities. Daily life lacked safe harbors; any stability was fragile.

The Wolfhounds had walked through this market perhaps ten or twelve times. They drove by approximately twice a week. Every third or fourth time they passed through the area, the Wolfhounds dismounted a patrol and walked the market.

As Cooke's team worked its way into the market, Kale recognized other vendors from previous visits. The one-eyed, one-legged tennis shoe salesman was there. He had a stand with three folding tables near the south entrance, his tables arranged like a horseshoe. From left to right around the horseshoe the shoe sizes went from smaller to larger.

Now Cooke led the team down a side alley no wider than a medieval city's. Several vendors had stands inside this alley, the furthest about 100 feet from the main street.

"Let's check a few of these out," Cooke ordered.

Kale hoped the team wouldn't go too far down the alley, which was too narrow for Humvees, so their trucks couldn't follow. The first stalls included vendors selling clothes. From a distance, the multi-colored clothing on display made the stand look like a flower shop. Mostly clothes for children and teenagers. Some dresses were stored inside thin plastic sleeves, like clothing in a dry cleaner. Kale touched one. The plastic was stiff and crinkly, like the plastic covering of frozen foods. Tables below the clothing displayed jewelry. Farther down the alley a perfume stand hugged the building wall. A vendor displayed little bottles of perfume on top of boxes covered with carpets.

Then Kale noticed a tall thin man standing in the shadows beside larger boxes. Kale couldn't see his face, so he was unsure whether the man watched the Americans. One of the man's hands was hidden behind his back. Something about the way the man stood looked wrong. Kale's senses alerted like a dog's ears going erect. Cooke noticed the man too, raking him hard with a stare. The other Americans hadn't noticed. Cooke moved sideways to get closer to the man. Then Cooke feigned a glance elsewhere, trying to look indifferent.

The Iraqi took a tentative half-step back, dropping the edge of the shadow down from his face to his chest. That triggered Cooke. Kale saw him pivot and bound two steps between the tables to get in front of the man, moving like a cat going after a toy. Cooke's move surprised the Iraqi, and he stepped abruptly out into the light. He looked as if he'd been caught stealing. He was a tall young man with a pocked face and thin mustache. A thin line of smoke rose out of the shadow—the previously hidden hand held a cigarette. The man had merely been smoking.

Cooke beamed at the man, exposing his white teeth as if he were auditioning for toothpaste commercials. He offered a handshake and the man took it.

Kale felt like he got out of race car and into a sauna.

"Perfume?" Cooke asked.

"The best," said the man in scratchy English.

"Do you sell for men and women?"

"Yes, of course."

Cooke made a show of sniffing several bottles. He grinned widely, when encountering one he favored.

"Where from?" Cooke asked him.

"Best places."

"I need to send some of this back to Nada," Cooke commented to Kale, but put the small bottle back on the table. "Very nice," he told the vendor. "Best of luck in your business, Sadi."

"Thank you, Sir," said the Iraqi.

The team turned around and went back out to the main street. The Wolfhounds passed spice dealers with their wares displayed in sacks inside wicker baskets. Next, a heavyset guy worked a couple of wicker baskets full of used cell phones, and a smaller basket of SIM cards. A little further down, on the other side of the street, a man with white-poodle hair displayed 15 or 20 blankets packed in transparent plastic suitcases.

After a few more minutes of walking, the team arrived at the egg ladies' stand. The two sisters acknowledged the Americans with modest familiarity. Cooke picked up an egg and playfully tossed it from hand to hand like a ball. The more elderly and assertive of the two ladies reached half-heartedly to snatch it back from him. She missed. Kale suspected she'd missed intentionally.

Kale took this woman's measure. She looked distinguished. Deep eyes, delicate nose, a certain sad grace earned by survival, perhaps. What a mature Janet Jackson might look like. All he could see was her face. She wore a brown burka with a dark green headscarf and was unmistakably a woman whom life had ridden hard, but she had survived and even staged a recovery of sorts. Survival was now probably her proudest claim. Although the Wolfhounds had known her for months, they knew little about her.

She said something to Cooke in Arabic.

"This is your *baq-shish*," Cooke explained, shrugging her off, using the Arabic word for "payment." He still held the egg in his hand and a sly grin on his face. His expression made it clear that he was teasing her, and that he wasn't stealing an egg. Her eyes sparkled with complicity.

She didn't know what Cooke said. She spoke no English, but understood what he meant.

He had taken an egg from her before—the empty egg shell he kept on his desk.

She warmed as she interacted with Cooke, her mouth relaxing to expose a set of teeth colored like crackerjack candy. Her eyes softened into an appreciative gaze. Kale sensed, too, the never far distant self-protective tendencies that must reside in her, the constant worry about the present, and she must be hoping that her conversation in the market with the Americans would go largely unnoticed.

Cooke wouldn't tease her long. He knew Iraqis didn't want attention, especially not in a public place. The egg lady now spoke directly to Cengo, more quietly. Her face suddenly became serious and drawn, with what Kale read as sadness.

Cooke and Kale looked on as the two Iraqis spoke confidentially for a few seconds. Then, as if forced to convey bad news, her eyes clouded and she lowered her voice. Had she told Cengo about a personal matter, unrelated to the Americans? Her eyes blinked rapidly. She looked from side to side, worried about something. Then she nodded her head towards Cooke as a conspirator might finger a co-conspirator. A wave of urgency rushing over his face, Cengo turned towards Cooke.

"She tell me about talk about some foreigners hiding brick factory," the terp spit out.

"What?" questioned Cooke, confused.

"Terrorists, maybe. She say she hear talk about hiding in dead part brick factory."

"What?" snapped Cooke, still unsure he understood Cengo.

"She say some people talking they hiding there."

"What people? Hiding where?"

Understanding Cengo was difficult. He had taken on the woman's attitude, wanting to avoid drawing attention.

"Who say? How she hear that?"

The egg lady looked down, alarmed by Cooke's agitated voice. They had been there too long. She clinched her bony hands like an old woman at an accident scene. The egg ladies were now anxious for the Wolfhounds to leave.

"Egg Lady say this," Cengo continued

"What factory?" Cooke asked.

Cengo asked the egg lady another question. Though he was speaking Arabic, Kale could tell Cengo was entreating her.

She answered quietly, looking as if she'd entered a place she wanted no part of.

Shoppers continued walking through the area. A few eyed the soldiers the way patients look at cancer doctors. At the far end of the stand, a young woman carrying a baby strapped to her chest stopped to look at the eggs, then moved on.

Kale felt his hands starting to twitch. He had to breathe harder to get the same oxygen.

Cengo translated the egg lady's reply. "She say she hear this from someone she talk to here. Somebody talking. That person angry. Other people angry from the killing of boy. That person say they hear terrorist that kill school boy hiding in old brick factory area. She trust person gave her this information."

Cooke spoke, authority in this voice. "Tell her thank you very much for the information. Tell her to contact us if she hears anything else—and, of course, she shouldn't tell anyone she told us."

The team walked away from the egg stand. Kale could see that Cooke had become highly focused, restless to move on, like a basketball player waiting for the jump. Nevertheless, on Cooke's direction, the team lingered three or four more minutes at other stands. Kale interpreted this to mean the platoon sergeant didn't want to draw too much attention to the egg stand by an abrupt departure.

Kale scanned constantly, trying to notice anyone watching them. Dozens of people were nearby. He sensed strange eyes inspecting him, but he tried not to worry too much. Hopefully none had been within earshot of their conversations with the sisters. He looked back at Cooke. Cooke's eyes were lit. Could these be the people behind the sniper? Surely that's what he was hoping. The excitement of discovery burned inside them and they were silent walking out of the market. The brick factory was several kilometers to the west.

Wynn sat in his Humvee, door ajar, reviewing notes. Cooke walked up unnoticed and leaned in. The two men's faces were within inches of each other. Cooke spoke low and slow, as if he worried that too much enthusiasm would spook the prey, relaying what he had heard from the egg lady. On hearing the news, Wynn churned in thought. Cooke looked like a man thinking he was nearing retribution.

"It's not far from here, Sir," Cooke added, "at most maybe five clicks due west. We can get there in less than thirty minutes."

Both men realized that in this environment five kilometers was far, and it would take longer than that to get there.

"Maybe. But it's a spread-out place we don't know." Wynn replied, uncertain. "We haven't been there and know next to nothing about it. I think the whole place, the factory complex, is about a kilometer long. Big building and lots of little buildings with open spaces around those big smoke stacks. Could be IEDs all over."

Initially, when Cooke had told him what the egg lady had reported, Wynn's hopes had surged, like an athlete sensing triumph—finally a solid clue on another PFA location. But caution and deliberation crept back in, and he let Cooke talk without showing his own hand. They had to get this right.

"We can cordon the whole damn thing. Get the QRF out to reinforce us," Cooke offered.

"That would take a lot of men. Don't think we can get the QRF for this. No imminent danger. You know they rarely scramble the QRF simply because of a suspected insurgent position. No shots have even been fired."

If they went for it now, they would have to go it alone, Wynn thought. He'd need permission from Baumann to leave his battlespace again. Probably could get that. Doubtful about the QRF. They would need more than just the egg lady's second-hand information.

"Problem is, only one road most of the way out there," Cooke continued. "If they have any spotters, and they surely do, they would see us coming."

"Yeah. It's a single two-lane hardball. You go out that road and the brick factory is your destination. Everybody knows it," Wynn replied. "They would see us for miles."

"What about from the north, from Route Orange? Must be access from up there," Cooke said.

"It's also way out of our area. It's not in anybody's active sector. We've never been there."

Reports from the three other platoon trucks came in sequence over the radio. The buzz and beeping sound from all the electronics was comforting. The market patrol had all re-mounted their Humvees, except for Cooke, and maintained security. Wynn and Cooke said nothing for a moment, contemplating their options in heavy silence. Thoughts in the mind are like boats on water; they never stay completely still. Ideas tumble over assumptions. Uncertainty surrounds everything. Swells of emotions jostle analysis. And their boat was riding the edge of a storm.

He remembered the platoon's hasty warehouse mission. They had busted a torture operation, but if they'd been more deliberate and developed the situation, they might have captured or killed more insurgents.

"The advantage to a quick strike is always surprise," Cooke argued. "If we wait or do nothing, the opportunity could be lost."

Wynn hesitated, still deliberating, wanting to be selective in his words. Cooke waited on the decision. The rest of the Wolfhounds, nineteen men in four up-armored Humvees, engines running, waited too.

"Don't think anybody suspected you of getting important information from her, do you?" Wynn asked, referring to the egg lady, and changing the subject slightly.

"Never sure, Sir. Doubt it. We chitchatted as long with several vendors. And we don't always talk to the same ones."

Wynn had an uneasy feeling every time an informant told them anything. The informant inevitably was playing with fire. Retaliation by insurgents could be brutal. Torture. Murdered families. Beheadings. However, getting information from cooperative locals was the only way. Without the Iraqis taking risks, it was impossible to make gains against the insurgency.

He could call CPT Baumann and discuss the whole thing with him. Then however it turned out, the decision would get made.

"Let me call the CO. See what he thinks."

"OK," Cooke agreed.

Cooke stepped away, separating himself from Wynn's pending conversation with Baumann, but still close enough to hear. He'd given his professional opinion and now seemed resigned to any decision. Wynn picked up the radio to call the commander and looked at Cooke. SFC Cooke, wearing full battle rattle and protective glasses, looked like a gigantic insect ready to strike. He walked around to the driver's side of D21, opened the door, and gave Gung a playful punch in the arm.

"No Purple Heart today, Sarge," Gung protested. Gung's gloved hands gripped the steering wheel firmly. He wasn't in the debate and didn't appear to care one way or the other. He was ready either way.

Within minutes, Wynn had Baumann on the radio. The commander had the same view that Wynn did. Don't be hasty. They should develop the situation more. Do deliberate planning. Baumann felt they would be able to get eyes on the site with UAVs. So that was it.

Wynn signaled to Cooke to come back over, and told him.

"We need better Intel to confirm. Do deliberate planning, the CO said. We can't rush out of sector without better Intel. To make this work we have to be sure. Then plan an operation. We rush and we could ruin it. If something's there, we should find out exactly where and what. Then strike. Strike smart and hard."

Cooke stayed quiet and chewed his disappointment.

Wynn took another look at the computer map, then continued. "I'll put it all into HQ on the way back. The CO thinks he can make a UAV flyover happen. See if we can get a read on whether someone is really camping out in the brick factory. Maybe specify the location for us. See what we're up against. Then he'll decide what kind of force package to put together."

Wynn saw Cooke wasn't happy with the decision. He was a man of action. Win with boldness. No taking a knee when the fight was on. But they had to be smart before they could fight well. Baumann thought the same. Aerial surveillance could see the whole complex, see evidence of people, and maybe confirm any vehicular traffic.

Cooke was still unconvinced.

"Sergeant Cooke, you said yourself it would be hard to get out there undetected. Since we have suspicions, but know next to nothing about the factory, we have to be careful. Tip them off or don't find them and we might fuck up our chances."

Cooke puckered his lips. He looked down, as if studying his boots, considering what Wynn had said. Deep creases lined his forehead like lost opportunity marks. Sweat glistened on his temples and jaw, soaking his helmet chin strap.

"Roger," Cooke blurted out finally, the 14 years of military subordination and loyalty evident.

"Let's get back, Sergeant Cooke, and get this thing rolling."

"Ever gotten your ass kicked, Sir?" Cooke asked Wynn, in the messhall about two hours later.

It was 1935, and the two men were having dinner together.

"No," Wynn answered, quashing a grin.

Cooke said, "Had mine kicked four or five times. The first time, I remember it well, was in the second grade. A fifth-grade kid yanked me up on the playground and knee-butted me to the head. Almost knocked me out. Growing up in Milwaukee, the rivalry between the Packers and the Bears was fierce. The biggest kid in the fifth grade was a dumb Bears fan. And you know me, I wore a Packers jersey two or three times a week already in the second grade. That was my first experience with bullies. Haven't had any tolerance for bullies since."

Wynn watched Cooke take a deep breath. His massive chest looked like a sea turtle shell. Few bullies would mess with Cooke today.

"And these terrorist motherfuckers," Cooke continued, "Deliberately killing women and children—they're just the latest incarnation of bullies."

Wynn caught something in his peripheral vision. Gung headed towards them.

"They say we're the world's policeman," Cooke added. "And, by God, the world still does need policing."

"Sir, the CO is calling for you," Gung said, now standing beside Wynn's table.

"Where is he?"

"Back at the company, Sir. He said find you and send you back."

"OK, thanks."

Wynn turned to Cooke and said, "I bet it has to do with the brick factory. Hope they got the fly over."

"Me too," Cooke replied. "We gotta nail that bitch."

Wynn admired Cooke's can-do attitude. Ever ready to go right back at it. The guy was like a fullback who always wants the ball.

"I'll go see him now, see the latest." Wynn left. Cooke remained seated, not ready to leave. Wynn sensed Cooke's eyes on him, a sharp hopefulness in his face. He remembered Cooke wanting to go straight to the brick factory earlier. Wynn, too, was anxious for the mission. Either the UAV over-flight hadn't happened or it had. And if what the bird saw in the brick factory confirmed possible insurgent activity, that meant a mission to investigate on the ground would follow shortly. He hoped the Wolfhounds would be part of it.

"I'll be back in my hooch by 2100, Sir," Cooke, looking at his watch, called after Wynn. "Come see me after. Meantime I'll knock on some doors."

By his comment, Wynn knew Cooke intended to go check on the platoon's soldiers. Cooke, at night, would regularly go door-to-door of the Wolfhound trailers, making sure the men were OK. Wynn thought again about Kale. Maybe Cooke would get some one-on-one time with him.

It was grey dusk outside now, nearly 2000. A thin stripe of orange lay on the horizon, the sun's final lingering kiss. Wynn watched the slowly sinking orange as he made his way westward across the gravel-covered parking lot and the dirt road bisecting the FOB to the passage leading down the long row of company headquarters buildings. Fine powder from the road surface wafted upward, filling his nostrils with a dry chalk-like scent.

All four battalion companies' headquarters stood side-by-side on this road. Wynn hurried, pondering options the whole way. If insurgents were hiding in the brick factory, how heavily would they be armed? What would Baumann plan? A night operation?

Wynn's men had been provisionally released and not scheduled to meet up again until 0630 tomorrow. If something had to happen earlier, he'd have to get the word out. By time he got back, his men might be in bed.

Wynn arrived at D Company headquarters and went inside. Baumann's office door was closed. Wynn knocked, then opened the door.

"Hold on. Need another minute here," Baumann shouted from inside as soon as Wynn cracked the door. As he shut the door again, Wynn could see First Sergeant Keith inside. The crusty Keith had an exasperated, plaintive look on his face, as if he was asking for something he knew he couldn't get. Wynn suspected Keith might be talking to the CO about the unit leave schedule. Soldiers had been rotating out for their two-week vacations back home. Baumann had recently re-juggled the list. That had caused grumbling in the ranks. The numbers of soldiers that could be gone at any one time was restricted, and the guys didn't understand the timing. Each man wanted leave when he wanted it. Of course that couldn't happen. Manpower had to remain sufficient to take care of all missions. The approved ratios meant the leave schedule would drag out past the ninth month in country for some of the soldiers. Keith had taken it on as a personal project to get everyone out and back before the battalion reached its eight-month mark in Iraq. Baumann argued his hands were tied.

In less than a minute, Baumann opened the door. "Come on in," he said to Wynn. The First Sergeant walked out without comment, expressionless.

Wynn saw agitation on his commander's face. Baumann's day never ended. Men constantly came to him with problems, looking for decisions. Wynn had more than enough to keep him busy with just one platoon. He shut the door.

"Battalion sent a UAV over the brick factory," Baumann said straightaway. "It looks like we've got bad dudes there. You guys did well. I got to watch some video stream at the TOC earlier. People appear holed-up in the old brick kilns, and maybe in the big building. A couple vehicles parked. And two guys carried some heavy stuff wrapped in blankets out of a car, possibly weapons, inside one of the kilns. Another two guys outside holding AKs. Not a typical family dinner party. Had the look of the usual thugs. The place definitely needs checking out."

Wynn hadn't said anything. He listened to Baumann, wondering what would come next.

"Battalion will let me know if they see anything else. They're going to make several more over flights tonight, and give us any updates. I'm going to sit down now and plan the operation. I want you and the rest of the platoon leaders to come back here at 2100."

"Roger, Sir," Wynn said. "I'll be back then."

In a few minutes, Wynn was at Cooke's trailer. Wynn knocked. No answer. He waited by the door a moment. He couldn't call Cooke on the radio; Wynn's radio was recharging in his trailer. Only Wynn had an Iraqi cell phone. Cooke must be out doing his door knocking, so Wynn started walking around the company trailer area to see if he would see or hear Cooke. The area was quiet. He saw several men playing cards between the trailers. He walked past the three quads of trailers where his men had assigned quarters and every door was shut. Dim interior light leaked out of curtained windows and between cracks in doors. Cooke might be inside a trailer doing footlocker counseling with a platoon soldier. Wynn decided not to interrupt. These guys needed all the close attention their platoon sergeant could give them. He decided to leave a note under Cooke's door and went back to Cooke's trailer. Taking a notepad out of his shoulder pocket, he wrote: *OPORD at 2100.*

LOOKS LIKE IT'S A GO. WILL COME BY AFTER. He slid the note under the bottom of Cooke's trailer door.

Cooke had about finished his rounds. He'd tried to share a gut-check moment with most of the men. Some had welcomed him with distant questioning eyes, stares of men grown tired by unsatisfactory waiting, the desire for something better and more conclusive radiating out of their bones. His response to each man was a positive phrase or two, intended as verbal caffeine, or maybe a head rub—he'd grind his big brown fingers into the man's scalp—hoping to impart motivation by physical contact. He loved his men. He loved leading them. It was a kind of warrior's romance.

He'd spotted Kale and Moose walking back from the latrine to their trailers. Cooke was pleased to see them together. The pair stopped when they saw him. Cooke greeted them. "How are my two favorite heathens tonight?" Neither man responded right away.

After long seconds of motionless dancing, while Cooke sampled their vitals with his eyes, Kale blurted, "Moose needed an escort to the little boys' facilities."

"That's bullshit," Moose retorted, and looked at Kale in amazement.

All three men laughed.

Cooke toyed with them a few moments longer; the exchange of words an obvious attempt by him to take a sample and check reflexes. He wanted them to know, and they knew. Cooke was happy Kale had played a comic card. Things seemed stabler. Reading Moose's eyes, Cooke concluded that Moose sensed that the platoon sergeant wanted a personal report on Kale.

"Truth is, Sarge, Kale don't need me to help him pull up his pants anymore. And if he asked me to pull them down, I wouldn't fucking do it," Moose said.

Cooke had his answer. Kale remained stable, if guarded.

No man wanted to be on the ground when others around him were walking erect. He felt Kale would keep walking.

Now Cooke sat in the trailer shared by Turnbeck, Pauls and Singleton, and listened to them brief him on the readiness of their trucks and their men. Each man had extra gravity in his voice and Cooke sensed the approach of something absolutely inevitable. He couldn't stop it, and didn't want to. Wynn would be back soon. They would have orders for an operation to the brick factory. Then, when the designated time came, the platoon would mount up, the gates of FOB Apache would open, their convoy would ride out, and the men and their equipment would again become a martial projectile to be thrown by U.S. Army at a hostile world.

"Super," Cooke said, when his NCOs had finished. "This much I know: whatever they have us do, every man will put his whole ass into it."

Everybody would be OK. Those fuckers in PFA better be saying their prayers. He slid his hand into his left pants pocket and felt Ramirez's name tape.

24

CPT Baumann had decided to lead the brick factory operation himself, using 2nd and 3rd platoons. Third platoon would take a blocking position south of the brick factory complex, and provide covering fire. The Wolfhounds would conduct the raid.

One platoon of soldiers didn't give Baumann the manpower he needed to dominate the area. Attempting the operation with too few men increased the likelihood of failure. Baumann wanted the extra assurance of larger numbers. This meant that D Company would have two platoons outside their assigned sectors for the duration of the operation.

After Baumann's initial comments, Wynn and the others waited in silence while their commander made a final check of his notes and prepared to brief the Operations Order. Baumann now wore glasses, magnifying his blue eyes and making him look older and more intelligent. His prominent forehead had chased his hairline rearward more rapidly than his youth would have suggested. His large mouth and puffy cheeks were swollen like a boxer's. He must have gotten a haircut today; his remaining hair was mere stubble, giving him the look of a man expecting a very serious appointment. Sometimes Baumann acted aloof, but Wynn didn't think this was the impression he intended to convey. Wynn believed the captain was a fair man. He was thoughtful. He wasn't a screamer. Didn't micromanage. A bit distant perhaps, but fair. The same general description had been used about Wynn.

Wynn was energized by the pending operation, but maintained his usual outer calm. He kept thinking how lucky they would be if the egg lady's tip proved correct. Could the brick factory people be PFA? Maybe merely squatters. Normally the insurgent cells tried to embed deep in the communities, so they could blend in. Hiding out in the isolated brick factory didn't fit with that. If they were insurgents, would the group include the female sniper?

Aerial surveillance had confirmed the presence of a small number of people in the brick factory. Vehicular traffic had been seen coming in and out of the complex. Photos showed two cars parked. Two or three structures showed evidence of activity. Most of the structures in the brick factory complex— actually abandoned brick kilns—looked like clay igloos. The kilns were maybe 20 feet in diameter, each penetrated by a cylindrical chimney. Saddam had built a new brick factory on the site in the early 1980s. This factory, which had tall smoke stacks like a power plant, appeared abandoned and stripped. As far as anyone knew, no bricks had been produced in any of the buildings since before the war.

Baumann stood up and walked the few feet over to a white marking board hanging on the wall, and began to sketch with a black felt pen. Each lieutenant already had a map in his hands. Baumann sketched for several minutes as the others waited.

1LT Smith took notes on a pad he held on his knee. He looked especially tired; his bloodshot eyes bulged like mushrooms. He was taking sleeping pills again.

2LT D'Augostino sat back with his arms folded and every minute or so he'd pull his mustache with his lower lip. D'Augostino had prior enlisted service. Wynn envied him for that, because of the extra experience it gave him.

About a minute later, back still turned to the room, Baumann started briefing the formal operations order by describing the enemy situation. He continued drawing on the board.

"In our battlespace the enemy continues to strike at Coalition and Iraqi forces with a combination of improvised explosives, small arms fire, periodic rocket attacks, and direct fire. Recent use of IEDs includes multi-shell explosives. One detonation in 3rd Battalion's AOR three days ago destroyed a tank. The bomb was constructed of four 155mm rounds stacked vertically, wired to a rudimentary pressure plate. The enemy followed up the IED with small arms fire. About one-third of recent IED attacks involve complex attacks, where a secondary attack follows the first. The composition of the anti-Iraq forces continues to be a combination of religious radicals, foreign terrorist groups such as Al Qaeda, former Saddam regime members, Iranian special militia members, and other criminal elements, with those groups with foreign connections reported to be on the increase. Two days ago Alpha Company discovered a large munitions cache. That cache included several old Soviet anti-tank mines. And, of course," he paused, "all of you know the purpose of this particular mission is a follow-up on a lead indicating insurgents might be hiding in this brick factory."

Baumann tapped the board periodically for emphasis. He spoke officiously, without nuance or elaboration, confident that those in the room were well informed. To him it was all business. While Baumann reviewed recent enemy activities, Wynn marveled at the diversity of the forces arrayed against them. It would be so much more straightforward if they had only one enemy, like the Nazis, instead of this assortment of nebulous bad characters. Why did this war have to be so complex? A futile question. It was what it was. You don't get to pick your wars.

Baumann continued, "The enemy may have emplaced booby traps along our planned routes of march. This could include both remote and command detonated devices. The brick factory complex might be wired with different explosives, and I've requested that an EOD team be on quick standby. We can expect the enemy to shoot at us with small arms and possibly light machine guns. Observation from positions inside the complex on our access routes is good. They'll likely see us coming. And you all know they may have a capable sniper on their team. But during early movement, we'll have darkness on our side."

Baumann hadn't looked at them, speaking while facing the white board. Then he turned away from the board, stepping aside so they could see what he'd sketched. Wynn slid his chair over to see. Baumann pointed to three lines on the board sequentially, all of which represented the access roads into the complex.

"These are the access roads. Refer to your maps if you need to. Two—these two," Baumann said, pointing to the roads entering from the east and north, taping the white board with his pen, "appear to be the most used. Twice in the last six hours vehicular traffic was seen using the north route. We know the road is OK on the east route, too, but haven't seen it used in the last six hours. The exact condition of the south route is unknown, but that road appears to be abandoned. It has a half-broken bridge on it located here, making it impassable for cars." He pointed to the bridge he drew on the sketch that wasn't visible on their military maps.

"For Friendly forces, we'll have an attack helicopter team on stand-by, a UAV in the air, as well as the EOD team. Fox Battery is in support with the big guns. As we close on the objective, as I said, the UAV asset will give me real-time information.

"First Platoon will continue operations in their sector." Baumann turned to look at Smith, "and will not be impacted by this operation. Battalion QRF remains designated as the QRF, and would be the go-to element—not 1st platoon—if we need more guns. Hopefully we won't. Any questions so far?"

No one spoke.

Baumann's eyes circled the room, lingering a couple of seconds on each man. Wynn could see he enjoyed the audience, his own performance, and the control he had over them. Like an orchestra conductor in the middle of a concert, except this orchestra carried guns instead of musical instruments. Power always felt good. Even dangerous power.

"Our mission. Delta Company will advance to objective Endzone, secure it, searching for any insurgent activity in the area, seize the objective, and destroy or capture any enemy discovered. OK?" *Endzone* was one of a number of sports terms Baumann chose as names to identify locations on his sketch.

The commander again surveyed the room, looking at each of his subordinates. Nothing communicated silently from any of them suggested he should stop or restate anything, so he began again.

"We'll execute like this. 2nd platoon will be the assault force."

Baumann began describing the details of how they would execute the mission. Wynn listened and watched attentively, ticking off in his mind the things he knew should be addressed, paying particular attention to time schedules, such as departure times, noting the black lines and circles Baumann had sketched on the white board. Both platoons, he ordered, would depart the FOB at 0345, 3rd platoon leading the company convoy. Each would arrive at the route turn-off checkpoints at approximately 0415, then at their respective second checkpoints at approximately 0445. Assault time for 2nd platoon on the objective would then be approximately 0515. Baumann emphasized he wanted 3rd platoon to have enough time to set up their blocking position.

"I don't want any squirters getting away."

Wynn tried to picture the operation. The satellite photographs of the ground passed around earlier had helped. Periodically, he referred to the map on his lap. But nobody in the room had been to the brick factory before. Everything they talked about, everything Baumann told them, was all based on maps and aerial reconnaissance. But Wynn wasn't concerned about that. Neither, evidently, was Baumann.

Baumann now described how 3rd platoon would approach the brick factory from the east route. To do this he used the sketch to show D'Augostino how he wanted 3rd platoon to travel and where it should set up. Baumann moved his finger along the sketch markings like a man examining a big city map. He left the exact positioning up to D'Augostino, and said so, but he mentioned issues and places he was most concerned about. Baumann spoke without notes for several minutes, explaining the terrain and the likely best places for clear observation outward away from the objective and inward towards the objective. Wynn waited patiently for 2nd platoon's orders.

The Wolfhounds would be anxious to go no matter the dangers. They were hungry to avenge the sniper, hungry to retaliate for the death of that boy, hungry to achieve anything they could rightly call a victory. On most days the platoon was in reaction mode, visiting scenes of calamity, or combing for information or investigating thin leads, which often felt like stumbling around in the dark. This day would be different.

Baumann described the structures in the vicinity of Objective Endzone. "The main building is about one-hundred-fifty by five-hundred feet. We believe it's been stripped. There are penetrations in the roof and numerous openings in the walls. Speculation is that everything useful was stolen. Aerial observation shows no recent activity."

1SG Keith spoke up. "Simply because we haven't seen anyone during the short periods the UAV flew over don't mean nobody's home. Might be the best place to hide people or things."

"Absolutely," Baumann answered. "We'll check it out."

"Walls, brick or sheet metal on that thing, Sir?" Keith asked.

"Looks like a combination. I suspect all the sheet metal would have been stolen."

"Yeah."

Baumann continued, "The Wolfhounds will proceed via the north route, passing checkpoint Third Base before turning south towards the objective. Christian, by the time you get here," Baumann tapped a place on the sketch, "you'll want to notify your assault teams to get ready for dismount. If we have not encountered enemy fire by this point, you'll position two of your vehicles here." Baumann again used his marker to trace this proposed movement on the board. He looked to Wynn for a confirmation, then continued.

"2nd platoon, leaving gunners and drivers in the trucks, will proceed dismounted towards these kilns." He drew another circle around the Endzone area. "Once reaching the objective area, you will search each of these six kilns here."

Baumann sharply tapped a few smaller, numbered circles he'd made on the white board sketch. "Here are the six kilns nearest to where activity has been seen."

"This area about a hundred meters southwest of the factory is where we saw two vehicles. And this one..." He placed his pen on a three-inch diameter circle on the sketch and pressed against it, as if he were holding it in place. "This kiln is the one people were seen coming in and out of." All the kilns he had pointed to were inside the larger circle labeled Endzone. "Make sure you get the kiln numbers correct.

"This is the area I want you to hit hardest."

Baumann's eyes drilled into Wynn's, seeking acknowledgement. Wynn understood and nodded affirmatively, but said nothing.

"Take the platoon here." Baumann pointed to an area just north of Endzone, "Confirm with me that 3rd platoon is in position, then hit these kilns one by one. Once you have eyes on, you can use your best judgment which one to start with. I'll be in my Humvee in your convoy. Keep me informed. I've numbered these kilns one through six on the board, starting with this one, going clockwise."

Wynn focused on the white board sketch. He carefully drew a sketch in his notebook and numbered the kilns, duplicating what Baumann had drawn. Baumann, noticing Wynn drawing, paused briefly.

Wynn wanted to ask when they would get their last aerial report from the drone. He wanted timely information before sending his platoon in, but decided to wait until the end of the brief to ask.

Baumann kept going. "Service and Support by Standard Operating Procedures. Top will have extra Class V in his truck for crew-served resupply. When the Wolfhounds turn here," Baumann pointed to the intersection of Route Cherry and the north route into the brick factory, "position yourself about a hundred meters in from that intersection and wait. Each platoon retains its organic medics."

"As I mentioned, I'll be with 2nd platoon. SOP remains in effect for communications."

After reminding them of several other standard procedures, Baumann turned around, hands on hips, and asked again whether the group had any questions. His eyes broadcast performance satisfaction.

"Will we get a final aerial confirmation of what's on the ground at the objective before we hit it?" Wynn asked.

"Yes, I have a bird on target at 0500 to do one more survey. That UAV will be on station until 0600. That should give us the latest information before we arrive on the objective."

The lieutenants asked Baumann additional questions, then Keith spoke up, a mischievous look on his face, "Sir, I have one more question. If the bitch sniper is there, can we scalp her?"

Everyone laughed. Even Baumann cracked a smile. He looked around the room, thinking about what to reply.

"Sometimes, First Sergeant, we can wish we lived in the eighteenth century."

DAY SEVEN

25

WYNN WOKE EARLY, very early. He looked at his watch—0253. He'd slept fitfully, never more than 30 minutes consecutively, feeling suspended between dreams and full consciousness. Details of the pending brick factory operation cycled over and over in his head, hard pieces of information tumbling in his semi-consciousness, like ice from an ice maker. Awake now, guilt came knocking, as if he was forgetting something but didn't know what. He'd rarely had trouble sleeping, even here. His body always needed sleep, took it ravenously, but never too much. He got out of bed. Still in his skivvies, he cracked his door and looked outside. Soon they would once again face the hot beating sun, each man paying tribute with his sweat.

Every sound around him was manmade. The fans of hundreds of Chinese air conditioners spun. Generators groaned steadily. The ever-present hum of modern technology on the FOB droned monotonously, a long, low echo of industrialization.

Fully awake now, Wynn felt his confidence coming back, measured but there. He and his men would go on the mission this morning because that is what they had to do. It was like that, day in and day out, and why they were here. Part of it was that simple. He knew that each man might ponder it, second guess their purpose—and that wasn't wrong. He did, too. Inevitably, a worthy man journeyed alone every day on a rocky trail of questions, resolutely, honorably, knowing that what he could control or change was minor, satisfied to take the good journey and stay the course. Sometimes just being there was the main thing.

They had a solid plan today. With two platoons they should have enough firepower for most contingencies. The biggest negative was their lack of familiarity with the ground. During the preceding months, the battalion had focused on the city. Most American units were near larger urban areas, leaving thousands of square miles of rural country relatively unattended. Hence they knew little about large parts of Iraq. Everybody talked about boots on the ground. Not enough boots meant economizing resources, particularly manpower. Developing the Iraqi security forces was the answer. Most questions had one answer: The Iraqis. Need more security: get the Iraqi Forces up and running. Need to improve the local communities' connection with the government: get the Iraqi Forces to do it. Need to increase information flow between different tribal groups: get the Iraqis to do it. The problem was that the Iraqis weren't ready. Could they ever be? The same ethnic and religious conflicts that riddled Iraqi society inevitably existed in their Army and Police.

Had to get his mind off the big questions. Can't debate those ideas right now. They had a specific mission today— their little part of the war. He didn't know whether all the pieces would eventually come together or not. If they were successful in clearing out an insurgent cell today, then they would have a little victory. Little victories might be all they could get in this kind of war.

"Gimme another rag," Ortiz yelled up at Moose.

"What—ya eating those things, buddy?" Moose, in D24's turret, badgered Ortiz while reaching into a box of rags, mostly cut-up pieces of Army T-shirts. He tossed a rag down.

The two men made sure D24 was ready to go. Ortiz checked the Humvee fluids. Moose continued working his .50 caliber. He felt the resistance of the bolt as he pulled and watched the sliding mechanism glide easily back and forth. It was good. He enjoyed a business relationship with his gun. He could feel a partnership in violence in his bones. I take care of you; you take care of me. He closed the weapon cover and did another function check, enjoying the sounds of the devil's engineering.

Moose looked down inside the truck. Eight green ammo cans. He wanted more. Usually he carried ten. Probably no one had extra, but he would check with the other gunners once everyone was in the motor pool.

Ortiz was now below him in the driver's seat, checking the vehicle's lights, wipers, gauges, locks, radios, running the truck through the motions. Moose marveled how the short and stocky Hispanic, a package of spiny arms and legs and slightly overweight torso, moved nimbly about. Inside the truck, Ortiz was like a spider dancing in its web. The spider had already walked around the truck several times, ducking underneath, opening the hood, looking for any indicators of trouble. It had been weeks, fortunately, since any of the Wolfhound trucks had had serious maintenance problems. But shit happened. Three of the platoon's Humvees had been in country for about two years and each had nearly 100,000 miles. The fourth vehicle, seven months newer, had replaced another vehicle after a culvert roll-over accident.

The Wolfhounds did what maintenance they could on the trucks. More complicated stuff, the maintenance unit and KBR took care of.

"Hey, man, think we'll get into some shit today?" Ortiz yelled up to Moose. The big gunner was silent a second as he glanced down at Ortiz.

Moose grinned. "We need some, man. My gun's hungry."

"Hungry, eh," Ortiz chortled. "Need to feed it some Hajjis?" Ortiz laughed at his own logic, and his two gold-capped teeth said hello.

"Like an Aztec sacrifice or something? Get some blood for America?" Ortiz offered as answer to his own question.

Moose liked that. He stroked his hand along the heavy black weapon's feed tray as if he was soothing a restless animal.

"That's why Uncle Sam bought this baby," Moose replied, pointing to the big .50 cal. "Need to get our money's worth."

Cooke walked over to their truck. The platoon sergeant looked as if his favorite football team had lost in overtime. Was he angry? Moose wondered. Probably he wasn't. Just ready to go, bleeding anticipation. The man ate angry for breakfast and was always ready to go, always loaded. He wouldn't tolerate wasting time. Cooke, sweat already collecting in the deep black wrinkles lining his forehead, eyed Moose and Ortiz and fired a question barbed with paternalism.

"You knuckleheads got my honey ready?"

Nobody answered him.

Moose looked back and forth from Cooke to Ortiz to the truck. Cooke was talking about the truck. It was his truck. Everyone considered their Humvee their truck. Of course, being platoon sergeant, Cooke had a more authoritative claim than the rest of them. Cooke looked straight at him, expecting an answer.

"Some Iraqi crud eat your tongue overnight, big boy?" Cooke asked, his eyes fixed on Moose.

"Roger that," Moose sputtered finally, clumsily, suppressing a smile, hoping to avoid more of Cooke's criticism.

When leadership cared, things got maintained, and the Wolfhounds couldn't get anywhere without their trucks. Some guys got possessive about the four-wheeled monsters—hence the lingo of ownership. Trucks typically had nicknames, so D24 was Cooke's "Honey."

Cooke now stared at Ortiz. Ortiz finally snapped out of whatever he was thinking about and addressed Cooke. "We due a sacrifice, Papa—my thousand-year-old Aztec blood tells me we gonna get some today."

Wynn and Cooke briefed the platoon on CPT Baumann's plan. Wynn spoke without emotion, sternly, rarely looking up, repeatedly pointing to the map and sketch he'd drawn, making sure that the target kilns were identified and understood by everyone. He gave the others time to take notes and make their own sketches. Several times, Wynn looked over the sketches his subordinates were making, checking for accuracy.

Cooke explained who would man the two dismounted teams, and how they would operate. Wynn would lead Wolf One, and Pauls would lead Wolf Two. Cooke would command the gun trucks.

Wynn briefed that Baumann would choose one of two options before reaching the objective. The option chosen would depend on whether the newer brick factory would be bypassed or searched. Either way, the target kilns were the main objective.

The men asked questions about the plan. Wynn answered several; Cooke, the others. Pauls asked about friendly fire. Since more than one platoon was involved in this operation, communication and coordination would be even more important.

Then Wynn and Cooke asked questions, in turn, testing the men's recall of the plan, making sure they were ready.

After a few more minutes of discussion, Wynn said, "We have a chance to do some real good here today. Ready to go?"

He looked around at the men. Every man returned the look. Some had that flat, distant look men have when the pressure of the group, more than the motivation of the individual, pushes them on. Silent anticipation washed over them all. They were with him. He felt stronger because of that.

He checked his watch. They'd kept within the 30 minutes he'd intended for the briefing.

"I hope we get that bitch," said Ulricht, as if he would kill her with his teeth.

"HOOAH!" someone shouted.

26

The Wolfhounds left FOB Apache on schedule with Baumann's truck following their convoy. After they had passed out of the company battlespace, the first four kilometers of road, clean and straight, cut through former agricultural areas. Then came areas of poorer-quality residential construction, the houses not much more than undistinguishable concrete boxes.

Because of the infrequent Coalition use of this particular road, the history of IED attacks was low. Even so, Wynn watched the surroundings closely as the Wolfhounds drove fast in the final 30 minutes before daylight. They made good progress. He remained cautiously optimistic that the patrol would arrive at the final checkpoint according to schedule.

Around a long curve in the road ahead, a car was parked on the roadside. Even from nearly half a kilometer away, Wynn could tell it was a small dark-color car. It appeared empty, probably belonging to a resident on this street. A dilapidated building stood about 30 meters from the car. Wynn focused hard on the car. No radio comment yet from Turnbeck.

Was the car lower to the ground than normal? One VBIED packed ten artillery rounds in a trunk. Ten rounds—that's more than 500 pounds. That car's backend must have nearly touched the road. Maybe blankets or boxes or something inside concealed things? The usual tension rose. He had to trust Turnbeck's evaluation.

The convoy got closer. Turnbeck still hadn't spoken. Then, very close, the car looked empty.

"Not a problem," reported Turnbeck sharply, as if hearing Wynn's question.

D22 passed the car. Then D21. Then the others. Nothing happened.

Wynn concentrated on what was to come. For the next few minutes, he did another methodical review of the assault plan, going over all the important details. Achieving surprise was important. Undetected, they would be much more likely to kill or capture whoever was in the brick factory. He clicked off each requirement in his mind like a man checking a grocery list.

He checked his watch again. 0407. The intersection where they would turn-off the paved road was 5 to 7 minutes away. At that turn-off, Baumann would check with battalion on any new activity observed by the UAV. Baumann would then give final orders to go in.

If the egg lady was right, the Wolfhounds would have to find another way to reward her. Wynn hoped she was still safe. The fact of her revealing this information was interesting. Undoubtedly, something about her relationship with the Wolfhounds had encouraged her to confide.

Moose felt amped as the Wolfhound convoy moved rapidly toward the brick factory: four screaming truck engines, 16 rubber tires grinding away at the road, electronics packages singing and blinking inside each machine, every man in his place, all a part of the motion and purpose and anticipation of the mission. Today was another great adventure, and he was part of it. It always amazed him how the platoon operated as a team, as part of a big team: Team Army. It was as if they'd broken huddle and were on the line of scrimmage waiting for the snap of the ball in a championship game.

He kept focusing on what was coming next, of his part in it, of what might go wrong and how to respond. Any violence encountered was a necessary part of the journey. No reconsiderations. No going back. This was it.

Although it was 0415, the outside temperature was inching up. A thin crack of sun like spilled orange juice seeped out from the horizon. He glanced down inside the truck, wondering what the others were thinking. Then he thought about Kale. Kale, like Moose, was assigned to one of the dismount teams. Maybe Cooke's idea of a confidence builder. Moose felt resigned about Kale. No matter what, it was up to each man to acquit himself well.

He disengaged the lock on the gun turret and rotated it around to the right, and practiced picking up targets while on the move.

"Anything up?" Cooke asked from below, when he noticed Moose's movement.

"No. Just getting ready."

Part of why he'd joined the Army was because it still celebrated the manly virtues. Traits he felt were right for real men were embodied in the Army. Strength. Fortitude. Courage. Skill under extreme stress.

The convoy approached the turn-off, and Moose could see the lead vehicle begin to slow down.

"Get ready to kick ass!" Cooke said loudly.

Cuebas saw it first: a black blur in his peripheral vision, like a bird taking off. The rocket came at them like a star drilling down, racing, screaming across the sky, passing over D24's turret. TRUNUNK! Didn't hit them, he thought. Frantic perceptions tumbled over his sensations so fast he felt dizzy. Nothing obviously wrong inside the Humvee. Did it hit Moose? He was partly exposed out of the turret. Jesus! Bastards are shooting RPGs at us. His sphincter muscle tensed as if he'd been electrocuted. Jesus. Slow enough you could see it fly at you.

Ortiz slammed the accelerator down. The truck leaped. Cuebas wished it would go faster.

PAASACKKK. The RPG skipped off the ground 75 meters past them and exploded. First time he'd had a rocket shot at him. No big fire burst. No mushroom cloud.

Cooke shouted on the radio, reporting the RPG.

Seconds later, Ortiz turned the truck to the right and stopped fast, jolting everyone. He hoped to give Moose a better chance to engage the target, but Moose hadn't seen a shooter.

"Go. Go. Go..." Cooke howled. "Keep this mother going! What the fuck you doing? I didn't say stop."

Ortiz took off again. A cloud of dust rolled over the vehicle from the back, hiding it, as if the temporary disappearance was the desert's way of chastising a scurrilous American presence. Nobody in the truck could see anything.

Moose, head out of the turret, wearing goggles, sand rag around his mouth, choked in the thick dust. He tasted sand, the atomized grit mixing with his saliva. He ignored it. Didn't matter. Would just make for a bigger spit when he had a chance. The rolling dust disappeared and visibility returned.

Everyone scanned, searched, questioned.

Moose coughed. And coughed again. Loud, raspy, as if he was suffocating.

"You good, man?" Cooke called up to him, without looking.

Cuebas looked frontwards now, trying to reorient. He felt dizzy, unsure, like he'd been sleeping and someone had cut the lights on. Moose hadn't answered Cooke.

"Hey, you OK?" Cooke asked again.

Still no answer.

Men in Humvees had been cut in half by RPGs. Cuebas turned to look at Moose. All he saw were Moose's legs, but no blood or anything to suggest Moose had been hit.

Moose needed to answer. Cuebas slapped Moose twice on the right leg with his hand to see if he was still with the living.

Moose reacted, and looked down straight at Cuebas. His eyes looked like a fat toad's behind the oversized goggles.

"What the fuck?" Moose mouthed. Cuebas couldn't hear him, but saw what he said. Cooke saw them communicating; that was enough to let him know Moose was unhurt.

The assault was launched. Any diversion, like chasing down whoever shot that RPG, would get them off track. Quick movement to the objective was their highest priority. For a second, Wynn questioned whether the shooter was even connected to the factory insurgent cell. Maybe some wiseass taking a pot shot. Probably was connected, though. Had to assume the worst. Anyone in the brick factory now knew they were coming.

That was Baumann's conclusion, too. He ordered the two platoons to switch to the alternate attack plan that anticipated loss of surprise. Wynn put Baumann's decision out on the platoon net. His people acknowledged.

Gung snorted. Wynn looked at him. Gung was tight and focused in the driver's seat, his hands firmly on the steering wheel, single-mindedness stamped on his face. Wynn looked frontwards. That men in extremely stressful situations had it in them to remain so focused and purposeful was a marvelous thing. Singleton, standing between the front and rear seats in the gunner position, took a step forward as he leaned into the big gun.

The radio crackled and Cooke confirmed assignments for the alternate plan, clarifying intended truck positions, and reminding the platoon of the increased importance of the dismount mission. He spoke like a coach shouting instructions from the sidelines. The alternate plan called for the Wolfhounds to clear the new brick factory building first, because it lay between the convoy's approach and the brick kilns. The change would increase the time it would take the platoon to get to the targeted brick kilns, but the delay was deemed necessary in order to lower the risk of being counterattacked from behind.

Ahead, through the gathering light, Wynn could now make out the roofline of the new factory. Close now, less than a kilometer away. Curves in the unfinished sunken road going into the factory area obscured further visibility. When the convoy turned slightly leftward, he could see more clearly. The road surface was powder. Soon a rolling cloud of this powder masked the convoy, blocking their vision. Like driving through an enormous exhaust plume.

Since the first RPG, it had been quiet. Wynn had expected additional small-arms fire by now. So far nobody else shot at them. Then, ahead, through the dust cloud, he saw the factory smoke stacks standing out like giant goal posts, at least 200 feet high. Then he spotted several of the old brick kilns beyond the new factory. In the dim light, the kilns, unevenly spaced, looked like warts on an otherwise featureless landscape.

Wynn squinted and scanned, looking for people or vehicles. Nothing.

"See anything?" Wynn shouted up to Singleton.

"No."

"Look for those cars."

Baumann came on the radio, sharply, sounding agitated. "Raptor 3 spots a squirter leaving the area, going south." Raptor 3 was the code name for the UAV. "He'll watch him. Break—Dobbie One, car leaving. Pick up the pace and catch 'em. No one leaves the area!"

The plan called for 3rd platoon to swing westward, secure that flank, and provide overwatching fire. Now Baumann wanted them to catch that squirter. Within the next two or three minutes, once the Wolfhounds were within 100 meters of the brick factory, Wynn would direct his platoon off the entrance road. He got on the platoon net.

"OK, less than a minute out. Wolf One and Two, get ready, move quick. A car spotted leaving the area. We do have company here!" The big factory was now straight ahead, rising up out of the dust like a phoenix. The convoy slowed. Dust enveloped them again.

"22, you split us off!" Wynn commanded Turnbeck.

Turnbeck would have to make the call now, tell the two rear trucks to peel off. The convoy was in single file. Dust from their movement filled the air and Wynn could see nothing clearly.

The convoy slowed. Seconds later, it almost stopped. Waiting. Waiting. Why nothing from Turnbeck? Was his visibility bad too? Wynn, restless, wished he was in the front vehicle so he could see better.

"Talk to me!" Wynn shouted on the radio.

They were in an open area, in front of the factory. Just as the dust cleared a bit, he heard Turnbeck's voice. "Go for it!" Turnbeck instructed.

In seconds, Wynn heard and felt the screaming rear trucks, 23 and 24, pass on his right and move toward the factory entrance. D22 and 21 sped up, moving towards the left side wall of the factory. He didn't have to say anything else for now. He felt a surge of pride as the platoon moved into place. D21's acceleration sounded like a prehistoric bird going after prey.

The factory was a prefab building with metal siding, some of it torn off, probably stolen, exposing rusting metal support beams. Its carcass looked like a dinosaur's ribcage. Pulling up alongside, he could see inside in places because of the missing siding. He watched for movement, his hunger to see someone—someone who could be a target for them—eating at his stomach. He turned to his front. Looking forward, he could just make out three kilns beyond the end of the factory. Still no signs of more insurgents or cars.

Baumann was quiet. Why? He'd be moving with 3rd platoon now. Should he radio and ask? No. Wynn would wait until Wolf Two entered the factory. Then he'd call Baumann, as agreed in the plan.

The brick kilns, spaced about 50 meters apart, looked defiant and stark, bleached almond white in the hot intensity of the sun, a reminder of the precarious existence of an ambitious people. The bricks once baked here must have been used in many local structures. A hard life had made this place; a hard people resulted from it. In the early light, the rutted and barren, yellow-moon openness of a thousand years surrounded the structures.

D 22 and 21 were at the back corner of the factory now.

"No bastards anywhere, Sir," Singleton reported, as if reading Wynn's mind.

"Look good," Wynn encouraged Singleton. When the dust cleared, Singleton, from up top, would have the best view.

"Let me know when and if you see any Dobbies come around from the other side."

As Wynn said that, Cooke came on the net. "21. 24, moving inside."

Wynn reported to Baumann, then dismounted his Wolf One team.

Wolf One went in through a gap in the factory wall. Kale crouched, stone-still. Seconds later, he had the impression he hadn't moved for a long time, as if time itself had slowed down, trapping him, pressing him, temporarily making him think he might be able to disappear and hide from this crazy world.

It was already very hot. Heat seeped through the factory walls, invincible, smoking him. It affected his vision, making it difficult to see the other men inside. His breathing was labored, rapid and heavy. He worried about hyperventilating. He looked around inside, hunting danger. With extended focus he could make out the walls and doorways. The next interior door was about 15 meters away. He tried peering through the dirty window of that door to the far side. Worry boiled his insides. His throat felt like a desert. He grabbed the tube of the almost-flat camelbak hanging over his shoulder; he'd nearly drained it. He sucked hard on the tube, taking several gulps of warm rancid water.

As he swallowed, the radio crackled. They got the signal to move. Now they weaved swiftly back outside through a break in the wall, in single file. Each man kept the right spacing, avoided bunching up, minimizing the chance for injury to more than one from explosions.

Other team voices called them forward. Kale was running again, without thinking, following the voices. Part of him felt powerless, propelled by irresistible force. They cut back inside the building, through another opening. Each team bounded forward again, alternating in short rapid bursts, like synchronized machines, then stop, take cover, and overwatch the other team's movement. Then do it again. Kale stopped again, waiting for Turnbeck's order. Movement was only on order, each team moving once the opposite team was set to overwatch. They held their rifles always at the ready, one hand on the trigger grip, one hand on the barrel guard.

Fractured images flittered about in Kale's field of vision, disconnected, gray and indistinct, disconcerting, mostly irrelevant. He passed another outer wall opening and could see the road encircling the factory. To the front and across the road, a scrawny dog scurried around the factory, hugging the wall. Something hanging from the ceiling, maybe 20 meters to his front, started swaying back and forth. He looked at it, unclear what it was. Electric wires maybe. No, too thick. A trip wire? No, too thick for that too. Maybe a rope of some sort, from which something had been hanging. He looked sideways again. A soldier kneeled not five meters from him. Who? Another opening in the wall. Outside, a long thin scrap of paper, possibly a newspaper or a wrapper, danced over the ground. Kale refocused. The inside of the factory looked zebra-striped with morning light coming in through the wall penetrations. He scanned the interior windows and doorways down the hall, hunting movement. Somebody spoke behind him. Kale looked back. Sims was ten meters behind him and appeared to be scrutinizing the pieces of junk equipment inside the building. All that Kale could make out were skeletons of abandoned machines.

Kale saw the Wolf Two team on the far side of the room. He watched the soldier's dark silhouettes traversing the interior of the factory's other side.

"Move your ass!" Turnbeck yelled at him, impatient, urgent.

Kale moved forward, uneasily eyeing the way, unsure what was ahead. The tension and the heat combined to make him feel as if he was drowning in air, unable to get enough breath, unable to think clearly. He heard the movement of other men. Boots scraping the ground. Plastic knee pads bumping surfaces. Grunts. Gear slapping. Men moving. Sudden stops. Urgent sharp voices. But no strange language. No explosions. No gunfire. His eyes struggled to possess everything around him. Anxiety and ambiguity consumed him. Still, inside this oxygen-less world, his eyes and mind worked together, like a giant optic vacuum cleaner, sucking in every-thing seen, but making sense of little.

After a few more short runs, both Wolf teams reached the back of the factory, near a door that looked like an exit. Kale saw Wynn on the far side. He watched the platoon leader as he lay down in the prone position and looked through a gap in the wall, immobile as a statue. Time crawled, each minute an hour.

What's next? Kale, uncertain, glanced to his rear. Damn, he was breathing hard, as if he'd climbed a cliff. Did others hear him breathing? Did Wynn? Kale saw nothing around him but the empty factory, dark and eerie.

Suddenly, Wynn was moving again. Kale got up and moved. He hadn't even heard the command, didn't know what actually got his body going. It was like a coupled train car effect, as if he were physically connected to the other men, pulled where they went without conscious decision. Moving, he heard the jingling of equipment on running men.

Outside again. Kale immediately saw several of the brick kilns ahead, within 150 meters. He stared at them, looking for signs of occupation. The kilns looked like massive ant hills, the scrap of millions of labor hours baking bricks spilled out of their tops, covering the round half-circle structures like crys-tallized lava. Breathing hard and gasping for air, he looked left and right. Other men ran at full speed, fury in their faces, as if chasing away damnation.

Exhausted, he reached the nearest kiln and dropped to one knee. People shouted, but he couldn't make out their words. Perspiration soaked him. His underwear stuck to his testicles. He grabbed the fabric bunched around his crotch and pulled. His desert camouflage blouse, flattened against his back by his protective vest, stuck to him like a second skin. His chin was the only place that didn't feel hot. Evaporating perspiration from his chinstrap cooled it. He struggled to get bearings on where he was and what to do.

Wynn halted behind a kiln. He rested momentarily, breathing hard, feeling as if he'd been underwater too long. An acute sensitivity came over him, as if all the circumstances and demands of existence clamored for his attention. His eyes adjusted rapidly, hungering to absorb everything he could see. Tyson was next to him.

Wynn radioed Cooke that Wolf One was in position, and ordered him to move the gun trucks up to the end of the building to overwatch.

Baumann came on the radio. Wynn pressed the headset closer to his ear to hear. Baumann reported that the Dobbies stopped the vehicle caught driving away. No shots had been fired. Two men and a teenager—who appeared retarded—were in the car, and all had now been flex-cuffed.

"Haven't seen anyone else?" Baumann asked, seeking confirmation from the platoon leaders.

"Negative," Wynn reported. Then D'Augostino did the same.

Wynn got back on the radio. "In front of *Endzone* now. Going forward in two mikes—if the Dobbies are in place," he reported. Then, realizing his thumb had slipped off the mike-key button, he repeated his report.

"Roger," Baumann answered.

Wynn waited for confirmation. Either Dobbie One would report or Baumann would.

Baumann's vehicle should be behind Cooke's team now. Wynn could not see them. A low rise in the ground to the west shielded visibility in that direction. Cooke would come up on the net when he was in position.

Wynn peered around the kiln edge cautiously, looking for signs that other kilns were occupied. Were those guys captured, insurgents? A retarded boy? What was he doing here? More would be to his right, but he couldn't see them.

Wynn twisted around, looking for dismounted Wolfhounds. Two of his men were behind the kiln to his left rear. The other two would be further left, but he couldn't see them.

A cloud of dust rolled into the sky behind him. Cooke's trucks must be moving into place.

No other vehicles had been reported. What about the earlier UAV report identifying several vehicles? Had they left? Who shot the rocket? One of the captured guys? Unanswered queries accumulated. They always did. As tension increased, and the mind awaited violence, questions broiled like a volcano nearing eruption. He bottled up parts of his mind to prevent drowning in information overload. Free space for what's most important. Concentrate. No other insurgents, so far. He hadn't seen any, and from inside the factory he'd had a good look at the ground ahead, at all the kilns. It could be ridiculously quiet in the buildup to combat, as if impending violence stilled all noise. Did they miss something? Were insurgents hiding somewhere? Inside kilns? Most likely. Other than inside the factory, which they had just finished searching, that's what the UAV pictures suggested.

Movement caught his eye. In the distance, he saw Dobbie Humvees. Two of them had taken stand-off positions, perhaps 300 meters away, behind a lip of ground. With their large round headlights they looked like colossal desert bugs. Friendly bugs, fortunately.

Wynn still hadn't received an update from Cooke. Should he call him? No, he'd wait longer. He didn't want those hearing to sense his concern. He kept his focus forward.

Things happened so fast. So many moving parts. It was like steering an out-of-control car, and he scrambled to slow things down. No time for reflection. What was next? Every man in the platoon waited on him for leadership. They expected that of him. He could not disappoint them.

The plan had been to make sure all the kilns were clear. He crawled along his and peered around the edge. He couldn't get a good view of the other kilns, each about the size of a one-car garage, but he needed to see. Then he slid backwards, reducing his exposure. He again checked his map to confirm. Kilns number three, four, and five were the main targets, the Endzone objective. Wynn decided to clear number three first, while Wolf Two provided overwatch. According to his map, one kiln was between where he now was and number five, which was perhaps 60 meters away. He took a deep breath and slid forward again, taking nearly a minute to inch far enough around the circumference to see what he thought was the objective. The ground around them was dry, no scrub grass, the soil brittle and impotent. He felt as if he was crawling on the moon.

To his left, other Wolfhounds positioned behind kilns. They waited for his orders.

He took out his binoculars and looked. He refocused, resting his elbows on the ground, hoping to see inside the door of number three kiln, but no door was visible from this angle. As he watched, two black birds flew off the kiln roof. Why? Movement inside? The kiln leaned slightly, as if bent by years of fighting a steady wind. Perhaps it was damaged. Wynn thought he saw cracks in the wall, but not big enough to penetrate into the interior. The door must be on the opposite side. Was somebody inside?

He scanned the other kilns. Then he studied the surrounding ground, looking for signs the area might be booby trapped or mined. Leaning out beyond the edge of the kiln, he was exposed. The binoculars would make him a favorite target. But he had no choice. He had to see what was ahead.

A hollow feeling grew inside him. Maybe they wouldn't find this sniper today. This fear, more than getting shot, began dominating his mind. The men would be disappointed. But the Dobbies had captured the squirting car. Something was going on here.

Were they interrogating the prisoners already? Baumann had said nothing else on the radio. His last report had been minutes ago, when they'd apprehended them. In combat, what he wanted to know to sharpen his analysis came to him slowly, if at all. Wynn looked back around at his men.

His uncertainty grew like a fever. Was somebody else here? Why wasn't Baumann giving the go ahead?

Wynn tightened, pressing his lips together as if compressing his thoughts. Everything was very still, waiting. His body was in the eye of the storm.

Suddenly, he sensed movement behind him. The rest of the platoon had worked its way into position. Men positioned themselves around the south side of the factory. Anyone in these kilns could not escape now. The target was caged.

Cooke reported. He was in position. Wynn listened.

Then Baumann said GO. Wynn told Wolf Two to move.

Just as the team moved, Wynn heard gunfire. AK47s: that poison crack in the air they immediately recognized. It was close. Then again.

"TUSSS!" Wynn heard a sound like a punctured tire. Tyson fell hard to the ground. Wynn went down too. Tyson lay with the left part of his face on the ground. His hands covered his mouth, as if he was trying to prevent himself from throwing up. Wynn darted over to him. Blood spurted from the back of Tyson's neck.

More gunfire. More sharp knocking.

Wynn rolled over and looked to the front. Then back at Tyson. Wynn got up on his knees and shouted. "Medic! Medic!"

Wynn put his hand on Tyson's neck. Blood coated his hand. Tyson made low mumbling sounds, but didn't move. Wynn looked back. "Medic!" he shouted again.

Tyson lay mostly on his chest, so his first aid bandage pouch was under his body. Wynn, not wanting to move Tyson hastily in case he had a spinal wound, took out his own bandage, stripped the plastic covering off, unfolded it, and pressed in on top of the hole in Tyson's neck.

More gunfire. American M4s this time. Then the AK47s again.

Then the knocking sound blended with the gunfire, like someone tapping rapidly on bricks with a hammer. It was the sound of bullets hitting Wynn's kiln.

Cruz arrived, and slid down beside Tyson.

Tyson's wounding had sucked Wynn out of the battle for a moment. Cruz worked Tyson. Wynn had to get back to leading his platoon. He couldn't let a medical emergency divert him.

"Shit. Shit. Shit," he heard Cruz say. But Wynn had already turned away. The gunfire continued, the loud air cracks chaotic.

Who was firing? From where? Confusion reigned. He wanted certainty; couldn't get it. Had to stay calm. A gunfight burned around him. Both AK47s and M4s fired. No heavy guns yet.

Wynn grabbed his radio and called Cooke. "4, this is 1, what do you see? We're going to need a MEDEVAC. Tyson's been hit."

More gunfire hammered.

A .50 cal opened up. It was a 3rd platoon weapon. Wynn rolled back to the other side of the kiln where he could see it. The .50 barked short bursts, spitting fire. Even from this distance, he could see the brass from the expended rounds ejecting like a shower.

Cooke hadn't answered.

Wynn rolled back flat on his back and called again. "Four, you hear me?" Still no answer.

He waited for what seemed like an eternity. He took a quick glance back at Tyson, who Cruz had rolled over on his back. Weapons kept firing. Intermittent now. The breaks of silence oddly unreal. Then the .50 shot again, smothering other sounds.

The firing was to his left. Wynn had to move there to see better. To see what was happening. But Tyson had been shot there. He'd have to pass Tyson and Cruz to get there.

"Got it," Cooke said on the radio. Wynn took that as confirmation that Cooke acknowledged his previous message.

Wynn moved. He circled around Tyson and Cruz. He did it on impulse, disregarding the fire, everything in him screaming he had to do it, running full speed to the next nearest kiln to his left, hearing bullets hitting nearby, whizzing past, skipping across the ground. He slid into the next kiln. Then he heard hammering on the back side of this kiln.

POP! POP! POP! A shooter fired at Wynn's new position. Where were they?

"Moving forward!" somebody said on the radio. Cooke? Wynn thought it was Cooke.

More crew-served weapons opened up. From Cooke's side now. A 240B this time. A crisp, buzzing sound, stitching across the ground. Hitting something, Wynn hoped.

Wynn moved further around the edge of this kiln, without hesitation, not thinking about it.

He could see Turnbeck across from him, behind another kiln. Kale would be— should be—on his far side.

The gunfire continued. Quieted a few seconds. Then started up again. A kiln stood about 50 meters ahead of Wynn. From there he could see number five better, and number five might be the source of the AK fire. He wasn't sure.

Turnbeck should have smoke grenades. Wynn looked across the separation between where he was and Turnbeck. Turnbeck looked back.

Wynn called Cooke again. This time he answered immediately, his voice stressed.

"Roger, we're moving forward. Think Ulricht nailed a few bastards. We're getting into better position."

Wynn twisted, taking another look frontwards. Then he looked at Turnbeck again while gesticulating his plans to move. "We go to that kiln ahead! You got smoke, right?" Wynn shouted. He pointed with his gun to the kiln he wanted to move to.

Turnbeck looked startled, but acknowledged.

"Put smoke there, as far out front as possible." Wynn pointed and shouted, mouthing his words like man screaming behind glass.

Turnbeck again nodded his head, but didn't act. Was the usually unflappable Turnbeck rattled?

More gunfire. A long burst by the .50 cal, deep and angry.

"Understand?" Wynn yelled again, as loud as he could.

Wynn was baffled by the radio silence. In other firefights the radio had been crazy noisy. He didn't have time to think about it. Their plan had specified that friendly firing from the Humvees would cease while dismounts cleared the kilns, unless specifically requested. Maybe he should warn them. He got on the radio.

"Wolf One and Two moving. Hold your fire."

Wynn waited for an acknowledgement. Turnbeck still looked at him.

"Check fire, check fire," came a command on the radio. Wynn didn't recognize the voice.

He looked at Turnbeck again. Now Turnbeck, smoke grenade in hand, waited for Wynn's command.

Wynn made the hand gesture, simulating a throw.

Turnbeck threw the grenade.

Now they moved. As fast as they could. Kale thought he'd never run faster. He ran lightly, imagining he was floating, his body tense for explosions. Then he was on the ground, again. Other Wolfhounds were on the ground, too. They were still moving. Kale started crawling, almost effortlessly, like he was being sucked towards a black hole. He kept checking his extremities. No, he wasn't hit. He felt the hard weapon in his hands. He looked forward in the direction of the kilns and tried to get his composure back, grasping for stable thinking, filtering rebounding sensations, trying to make sense of it all. He saw nothing ahead. Smoke from the grenade obscured his vision.

Suddenly he sensed a weird sound suppression. All he heard was moving, grunting men. No .50 cal. No 240B. No more AK fire. Then he noticed a sour smell, like fresh urine. Sand stuck to his left hand. He looked at it. Had to be piss. He was crawling through a place where someone had recently urinated.

Someone fired, a ripping, cutting stream of bullets lasting five, six, seven seconds. A desperately defiant sound. Someone wasted a mag, for sure. He checked his body again, looking for blood. Nothing. Hadn't been hit. Would friendly or enemy bullets feel different? Stupid thought. He kept moving, still crawling, feeling exhilarated. Maybe too much adrenaline to feel more fear. He was calmer now than minutes before. Maybe you reached a sort of combat equilibrium at moments like this.

He looked at the kiln ahead of him.

"Move! Move!" Pauls commanded.

Kale was up on his feet and running before he realized it, his body responding faster than his mind. Maybe the training made that possible. Good training overcomes stress, they'd been told countless times.

He ran full speed toward the kiln's wall, hard, unthinking, unable or unwilling to slow down, and smacked into the side of the kiln. Smoke rolled into his face, flooding his mouth. Bitter grit coated his teeth and tongue, as if he'd licked sand. He spat and nearly gagged. If not for his goggles, the same grit would be in his eyes.

He slid around the wall of the kiln, hugging the surface with his back as if he was edging around the rim of a cliff. Pauls moved ahead of him. Follow Pauls. Follow Pauls. The kiln entrance was to his left.

"Grenade!"

The word hit him like a passing train. He dropped, face down, closing his eyes so hard it hurt. Every sinew in his body tried to burrow into the dirt.

TEECACCKKK!!

The explosion screamed past him. He hugged the ground as if he was spinning, clawing the dirt like a frantic dog.

Whose grenade? Had Pauls thrown it? Had it come from inside the kiln?

Then close M4 fire split the air.

He opened his eyes. The concussion of the grenade still echoed inside him, disorienting him.

Pauls, now on his knees beside him, held his rifle in one hand inside the kiln and sprayed bullets. "Take that, fucker-rrrrrrrrssssss!" he yelled, mouth open, teeth exposed like fangs, his face like a beast's.

Sprinkles of debris still rained down from the grenade explosion. It must have exploded outside. Must have come from inside. Kale tried to stand, but couldn't. Was he hurt? He felt unhinged, as if he'd fallen irretrievably into an impossible chasm, the walls around him shouting inexplicable accusations. He saw Pauls standing firm, still firing. Kale watched, still on the ground, fixated on Pauls' open mouth as he screamed.

Pauls dropped to his knees, on all fours. Then he was gone through the kiln door. Not right. Can't be alone. He can't leave me. I can't leave him. Kale got to his feet and slid rapidly around the rest of the kiln to the entrance, as if pulled a magnet.

Pauls' boot soles extended outside the entrance. The rest of his body was inside. Kale knelt again, hesitating to lean down. He must peer inside the kiln, inside to where Pauls was. Then Pauls' boots slithered inside, disappearing like an animal's tail. His turn now. He must go in. For a second, Kale observed the scene as if it was all a paused movie, a tense scene in which a main character had gone through a door that the audience knew he shouldn't have. Everything waited on what would follow.

TEECACKKK!!

Another rattling explosion, not quite as close. Grenade near another kiln? The blast broke Kale from a trance. He bent forward, low enough that he thought he could go through the door, and charged in. Inside he expected he'd see a chaotic scene, the flashing of muzzle shots, angry expressions on the faces of men facing death, but it was pitch dark, and he saw nothing. He stumbled, catching his balance by dropping to a knee. His breathing was stressed, as if he were deep in a mine. Then he made out indistinct lumps against walls. He knew they were bodies, crashed on the floor from their wounds.

"You motherfuckerrrrrrrs!" Pauls screamed again.

Cuebas and Moose rushed up to the last target kiln, number five, alone. The rest of Wolf One and Two remained in over-watch, some behind other kilns, some in prone positions nearby. To Moose, the 25 meters he had to cross was a magnificent space: the distance between steel and power and money, and insignificance. The war in Iraq had brought him and the others to this place. Every day he felt as if he understood it less, but that whether or not he understood it mattered less, too. What mattered was how it made him feel. And he felt good. The thrill kept coming back and made him reach farther than ever before. He looked at the kiln with a mixture of pity and ferocity. No way would whatever was in there survive.

They arrived in a full run, his body starved for oxygen. He saw a freshly bloody sandal lying outside the kiln. He listened, trying to determine whether anyone was inside. No sound. Could it be empty? The kiln was no more than an 18-foot diameter blister of earth: a manmade place, where struggling men had gone to work and produced bricks, to feed and shelter and rest and dream. Cuebas waited across from Moose, on the other side of the kiln. The two of them spoke with their eyes. Cuebas had seen the bloody sandal too. The kiln door was on the other side. They needed to slide around to it. Like the other kilns, this entrance was low, no more than four feet high, like the opening to an igloo.

Moose saw Cuebas' eyes awash with anxiety. What did his own eyes show? He wanted to project firmness and fearlessness. Gunfire had ceased again. Everything waited on clearing this kiln. He could no longer smell the smoke from the grenades and gunfire, nor the dry chalky desert. They circled slowly around to the kiln door. To call it a door would be too much. No door left. No hinges. A roughed-out rectangular hole with a sheet covering it. A sheet? That wasn't normal. Someone must be using the kiln. Moose inched closer to the entrance. His hand held a grenade. Cuebas followed.

So far the platoon had done well. Right by the book. No way would he lower the standard.

He and Cuebas continued to edge around the kiln.

An arm's reach from the entrance now, Moose looked for any signs of booby traps, for wires on the ground or across the entrance, or roughed-up dirt. He saw none. No signs of digging. No wires. No signs of anything in the ground. Just the sandal.

The sheet was slightly ajar but hadn't moved. Bright sunlight now illuminated the entrance like a stage. He couldn't see inside enough to see anything. He reached back and tapped Cuebas. Cuebas dashed to the other side of the door. Weapons were up. Both men crouched slightly and leaned forward toward the kiln entrance. An eye signal decided it. Moose had the grenade in his hand.

"Come out!" Moose yelled.

No answer. One second. Two seconds.

"Last chance, come out!" Nothing.

More eye talk. Moose stowed his grenade.

Without further hesitation, they went in, Moose first. He had the left side wall. Snap: he took a mental picture of the inside of the structure, hoping to instantaneously detect any suspicious object or person. His eyes blazed. Nothing. Too dark. Keep moving. By then Moose had lunged across most of the width of the kiln. His eyes swept the walls and the ceiling. Cuebas did the same with the other side and the floor. Clear. Nothing on the walls. Nothing there. Too fucking dark. The place was remarkably quiet, insultingly quiet. Empty? An underground passage?

"What the fuck?" Cuebas exclaimed. He went to his knees.

"What? What?" Moose asked urgently.

Cuebas examined something by his feet. Both men turned on their lights.

A long bulky roll of dirty sheeting lay on the floor, extending half the kiln's diameter.

Both men stared silently.

Both shone their lights. Moose remembered the warehouse. He knew what was on the floor.

"Think there's a body in that," he said, wiggling his light on it.

"Ayeee, no fucking welcoming party," Cuebas cracked.

27

Wynn stood over her body. They'd pulled her out of the kiln and opened the sheets she was wrapped in. He stood over her in the full glare of the daylight now, strong, tall, dominating, like an executioner after an execution. He hadn't personally killed her, but that didn't prevent him from feeling a measure of success. The sun warmed rapidly, relentless, shining on the scene around them like a spotlight on a dissection table. A voracious curiosity simmered in him. He wanted to know the mind of this woman, what had made her who she was. Alive, she might answer a ton of questions. Of course, the answers would be unsatisfactory. He never expected to understand her world. Probably no westerner could.

Her corpse lay on its side, arms crossed and folded over her chest, head tilted forward, knees bent slightly, as if sleeping, lifeless as the brick kilns. A large brown patch of dried blood stained her midsection, evidence of the wound that killed her. She now lay exposed, and fat green flies buzzed her nose and mouth in growing fury, as if repossessing something that was rightfully theirs. Rigor mortis was well advanced. If they turned the corpse upright and sat her on her backside, she would be frozen in a pose not unlike a woman in the middle of a sit-up. Alternatively, if they flipped her over, putting her weight on her arms, face down, she'd almost look as if she'd assumed the position of Islamic prayer. But she lay as she did on the soiled sheets. Her face held a fierce grimace, a look she would take to eternity.

They estimated that she'd been dead for more than a day. Her skin was taut from body thickening, purplish-gray, and drying, but she was not yet grotesquely bloated. Her hands, thin and boney, had long gnarled fingers stuck out like stalks of young bamboo. Wynn was surprised how ordinary she looked, maybe five-foot-three or -four, with small facial features, typical coal-black hair, not unlike someone you could imagine as a nanny or a music tutor. He felt she should look special. She had shot and killed American soldiers and an Iraqi child. Why? Her eyelids were closed. Not being able to see those eyes was somehow unfair, as if there would be no knowing without looking into that cavern. Whatever thoughts or vision she'd had were gone forever.

The body was not washed or shrouded. Since among her group she would surely be considered a martyr, Islamic custom required that she be buried uncleaned in the clothes she died in within a day or two of death. The white cloth in which she'd been wrapped was part of the customary burial prep, too. So this was how they found her: as she had died, ready for burial. Islamic extremists rarely bothered to send their dead back to their home countries.

The Wolfhounds had not killed her today. All the men knew it. And they all had the same unanswered questions. How had she died? If the Wolfhounds had killed her, it could only have been on the day of the school shooting. But he doubted that was the case. If that were true, her body would have swollen more by now. And she hadn't been hit by a .50 caliber round—the damage to her torso wasn't that massive. Nor had the Wolfhounds had an extended firefight at the warehouse. No shots were fired at the checkpoint explosion site, nor did they have any information that PFA was even involved in that attack. Maybe she had been shot by another platoon. Her companions had probably dragged her away and given her rudimentary medical care. He didn't think she'd lived long after being wounded. She had no padding under the clothing around her belly to indicate any bandaging. Curious, he knelt down and patted the brown stain in her stomach area. The wound area remained a little spongy, but was dry and crinkly, the blood long since coagulated. She'd probably bled out from the wound and been carried here soon after.

Moose and Cuebas stood near Wynn. Wynn looked at them; each man was nearly expressionless, eyes just visible under their helmets, weapons still ready in their hands. Wynn thought he might read disappointment in their eyes, but wasn't sure.

"You guys all right?" he asked.

Both men nodded, but remained quiet.

They'd be happy about the success, Wynn was sure, but less happy than they would have been had the winning shot been one of theirs. Though they found the sniper, no one could claim credit for having fired the kill shot. But adrenaline still rode high, and other than a hint of weariness in their postures, he was confident each man was ready to go.

"The bitch," Wynn heard Moose mumble.

Wynn saw Cooke walking towards them. He expected CPT Baumann shortly. Baumann would be pleased. The operation had been a success. They'd clearly damaged an insurgent cell. The count of enemy dead was seven, including a one-sandaled man near this kiln. At least four were killed by the Wolfhounds. Two bodies lay outside the kilns, two others inside. One was killed by 3rd platoon. Another body—a man with a red Santa Claus beard—looked, strangely, as if he had been dead a couple of days. One wounded insurgent was barely conscious, but alive. He had a bullet hole in the shoulder and a dirty bandage strapped around his head and one eye. Two Americans had been wounded.

A shadow of skepticism passed through Wynn's mind like a cold draft of air. What if she wasn't the sniper? Nothing identified her. None of the Wolfhounds had actually seen this woman fire a shot. For that matter, no reports had come to the battalion, other than from the information discovered in the warehouse, even confirming the existence of a female sniper. But a few minutes ago a Tabuk Dragunov sniper rifle had been found inside one of the other kilns. That confirmed the likelihood of a sniper being among them. They might never know for sure whether she was, in fact, the sniper. But he felt pretty certain she was. The woman had been wrapped, but not buried. Maybe they hadn't had time to bury her, or perhaps they were trying to protect her body. To show her to someone? Word had been on the street. The insurgents had been holed up exactly where the egg lady heard they were. Women involved in insurgent groups were rare, yet here she was. All this suggested she was the sniper. Back in America it would be much easier. Fingerprints or other forensic evidence could be used to confirm. She would have had a known past. Investigators back home would be able to determine all that with about a 99 percent probability. None of that was possible here.

Wynn went over to see Tyson. The MEDEVAC bird was expected any minute. Lee and Cruz still worked on Tyson, who was in very serious condition, drifting in and out of consciousness. He'd hardly moved. His whole head was now wrapped in bandages. Wynn took a knee and kissed Tyson on the top of the head. Cruz said the bullet had smashed into his cheek and exited the back of his neck. Tyson had a tube stuck down his nose to keep the airway open, and he hadn't spoken, but occasionally made gurgling sounds, like a man might make prior to spitting out mouthwash. The wound in this cheek had grotesquely swollen. His mouth was open more than it ought to be. The injury swelled his nose, internal bleeding turned it purple.

Cruz took Wynn aside and said the bullet trajectory took out at least a half dozen of Tyson's upper teeth, and had speared teeth splinters throughout his mouth. The wound on the back of his neck was slightly off-set from the spine and about the size of a soda bottle opening.

"His face looks like a screaming eagle," Cruz said. "I hope the bullet missed his spine."

On the drive back to the FOB, Moose felt vindicated and purified. He didn't understand why. Some claimed they felt dirty after killing. That killing was something so incomprehensible, so disgusting, and that you could never clear the brutality of the act out of your psyche—from then on dark stains clung to your soul like coal dust on a miner. Moose didn't think like that. Kale had his trouble—he overthought things. Killing might crush him. Today, at the brick factory, others had killed. They had achieved something uncommon and momentous, almost beautiful, Moose thought. No, not beautiful. Not in a physical sense. He realized death was an ugly thing, so decisive, so final. Death stole whatever worth life possessed.

Of course violent death wasn't the only thing that stole worth. Moose thought about Tyson. He'd almost had his face ripped off. Moose hadn't seen him before the MEDEVAC carried him away, but others had described the severity of his injuries. A couple of the men had cried. Tyson would not be back in the fight anytime soon, if at all. If he survived, the Wolfhounds probably wouldn't see him again until they got back to the States. Bad things happened to people; Tyson knew that. They all did. Being in Iraq was playing Russian roulette.

Moose, in the trail vehicle of the convoy, leaned back against the back of the turret triumphantly, resting an open palm on the hand grips of the gun, like a trainer's hand on a boxer's shoulder, and watched the disappearing world behind them.

"Ayeee. We put a hurt on them," Cuebas said over the intercom, as if he read Moose's thinking.

"Damn sure did, buddy."

Moose thought about death. When a man kills, an act that society proclaims men can't or shouldn't do, and he gets away with it, it's weirdly liberating—a matchless defiance of civil restrictions that's so slap-face bold, that he thinks himself some kind of superman. He had met a soldier once, a guy in another company, who joked about wearing a Superman shirt under his army-issued brown T-shirt. Now Moose felt as if he had Superman tattooed on his soul.

Kale—what was he thinking? How did he do at the brick factory? They would talk later this evening.

The sniper was interesting. Moose believed that girl had to be the sniper. The Dragunov rifle was proof. He hadn't had an expectation of what she might look like, and now he wasn't sure if how they found her was relevant in any way. He agreed she had been dead for at least a day.

The Wolfhounds now carried her body back to the FOB, her corpse loosely wrapped in three or four black plastic trash bags, secured with 100 mile-per-hour tape, and tied on the hood of D23. They'd decided against the honor of placing her in an American body bag.

A mature sun pressed relentless heat and light against the almond-colored landscape. The ground around them responded with blinking silver sparkles and shimmering reflections, the protest of billions of atoms in billions of separate places. Light didn't always illuminate.

The Wolfhounds brought Mongrel to the Aid Station. Grenade fragments had lightly peppered his hand. Because his wounds were superficial, he had insisted he wouldn't be left behind, and wanted the platoon to wait for him so he could go out for the afternoon's mission. Wynn had agreed to wait if the Doc said Mongrel would be ready in an hour. The Doc did. So the platoon went to lunch and then came back. Halliburton, his mouth white with paper pulp, brought Mongrel a plate from the DFAC. The Aid Station had no further info on Tyson's condition because the MEDEVAC aircraft had bypassed FOB Apache and taken Tyson to a FOB with a larger hospital.

After picking up Mongrel, the Wolfhounds had to continue with census work. Any victory celebration would have to wait, CPT Baumann said. Higher headquarters was giving him flack about the census. Some Wolfhounds questioned the brevity of brick factory operation. After all, they'd taken fire from the village going in, and it might be worth investigating that route and area further, visiting with the residents in the area to try to find out who might have cooperated with the insurgents. But Baumann had concluded that an insurgent lookout had seen them coming. Since the brick factory was located outside the battalion's area, headquarters wouldn't approve more time for searching. The insurgent cell was smashed; the kilns thoroughly searched. Little was found. Further investigation might be undertaken by other agencies—after interrogations of the three captured men. For now, the Dog Platoons would return to their respective battlespaces to continue operations.

During the trip back downtown, the men were quiet. Quieter than usual. The few hours at the brick factory had seemed like days. Each man was absorbed by thoughts of the morning's activities and his convoy responsibilities. Despite weariness, most of the men's minds hummed with contentment.

Kale ruminated about the brick factory operation. During the next few days, the men would talk about their individual experiences, where they had been in the fight and what they thought of the outcome. He would listen, but mostly remain silent. The topic of the female sniper would feature prominently in the conversations. Most of the men would be thinking about the next mission, or what Cooke sometimes called the platoon's business. That business—the urgent real time work required of them—put each man back in a state of mind where most thoughts remain private, and the questions and what-ifs submerge fast and deep into that place where the questioning never ends, and the answers found are never entirely satisfactory. Work and duty made them go on. Should there be something more? Something was still missing, but he didn't know what. He sensed the new satisfaction present in the men. He felt it too, and he liked that feeling, wondering how long it would last. Tyson being badly wounded took away from it and Kale wondered how much the others thought about Tyson.

"Think that fucking sniper lady had ever had a dude?" Randall asked abruptly.

"Knock the shit, pretty boy," reprimanded Pauls. "Get your mind right. Watch your zone."

Pauls' sharp words made Kale scan the surroundings again. The grim brown landscape offered no revelations. Something important had happened today, that was sure; the Wolfhounds had participated in an operation that netted several insurgents and found the sniper that had killed the boy. She was dead. The brick factory had been cleared out. Even if the war was far from over, this was progress, wasn't it? He could claim to have been part of that progress. Sure, he'd been scared. And he hadn't fired a shot. But he was there, was part of the team, the effort, and could claim some of the result. That would be part of his story, too.

28

By 1725, the Wolfhounds were back on FOB Apache. They'd conducted another 25 home censuses and called it quits.

Half an hour later Wynn sat with Petty in the JOC, discussing the morning's operation. Initially, Petty conducted a kind of clinical evaluation, as if neither one of them had been personally involved. He had a way of doing that, as if he was analyzing an experiment he'd read about. After a while, Wynn slowed the conversation down, explaining in greater detail key points of the operation. He told Petty about the hurried approach, the excitement of the men, the RPG firing, going in, the layout of the brick factory, and assaulting the kilns. Finally, he talked about finding the female sniper. Finding her dead. After less than an hour, Petty knew all the essentials.

Petty, pleased, had the jovial grin of a boy who won a game convincingly. He liked to win. Wynn hadn't used the word "win" to describe what happened, but it didn't matter. Wins had not come often enough, and that's how Petty interpreted this.

Both hated the thought of losing. Even a half win was fantastic.

"The warehouse papers had a goldmine of information," Petty said. "Without you guys getting those we had squat. Now we got info on money trails, safe houses, and informants, a big catch on the female Chechen. They'd been using that place for storage and hideaways for months. It's amazing how connected internationally some of these groups are. It's like terrorism's the new frontier for globalization."

"Why do you think nobody talked before?" Wynn asked. "With all the detainees. All the interviews and questioning. Nobody spilled the beans on that place."

"Same reason why we don't ever get much valuable information. I'll give you a one-word answer: fear. Folks are scared. Their lives, their families' lives—everything they have is on the line. Why talk? Think about it. Why should they talk?"

Petty paused, looking for Wynn to express an opinion. Wynn said nothing. Petty gave his own answer. "People don't talk when silence is the better option. Silence is safer. Less risky. Think about it—rarely does not talking get you in trouble. If talking doesn't improve their odds, doesn't help them get safer than they are, people keep quiet. Play it safe. Don't rock the boat. Mind your own business. That's true everywhere. Especially in wartime. It's as old as time, man."

Wynn didn't respond. Petty was exactly right. Wynn looked out the small window. The view outside was unpleasant, the dry ground, mottled with a pale grass, contesting a muddy spot where someone overwatered an under-tended garden. The land here was hungry for improvement. Anything alive was fragile and uncertain. True, too, of her citizens. A weak mango-colored light bathed the yard outside as the sun softened steadily, the heat less dominant. A subdued atmosphere, tired, less sure of itself, settled over the late day. Soon night would hide it all again. Another day done. Another task tomorrow.

Ordinary people were almost helpless in this situation. The huge weight of their immediate dangers, their brittle everyday lives, all the uncertainty of the present, the corrosive fear of the future, left them adrift. They were either pawns in a big chess game or sand on the beach. Used ruthlessly, or irrelevant.

Petty looked at Wynn as a tenured professor looks at his student, and said, "Intelligence information is a funny thing. Most days we get nothing but trash. Just garbage, everyday writings and jabberings. With only a handful of analysts, the work we can process locally is pitiful. We send lots of stuff higher, of course. They have more analysts. Some of it might be good, but we get little back. If it's local stuff, you want to look at it. At least try to determine the motives of who provided the info. Sometimes it's vendetta action going on."

Petty let out a long sigh, as if he was resigned to accepting all the usual limitations. Then he started again. "But then something like this warehouse stuff comes in. Makes you forget your bad days."

"Remember the warehouse stuff didn't tell us where the sniper was. A little old lady did that," Wynn reminded him.

"I realize that."

Petty now had the look of a man trying to get a valuable contract signed. Wynn could tell that something had been left unsaid. Both men waited, quieted by a mutual recognition of how little they could be confident about, but how nice it felt to get something right.

Then there was the core human element: why men did what they did.

"You get to be out there, man," Petty said, making reference to the Wolfhounds' combat role. "You're out front. The lead dog, so to speak. We Intel geeks are back here in the bowels, working the shit. Then spitting it out."

"Yeah, and we have to eat it."

Petty smiled at the reply. A long pause separated them. When he continued, his voiced buzzed with derision. "You know that retarded boy. He was there with his father. The father told interrogators this afternoon that he believed that by having his son with him in PFA, he would get him closer to God. Can you believe that? "

Wynn couldn't believe it, but he said nothing right away.

"I still can't get the female bit," Wynn said, after another delay. "Never will. Female Chechen sniper? Who would have thought."

"It's crazy that nothing makes sense," said Petty, as if he read Wynn's mind.

"I wonder who shot her," said Wynn. "There's no way to be sure."

Wynn stopped talking again. Part of him still wanted to believe the Wolfhounds had killed the sniper.

"Maybe they killed her themselves to turn off the heat," offered Petty, alternatively, without believing it.

"I doubt that. And the truth is we got her more by luck than detailed investigation."

"Relationships. Relationships with locals made it happen," Petty said.

Wynn looked across the room at the large flat screen with the electronic map. A scattering of multicolored symbols marked the map. The screen radiated sophistication and purposefulness, possible only through man's ingenuity and inventiveness. Thousands of miniature special parts constructed of thousands of different types of materials. Each color meant something. Geometric shapes on the screen meant things. Other lines and markings on the map helped the viewer organize his thoughts. All so ordered, so technical. Man mastered the atom, but continued to struggle to understand the basics of human nature.

Wynn looked at Petty and spoke. "A little old lady who sells eggs told us what we needed," he said quietly, as if he still needed to persuade himself.

Petty stared at him. Could he tell he was dog-tired? Wynn was unshaven. Stains smudged his brow and cheeks; his lips were cracked and dry. He needed a meal and a good sleep.

"We won one. Let's get some more," Petty added.

Wynn left the headquarters. As he walked towards the exit gate, CPT Baumann came out of an adjacent building where the battalion commander had his office and called out to him.

As Baumann neared, Wynn studied his face for portent. Bad news on Tyson? Baumann would probably hear first.

"You did well today, Christian. Your platoon did well. I'm happy. So is battalion."

Wynn breathed easier, absorbing the praise. Baumann was rather sparing with positive comments, so when he did spread praise it meant more. Their gazes met and lingered, and Wynn had a sudden feeling that Baumann was monitoring something deep inside him that he couldn't put into words.

"Thanks, Sir. The guys did super."

He studied Baumann the way a musician studies his conductor, attentive, anticipating, wanting to please. Wynn felt uneasy about raising the subject of Tyson, as if it would be bad luck.

"Tyson's serious but stable. That's the word they're giving us. He's going to make it. He's in Baghdad now," Baumann reported, anticipating Wynn's question.

"Good to hear. It was a very bad wound," Wynn said. The report wasn't much information, but it was positive. A feeling of relief came into him as he thought about telling his men. They would be glad for the news. Making them feel better would make him feel better.

"Poor bastard," Baumann added. "But apparently the bullet missed his spine. That was the main thing. Of course they'll have to rebuild this face. I have no idea how much damage to his mouth. Probably major."

"Got to be."

"We'll keep getting updates on him to you guys. He'll probably be back in the States within a week."

"Thanks, Sir."

"How's Mongrel?"

"He's fine. He's already back to duty, Sir."

"Tell those Wolfhounds of yours, I said, 'Well done.'"

"Yes, Sir."

"One more thing," continued Baumann, "and this is kind of odd. Remember that wounded guy we captured at the brick factory?"

"Yeah."

"Well, they've had him in the Aid Station here since we brought him. Apparently he's been hallucinating and talking a lot whenever he's conscious. He was talking so much the Docs brought in an interpreter. He's missing an eye, and he told the Docs that a man with just a thumb gouged his eye out. That made me think of the report you wrote me about your last Amir visit, when you mentioned a Mr. Thumb."

Wynn went rigid. Could Sheikh Amir's Haider have anything to do with this?

"Hmmm. I'll check it out."

After Baumann dismissed him, Wynn walked back to the platoon area. He found Cooke and told him about Tyson. He told Cooke to go tell the men. Wynn went to find Cengo and call Amir.

About an hour after Cooke had come by with the news of Tyson, Kale and Moose sat across from each other in Kale's trailer. They were alone. Moose had come back from the gym. Sweat glistened on his neck. Kale had told him about Tyson. Kale now eyed his friend, a mixture of admiration and envy coursing through him as he measured Moose the way a man at a horse race might evaluate the winner.

"Pretty rough what happened to Tyson," Kale said.

"Yeah. I went by the Aid Station on the way to the gym, to see if they'd heard any more details. Nobody had. Figured he'd have left me a love note at least, but no. He didn't do that either."

"I hope he makes out OK. The bastard has him a ticket home now," Kale said, scratching his head with the nubs of his fingernails. "Fucking raw deal." He looked for emotion in Moose and saw none.

Moose turned his head to the left and looked down at the floor. He stared downwards for several long seconds, as if checking his shoes. He must be thinking about Tyson, Kale thought, waiting for Moose to take up the conversation. He wanted him to say something that would reveal weakness. But Moose stayed mute.

Finally, Kale changed the subject. "When we got back, I heard Cengo say that the Iraqis will be grateful. I hope he is right."

"Fucking Iraqis," Moose said, "I don't see much gratitude in his country."

"Come on, man. He's not part of all that. He's a Kurd anyways. The dude loves us."

"We need to put a wall around this place. Nobody gets in or out. We come back in a thousand years and see what's left."

"Huh? The Kurds are different. You know that. Even a lot of the other Iraqis are. They don't want this mess. Nobody would."

Moose didn't reply right away. He wiped his dripping brow with the open palm of his hand, looking firmly at Kale. Skepticism sparked from Moose's eyes.

"Speaking of different, I heard you did well today, buddy. The guys were talking,"

Kale suppressed a grin. Was it true, or just Moose trying to make him happy? "Don't know about that. I did my job."

"Fuck, dude. You were right there in it, on one of the teams. We got that bitch. You ought to feel good about that, soldier!"

Moose's voice showed no condescension. He meant it. Kale let the positive feeling rise up inside him. Yes—he had been out in it. And the whole time he'd felt as if someone was tattooing directions to hell on his nerves. But he *had* been there. Being there—as he'd told himself before—was pretty damn important.

"It does feel great to have smacked the bastards that killed that boy," Kale said softly, as if he was explaining something complicated to a child.

"You bet it does. OK. I'm off to the shower to wash this nasty ass."

Moose stood up, looking down at Kale. His expression said that he was assessing a yet-to-be-finished story.

Kale fidgeted with his boot. "OK. I think I'll walk down to the phone bank and try to call Serena again."

"Tell her for me that if she ever gets tired of you, I'm still available. But I can't promise her for how long," Moose ribbed, a devil's smile on his face.

"Fuck you. You ain't got what it takes. She wouldn't give you the time of day."

"Shittt!"

Moose walked out and left the door open. Kale watched him go. He strode away with the assurance of a winner, hulking, carefree, bath towel over his shoulder, shower kit dangling at the end of long rope that he held in a massive hand. Kale watched him for maybe half a minute, until he passed around a corner of a group of trailers and disappeared down the path to the shower stalls. Kale got up slowly and went over to the door. He looked skyward, through the dim illumination of the FOB lights, and beyond, to the gray gulf of space, and far away towards what some men called the heavens. Then he closed the door and turned off the light in the trailer, and sat back down in the dark.

29

Wynn and Cengo waited just inside FOB Apache's main gate. They waited on Amir. It was almost 2200, the scheduled time for Sheikh Amir to arrive. The night air felt like warm broth. After hearing Baumann's report that Haider, also-known-as Mr. Thumb, might have had an encounter with one of the wounded insurgents found at the brick factory, Wynn had called Amir. He asked Amir bluntly if he knew whether Haider had some connection to the PFA insurgent group. At first Amir pleaded ignorance, but didn't make an outright denial. When Wynn had finally said that he wanted to question Haider, Amir offered to come talk. "Not on cell phone," he said. Wynn accepted that, and was happy to meet face-to-face. Amir, surprisingly, was agreeable to meeting right away.

Soon the gate security guards told Wynn his visitor had arrived. Wynn walked to the checkpoint. A black BMW with dark-tinted windows waited outside the barrier. FOB security personnel checked the car and scanned the undercarriage. A rear window rolled down. Amir held out his hand to Wynn, who took it. An Iraqi driver and one other man, not Haider, were in the car with Amir.

"It's them," Wynn said to the FOB guards.

Within a couple of minutes, the BMW was allowed to proceed through the gate to a small parking lot on the other side. Wynn and Cengo followed on foot. When they arrived at the car, Amir and the other Iraqis got out and met them.

"Amir suggest you and I sit in car with him and talk," Cengo said to Wynn.

The three men—Amir, Wynn and Cengo—got in the car, Amir and Wynn in the back seat.

Amir smiled at Wynn respectfully and said, in Arabic, "I know you have questions. I have come here to tell you a story. Please let me tell it. I think you will understand," Cengo translating.

"You have a story. I have questions, but I will listen to your story and see if it answers my questions," Wynn said.

Amir proceeded, at length. He had the look and voice tone of a lawyer negotiating a divorce settlement, trying delicately to bridge the difference between hopes and reality. His big nose appeared to grow even larger, as if it were serving as a shield for his mind's calculations. After some time, Amir stopped and Cengo turned to Wynn.

"I try explain this, Sir," Cengo began, breathing deeply before attempting. "Sheikh Amir tell me many things. I try carefully. He say he knew for some days already about the torture warehouse before we go. He trying many days to ransom his friend's son. They, the *Takfiri*, negotiate hard. Sheikh Amir say they lie to him, then they kill his friend's son. Amir he find this out before he call us go *warehouse*. He find out because his friend call him and say his son's head left at his house. Early that morning the *Takfiri* bring head and leave it at front door doctor's house. So then Amir know it over. Then he call you to help get revenge."

"So Sheikh Amir knew his friend's son was dead before we even went to the warehouse?"

"Yes. He learn that morning."

"Why didn't he call me sooner?"

"He say that not possible. He say if he call you sooner, and you go warehouse, they surely kill his friend's son. He say PFA no really interested in negotiation, they only want kill those working with Americans."

"What else he say? What about Haider?" Wynn looked at Amir as he asked these questions. The sheikh sat resolutely. Wynn didn't think he'd moved once during Cengo's translation.

Cengo continued. "There's more, Sir. Amir say he have someone watching warehouse when we come there. This person, he saw several cars and nine or ten people leave in hurry. He, that person, tell Amir this. Then Amir get worried. He say, he say to himself, 'why when he tell Americans something, and they go there, the *Takfiri* leave in hurry few minutes before American soldiers come.' Amir, he very worried, he say to me 'maybe information I give Americans not private, maybe they have spy, maybe *Takfiri* somehow know what I say to Americans on cell phone.' So Amir say to me he have other plan. He say doctor friend beg him for revenge. And Amir say he want stop PFA too, but use *his* way. This what he do. He hear from Manah."

"Manah? What did he hear from Manah?" Wynn interrupted, his mind simultaneously scrambling back to the school shooting.

"Amir, he say this. Manah his old friend. After boy shooting, Manah call Amir. Manah say something interesting. He tell Amir that the schoolmaster, Albadi, he have son-in-law that maybe friendly with *Takfiri*."

"A son-in-law friendly with insurgents?" Wynn asked. Albadi had earlier acknowledged two daughters, but their ages were supposedly younger.

"Yes, Sir. He say Manah tell him this. He say after shooting, Manah hear Albadi talk to his daughter on phone. That he very worried about way daughter's husband talk. He think, I mean talk, like daughter's husband maybe terrorist. Manah wonder if this husband help PFA. And Amir hear all this from Manah. Then he say to me this what he do."

"What?"

"This information make Amir send strong people, his people, to the house, to Albadi's house, the night after we go warehouse. The same night of the day Amir's friend get son's head. Haider lead these people."

On hearing this about Manah and Albadi's son-in-law, and then Haider's name mentioned, Wynn's mind neared eruption. He felt like information-seeking rockets were about to blast out of his head.

"Sir, Amir say Haider talk hard to this man, Albadi's daughter's husband."

"Wait. Wait. Why did Amir think that this man had any connection to PFA?"

Cengo turned to Amir, who had been quiet and waiting patiently, and asked that question. Before Amir answered, he looked down at his right hand, made a fist, and then looked back at Cengo. Was his fist-making a symbol of crushing something, maybe crushing his enemies?

After Amir had answered, Cengo continued: "Amir say he hear rumors that PFA female sniper shot the boy. And then this what Albadi's daughter's husband tell Haider. Amir say Haider call him after talking to that man. Haider tell Amir that the man definitely know something. He act funny. He act guilty. So they take him to special place, and they torture him. Haider take out his eye. Then Haider tell him if he not talk, he take one of everything he, that man, have two of. He say I take off one hand next. Then foot. Then take balls. That's what

Haider say to him. The man lose his eye—Haider use thumb to take eye out—but then man talk. He talk everything."

"So that prisoner we have is Albadi's daughter's husband?"

"Yes."

"What else did they learn from him?" Wynn asked, trying to imagine the horror of the scene.

"They find out he work with PFA. Amir say the man tell them the lady sniper shot boy because she cannot shoot Manah. He say Manah was inside school with you the whole time. She decide shoot boy to send message that anybody work with infidels, even talk with infidels, are bad Muslims. That even children be killed to stop infidel's plans for Iraq. Then, because he very scared they torture him more, he tell them more."

"What?"

"This what happen. He tell them he know other places PFA maybe go when they leave warehouse fast. One place is Mullah's house. The leader this PFA group have Mullah religious adviser here in Bejanas, he tell them. Sometimes, with just a few of the PFA people, the leader he go there to Mullah. Haider torture man more and learn from him where this Mullah live. Amir talk to Haider on phone. Amir, he then organize twenty of his men, men with guns."

Cengo paused and glanced down. He looked wearied by the complexity, almost too tired to continue. Amir remained silent and still.

"Go on. Give me the rest," Wynn said.

Cengo asked Amir another question. The answer was quick.

"Amir's people, they take the tortured man and go to the Mullah's house. That tortured man guide them to house. This happen maybe 1am in morning, I think. Only one car there. This mean PFA split up, and go different places. So Amir and Haider, they think they get lucky. Amir tell Haider on phone to kill everyone in house. So the men—everybody wearing masks—go in house. They kill the people. But Amir tell me the

Takfiri in house—not many, I think he said four or five—they fight back. The fighting hard. Two Amir's men killed. During fight, they, the *Takfiri*, they destroy the car Haider come in, the car that Albadi's son-in-law in. When Amir people leave, they leave very fast. They think maybe more *Takfiri* maybe come. The damaged car with Albadi's son-in-law is left behind. Haider tell Amir he shoot that man himself as he leave the place. But, like we know, that man live. He now in FOB hospital."

"Why did he take this risk?"

Cengo asked Amir Wynn's question.

Amir summoned a little smile and balled his hand into a fist again, then relaxed it. He spoke for about a minute.

"Sheikh Amir say," Cengo began, "that strong man sometimes have to take risks to stay strong. He also say, like old American Cowboy movies show, that the way kill a snake is cut off its head."

"Was the female sniper at this Mullah's house?"

"Amir say yes."

"Amir's people shot her?"

"Yes."

"How does he know he cut off the head? How does he know he got the leader?"

"Amir say the leader had a long red beard."

Wynn remembered the man with the red beard at the brick factory. He had been dead for more than a day. That would be this man.

"Tell Amir that we found the red-bearded man and the female at the brick factory."

Cengo translated. Amir nodded his head and looked at Wynn the way lawyer looked at his client when all the documents were signed.

Wynn went on to explain more about what happened at the brick factory. He asked Amir whether he knew about PFA having a hiding place in the brick factory before today. Amir said no. Amir added that PFA probably had several hiding places around the city, which Wynn also suspected. The brick factory must have been one of those, maybe a kind of last re-doubt. After further conversation, both men concluded that other PFA personnel must have recovered the casualties at the Mullah's house and taken them to the brick factory. Wynn didn't tell Amir how the Wolfhounds had heard about the brick factory. He wanted to maintain the confidentiality of the egg ladies.

"This good. American soldiers and my people, Iraqi people, we make very bad time for PFA," Amir said in rough English, summarizing his position.

"It seems so," Wynn said. "You certainly did things your way. I have one final question. Why didn't you ask us for more help? Well, maybe two questions. Why didn't you ask us for more help and why didn't you give me information sooner on PFA?"

Cengo translated.

Amir pondered the question, then put both hands in front of himself, palms up, before answering. He spoke for as long as necessary to make his point.

"Amir, he say he have to put his friends, his people first. He not act unless it for him and his friends. Albadi, the school-master, he from different tribe. So Amir no have problem deal-ing hard with him. But with PFA he must be careful. They very dangerous. He say when he decide they must attack Mullah's house he think that best and safest plan. Plus it make his doc-tor friend happy. His doctor friend, he go there with Haider. Amir, he use the word honor. It honor for them. Plus, like he say before, he not understand why when we go warehouse the *Takfiri* leave before we get there. Amir he say—and this he think very important—a wise man must act carefully, but when he do act, he must act very hard."

About an hour later, after midnight, Wynn leaned against a concrete barrier near his hooch. He had crunched every detail of what Amir had said, and decided to digest it overnight. He'd wait until morning to tell his men. Despite some anger about Amir's originally withholding significant information, Wynn recognized that from the Sheikh's perspective he had probably handled things the way Iraqis would. Amir's story resolved most things plausibly. Amir could not fabricate a whole tale like that. Amir's people had, evidently, decapitated PFA. The Wolfhounds, this morning, had cleaned up the rest.

Albadi wasn't honest. He probably lied about his girl's ages, to hide the fact that one of them was married. Based on the timing, the schoolmaster would probably have known his son-in-law had been kidnapped just prior to the second Wolfhound visit. He had looked particularly tired that day. He had no compelling reason to tell them. On the contrary, he would have wanted to suppress any knowledge that his son-in-law was involved with PFA, if he even knew.

On the issue of why the insurgents fled the warehouse prior to the Wolfhounds arriving, all Wynn could conclude was that somebody had seen them coming. This was not surprising. Perhaps someone at the market had heard them talking to the egg ladies. No way to know.

Sheikh Amir had taken a considerable risk in striking PFA. Amir and his people were very fortunate that they found the PFA leadership at an opportune time, when only a few key members of the group were at the Mullah's house. Amir wouldn't risk attacking a larger group. Since the remains of the group got destroyed at the brick factory, the chances of PFA retaliation against Amir was low, at least for now.

Then Wynn thought about the way things looked to him overall. What was happening in Iraq was both complicated and simple. Was it possible for America to achieve its goals? Echoes of the past always pummeled the present. Man's ambitions drove everything; his abilities perhaps insufficient.

It was simple because it was basic, he thought. All was struggle. Survival was in jeopardy. Danger was a constant. Only those close to you would help. It had always been such. Blood connections are the surest bond, man's most important asset.

It was complicated because it was so hard to understand. What had Iraqi's experiences taught them? Their stories?

Their traditions? Maybe the answer was different from what rational western minds might conclude. Maybe we couldn't understand them. Maybe we lost ourselves in a safe imagination of civil structure and domestic comfort.

At best, if they're fortunate, good soldiers can feel it. They can feel things like the tribal attachments, detect it by being deep in—by watching, by thinking, by experiencing.

The world every man lived in also lived inside him. That much they knew.

Then he reflected on his soldiers—the Wolfhounds.

Like all others, present and past, they were temporary players on a larger stage. Many had played in the past. Others would play in the future. They would look to the past and ask the same questions, whether as nations or as individuals. The Wolfhounds' time to be soldiers was now. That would come to an end. All was transitory. Life was too.

They had taken two casualties today and were lucky it was not more. The insurgents could have planted IEDs on the roads leading into the brick factory. The Americans had been spotted coming in. They'd come under fire. But no IEDs were used. Why? Perhaps the enemy had been too busy.

In the meantime, Tyson had many months of care ahead. Ramirez's family, and the others that had lost loved ones, would deal with that for the rest of their lives. That was the cost of war. And being wounded—or even killed—was the highest form of payment. Some would pay that price. No way around it.

Transcending questions existed. And to Wynn the most important one was this: why was each Wolfhound here? Their actions gave the answer. Whether in garrison in a loose formation of laughing and strutting soldiers, or when working and fighting together, each willingly put his body and life at risk. That willingness to serve was an expression of the sinew of their experience and ambition. Each man wanted it. It was a volunteer Army. Had a man not wanted it, he wouldn't be here. The most common motivation: respect. Each of them wanted respect. Not only the respect of outsiders, or the respect of the unit. But the strongest and most durable form of respect: self-respect. Earning respect before a personal altar of courage was what made the whole thing work. To each man, more than big and heavy words like democracy, or nation-building, it boiled down to a simple thing, a far more elementary emotion: an affirmation of courage. In their minds, the men were proud that no one could say that when the call came, they were wanting. The Wolfhounds were not wanting. They were here. Them, not others. This was stuff that built a strong masculine bond. And yet it was an ultimate assertion of individualism. Embracing the warrior brotherhood brought the two-component ingredient together and made the whole stronger.

He moved away from the wall and started ambling back to his trailer. The night sky was mostly clear. Thousands of stars threw a cascade of light across the immensity of space and a blue band of clouds hung low on the edge of the horizon. As he walked, Wynn saw the cloud band edge skyward. Perhaps a storm was building out there, or perhaps an incomprehensible power silently pulled a heavy blanket over a sinful world.

At 2000 the following evening, Wynn and CPT Baumann sat next to each other in the battalion headquarters awaiting BG Craig's call. After the report on the brick factory operation and the take down of PFA had gone up channels, word had come down that Craig wanted to talk personally with Baumann and commend him. Baumann, recognizing the crucial role the Wolfhounds had played, brought Wynn along.

Wynn, after Baumann had informed him of the pending call, couldn't help but feel positive about the reasons. The Wolfhounds had performed well. Recognition of that was now being acknowledged all the way up to division headquarters. He tried to anticipate what Craig might say. Baumann, as the company commander, would get a lot of the credit. Wynn understood the rules of hierarchy. But he appreciated Baumann's including him in the call. That said a lot about Baumann's view of things and his leadership style. It also reflected well on Craig. For the second highest ranking officer in the division to so quickly take the time to offer a personal commendation said something important.

A staff officer came up on the line and told Baumann to standby for BG Craig.

"Roger, Sir," Baumann answered.

Baumann looked at Wynn. Wynn read his look as one part pride and one part uncertainty, aware that things were always a bit unpredictable when a general entered the conversation.

He thought about the talk with Amir last night. He'd informed Baumann of the details early this morning. After shaking his head for a while, Baumann had evidently accepted, as Wynn did, that the facts revealed by Amir needed to be viewed as something unchanging and essential, like the weather, or like the birth and death cycle of life—as something to take benefit from when possible, and to endure with stoicism when no other answer was reasonable. Baumann had told Wynn that he'd included some comments on Amir in his report.

"Ben, you there?" Wynn could tell it was the powerful voice of BG Craig.

"Roger, Sir," Baumann answered.

The conversation grew muffled and Wynn couldn't hear most of Craig's words. Baumann received the statements like a man on stage getting a trophy.

After about two minutes, Baumann, when he saw a window of opportunity, said, "Sir, Christian Wynn's platoon made this possible. Those guys did the leg work and had the connections. I have him here with me. Could I ask you to say a word to him?"

Baumann handed Wynn the phone.

"Lieutenant Wynn here, Sir,"

"Christian, your boss and I just had a short chat. He tells me you guys did most of the ball running. That's great! Look,

I'm going to make this quick, but it's important. Tell your men, 'Job well done!' And tell them I know it's hard. Remember this—if you're a surgeon cutting out a cancer, every step is a big deal. No matter how many or how simple or complex they are, every one of them counts. But everybody in that operating room knows that, without the surgeon, it ain't happening. That surgeon is the indispensable man. Your platoon, Christian, you guys are the surgeons in your piece of the war. Without you and your boys the operation has no chance of success."

"Thank you, Sir."

"Nobody knows for sure how this thing plays out, Christian. Not us up here, not Washington, not you guys down in the dirt. What we do is what we always do: soldier up and drive on."

ABOUT THE AUTHOR

Colonel Claude Schmid retired from the Army in 2013 after 31 years of military service in combat units around the world. During his two tours of duty in Iraq, he commanded a combined US-Iraqi Infrastructure Security Force which secured, defended, and assisted in the rebuilding of Iraq's Northern Energy Infrastructure. He returned to Iraq as Commandant of the new Iraqi Military School System. Before retiring, Claude served as the Chief of the Army's Wounded Warrior Flight Program, which welcomed thousands of wounded warriors back from Iraq and Afghanistan for medical treatment. Serving in this capacity—witnessing their hardship and pain, and hearing their stories—reaffirmed for him the unbreakable strength of America's Soldiers, Marines, Sailors, and Airmen.

A first-generation American, Claude was born in New Jersey of Swiss parents. He went from childhood to manhood in Spartanburg, South Carolina. He is an avid student of history, politics, and good books. He holds degrees in economics and government, a Master's Degree in Business Administration, and a Master's in Strategic Studies from the Army War College. He is a member of the American Legion, the Veterans of Foreign Wars, and the International Churchill Society, and serves on the New Jersey Board of Directors of Operation Homefront.

Dedication

This book is dedicated to a soldier without uniform. In fact, he wasn't a real soldier at all. But he fought as hard as any soldier I've ever known or read about, and eventually what he fought against killed him. That man was my brother, Kevin Walter Schmid. Kevin was born with Muscular Dystrophy and spent his whole life at war with it. That disease ravishes your muscles. It kills slowly, by convincing your body that it should prematurely self-destruct. Muscular Dystrophy has killed millions. Kevin's battle started early; I remember him going from a slow limp in elementary school to a wheelchair in high school to what was essentially paralysis in a hospital bed at home late in his life. Like the best soldiers, Kevin had a quiet resiliency that manifested itself most clearly when the going was roughest. He kept his cool during the whole fight. He worked hard to make himself better long after most of us were done. He didn't complain. He just fought harder. Like the best soldiers, Kevin was made stronger by being part of a good team. The most important members of his team were his devoted parents. They helped give him the best life possible and loved him to the end and even now. Like the best soldiers, he had other teammates who were proud to know him and admire him, and surely ask themselves whether they could have ever shown that much courage. In 31 years in the military, I was honored to serve with and meet some of the bravest men on this planet. My brother was one such man. Kevin, I salute you.

ACKNOWLEDGMENTS

It's been said that writing a book is like giving birth. I like that analogy. The process is long and physically exhausting. You see and feel changes going on inside you that you strive to convince yourself that you are in control of but you are never quite sure. Yes, you, the author, get most of the credit in the end. However, around me figuratively in the hospital as I'm delivering this child are hundreds of crucial staff members that I've too often called on. First of all, there are my fellow warriors, America's Soldiers, Sailors, Airmen, Marines, and Coast Guardians. Those guys built the hospital where I went to give birth. They consummated the enterprise and made this novel possible. Without them, there is no life-experience, no context, and no story. Some exceptional people came into the delivery room, having taken a more personal role in gestation. I would like to thank Mr. Hugh Cook, the Canadian writer and professor, for very early editing advice and for making me think I could do it. I owe the beautiful Ms. Ludmila Bogomolova special thanks for checking my pulse and wiping my brow as the time got closer and we read and reread the text together. There were times when I wanted to abort. Ludmila didn't let me. Once contractions started, the stern doctors with the forceps in the room were Dale and Julia Dye. That noble team at Warriors Publishing Group gave me a chance and did the close-in delivery. They have my utmost gratitude for dealing professionally throughout this amazing experience of bringing a very vocal beast out into the world.

WWW.WARRIORSPUBLISHING.COM

WE PUBLISH
BOOKS YOU
LIKE TO READ

WARRIORS PUBLISHING GROUP

FOR THE BEST IN MILITARY FICTION AND NONFICTION

www.ingramcontent.com/pod-product-compliance
Lightning Source LLC
Chambersburg PA
CBHW060245210726
48292CB00002BA/495

* 9 7 8 1 9 4 4 3 5 3 1 0 0 *